"March? That's months and months away!"

"Right. Listen, Ange, you don't just add water and stir. It takes a while to produce a book. There's a lot that goes into it. And you'll be learning all about it as you go. In fact, your first lesson starts in two weeks. Mark Green wants to meet you to discuss his editorial suggestions. Mmm. Pass the pâté!"

"Who *is* Mark Green?"

"He's your editor. He's first rate. And he's H and H's editor in chief, so he's got plenty of clout."

"When does Mark Green want to see me?"

"He'll probably call you tomorrow to set up an appointment. And Angie, when you go in, you've got to look gorgeous. I mean stunning. You may need some coaching. . . ."

"Coaching? For what?"

"Oh, you know. Nothing major. A little PR training just to get you used to appearances, interviews, TV talk shows, touring, that stuff."

"I think I'm going to be sick. . . ."

ADVANCES

SAMANTHA JOSEPH

PINNACLE BOOKS NEW YORK

This is a work of fiction. All the characters and events portrayed in
this book are fictional, and any resemblance to real people or
incidents is purely coincidental.

ADVANCES

Copyright © 1983 by Ronni Stolzenberg and Ken Sansone

A Pinnacle Books edition, published by special arrangement with
Macmillan Publishing Company.

Macmillan edition published 1983
Pinnacle edition/July 1984

ISBN: 0-523-42217-2

Can. ISBN: 0-523-43209-7

Printed in the United States of America

PINNACLE BOOKS, INC.
1430 Broadway
New York, New York 10018

9   8   7   6   5   4   3   2   1

For Marty and John

Many thanks to Rochelle Stolzenberg, Amy Schildhouse, Wendy Cohen, Esther Mitgang, Jeffrey Carlton Green, Michelle Sidrane, Carl Apollonio, Manuela Soares, Dana Rae Landry, Sandy Pollack, Gail Kinn, Lindley Boegehold, Marion Wheeler, and Diane Cleaver; and especially to our families—at home and at Crown.

We'd like to acknowledge the contribution of inspiration made by Samuel Stolzenberg, Josef Sansone, David Stolzenberg, and Thomas Christie Pallante.

ADVANCES

CHAPTER
1

ANGELA VACCARO'S large green almond-shaped eyes darted from the sheet of paper in the typewriter to the antique mantel clock at the edge of her oak desk.

"Enough!" she cried as she shoved her chair back. It was twelve-thirty. Damn! she thought to herself, I'm running late. She rolled up the sleeves of her blue oxford-cloth Brooks Brothers shirt, the sole garment she wore when she worked at home. It was at least three sizes too big, and it covered her down to the tops of her thighs.

She leapt from the secure depths of her overstuffed wing chair and ran to the bedroom. The unmade bed lay in the path of the streaming July sunlight, its sheets and covers spilling onto the floor. Under the pile of bedclothes, Angela located her Levis and hastily drew them up over her long legs and bare, firm buttocks. She stuffed the shirt hurriedly into her jeans and dove to the floor to find her strappy Maud Frizon sandals. Moments later, with giant sunglasses perched on her aquiline nose and a straw basket she used as a summer handbag slung over her shoulder, she was in the elevator, descending from her eighth-floor Gramercy Park co-op apartment to the streets below.

The heat hit her with the force of a heavy blow as she ran to Third Avenue, anxiously scanning the traffic for an air-conditioned taxi. Waving her long arms, her large, high, unbound breasts bouncing beneath the cotton of her shirt, Angela flagged down a cab.

"Georgette Klinger," she said, aiming her instructions through the Plexiglas shield at the back of the driver's head.

Routinely, he checked her out in the rearview mirror. "It's on Madison, near Fifty-third," Angela added.

As the cab crawled like a yellow snail up Third Avenue in the noontime traffic, Angela had time to compose herself and think. It was finally finished. Her second novel was complete. The manuscript would be submitted to her publisher, Heywood & Horne, who had bought it based on her outline by her agent—and best friend—Elizabeth Walsh. Then she would have to wait for her editor's and the marketing people's reactions, suffering like a nervous defendant awaiting the jury's verdict. What if this book wasn't as successful as her first? The overwhelming commercial success of her first book, *Blue Grotto*, was a hard act to follow.

And what the world had to say about this new book, *Emerald Isle*, meant everything to Angela. In it she had tried to say something important, to go beyond entertainment.

Shaking her long mane of mahogany-colored hair, Angela idly gazed out the window at the lunchtime crowds swarming purposefully and swiftly along the sidewalks of midtown Manhattan. Angela took pleasure in watching the parade of colors, the fashionable New Yorkers having now discarded their spring pastels in favor of bold, bright summertime hues. The reds, yellows, purples, and greens created an air of carnival, contrasting vividly with the serious grays of the stern office buildings that stood like some giant's picket fence along Third Avenue.

The summer-tanned pedestrians reminded Angela that she had been out of circulation for a long time. More than a year of her life had been spent inside her apartment, behind closed doors, while she slavishly dedicated herself to her work. If Mark Green hadn't called her this morning, she would still be writing and rewriting, even though she had finally hammered out the words "The End." Thank God for Mark! Mark, she mused, who was not just her editor, but also a friend. Not just a friend, but also . . .

Suddenly the cabbie turned around in his seat, craning his neck to peer at his passenger.

"Hey, you famous or something?" he asked affably. "You look familiar, you know," the driver continued. "Anyone ever tell you, you look like Sophia Loren? Only younger, of course.

You her daughter? I mean, you could be. I drove a lotta famous people in this cab."

"No, I'm not Sophia—or her daughter, but thanks," Angela said, laughing. As she smiled, she revealed straight, white teeth. Her face boasted wide, high cheekbones and a sensual mouth. She laughed again, thinking that Miss Loren would be horrified to think that she, Angela, at age thirty-one, had been taken for her daughter.

When the cab pulled up in front of the silver sculpted doors of Georgette Klinger's salon, Angela paid the driver and quickly strode inside, where she was warmly greeted by Irina, the receptionist. After exchanging pleasantries, she gently chided Angela for waiting so long between visits.

"Oh, Irina, I know I've been lax," Angela responded, clasping her hands in mock penitence, "but I've been working on my new book. In fact, I just finished today! You're the second person to know."

"Who's the first, Miss Vaccaro? Your boyfriend?"

"My editor."

Angela walked through plush and chrome-furnished rooms on densely carpeted floors to the elevator that took her to the massage room. She stripped off her clothes and lay tummy-down on the table. Sweet relaxation at last, she thought as she prepared herself for a massage. She rested her head on her folded arms and let her mind wander as trained and supple fingers firmly caressed her cares into oblivion. Now was the time to think of pleasure. Of her date with Mark tonight. The first date she had made in months. And it was going to be really special. Something to celebrate. She had told him this morning that she had finished the manuscript. She had made the changes her agent had suggested—cleaned it up here, expanded there—and it was ready to be returned to the Elizabeth Walsh Literary Agency, where it would be retyped, copied, and delivered to Mark at Heywood & Horne.

Too soon the massage was over. Angela slipped into her blue and white Klinger wrapper and terry-cloth scuffs. Hair treatment next. That consisted of a divinely sensual scalp massage, then a shampoo with a mysterious liquid that smelled temptingly like marzipan, and finally the hot oil pack. Angela sat back dreamily in the blue plush chair with a hot, wet blue towel wrapped around her head. It pleased her to think that her neglected tresses were absorbing nourishment while the hot towel kept the pores of her scalp open. How sybaritic she felt having her manicure and pedicure done at the same time, while André, Georgette Klinger's hair expert, massaged her long neck and murmured extravagant compliments in her ear.

"You know you're my favorite client, Angela. It's a treat to work on such gorgeous hair. And you have the best skin of anyone I've ever seen walk in here. Perfect. Absolutely flawless. When you get tired of writing, you could have a fabulous career in show business. I mean fabulous," he cooed. Angela only smiled in response.

"I told you I read your book, right? *Blue Grotto*. Fabulous. I lent the copy you autographed to my roommate. Can you believe it? When that bitch left, he took the book with him. I had to buy the paperback. Could you die?" He looked at his watch. "Are you cooked? Yeah, you're cooked." He unwound the towel and ran his hands through her hair.

"Okay, hon. Go get your facial. What are you doing today? On television again, or what?"

"No, no," she replied, rising out of the chair. "Not today. Nope. I got a hot date tonight!" and she winked at him as she rushed on to the facial salon.

After undergoing a thorough cleaning, moisturizing, and conditioning of her famous face, Angela was beginning to feel ready to greet the world. She decided to forgo "the works," preferring to do her own makeup. The pros always managed to make her look ready for a black-tie New Year's Eve party when a Tuesday night out-for-dinner look would suffice. After she was shampooed a second time and her hair blown dry, Angela was more than ready to head back to the velvet-curtained dressing room and retrieve her clothes. She slipped back into her jeans and sandals but buttoned her shirt only halfway, mischievously revealing deep cleavage and a glimpse of the firm curves of her spectacular breasts. Between them sparkled an eighteen-carat tear-shaped sapphire, hung on a simple gold chain. Angela readjusted her hair (they never combed it *exactly* as she liked to wear it) and looked at herself in the full-length mirror. She smiled, pleased at what a few hours in the right salon could do for a woman's looks—and morale. A few hours! Angela looked at her gold Rolex. It was four-thirty. God, was she running late! She still had to straighten her apartment—it was the maid's day off—and she wanted to make this night even more special by buying something new to wear. Well, I'll just have to hustle, she told herself.

Out on the oppressively hot street again, Angela headed up Madison Avenue to Fifty-seventh Street and made a beeline west to Henri Bendel's. Nowhere else would she be able to find what she was looking for—something wonderful and daring, sexy and slightly outrageous. And it didn't take her long to find what she wanted. After Angela charged Anne Klein's dramatic scarlet silk pajamas to her account, she went straight to the Delman shoe boutique on the first floor of Bergdorf Goodman and bought a pair of dangerously high-heeled gold sandals.

By six-thirty, Angela had fought for and claimed a precious rush-hour cab, straightened her apartment, and was luxuriating in her black marble bathtub with an icy bottle of Pinot Grigio beside her on the thick, white carpet. She raised her wineglass in a toast to herself, her book, and to the nice man who invented air-conditioning, whoever he was. It was so deliciously cool in her apartment that she could comfortably run a hot bath that steamed the art-deco-mirrored walls all around her. Sitting in the bath, sipping the fruity but tangy Italian wine, Angela recaptured the deep sense of relaxation she had lost when she left Georgette Klinger's.

She let her mind wander, and as she soaped her long, voluptuous body, she let her right hand linger over her breasts. Slowly, she allowed her fingertips to play over her nipples, hardening them. With her left hand, she languorously reached between her thighs, rubbing and stroking, finally pushing her finger deep inside. Her mouth opened wide, and her green eyes shone as she brought herself closer to climax.

Suddenly, she heard footsteps in the hallway. Mark had let himself in and was calling her. Cursing under her breath, Angela quickly opened the drain, rose, and began to rinse herself off with a hand-held shower head. I'd better use cold water, she thought, smiling to herself.

When Mark found her she was wrapped prettily in a thick, white bath sheet. He stood in the bathroom doorway, reflected on the walls all around her. He was deeply tanned and, at forty-two, in perfect condition, thanks to his frequent and ardent tennis-playing both at his club and at his Long Island home. He had just come from the office and was wearing a carefully tailored khaki-colored summer suit, a crisp, white button-down shirt, and a madras plaid tie. His gray eyes gleamed at the sight of Angela in her towel. As he smiled, showing even white teeth, deep creases appeared on his fine-featured face. He removed his horn-rimmed glasses, which were fogged over by the conjunction of the cool air of the hallway and the warm air coming from the bathroom, and ran his hand through his brown and silver hair.

"Hey! It's bloody hot in here!"

You don't know the half of it, Angela thought as she greeted Mark with a hug. Wordlessly, he held her close, and she felt him growing hard beneath the impeccably tailored pants of his light summer suit. She broke away, not wanting to arouse him until the very end of the evening. Her satisfaction, thwarted by his unexpectedly early arrival, would be that much greater if she delayed it even longer. First a little dinner, a little wine, some talk. There was time. . . .

Mark had chosen Vanessa's, a chic Greenwich Village restaurant, for dinner, where they could enjoy quiet intimacy away from Mark's colleagues who were dining uptown at Le Cirque, Elaine's, or Mr. Chow's. While they waited for a table at the oak and art-deco bar, Mark reached for Angela's hand. He wanted to draw her closer—closer in every way. He adored her. And although he had never entertained thoughts of ending his marriage, he wanted desperately to possess her completely. Minutes sped by as he watched her silently.

There often were stretches of silence between them. Mark Green, who had dedicated his life to words—fifteen years of working up through the ranks of publishing to become editor in chief at the prestigious house of Heywood & Horne—was at a total loss when it came time to express his feelings. He was dramatic and convincing at editorial meetings, adept at creating any impression he chose to dazzle his colleagues. They cried when he presented a tragedy and howled when he described the new comic masterpiece he proposed to publish. Words stood at his beck and call when his intellect summoned them—but when his heart called on them, they stood mute as stubborn enemies.

At this moment, Mark was happy just to gaze at Angela. Being with her filled him with a schoolboyish pride that he liked to think he had outgrown. But Angela turned heads wherever they went. At times Mark was actually embarrassed by her ripe beauty. It was so frank, so obvious, so openly sexual, that he felt his private self was on display for all to see. For how could anyone be with her and not feel desire? Mark didn't worry about his wife's response when he and Angela were seen together. An "agreement" existed between Mr. and Mrs. Green. Mark knew of his wife's affair with her tennis instructor and knew it was no threat to their marriage. Mark stayed at his pied à terre in Manhattan during the week. His wife never asked for or received a key. Neither spouse would have dreamed of intruding on the other's Monday-to-Friday life. Both were happy and neither would ever consider divorce.

As Mark followed Angela and the waiter to their table, he noticed admiringly that Angela wore no underwear under the shimmering silk pajamas.

After a second glass of Pouilly-Fuissé, Angela grew animated. She wanted to discuss her manuscript and share her doubts.

"I think it's good. Eli read the rough draft and thought it was good, but will you like it? Will the house like it? It's not at all like *Blue Grotto*, you know."

"Look, Angela. Eli knows what's good. If he thinks it's good, it's good. I want you to stop worrying. If the manuscript's as good as the outline, I think you've got a damn good shot at the best-seller list, too. There's very little in the way of competition from other publishers' lists coming up." He paused. "There *is* our Jessica Simon book, of course. So far, all we've gotten is the title—*Lovers and Losers*. She hasn't delivered a word yet. She may not even make the spring list at all, so buck up and start thinking about that big, beautiful check you'll get once your manuscript is in house."

He raised his glass to her as the waiter brought their food. Angela smiled appreciatively at the steaming plate of chicken tarragon. Mark barely acknowledged the arrival of his meal and automatically began to pick at the soft shell crabs amandine. Food was not foremost in Mark's mind tonight. He hoped Angela would eat quickly. The more time he spent with her, the more he wanted her. It had been such a long time since he had made love to her. Underneath the starched, white cloth covering the table, Mark Green had a full erection.

Walking arm in arm along Bleecker Street in the soft

summer night air, Mark and Angela drew a blanket of intimacy
around them. Other couples strolled the Village streets enjoying the romance of the perfect night. Gay men promenaded,
arms around each other, and lesbian women courted openly
while groups of visitors from Long Island and New Jersey
gawked. Because most of Greenwich Village's well-to-do gay
community summered on Fire Island, Angela was surprised to
encounter Scott David and Paul Jameson.

Scott's arms opened wide. "Angela. You look great. Terrific
outfit—but it's *not* a Scott David." He wagged his finger at her,
then bent forward to give her a hearty kiss. She got a strong
whiff of Scott David cologne. She grasped his hands and stood
back to appraise him. She had not seen him for a long, long
time. He stood tall, lean, and firm. His deep tan, dark hair, and
velvety black moustache were set off by a light blue golf shirt
with a red sailboat—the Scott David insignia—on the breast.
He wore tight, faded dungarees—Scott David Jeans, of course.
His bare feet were slipped comfortably into properly scuffed
Top-Siders. Despite the preppy outfit, Scott David, born Scott
David Schwartzbarth, was still the boy from the Bronx who
had parlayed his considerable design talent into a sizable
fortune as one of the five top American fashion designers. His
sporty and trendy fashions for men and women comprised only
a small part of a design empire that conferred the ubiquitous
sailboat trademark on linens, tablecloths, jewelry, cologne,
leather goods, and even kitchenware.

His friend and sometime lover, Paul Jameson, struck a
definitive contrast to Scott's exotic darkness. Paul, blond and
bearded, blue-eyed and golden-skinned, was dressed exactly
like Scott except that his golf shirt was black.

Introductions were unnecessary. Paul was the art director at
Heywood & Horne. After greetings were exchanged, Paul
suggested they all go to David's Potbelly on Christopher Street
for dessert. Angela let visions of chocolate-chocolate chip
Häagen-Dazs ice cream dance in her head and was about to
take him up on his offer when Mark cut in.

"No, I don't think we can. We have to make it an early
evening."

Paul was obviously disappointed. "Well, okay, but Angela,
you'd better call me. We have a lot to talk about."

"I'll call you tomorrow. I've missed you." Impulsively,

Angela reached up and kissed him, breaking away quickly as Mark took her arm. Over her shoulder she called back to him, "Hey, I finished *Emerald Isle*. We've got to talk about a jacket!"

Uptown on Central Park West, Mark sat in his favorite armchair in his studio apartment in the San Remo, the luxurious building that was once a hotel, and waited. Suddenly, the bathroom door opened and there she stood. All five feet and seven inches of naked, womanly glory. He inhaled deeply and took in every inch of her body: the long, slender neck, snowy shoulders, the extraordinary breasts standing out full, round, and heavy, their deep rose nipples startling against the stark whiteness of her flesh. A tapered waist curved and swelled gently into rounded hips, and a mound of fine reddish brown hair surmounted well-molded, firm thighs. Her legs were long and shapely, her feet slender and highly arched.

Mark led her into the alcove that surrounded the large platform bed, where Angela teased him by posing languorously and suggestively on the bed, first on her back with an arm flung underneath her head, pushing the proud breasts into prominence while she coyly covered her sex with her other hand. As he quickly undressed, she turned over on her belly and gave him a full view of her round, shapely buttocks and beautiful back. She knew she was gorgeous, and she reveled in it. She knew that men enjoyed her body, and she shared that pleasure with them.

As Mark pulled at his tie and fumbled with his shirt buttons, he silently prayed that he would be able to contain himself inside her long enough to give her the pleasure she obviously sought. Seconds later, naked and lying beside her, he began to caress her breasts, concentrating on her hard nipples. She began to moan as he moved his head down to playfully jab at her nipples with his tongue. Angela grasped his erect penis and massaged it until Mark gasped. As he entered her, her muscles tightened around him, and they began the slow, undulating voyage to climax. Angela felt it first. She tensed, but as he urged her on, she let go and came in heaving waves, thrashing wildly, grasping his shoulders. Then he thrust violently. It was over quickly, and the air was perfectly still.

After lying silently for a few moments, Angela jumped out of bed. "I've got to go, Mark."

"Angela, please. Spend the night with me. Why won't you ever spend the night with me?"

Angela shook her head.

Mark continued pleading. "Look, we'll have a nice breakfast, then spend the day together. I could use a day off. What do you say, Angela? We could have a whole day together."

"Mark, you know I like to sleep at home. We've been over this a thousand times. Now help me find my earrings. I can't remember if I took them off here or in the bathroom."

Angela told the cab driver to drive slowly through Central Park on the way downtown. She was in no hurry to confront the loneliness of her dark, empty apartment. Yet the alternative was out of the question. She would not sleep with Mark. Or any other man. What if the nightmare should come? What if she awakened in the middle of the night, screaming and crying out as she had so many, many times before? She'd have to explain. Mark would want to hold her, to know all about it. And bind her closer, with intimacies deeper than the ones their bodies had known. No. It was best to keep things just as they were. Light. Breezy. Simple and fun. No, it would not do to tie herself to anyone. Not now, not ever. It would only turn out badly in the end. It would only hurt, and pain was something she knew only too well.

CHAPTER
2

"MAKE a wish, darling," cried Marie Vaccaro, putting her arms around her taller, thin daughter and squeezing her close. Her voice still carried the Irish lilt that years of training from the nuns at the orphanage where Marie was educated could not erase.

"Wish for a new dog for me!" called Jimmy, jumping up and down beside the kitchen table.

"Jimmy! Take it easy. You'll knock over the whole table." Sal Vaccaro ruffled his son's thick, light brown hair.

"Angela's got to make a wish for something for herself," Marie admonished. "It's her birthday."

Radiant behind the chocolate cake her mother had baked that morning, Angela's merry eyes reflected the light of fourteen—one for good luck—candles.

"Hurry, Angie," Jimmy cried, "the candles are melting."

Angela shut her eyes and made her wish. Then, as she drew in her breath, Jimmy, Sal, and Marie bent with her over the cake to help her extinguish the dancing flames.

"What did ya wish for, Angie?" Jimmy wanted to know.

As Angela cut and served the rich devil's food cake, she silently pondered her wish. She could *never* tell anyone about this! It was not like wishing for a new Sunday dress or the smallest, best transistor radio. This was a lot more private than wishing for straight nineties on her final exams. Angela had wished for a miracle. And the miracle was to happen to her. She had wished to "develop."

All the other girls in the seventh grade were way ahead of her. They were developing right before her eyes. Almost all of them wore "training" bras at least. All the other girls in her

class were wearing underwear with names like Maidenform
and Playtex. She was still in Carter's.

What a curse it was to look like Angela! Tall, painfully
skinny, with a shapeless body that seemed to be all gangly,
ungainly legs. Yes, it would be nice if her body would hurry up
and develop.

And there was something more. To Angela, her *thirteenth*
birthday was especially important. She wasn't a kid anymore.
She was thir*teen*. A teenager. Something was bound to happen.
She made a wish to find out soon just what she was meant to
be.

Everyone was special in his or her own way, it seemed to
Angela. Everyone but her. Everybody she knew had a quality
or talent that set them apart and gave them an identity. But
where was hers? Even Jimmy, her younger brother, had *something*. Ever since he was a little boy he had drawn and painted.
Mama always said that he was a regular Michelangelo, the way
he liked to make things out of clay or bits of colored paper.
Jimmy was only nine, but everyone knew that someday he'd be
a real artist.

But what was special about Angela? What *could* be special
about an awkward girl who liked to read and make up stories?

Marie placed a gaily wrapped box in front of Angela.

"Open it, Angie, open it," Jimmy demanded excitedly.

Angela carefully unwrapped the box, so she could save the
white daisy-patterned wrapping paper and full yellow bow.
Reaching inside it, she produced a baby blue leather-bound
book bearing the gold-stamped inscription "My Diary." It had
a gold clasp lock and key.

"Oh, Mama. This is great. Really neat. I'm going to write in
it every day," promised Angela. Maybe, thought Angela, the
diary would help her find out what she needed to know about
herself. Maybe it was the beginning of her wish coming true.
This *was* a happy birthday.

But Angela was not quite finished with birthday surprises.
Marie had yet another gift for her daughter. When the house
was dark and still, when Jimmy and Sal were in their beds,
Marie tapped lightly on Angela's door.

"Angela, honey, you asleep?"

"No, Mama, I'm awake."

Angela was sitting up in her narrow bed carefully writing the first entry in her new diary. Marie sat down on the edge of the bed.

"I want to show you something, Angela," Marie began as she removed a bank book from the envelope in her hand. "I've been saving out of my household money for you for a long time."

"But Mama, why? . . ."

"Hush, darling, and just listen. You're a real bright girl, Angela. Your dad and I are very proud of you. You know that, don't you?"

Angela nodded.

"If you do well on your exams this fall, you'll be going on to a good high school. And Daddy and I have always planned on that, that you'd go to a good Catholic high school and get a good education. It costs money, but we're ready for that now. But Angela, if you do well in high school and you take to your studies like you're taking to them now, there's no reason why you can't go on. You see what I'm getting at? You could go to college, Angela. A good college. The best. But that costs a lot of money. And I'm not so sure your dad will go along with all that. He can see Jimmy maybe wanting to go, but he won't see any need for you to continue. So, much as I hate going against your father or having secrets, I decided to do something on my own about it. I saved some money that I've put in a savings account in trust for you. Now what do you think?"

"Mama! I think it's great. I mean, thank you, Mama. I know I'll do well. I just know I will, and I'll make you both so proud. Oh, Mama!" Angela hugged her mother.

Marie tucked in her daughter, as she did when she was a little girl, and kissed her good night.

"Good night, Mama. It's been a great birthday."

Soon all the lights but one were out and the house was very still. Angela fell asleep to the gentle rhythmic groaning of her parents' stately old bed. She did not hear her father whisper to his wife, as he smiled down and winked at her transfigured face, "Marie, hey, Marie, you're still my sweetheart."

Angela was thinking about Mama's secret savings account that day in October as she walked home from St. Luke's School. She had missed the bus again, and was progressing slowly, because she had many books to carry.

She had chosen the books from the school library slowly and thoughtfully, as she always did. Once she entered that large, well-lit room with its special dry smell of old paper, paste, and dust, she lost all track of time. So of course the bus was long gone.

The walk home through the clean, neatly paved streets of Whitestone, Queens, was so familiar to her that the sights along the route held no surprises. To make the time pass faster, Angela usually made up stories in her head about the people she passed and the houses she walked by.

But today Angela's thoughts were far from flights of fancy. Catholic high school entrance exams were finally over, and she hoped she had placed well enough to be assured acceptance by the Catholic girls' high of her choice. She would consider all those in New York City and pick the one that offered the best college preparatory program. If she worked hard, got summer jobs, and if Mama kept adding to that bank account, Angela would go to college for sure.

Angela's thoughts were interrupted by the sound of angry voices up the street. As she approached the three girls wearing St. Luke's green jumpers and white cotton blouses, Angela recognized Elizabeth Walsh, the new girl in school who worked in the library, with Patricia Conlin and Mary Ann Donato, the "fastest" and most "well-developed" girls in the eighth grade.

"You stupid four-eyes fag!" Mary Ann jeered, holding Elizabeth's arms tightly behind her back.

"Wanna smoke, goody two-shoes?" Patricia sneered, threatening Elizabeth with the lit end of a cigarette.

"Let go of me, you dirty tramps," Elizabeth screamed, her chubby-cheeked face aflame with rage.

"Listen, curly locks," Patricia said, grabbing a handful of Elizabeth's unfashionably spirally white-blond hair, "you better watch what you call us, or we'll *really* have to teach you a lesson."

"That's right, Miss Librarian. You think you know it all?" added Mary Ann. "You don't know anything, you stupid baby."

Elizabeth lunged at Mary Ann, and her square-shaped, thick-lensed glasses flew off her nose and skidded across the sidewalk, landing at Angela's feet. Angela quickly picked them up, and strode into the tangle of girls.

"Okay," Angela said crisply, handing Elizabeth her glasses, "that's enough. Let go of Elizabeth *now*."

The action stopped abruptly.

"Well, look who's here," said Mary Ann, patting her teased hair into place. "It figures she'd be friends with Walsh. You faggy girls gotta stick together. Hey, Vaccaro, how's the view up there, ya beanpole!"

"Come on, Elizabeth," Angela said, ignoring the jeer. "The guys are waiting for us at my house."

Awed and astonished by Angela's face-saving fib, Elizabeth nodded and hurried to fall into step with Angela's long strides, ignoring Patricia and Mary Ann's jeers.

"Two against one," Angela said. "Those girls are *gross*."

"Thanks for helping me out. I'm Elizabeth Walsh, but in my old neighborhood in Brooklyn everybody called me Eli."

"I know you. You're new at St. Luke's. You work in the library. I see you there almost every day."

"I know. I've seen you, too. I was going to start saying 'hi' to you, but, well, I didn't, and then I couldn't. You know what I mean?"

"Sure. You probably thought I was stuck-up anyway. Everyone does."

"Oh, no," Eli protested. "It's just that you always look so serious. And, besides, Sister Immaculata told me not to talk to anyone. I'm her slowest worker."

"That Sister Immaculata is strict."

"You're telling me! But in a way I don't blame her. When I'm supposed to be putting the books back on the shelves, I always start reading them. If they look interesting, that is. Right now I'm reading biographies."

"Me too!" cried Angela, and she showed Eli her books. The girls continued in silence.

"Wow," Eli began, "I can't get over how brave you were. I don't know how you just walked over and stopped them. I mean, weren't you scared?"

Angela laughed. "I guess I should've been, but I got so mad when I saw them, I didn't think about it. By the way, I'm Angela Vaccaro."

"Angela Vaccaro! You're the one who left a composition in the library. Did you ever get it back?"

"Oh, yeah, thanks."

"I read it, you know. You wrote a really good story."

"Oh . . . that was nothing. I meant to throw it away," Angela said, turning her head from Eli.

"Nothing? Are you kidding? It was great. I wish I could write like that. You should enter Sister Ursula's composition contest."

"I thought about it, but I don't know. I'd never win. Besides, if I did, I'd have creeps like Mary Ann and Patricia giving me a hard time."

"I know what you mean. They hate the girls who get good grades, but boy, they don't mind cheating off your test papers when they get a chance. Look, Angela, you've got to enter the composition contest. You're really good."

"Nah, I can't write. Not the way these guys can," Angela said, holding up a library book. "My stuff's just kid stuff. It's no good."

"Why don't you give it a try? If you won, I'd be happy for you and besides it would confirm my literary judgment."

Angela looked hard at Eli for a moment. "It would?"

"Yes, it would." And then she added lightly, "And, anyway, us faggy girls gotta stick together. Well, here's my house. See you tomorrow."

Angela rounded the corner and headed toward the modest Vaccaro house with its neat front yard. She was surprised to see her father's green *Vaccaro Brothers Tile Company* van parked in the driveway.

"Daddy? Daddy?" she called as she walked through the door. "You home?"

"In the living room," her father answered softly.

Angela found him sitting in his TV chair, still in his dust and grout-covered work clothes.

"What's wrong, Daddy? Where's Mama?"

"Your mama's in the hospital."

"What's wrong?"

"She went for a checkup and the doctor saw something that wasn't supposed to be there, so he wanted her to go over to Whitestone Hospital and get it checked out," Sal said, his dark Italian face drawn and sallow. "I want to go over and see her.

Do you think you can take care of Jimmy for a while and make some dinner for the two of you?" He stood up wearily and kissed the top of his daughter's head. "Be a good girl. And don't worry."

Colored lights shed their red and green glow on the thin layer of crusty snow that had fallen days before. It was almost Christmas, and all the houses lining both sides of the Whitestone block displayed elaborate decorations.

Jimmy and Angela had dutifully brought the cartons that held the strings of lights and miniature sleigh from the basement, but Sal never brought the ladder from the garage and decorated the house. He couldn't bring himself to do it this year. Not with Marie still in the hospital and the prognosis so grim.

Angela put dinner on the table and waited for Sal to come home from the hospital. He was unusually late tonight, and Angela was beginning to worry when Sal burst through the door, bringing a blast of cold air with him. He was smiling triumphantly, and he carried a small Christmas tree in his arms.

"They're letting Mama come home for Christmas!" he shouted as Angela ran to help him with the tree. "She's gotta go back right after, but she can spend the whole day with us!"

After dinner, they decorated the tree together. Angela felt sure that the news meant that Mama was getting better.

On Christmas Day, Sal carried Marie into the living room and laid her down on the couch. The ease with which he was able to lift and carry her shocked and saddened him. She no longer felt like a flesh-and-blood person but like a doll made of corn husks and rags. He covered her with an afghan and propped her up with pillows so she could watch the children open the gifts that lay under the tree. Angela tried not to notice the change in her mother since her hospitalization two months before. She had even changed since the last time Angela had been allowed to visit her—just days ago. She looked paler, more fragile. Her hair lay limp and dull on the pillowcase, and deep, bruiselike circles ringed her lusterless eyes.

"Angela, come here," Marie called to her daughter. "You see that big box with the red ribbon? That's your special gift from Daddy and me. Bring it here, honey."

Angela lifted the heavy box and took it to her mother's side.

"Open it."

Inside, Angela found a portable typewriter. It was more than Angela had ever dreamed of asking for. Forgetting her mother's frailty for a moment, she exuberantly hugged and kissed her, then ran to Sal and grabbed him around the neck, kissing him and breathlessly thanking them both.

Marie smiled and motioned Angela to sit down beside her on the couch. "Listen to me, Angela. You have a God-given talent. You're a natural-born writer. You're a very special girl with special talents and special dreams. Don't waste it all. I want you to be happy. I want you to have your dreams come true."

Angela nodded her head. She had listened and would try to do as her mother asked, although she didn't quite understand why her mother was telling her this now; why she looked so serious, so intense.

All too soon the day came to an end. As Angela took her typewriter upstairs to her room to try it out, Jimmy busied himself looking for his paintbrushes to experiment with his new set of watercolors. Alone with his wife at last, Sal knelt at the side of the couch. As Marie stroked Sal's dark hair, he buried his face in her lap and held her until it was time for her to go.

By the time she was seventeen, Angela knew better than most girls her age that life can hold many surprises. No one could have predicted that Marie Dugan Vaccaro would die of cancer at age thirty-two, but she did. And after that Angela's life changed drastically. Sal changed too. Sal's genial good humor turned to bewilderment. The reality of raising two children without a wife confused and intimidated him, but he did his best, often asking himself: What would Marie have done?

Jimmy and Angela grew closer, seeking solace in each other. They were the only two kids they knew whose mother had died, and they felt less freakish and alienated when they could huddle together.

Mama's secret savings account was depleted by her long illness and the funeral that followed, and Angela had to go to public school although her exams had placed her at the top of her class. The dreams of a Catholic prep school was gone, but

Eli's steadfast presence at Whitestone High School made the transition from dashed dream to mundane reality much easier for Angela to bear.

Because Eli's parents thought a parochial high school education would be limiting, Eli went to Whitestone High too, and the best friends weren't separated. They also encouraged Eli to think about and discuss politics, art, religion, and sex and took her to the theater and museums. But the Walshes' liberal attitudes separated Eli from the other mostly working-class kids, who thought her "weird." It was true; Eli was different. And she reveled in it.

She wore wire-rimmed glasses and lots of silver jewelry. Her white-blond hair fell naturally to her shoulders in bouncy ringlets. While the other girls experimented with teasing, spraying, and bleaching their hair, Eli experimented with chord changes on the guitar she had bought in a secondhand shop.

To Angela, Eli was a marvel of spunkiness and individuality. Her ideas were off the wall sometimes, but they always made Angela stop and think. The two girls got together after school and discussed their English assignments and the books they borrowed from the library and exchanged. Only Eli read what Angela wrote in her journals. The diary Angela had received for her thirteenth birthday had been quickly filled with daily thoughts and experiences. She had locked the little book with its gold key and put it away on the top shelf of her closet, but she continued writing her daily entries in what she now called her "journal." Starry-eyed teen-agers wrote about their crushes in *diaries*, a future famous author kept a *journal*.

Luis took a deep drag on the joint gripped between his lips. He was clapping his hands and shaking his shoulders in time to the heavy beat pounding through the headset of the Sony Walkman hidden in his pocket when he spotted the taxi slowing down as it approached the building. He ran to the curb and opened the door, extending his hand to help Angela out.

"Shee-eet!" The doorman hissed under his breath. "What a woman! This job's okay!"

Once upstairs, Angela began pulling off her clothes before she got to the bedroom. She was exhausted. It had been a full day . . . finishing the novel, shopping . . . then Mark. Now she wanted to sleep.

Stripped to the skin, she slipped between cool sheets and settled into her habitual place on the right side of the queen-size bed, as though leaving room for someone else next to her. Pulling the extra pillow in close to her body, she whispered, "Please not the nightmare, please, no dreams tonight."

As loneliness enveloped her, she reminded herself that it was her choice. She slept alone because she *chose* to. Still, it was hard for a woman who had been married . . . twice.

It was Frankie Marino's interest in her that convinced Angela that she must have changed, that she must have shed her ugly-duckling feathers for swansdown; or Frankie, the most popular and best-looking guy in Whitestone High, would never have asked her out.

Eli tried to convince Angela she was beautiful, had even dragged her to the mirror and said, "Look! Look at you, for God's sake. You're gorgeous!" But Angela had remained unconvinced. Even when she went to Jones Beach with Eli and boys swarmed around, she was sure that it was Eli's wild blond hair and lithe, small body with its compact rounded hips and small, plump breasts that attracted the excited catcalls and whistles. She could not see the new Angela, who was a miracle of curves and shapely limbs, of heightened and breathtaking coloring, of defined and classic features.

Eli had looked at Angela incredulously when she told her the news about Frankie. Frankie was handsome, of that there was no doubt, but he was certainly not Angela's "type." He never read anything except what he had to for class. He excelled in sports and in the auto shop, not in the classroom, where Angela and Eli shared the spotlight with a handful of other "college-bound" Whitestone High seniors.

Eli tried to talk Angela out of "going" with Frankie Marino, but when she saw the tilt of Angela's obstinate chin and the shine in her shamrock-green eyes each time Frankie was mentioned, Eli sighed and changed the subject.

As for Angela, she thought that life could not offer her more than a night in a parked car with Frankie's muscular brown arms around her. The inevitable happened just before graduation. Beneath the hedges circling the high school playing field, on soft, scented spring grass, Angela gave in to Frankie's persistent desire. It hurt a lot more than she thought it would, and it was over very quickly. Frankie lit a Camel cigarette pulled from the pack he kept folded in the sleeve of his T-shirt against the bulging muscle of his upper arm.

"I'm scared, Frankie," Angela said, as she pulled her panties and jeans on. Her blouse and bra were untouched. "What if I get pregnant?"

"You won't, dummy," he replied. "You can't get pregnant your first time."

"Eli, you've got to help me," Angela whispered into the telephone six weeks later. "I think I'm pregnant." She was calling on her friend as she had hundreds of times since her mother died, for help, advice, and comfort.

"Angela, oh, God! Are you sure? What are going to do? Do you want to have an abortion?"

"I can't, Eli. I would feel like a murderer. But I don't want to have a baby! I've been accepted by Queens College!"

"I know! Why don't you tell your father maybe—"

"No! My father can never know! He trusted me."

"What does Frankie say? Oh, Ange, you're not thinking of marrying him, are you?"

With that, Angela began to cry. "Yes, Eli. That's exactly what I'm doing. I don't see any other way out!"

Angela became Mrs. Francisco Marino on June thirtieth, nineteen sixty-eight, only weeks after her eighteenth birthday. She entered the date in the artists' sketchbook she now used as a journal.

"Today I married Frankie," she wrote. It was to be the last entry she would write for seven long years.

She blamed herself when she lost the baby. Three months after the hasty wedding, she was overwhelmed by intense cramps and woke up in the hospital. She was glad not to be a mother, but had her wishing made the baby die?

Angela's life was lonely. She missed Eli, who was a busy New York University co-ed living in a Greenwich Village dorm. As Eli's world broadened, Angela's seemed to shrink. She felt envy mixed with pleasure when Jimmy showed her projects he had done in his art class. She felt envy and frustration when Eli visited her on school holidays and described campus activities. And when, as the years passed, Eli graduated and got her first job as an assistant in the Brad Monroe Literary Agency, Angela despised herself for feeling envy—and for not keeping up with those who had expected so much of her.

After six years of marriage, Angela's loneliness was so great, her boredom so acute, that she became obsessed with the idea of having a child, surprising Frankie with a sudden burst of passion. Frankie had long ago accepted Angela's moody indifference. She made him feel awkward and stupid when he was with her. He found comfort away from her in easy sex with the neighborhood "fast" girl, in bowling with the guys, and watching "the game."

Angela felt a pleasure deep and rare when Dr. Blumberg told her she was pregnant again. Maybe now her life would have meaning. Someone would need and love her, and she would have fulfilling tasks to perform. She was wild and inconsolable when just three months into the pregnancy she lost that child, too.

After a spell of grief, Angela withdrew to her bed for many weeks. She barely spoke and ate little. Sal was frightened, Jimmy alarmed. They decided she needed a change of scene.

"I won't go," Angela said when Sal visited her apartment and handed her the passport.

"But Angela, you'll love it. It is beautiful in Italy, and my sister will take care of you. She was so happy when I wrote to her. She has been a widow for so many years. She must be very lonely. You would be doing her a great favor to visit."

Just then Angela heard Frankie rush into the apartment, home from his job behind the neighborhood delicatessen counter, then she heard the sound of the Yankee game coming from the TV set in the living room.

"Hey, Ange," Frankie's voice rang out, "we got any beer?"

Angela looked at her brother standing next to her father at her bedside. Deep concern and love filled their sad eyes.

"All right," she said, "I'll go."

Eli met her at Kennedy Airport, late as usual. Angela was just about to board when her friend came flying through the waiting room.

"Angela! Wait! Here's a going-away present!" Eli pressed a notebook into Angela's hand. "Take this, Ange. You're going to a foreign country, you lucky kid. You're going to have lots of adventures and experiences—so *don't forget to write!*"

CHAPTER
—————3—————

ANGELA wanted to drop her suitcase and scream. Standing in the Naples train station, she felt as though she were wide awake trapped in a nightmare. Total chaos reigned as people rushed, pushed, collided, and cursed their way through the cavernous station. How would she ever get any directions? No one would stop long enough even to notice her. After the long plane flight, Angela just wanted to collapse. If only she could lie down, close her eyes, and find herself back in her own bed! Panic began to climb from her stomach to her pounding heart and make its way to her throat, choking her and bringing tears to her tired, gritty eyes. Taking control, Angela reached into the flight bag slung over her shoulder and found Aunt Renata's letter. With her free hand, she took out the onionskin note and scanned the page for the directions she had underlined in red.

> You will be tired from the plane, but you must go to the train station and find the Circumvesuviano. It is very bad to be a young girl alone in Napoli. They steal here and also will bother the ladies, so you must come directly to Sorrento. You must hold tight to your possessions because they know many tricks in Napoli to fool the tourists. Don't pay for anything with traveler's checks. Change them at the booth marked CAMBIO for the good rate of exchange.

Cambio, Angela thought. Well, that's a start. Off to the side of the station she spotted a glass-enclosed area where the sign she sought hung outside like a shingle. Lifting her heavy suitcase, Angela began to make her way across the floor.

Suddenly, she was noticed. Dark-skinned men began to zero in on her from all corners of the station, each of them gesturing, speaking to the signorina, obviously wanting to "help" her with her suitcase. Angela shook her head vehemently and tried to keep walking in the direction of the cambio. But they would not leave her alone. "Bella signorina!" they kept repeating. One smiling moustachioed young man even tried to free the suitcase from Angela's tight grasp.

"Stop it!" she cried. "Please go away!" A circle of smiling, nodding, murmuring men and boys gathered around her. One older man, at least fifty, dressed in tight jeans and an open sports shirt, reached behind her and gave her backside a slow, deliberate squeeze. A pimple-faced teen-age boy reached forward quickly and pinched her breast painfully. Angela pulled away on the verge of tears. "Stop that!" she shrieked. Animals! They were all animals! Why wouldn't they leave her alone! Where was a policeman? When a policeman finally strolled by, she called out to him, but he shrugged, winked, and went on without breaking his leisurely stride. What kind of a place is this? Angela wondered as she rammed her suitcase through her group of admirers and made her way to the glass booth.

Calmer, and with fifty dollars' worth of colorful lire in her purse, Angela made her way to the train that would take her to Sorrento and Aunt Renata.

The hour-long ride on the crowded, odoriferous train did nothing to raise Angela's spirits. With a romantic-sounding name like Circumvesuviano, she had expected something a little better than a nonscenic ride in a train like the Long Island Rail Road at its worst. This is where they sent her to "get away from it all"?

As Angela stepped through the station door into the bright sunlight of Sorrento, she gasped, blinked, and stared. She felt as Dorothy must have in *The Wizard of Oz* when her house touched ground and the gray, dull world of Kansas was transformed into the blazing colors of the land of Oz. In the bright late-morning Mediterranean sun, Sorrento indeed looked like a fairyland.

The low pink, yellow, and white buildings awash in the golden light looked like gingerbread houses among the extravagant groupings of lemon and orange trees that lent sweet fragrance to the clean sea-swept air. Purple, scarlet, and pink flowers bloomed all along the narrow little streets Angela could see from the top step outside the station.

On the street below, a toothless, wizened man beckoned to Angela. In a daze, she walked down the steps to a picturesque donkey-drawn cart that stood as if waiting for her. The old man took off his straw hat, a match for the one worn by the lazy-eyed donkey, took her suitcase, and motioned her into the cart that would take them through the narrow streets of Sorrento to the sea.

The bright pink Hotel Vistamare appeared like a bead in the colorful necklace of resorts strung along the high plateau overlooking the Gulf of Naples. From its perch on the southern end of the edge, the Vistamare stood directly overlooking the Marina Grande of Sorrento. The smooth beach below, blackened by volcanic ash from the eruptions of Mount Vesuvius, was flung out like an opera cape between the base of the rock plateau and the sparkling crystal-blue sea. From the beach a high boardwalk extended to the Gulf. Cabanas and matching deck chairs lined the walk and dotted the dark sand beach, their bright yellow and red stripes standing out gaily against the cloudless blue sky and tranquil sea.

Inside the Vistamare, all was bustle and action. The hotel's proprietress, Renata Vaccaro Soluri, stood behind the reception desk in the lobby of the modest class-two hotel and cajoled, purred, barked, and scolded her staff into frantic, purposeful motion.

In a town that had been known as a resort for two thousand years, the season was once again upon the natives. Hordes of German businessmen and their wives and legions of middle-aged British couples were on their way to Sorrento, site of Roman emperors' villas, the very spot from which Ulysses had heard the songs of the sirens.

And Renata loved it all. It was a tremendous responsibility for a widow alone, but the spirited Renata welcomed each summer as another adventure. Although fifty, she admitted only to thirty-eight—and got away with it. Very thin and very tan, she had a strikingly handsome, well-structured face. Deep laugh lines formed around her huge brown eyes when she smiled, which was often. Black eyeliner and bright pink lipstick were her only makeup.

When Renata caught sight of a donkey cart through the glass front doors of the hotel, she clattered out the door and down the steps in her high-heeled mules to greet the niece she had never met.

The old man helped Angela out of the cart and made it clear that he expected twelve thousand lire for the trip. As Angela counted the money into his hand, he looked nervously at Renata. Not realizing that she had just paid about fifteen dollars for an unnecessarily circuitous trip, Angela was shocked when this intense-looking woman began screaming at the driver in Italian. They argued loudly for several minutes until Renata motioned the old man on his way. "Basta!" she cried. Enough! "Va va!" Go! Renata turned to her niece and deliberately looked her up and down.

"Che bella! Angela. No? You *must* be Angela. I am your Aunt Renata. Che bellissima! Very pretty. Why, you really are a beautiful young girl. You must be tired. Leave your bags. One of my boys will get them. Come inside, come." Exhausted and still stunned, Angela contentedly placed herself in this wiry and energetic woman's care. As Renata led her to the elevator that took them to Renata's private suite, she began to explain.

"Vincente took you for a tourist, cara mia. And he made you pay too much. He is a sneaky one. He waits at the station, and when he sees an unfamiliar face, he take advantage. You see? Only the tourists take the cart ride. It is—como se dice?—a gimmick. You see? And he take you the long way, and whew! he charge you much too much. He give me back half the money tomorrow, he say. But we'll see. I tell him he made a bad impression. I break his neck! But now you see—here we are."

They were on the fourth floor in front of a door that led to Renata's own living quarters: a suite of rooms occupying the entire top floor, decorated haphazardly with gaudy-colored lush fabrics draped everywhere and ornate knickknacks, creating a scene of mad opulence.

"Excuse the mess. I'm so busy making clean where the guests live, here I am myself. I can let down the hair. I want to show you the garden. It's on the terrace, very private, where I do the sunbathing. Just through the bedroom."

They walked into the bedroom, and there, on a huge, gilded and carved, clothes-heaped bed, a deeply tanned, completely naked sleeping man lay stretched out, his arm flung across the multicolored pillows. Angela stared.

"Ay, ay! Gianni!" Renata cried in dismay. "Get up! What's the matter with you? Pig! Get up. Lazy. Come on." Renata pulled his hair, and he rose sleepily. The beautiful young man looked from Angela to Renata and smiled as he stood up, extending his hand. "Hello. You must be Angela," he said in halting English. Before the astonished girl could recover her wits, Renata continued her tirade.

"All you want to do is make love, eh? Well, there is work to be done. Go on. Get us some vino. My niece has come a long way. And not to look at you, you fool. Now go." Gianni pulled on a pair of black pants and grabbed a short white waiter's jacket from the back of a chair. Slowly and insolently, he shuffled out the door, but not before flashing Angela a self-satisfied smile.

"Oh, that Gianni." Renata turned to her niece. "He is very pretty, no? But he takes too much for granted. He is a waiter here, and he has too much to do to be thinking all the time of making love, yes?"

Angela could think of no appropriate reply. But Renata did not seem to need one. She chattered on.

"But I am so happy to see you. And how's the family? Your father, Salvatore? Everything is good, yes? Don't worry, Angelina, cara, we will have you healthy and happy quick here, yes? But you are too pale. Come and sleep a little in the sun. Get comfortable, rest. Did you bring a bathing suit? Here they wear the bikini, yes? Well, we leave the unpacking for now. You wear one of mine."

Angela undressed self-consciously, keeping a wary eye on the door lest Gianni should burst in without warning, making her provide the show this time. When she had put on the white string bikini Renata handed her, her aunt clapped her hands and exclaimed:

"Angela! You are magnificent! The bikini is yours." She kissed her niece resoundingly on both her blushing cheeks and led her out to the terrace. When they had settled themselves on beach lounges, Gianni appeared carrying a tray with two wineglasses, a carafe of chilled white wine, and a glass bowl filled with ice water and ripe peaches and luminous green grapes. After he set the tray before them on a low table, Gianni stood staring at Angela. Angela's face reddened. Suddenly, Renata became aware of Gianni's rude scrutiny of her charge.

"Gianni!" she snapped. "Get lost!" Then she threw back her head and let out a deep throaty laugh as the waiter hurried off.

"You see? I was right! The bathing suit looks good, yes? Try this wine. It is special from this part of Italy only. Lacrima Cristi. The tears of Christ."

Angela shyly reached for the full glass her aunt held out to her. The wine looked like ordinary white wine but smelled different. Angela unwittingly crinkled her nose. Renata laughed. "That's the sulphur. The ashes from Vesuvius, the volcano, they fall everywhere for thousands of years—on the beach, in the vineyards, in the earth—so the grapes taste and smell like so. Capisce?"

Angela sipped the wine. It was delicious. She drained the entire glass and soon fell into a deep, much-needed sleep.

As each morning mist melted to reveal a golden afternoon, and as each bronze sunset gave way to a cool blue evening, Renata busied herself preparing the hotel for the tourist season. She had little time to spend with her forlorn and sullen niece, who did not seem to be getting any better. Angela remained lost in her own world, oblivious to the activity around her, scarcely aware of the opportunities at her fingertips. At first Renata had made suggestions. Why not go into Naples for the day? What about a trip to Pompeii? A shopping tour of Sorento? The girl's eyes remained vacant and her face expressionless. The only suggestion acceptable to Angela was that of going down to the sea to swim. Each day Angela walked the short distance from the hotel to the public garden. There she presented her hotel pass to the elevator man, who took her down, through the rock cliff, in a perfectly ordinary-looking elevator. She might have been in a New York apartment building instead of traveling down a tube hollowed through Sorrento's rocky ledge.

Once down on the beach, Angela rented a cabana, removed her shorts and T-shirt, and strode onto the pier in her white string bikini. After climbing down the ladder that led into the sea, Angela cut through the azure water smartly and arrived at the raft that floated a short distance from the beach. Every day she repeated the routine of wringing out her long hair and settling herself belly-down on the raft to sunbathe. Young men passing in small boats called out to her. Resting swimmers sharing the raft with her tried to strike up conversations. She ignored them all or merely said, "Non parlo italiano." But despite her quiet aloofness, she attracted considerable attention. Angela little realized that she had become a topic of conversation among the guests and natives. Who was this mysterious beauty? Why did she not speak? Where was she from? Someone had observed that she wore a wedding band, yet why was she always alone? The young Italian men, vacationers from parts north, conjectured endlessly, each cherishing the dream of being the one who would break through the ice barrier and charm the beautiful stranger into bed. She was fuel for endless fantasies. As she lay in the sun or swam laps from the raft to the pier and back, the young hopefuls discussed her attributes and bragged to each other of what they would do with her. Three teen-age boys from Rome had made her their obsession. They dared each other to approach, to speak with her. And when she ignored their courageous attempts, they cursed her, little suspecting that slowly, the intelligent and forlorn woman, but three weeks now in their country, was beginning to understand their language.

Sitting up in her bed, chewing on the end of her pen, Renata rested her pad of air-mail stationery on her knees. After two letters she was finding it difficult to find things to write to Sal. The fact was, his daughter's condition was showing no signs of improvement. She could assure him that a present had been bought in anticipation of Angela's twenty-fifth birthday on June 3, but she could not assure him that Angela would be pleased by the white linen sundress with Sal's birthday message tucked inside. It seemed as though nothing made any difference to Angela.

It was Sunday morning, still very early, and as the first rays of sunlight filtered into the room, Gianni, snoring softly beside Renata, began to stir. Absently, she stroked his hair as a plan began to take form in her mind. She would throw a little party

for Angela, to distract the troubled girl from mourning her loss
and to show her how much everyone cared. Everyone? Whom
could Renata invite? Angela had made no friends. Women
were put off by her beauty and remoteness. The scores of men
who had, at first, asked Renata if she knew who the beautiful
young lady was had begun to give up hope and to express
resentment. If only Angela knew what opportunities lay at her
feet! She could be having the adventure of a lifetime! Well,
they would have the little party anyway. On the terrace outside
the dining room, with the lights of Naples twinkling in the
distance. Who wouldn't enjoy that? And Gianni would be there
and a few of the others who worked in the hotel. The chef
could bake a special cake. They would have champagne. . . .

Renata felt fingers pinching her naked thighs. Gianni was
wide awake now, and he wanted to make love. Renata threw
back her head laughing and slid down under the sheets,
reaching for Gianni's full erection. In one swift motion, Gianni
pulled the pen from Renata's hand and threw it on the floor.
Soon Gianni was deep inside her, thrusting hard as Renata
screamed with pleasure. As she climaxed, Renata's shouts
intensified. She cursed, screamed, and laughed in her full,
hoarse voice, giving way entirely to her joy. Calling on God,
the Madonna, and Gianni with equal force, she had no idea that
her niece, passing her door, heard it all.

As Gianni joined Renata's chorus, Angela burst into the
room. Hurrying to the bed, she was stopped by a sight that
filled her with shock and embarrassment. Gianni suddenly
tensed and pulled away from his lover's arms. "Madonna!" he
exclaimed. Drawing her legs together and looking up, Renata
met her shamefaced niece's stare with silence.

"I . . . I thought you were hurt. I mean, I thought he
was . . ." Angela stammered and gave up. Renata blinked,
then began to chuckle. As did Gianni. Soon their chuckles
swelled into loud, full-bodied laughter. Tears ran down
Renata's flushed cheeks. Humiliated, Angela turned from the
couple and ran out, taking her usual route to the public
gardens.

Renata had tried, she truly had, but the birthday party was
not a success.

Gianni and the other hotel employees had done their best to

please Renata by attempting to cheer the sour-faced guest of
honor but to no avail. Gianni had flirted openly, with a winking
Renata encouraging him, but his attentions barely raised a
smile on Angela's lips. The headwaiter constantly refilled
Angela's champagne glass in the hope that wine would succeed
where wit had failed. And yes, Angela had drained the glass
time and time again. She got drunk. Morosely, sullenly drunk.
Finally, Renata motioned them all away, leaving her alone with
her niece. The table was cleared but for the glasses, a bowl of
fruit, and a full bottle of champagne. Renata decided to try the
direct approach.

"What is it, Angela? Why can't you smile? You have been
through tragedy, yes. But you are alive. You are young. You
are beautiful. You are here in Italy. Away from these things that
hurt you so. Why won't you let yourself enjoy this?"

With these words, offered warmly and with concern, the ice
finally cracked. Her aunt held her hand while she cried,
offering her a handkerchief as the tears subsided.

"You see, cara, I don't have all the answers. But I do have a
handkerchief."

Like the sun breaking through dark clouds, a smile appeared, stretching across Angela's face. She giggled as she
blew her nose and took another sip of champagne.

"I really have been awful. I'm sorry, Aunt Renata. And I'm
sorry for what happened Sunday morning, too. I feel like such
a fool."

Grasping Angela's hand again, Renata knitted her brows and
said, "Forgive me, Angela, but how did you not know there
were people making love? Have you never heard these sounds?
Have you never felt yourself as I felt with Gianni? You are a
beautiful young married woman. You and your husband
must . . ."

Angela shook her head and cast her eyes down. "No. I
mean, yes, we, uh, make love, but it never gets like that. I
mean, it's over so fast. And I don't feel, I mean . . ."

"I understand, cara. Your husband does not give you
pleasure like Gianni gives to me. Well, he is young; perhaps in
time he will learn how to make you scream for the Madonna,
yes?"

They both laughed. "No, Aunt Renata, I don't think so. I
mean, I don't even know if we have anything anymore. He

doesn't really care. He tries sometimes, but I guess we got married too young, and he's just not that interested."

"What about you? Do you love him?"

"I don't know. I guess so. I'm not sure. I do know that I miss Jimmy and Dad, but I don't miss Frankie, really. I don't even think I really know Frankie."

"But what about the lovemaking? How do you live so . . . so like a nun?"

"I don't know, Aunt Renata. I guess I just don't think about it that much."

It shocked Renata to think that her young niece had no sex life. She mused on the irony: Here was the girl that was charging the entire male population of Sorrento with sexual energy. She knew that all the males in her employ thought constantly of sleeping with their boss's niece. She herself had envied Angela's youth and extraordinary good looks. As the days went by, apart from her sour expression, Angela was growing even more beautiful as her coppery tan deepened and her voluptuous body grew firmer and leaner with the constant exercise her daily swim provided. All these gifts of beauty and sexuality were hers, yet they lay dormant as Angela dream-walked through the realm of the senses. Never an orgasm, never a hot fling with a romantic and ardent lover. Poor Angela.

Renata made up her mind. She would provide Angela with every opportunity to discover the sensual side of herself. And she would start tomorrow. She would expose Angela to the exquisite beauty of nature as lesson—one. She would immediately begin the program by awakening the girl's sleeping senses. Tomorrow Renata would send Angela to Capri.

Angela stood shivering on the deck in the early-morning air; she was sorry she had accepted Renata's advice. If she had taken the hydrofoil, as she had wanted to, she would have gotten to Capri much more quickly. She also would not have to stand in the cold for forty-five minutes with a bunch of silly middle-aged British tourists on the deck of a grubby-looking little boat, a boat that was transporting her reluctantly across the bay in an exercise in futility. What was a trip to Capri going to do for her anyway? Why had Renata been so insistent? If Renata hadn't been so good to her, she would never have agreed to go. But here she was, trembling in her thin-strapped new sundress and her high-heeled sandals, hoping the ride would be over soon and that the whole expedition would end so she could go back and have her swim.

Gazing out to the sea, Angela began to realize why Renata had recommended the slower boat trip. There before her, rising out of the mist that the early-morning sun had not yet grown strong enough to burn away, loomed a glistening mound of pure white rock. As the vessel slowly made its way through the calm water, the mist parted to reveal another mound rising higher than the first. They were nearing the Isle of Capri.

Angela had to admit that she had never seen anything quite so beautiful in her life. From the approaching boat, Capri appeared to rise out of the sea like a miracle, like an exquisite gem the gods, in their greed to possess, had fought over and dropped into the sea. A closer look revealed veins of green vegetation running through the honeycombed white rock. The boat circled around the inaccessible part of the island where the limestone rock, riddled with numerous grottoes, ran right into the most radiantly clear blue sea imaginable. The boat docked at Marina Grande where signs showed the way to the funicular that took passengers up the lower of the two mountains that comprised the island to the town of Capri. Disembarking, Angela decided to get on the next available run and sample that unique mode of transportation that she had heard about in a song her father often sang. But as she began to walk unsteadily in her high heels along the quay, one of her fellow boat passengers grabbed her hand.

"Why don't you follow us, love?" the Englishwoman inquired amiably. "We're going to the Blue Grotto. Morning's the best time to see it, they say. No need for you to wander off alone, is there now?"

Angela nodded her assent and allowed herself to be led across the dock where, after giving the ticket man five hundred lire, she found herself tucked into a motor-powered sailboat. The man at the rudder sullenly took her ticket, waited for the other boats around him to fill up with passengers, then began the four-mile trip along the coast to the opposite end of the island.

Once outside the grotto, the sailboats were met by rowboats to take passengers to the cove. The buoyant-spirited British tourists in their sensible shoes had had no trouble getting into the little boats, although the boatmen only grudgingly offered their hands in assistance. But Angela's high heel caught on the side of the rowboat. Desperately she reached her hand out to the boatman, but it was too late. As her British friend moaned "Oh, dear!" Angela fell into the sea.

Stunned and humiliated, Angela turned from the commotion she had caused in the boats and swam to the close-by shore of the cove. Alarmingly, she found herself rising out of the water and with her now bare feet planted on rock and gravel. She coughed and sputtered in a complete daze. Whatever had happened to her seemed to create an even greater uproar as the boatmen and tourists began to whistle and cheer.

She heard hearty masculine laughter coming from very near, and as she peeled the wet hair off her face, she looked up into the biggest, roundest, most beautiful deep, liquid-brown eyes she had ever seen. Those incredible eyes moved closer to hers as the stranger picked her up in his arms, chiding her good-humoredly in Italian. He draped a pale blue pullover loosely around her and carried her up a steep path to the road and a bright red, low-slung sports car. After he gently placed her in the leather bucket passenger seat, he eased himself into the car behind the small wooden and chrome steering wheel. Smiling and nodding in her direction, he thrust the shift stick into gear, and they zoomed up a narrow mountain road toward the town.

Angela trembled violently as they sped along: partly because she was still cold; partly because the whole incident had shaken her; and mostly because this maniac was driving on a treacherously winding, narrow road at top speed. The "maniac," however, was sanguine. He chatted in his native tongue, his tone of voice assuming she understood him, taking for granted that all was well with her, except for the minor discomfort of dampness. He turned to direct a comment at her from time to time, causing Angela to blanch as he took his eyes from the road. Finally, through clenched teeth, she said, "Non parlo italiano."

"Ah," the stranger replied, as though suddenly seeing the light. "Parlezvous français?"

"No, I don't."

"Oh, yes. English."

"American, in point of fact. And could you please slow down?"

"Oh, yes, mi dispiace. I'm sorry, I mean," he said as he downshifted. "It's just I want to get you into some dry clothes very soon. You see? You can get a cold. Yes?" There was a pause. "Oh, yes," he continued, "I don't mean to frighten you. I am Paolo di Fiori."

"Di Fiori?"

"Yes, like the car. Like this car. You have heard of us? Well, then, we are not strangers, and you don't have to be afraid. Yes? I saw you fall in the water, and I felt I must help you out. I did not mean to be rude, but you have no shoes, so I carry you to the car. We are going to my home so you can get dry. Are you still upset?"

"No. I guess not. I'm Angela Marino. This is my first time here, but I guess you could figure that one out yourself."

"Yes, Angela Marino." He laughed. "Welcome to Capri." They both laughed together now, Angela seeing the humor in her situation for the first time. And as his laughter rang out after hers, she studied the man who was taking her to his home.

She liked what she saw. Paolo di Fiori was exceptionally good looking. Tall for an Italian, he was well built without being especially muscular. His luxuriant hair, the color of mink, and thickly lashed velvety eyes and dark brows contrasted sharply with his fair skin. His nose, though a prominent wedge, was straight, and his firm chin and slightly squared jaw were softened by a surprisingly sensual mouth. He was dressed casually in a white open-necked cotton lisle shirt and white linen pleated pants. Watching him expertly work the clutch and brake of the custom di Fiori, Angela noticed he wore black Gucci loafers without socks.

Halfway up the mountain, Paolo veered the car onto a private road and stopped in front of twin iron gates. Paolo touched a button on the paneled dashboard, the gates swung open, and as they drove toward the end of a promontory that jutted into the sea, Angela caught sight of Paolo's home. It was all glass and wood and built into the rock above the sea. She could see parts of a stone stairway that led down to a private cove where various sea craft bobbed merrily in the little harbor.

Paolo pulled up the drive to the front doors, and two mastiffs ran out and jumped on the car, followed by two moustachioed

young men, wearing jeans and carrying walkie-talkies. When
Paolo shouted commands to the dogs, they immediately were
subdued. As he opened the door and helped Angela out of the
car, the two young men began berating Paolo for, from what
Angela could gather, going off and not telling them where to
find him. Paolo chided them good-naturedly and led her into
the house. A tiled gallery ran the length of the house to glass
doors that led to a terrace garden and a breathtaking view of the
rocks and sea below. A skylight in the center of the gallery shed
golden light on a modern concrete fountain surrounded by
sculptures and well-tended dwarf lemon trees.

Holding Angela's hand, Paolo called out, "Santina!"

A small, neat woman with bright birdlike eyes and hair
pulled back severely from a wrinkled, soft face appeared in the
hall, wiping her hands on her apron. Seeing Paolo, she too
berated him without restraint. Paolo laughed and kissed the
woman's gray head. He soothed her in Italian and explained in
English, for the benefit of his American guest, that the young
lady he had brought home with him had had a slight accident,
and that she needed to get out of her wet clothes and into some
dry ones.

Santina led the barefoot Angela down a wrought iron
staircase with highly polished wooden steps to what she
assumed was the master bedroom. The room was huge,
extending almost the entire length of the house. It was sparsely
furnished in Italian high-tech and only the oversize bed, set in
an ornately carved wooden bedstead, lacked the austerity and
functional look that was the room's unmistakable hallmark.
The thick carpeting was off-white, as were the walls. A black
onyx glass vase filled with tiger lilies sat on a chrome and glass
table that was surrounded by four black leather and chrome
Wassily chairs. The room would have appeared all too severe if
some very human touches had not been added: photographs
and blueprints of automobiles hung on the walls, unframed; a
bottle of suntan oil stood uncapped on the black-lacquered
dresser; a half-written letter lay on the bed next to a discarded
shirt; several tape cassettes lay on the floor next to the bed. It
was obvious that Santina did not approve of some of these
"touches," because as soon as she had shown Angela where
the dressing room was, she began to pick up after her
employer.

Santina had led Angela into what seemed to be a large closet. Three of the four mirrored walls were lined with suits, jackets, slacks, ties, and Plexiglas shelving holding shirts, sweaters, bathing suits—and shoes. Row upon row of leather, suede, and alligator shoes. Buttery-soft loafers, bright-colored sneakers, dashing suede oxfords, linen and leather sports shoes, hand-tooled lizard-skin cowboy boots, white kid jazz shoes. Angela had never seen so many shoes. The fourth wall was a full-length mirror. Angela was shocked to see herself. She was still clutching her rescuer's sweater, but it could not hide what her mishap had done to her. Her hair hung limply down her back in stringy strands, and her beautiful new still-damp sundress clung to her like a second skin, revealing her pink-flowered cotton underpants and dark nipples under the sweater around her shoulders.

"Signorina! My clothes will be too small for you. Signor di Fiori says you may wear his clothes till yours are dry."

Angela looked around her. What could she wear? There was no bathrobe in sight. Perhaps a large shirt? But which one? There were so many. Angela chose as casual and unimportant-looking shirt as she could find—a white cotton shirt with a button-down collar. The Armani label meant nothing to her. She gratefully wriggled out of the wet sundress and underpants and slipped into the shirt whose hem just reached the top of her thighs, affording her more modesty than the wet dress. Angela emerged tentatively from the dressing room. Once she was sure she was alone, she rapidly walked across the bedroom and out onto the terrace that overlooked the sea. Leaning her elbows on the far corner of the low limestone wall, Angela gazed out at the gulf shimmering far below under the afternoon sun. Majestic rock formations rose up from its sapphire surface punctuating a brilliant blue sky. Angela's tense body began to relax as the sun warmed her and the exquisite view lifted her spirits.

Lost in the glories of Capri, Angela stood mesmerized for almost an hour, her mind blank, her senses keenly aware. She did not notice Paolo come into the bedroom.

He could not see Angela at first. Then, out of the corner of his eye, he caught sight of her wind-blown hair through the terrace door. Shirtless and contemplatively stroking the dark hair below his breastbone, he walked over and stood silently behind her, knowing her to be lost in the beauty of the view that still thrilled him, even though he awoke to it daily whenever his whim brought him to his island home. Now, as he admired Angela's striking profile, her smooth, copper skin, long, lean legs, and abundant hair, Paolo felt he had never fully appreciated the view before.

When Angela turned and faced his frankly appreciative stare, she blushed deeply but his eyes held her. As he reached through the open door to draw her close, the loosely buttoned shirt slipped from her shoulder, exposing the full white curve of her breast. Paolo gripped her shoulders.

"You are beautiful, Angela. Very beautiful."

She did not respond but continued to stare into his eyes as he began to stroke her hair. She stood mute as he kissed her face, her neck, her shoulders, and finally her mouth. As his caressing hand reached her breast and its taut rosy nipple, she began to kiss him back. As her arms encircled his neck and shoulders, he lifted her easily and carried her to the bed. Almost in a trance, she watched him unbutton her shirt to bare her to him completely. He inhaled sharply as he explored her magnificent body with his eyes, his hands, and his lips, kissing her neck, her shoulders. Moving his head down the length of her torso, he kissed her breasts, her belly, her thighs.

"Your skin . . ." he murmured, "your breasts . . . you are so lovely, Angela. So beautiful," he sighed.

Tentatively, she rested her hand on his thick hair while he kissed and licked her nipples. As he continued, Angela felt she would melt. The warm sensation between her legs grew, until it became an insistent throbbing. Her breath came in short gasps as he ran one hand down to rest on her downy mound. With his other hand, he led Angela to feel his hardness. He gasped as she stroked him, then sat up and slipped off his pants. Rising from a mass of thick, curly, dark hair stood his fully erect penis. As Paolo led Angela to grasp it in her hand, he sighed with pleasure and closed his eyes.

Lying naked, and pressed together, they silently explored each other with hands, lips, tongues. Angela's avid hands wandered over Paolo's smooth body, touching his chest, his belly, his shoulders, always returning to the hardness between his legs, delighted with the dramatic effect her slightest touch had on him. Paolo stroked her thighs, taking his time, letting his fingers lightly play along the crevice between her legs. As desire consumed her, Angela's thighs parted, allowing him to reach the throbbing, wet place within. He was stroking her faster now, grazing her clitoris which he found easily. The rhythmic pressure of his touch began to send little electric shocks through her, and she heard a voice that sounded like her own, moaning and sighing.

When she thought she could not bear it any longer, he was inside her, easing his full length into her slowly. He held her tightly as he rode her. She shut her eyes and imagined herself to be climbing up a steep mountain—a mountain of pleasure. Each of his ardent thrusts brought her higher. Finally, she reached the peak. As he kept pushing her, riding her, she felt as though she had no choice but to jump off. She let go, expecting to plummet, but to her surprise she did not fall: she flew. And as she soared, waves of warmth and joy shot through her, starting inside her belly and extending to her toes and fingertips. Somewhere in the distance she heard herself scream and call out, "God, oh, God, oh, my God!"

Angela opened her eyes and saw Paolo. His face and chest were flushed and rosy. His eyes were tightly shut, his face contorted. He began to thrust wildly, forcefully, and rapidly, calling her name loudly as he gasped for air.

She held him tighter until he stopped and opened his eyes. Now they were both calm. Their faces and bodies glistened with sweat as he kissed and caressed her, murmuring into her ear, stroking her hair, kissing her eyes. At last, they drew apart and lay side by side, their hearts still pounding.

After a few moments of silence, Paolo reached for Angela's hand and led it to rest on his soft penis. Angela's mind was pleasantly blank when he turned toward her and began fondling her breasts. Then she was aware that his penis was getting hard again. She rubbed and stroked him until he was fully erect. Her nipples hardened as he licked and sucked them. She felt the throbbing between her legs begin anew. Then he was kissing her belly. Now her thighs. He spread her legs apart and began to kiss her there. She tensed. She was not ready for this next new experience. It frightened and confused her, and she tried to push his head away. But Paolo was insistent. His flicking tongue had found her clitoris again. As his mouth and tongue stimulated her, she was enveloped in a deep sense of pleasure.

Her second orgasm came swiftly and unexpectedly, and although it was not quite as dramatically intense as the first, it again filled her with a peaceful, blissful warmth.

"You are like cake, Angela. So sweet," he was saying as he lay beside her again.

"I never . . . I mean . . ."

He put his fingers over her lips and drew her into his arms. "Kiss me there, Angela," he said, placing her hand on his erection. The eyes that looked into his were blank with confusion.

"Come, Angela. I will show you how to give me very much pleasure."

He coaxed and coached her as she took him into her mouth. His sighs and moans told her what pleased him. Arching his back he thrust faster and harder until he cried out and her mouth was filled with creamy wetness.

It was over and he was holding her. She sobbed in his arms, and he did not try to stop her. When her shoulders stopped shaking, he turned her face up to look at his.

"Angela, you have never made love like this?"

"No. I never have. I never even . . . well, it never happened for me like this."

"You have never come before?" Paolo exclaimed in amazement. "But you are very . . . well, very warm. You are a sexy woman, Angela. You try to flatter me. Surely you have had this before?"

Lying there, nestled in the arms of this stranger who had just become her lover, Angela felt a closeness she had never felt with any man. The story of her life came tumbling out. Her marriage to Frankie, their crude, unsatisfying lovemaking, the two miscarriages, her wish to be a writer, everything. Paolo proved to be as good a confessor as a lover. He sympathetically listened to all she had to say, offering reassuring and supportive comments when she was too hard on herself. He was enchanted by this beautiful, melancholy girl. He was flattered that he was the one who had unleashed her pent-up sexuality. She was a refreshing change from the women he was used to sleeping with: the women who were used to having their way in bed, who barked their orders and preferences, who took pleasure selfishly, not caring if they returned it. Much to his delight, Angela was intelligent, too. He was intrigued by her desire to write. Although she was no international heiress, no jet-setting, decadent princess, she was special. And what a beauty! Si. Certo. She was very special.

Satiated and exhausted from lovemaking and conversation, Paolo and Angela drifted into sleep, their bodies entwined. When Angela awoke, Paolo stood beside the bed wearing a black silk robe and holding a tray of food. She sat up, looked into his eyes, and smiled happily.

"I made this myself," he announced as they settled in bed with the tray before them. They hungrily devoured mussels simmered in garlic and white wine and quickly drained glasses of Lacrima Cristi while they chatted intimately, like lovers who had known each other a long time. Paolo was telling Anglea about his plans for the garden outside the villa when she realized that the vista through the glass doors had grown dark.

"Paolo, it's late. I must have missed the last boat back to Sorrento by now!"

"Don't worry. I can take you in my boat. But why must you go? Stay the night and in the morning we can swim, or we can go into town. I'll show you the gardens, or we can—"

"No, Paolo. I've got to get back. Aunt Renata will be worrying about me."

"Go back? Go back and be sad? Swim alone every day at the beach? Stay here, Angela. I want to make you smile. Please."

"No. I can't. Please take me back to the hotel."

"Va bene. I take you."

Stairs led from the terrace to the cove by the sea. There they boarded a small motor launch. As a silence between them grew, Angela began to regret the glorious day. With a clear head, she looked at her behavior in retrospect. She had fallen into the sea. A strange (gorgeous, but strange) man had rescued her, had taken her to his house in a speeding sports car, and had easily, very easily seduced her. Now she had committed adultery, had been unfaithful to Frankie. And she had liked it. She had had not one but two orgasms. She had had the kind of sex with this stranger that she had never even dreamed of. But what did it all mean? What had really happened? Angela reduced it all to a cliché: Some sexy Italian guy picked up a dumb American tourist and laid her, that's what had happened. And now he had something to tell his hotshot friends, and she could be sure she'd never see him again. What a fool she had been!

Paolo maneuvered the boat while deep in thought. Angela's silence hurt and confused him. He thought she had enjoyed the day as much as he had. He had pleased her, he knew that. What had happened? Why did she refuse to stay with him? Had he only imagined that a warmth and intimacy had grown between them? Looking at her, Paolo saw only indifference in her face. He sighed in disappointment as they approached the dock at Sorrento's Marina Grande.

"Angela, let me take you back to the hotel," Paolo suggested.

"No, thank you." Angela did not want to have to explain to Renata who he was. "I'll be fine on my own."

Angela took her sunbathing spot on the raft early the next morning. She had managed to elude her aunt the night before and did not want to have to discuss the excursion to Capri with her this morning. Although guilt still plagued Angela, when she began to recall the details of her lovemaking with Paolo, she found herself aroused. Paolo was a perfect lover. There was no denying that. But the kindness and sympathy he had shown her, the compliments and care were clearly characteristic of the deadly infamous Latin charm that her friend Eli had warned her against. Paolo was probably prowling the streets of Capri at this very moment looking for another foreign pushover.

But she was wrong. Paolo, who knew where to find her, was heading toward Angela in his launch at that very moment. As he neared the raft, he cut the engine.

"Ciao, Angela," he greeted her. "How did you sleep? I was like a baby. I feel good. You too?" He flashed his devastating smile and tried to stand in the rocking boat. He nearly fell over as he waved to her.

She thought he looked wonderful in his khaki pleated pants and black Merona sport shirt. He wore Porsche sunglasses, and his hair was wind-swept and tousled.

What is this? Slim pickings on the Blue Grotto today? Angela thought. She smiled wanly at Paolo. "I'm fine, thank you."

"Come on. Get in the boat. We go for a ride!" Paolo called in high spirits.

But Angela was no fool now. He just wanted a repeat performance. She wasn't about to allow herself to be used again. Even if it was fun.

"No, I don't think so, Paolo. Not today. Arrivederci!" She turned her back before she could see Paolo's face turn red and his smile disappear. He started the engine and sharply turned the boat away. Humiliated and confused, he wondered what he could have done to offend her.

Angela did not return to the hotel until the sun had sunk to rest on the horizon. Renata was waiting for her.

"Angela. You were gone all day! Who is this Paolo? He called six times. He wants to see you, he wants my permission to call on you, he wants to apologize. He is crazy! Who is he?"

Angela shook her head wearily. "Oh, no one. He's Paolo. Paolo di Fiori. Just some guy I met on Capri. Next time he calls, just hang up on him."

Renata's eyes grew wide. "Angela, cara, listen to me. Are you sure it's *di Fiori*?"

"Yes. Di Fiori. Like the car."

"Like the car is right," Renata countered. "Angela, do you know who he is? Wait a minute." Renata dug through the bedclothes and found the magazine Gianni had been reading. It was a three-month-old copy of *Uomo*. There, on the cover, with his two mastiffs and dressed in a beautifully tailored three-piece suit, stood Paolo.

"Yes, that's him all right. I didn't know he was famous. I just thought he was rich."

Renata was impressed. "How well do you know him?"

Angela blushed. "Pretty well, in a way."

"Dio! You have made love with Paolo di Fiori and now you avoid his phone calls? Angela, what has happened? Do you know how lucky you are that he is interested in you? Of course you are beautiful, cara, but Paolo di Fiori is one of the wealthiest men in the world! And he wants to see *you!* Cara, do you know who he is? The cars! The di Fioris! He is the only son of Cesare di Fiori, who owns the whole company. He is a millionaire! Three times they try to kidnap him for ransom."

Angela was thoughtful. "That would explain a lot, then."

"What? Explain what?"

"Why those guys were hanging around his house. Big guys with walkie-talkies. I guess they're his bodyguards."

"Cara, you make me crazy! You spend the day with Paolo di Fiori, and this is all you have to say? Walkie-talkies?"

"Aunt Renata, tell me more about Paolo."

The two women sat on the bed while Renata translated the *Uomo* article for Angela. The story concentrated heavily on thirty-two-year-old Paolo di Fiori's legendary wealth, the money he was heir to, the kidnapping attempts that had been thwarted, and his casual lack of concern about them. Described as one of the world's most eligible bachelors, he was shown water-skiing off the French Riviera, strolling through the Borghese Gardens in Rome, and chatting at Wimbledon with Princess Caroline of Monaco. In a photo taken in Paris at the Place de la Concorde, Paolo was shown walking next to Jackie Onassis, his face in a scowl, his hand raised in anger toward the camera's eye. In a large, full-color picture, Paolo, wearing white coveralls with the di Fiori charging stallion emblem on his breast, flashed an expansive smile as he leaned against a red sports car. Renata read the caption:

Paolo involves himself with the design of the custom cars produced by the di Fioris. This, his own di Fiori, is constantly being modified. When it is ready, according to his own specifications, Paolo plans to race the car at Le Mans.

"Curiouser and curiouser," Angela mumbled.

"Now you must tell me what happened," Renata insisted.

Angela recounted the events of the day before, leaving out only the most intimate details. Renata was enthralled.

"He is wonderful. And of course he is crazy for you. Why do you not run to be with him?"

"Aunt Renata, I'm married. Did you forget? I have to admit that yesterday I thought Paolo was pretty wonderful too, but he's just having fun with me. I was a sucker for his gorgeous brown eyes, and he knows it. How will I ever face Frankie if I let this continue?"

"My dear niece, I think you are making a very big mistake. Paolo di Fiori has made love before. And he does not have to beg for it. He also doesn't have to play games for it. He likes you. Very much, it seems. And you cannot deny that you like him. You are here. It is now. He makes you happy. You need a little joy right now. There will be many times in your life for sorrow. I know. I have lived longer. And had much sorrow. So when a little joy comes along and bites me on the ass, I don't turn away. You understand? Hey, cara, I'll never tell!" Renata winked and hugged Angela.

"I guess you're right about there being time for sorrow. I'm pretty young, and I feel like I've seen a lot of it already. But I'm not sure I can go on being unfaithful to Frankie. I'm not really sure that I love him, but he *is* my husband."

"Think about it, cara. Paolo is a special man. How much joy has your husband given you?"

Angela made up her mind. She would place herself on the raft again tomorrow, and when Paolo came by, as she was sure he would, she would go off with him. She would reach out for the happiness that had eluded her.

But Paolo surprised her. He did not come by the raft the next day. Not in the morning, not at noon, and not even when the day grew chilly and the sun sank into the sea. Sadly, Angela made her way back to the hotel.

Angela found Renata in the sitting room, happily chatting in Italian while arranging a bouquet of tiger lilies in a vase. The visitor to whom Renata was addressing her exclamations sat in a rattan peacock chair, its high back facing the door. Angela was about to leave when Renata caught her eye and motioned her inside.

"I believe you two have already met," Renata crooned as Angela turned to face Paolo di Fiori.

"I am so sorry," they said simultaneously, and laughed.

"You have nothing to apologize for, Paolo. I've been rude . . . and silly."

"I would like you to have dinner with me tonight," he replied, locking eyes with her, "and you, too, of course, Signora."

Renata laughed. "Of course. But no. I have plans this evening. Grazie, Signor di Fiori. Now go, Angela. You can't very well go to dinner in your bikini!"

Angela hugged her aunt and dashed to her room. Thirty minutes later, she emerged, showered and dressed, carrying an overnight bag discreetly under her arm.

CHAPTER
4

"PARTY? Oh, God! I don't know. I mean, it sounds great, but, well, I didn't bring any nice clothes. I mean, what'll I wear?"

"Angela, don't move. I'm trying to get this shot of you with the sun on your hair. . . . Be still, cara."

They stood on Paolo's terrace, Angela again clad only in one of her lover's shirts; he barechested, in jeans, his Nikon held against a squinting eye, a Gitane dangling from his lips. Angela had been posing all morning. They chatted as he circled her, his tanned, bare feet moving constantly to catch her from this angle and that, with the sun above her, the sea behind her.

"Gino! Ettore! Va! You are getting in the picture!" Paolo called to the two guards standing on the rocks below the terrace. They had been climbing around the promontory all morning, scanning the cove from behind dark glasses, walkie-talkies at their hips. They were necessary, yes, but Paolo preferred it when they kept discreetly out of his view. Especially when he wanted to enjoy the illusion of privacy.

Angela would not be distracted. "Paolo, what about this party?"

"Well, some of my friends are going to be here soon, and I want them to meet you. And I am going to arrange for you to meet some people who will help you with your career. Now look at me. Good. Don't hide your smile, Angela. I love it."

"Paolo, what career? What are you talking about?"

"You are a writer, yes? So you can meet some writers."

"Oh, God, Paolo. No!" Angela fled from the terrace. She took refuge in the bedroom, between the bed's cool sheets. Paolo tossed his cigarette over the terrace wall and followed

her, pulling the camera strap over his head. Carelessly, he
flipped the Nikon onto a chair and stretched out beside Angela.

"You want to make love?" he whispered in her ear.

Angela flushed. In the three weeks since she had left Aunt
Renata and the Vistamare to stay at the villa, she still had not
accustomed herself to his directness—or his ever-readiness for
sex.

"No, Paolo," she said demurely, covering her head with a
pillow. She was embarrassed that her retreat to bed had been
mistaken for seduction.

"What is it, Angelina? You are upset?"

Angela's mind raced as her heart pounded. Why must they
have this party? Why couldn't they just leave things as they
were? Here, alone in the villa, they could forget that Angela
was a girl from Queens, New York—a frustrated housewife
whose husband worked in a delicatessen shop. If Paolo brought
his friends here, they would want to know who she was, what
she did. They would know that she was different—certainly
not one of them. And writers! Real writers! People who really
did what Angela had only dreamed of and only talked about.
Why ever had she told Paolo about her silly hopes? He had
taken her too seriously. Now she would be shown up for what
she was—a nobody from nowhere. And worst of all, Paolo
would see it, and the fantasy spell of these blissful weeks
would be broken: she would lose him and the perfect memories
she had hoped to take home and treasure a lifetime.

And what beautiful memories they could be! Each golden
day had been filled with delight and surprise. Angela did not
think it possible, but the lovemaking got better each time.
Paolo was introducing Angela to a world of sensations that she
never knew existed. He made her feel like an exquisite, exotic
princess who existed only to be tantalized and amused.

The piquant taste of the delicate and simply prepared foods
served by Santina on heavy white stoneware plates; the tang of
dry wine, drunk from tall, fluted glasses; the feel of satin sheets
against her bare, sated flesh; the murmur of the sea and Paolo's
soft whispering in her ear; the perfect blue of the cloudless sky;
the clean white of the Capri limestone; and the deep, liquid
darkness of Paolo's eyes held her in thrall, suspended in a
world of extravagant sensation. Her mind almost drugged by

it, relaxed into an open state, while her body was vibrantly
alive, every pore responsive to touch, sound, and sight.

Angela spent a few of the delirious days alone. On those
days, Paolo left their bed early, kissing her and saying,
"Business, cara. See you tonight." When he offered to take
her into town with him so she could shop at Capri's elegant
boutiques while he met with his associates, she refused,
preferring to stay at the villa swimming, sunbathing, and
occasionally writing in her journal. She spent hours gazing at
the horizon or exploring the house, or following Santina about
the huge, well-appointed kitchen—touching, tasting, inhaling
the aromas of herbs freshly picked from the gardens and of
sauces simmering on the stove.

How sweet and voluptuous it all was. But now reality in the
form of a posh party was going to dash it all to pieces.

"Cara, you must tell me. Why are you so upset?" Paolo
stroked her hair, waiting for her to answer. She felt ashamed
and knew she could not explain without revealing her most
deep-seated fears and insecurities to him. And something
worse. She couldn't bear to let him know how much he meant
to her now. She was just discovering this herself—and it
terrified her.

"Cara, you're not afraid of a little party, are you? It's just my
friends. The usual people with some others I invited just for
you. I thought this would make you very happy."

Angela sat up and shook the long hair from her face. She put
her arms around Paolo's neck and kissed his cheek.

"Yes, caro," she said, imitating his accent, "it weel be—
how you say?—fantastico!"

"Oh, you are a witch!" Paolo cried, pulling her down on the
bed. As the playful wrestling turned to serious lovemaking,
Angela vowed to bury her anxieties—for Paolo's sake.

Buttery sunlight filled the room as Angela awoke from a
nap. Stealing from the bed as Paolo lay in a heavy sleep, she
drew on his shirt and slipped up the stairs to the kitchen to find
a snack. As she reached the top step, she drew back and
gasped. Dozens of workmen and crisply uniformed waiters and
maids swarmed the main gallery and buzzed in and out of the
kitchen carrying trays, flowers, cases of champagne, and small
potted palms and trees.

At Angela's appearance, they stopped in mid-task and turned as one man to face her.

"Buona sera, Signorina," they greeted her, nodding and smiling.

"What? Oh. Buona sera," Angela replied as she backed down the stairs. Excitedly, she shook Paolo awake.

"Paolo, there are people here. The party is *tonight*?"

Paolo grinned sleepily and tried to pull Angela back into bed. He reached inside her shirt and began to caress her nipple.

"Paolo, stop. Listen to me. It's Thursday, for God's sake. I thought the party would be Saturday or something. It's tonight?"

"Yes, yes, it's tonight. Why not? It's just a very little party. A festiccola, eh? So come back to bed."

"But what will I wear? I'm not ready for this!"

"Wear nothing, cara. It's how I like you best!"

In exasperation, Angela threw a pillow at the laughing man.

"Relax, relax. Trust me, Angelina. You will be the most bella donna here tonight. Signor Halston and I have seen to that."

Paolo swung out of bed and produced from behind his suits in the dressing room a white silk jersey gown.

"Now, cara, it doesn't look like much just hanging, I know. It needs you inside it."

Angela was thrilled that he had bought her the gown, but she didn't see how the limp fabric on the hanger was going to transform her into the "most bella donna." The dress looked like a droopy sheet. But if the last three weeks had taught her anything, they had taught her to trust Paolo's taste and sense of style.

"I'll get ready right now. Oh, thank you, Paolo!"

"Wait, Angela. We have hours. No one will be coming until ten." He returned the dress to the wardrobe.

"Now will you please come back to bed? Please . . . per favore . . . cara . . . `ragazza mia, bella donna, Angela, Angela mia, Angelina cara mia. . . ." He moved his lips, trailing endearments from her neck to the mound between her legs. She felt the hot, familiar moistness as she allowed him to pull her back down on the bed. She raised her arms over her head and sighed as he brought her to the edge of her climax with his knowing tongue. Then, abruptly, he stopped. He drew himself up beside her and began running his hands over her body. Angela panted and writhed in high anticipation. Suddenly, Paolo pulled her by the hair so that she was face to face with him, staring into the deep pools of his dark eyes. Hoarsely, he whispered, "Do you love me, Angela?" His other hand stole between her thighs. It was more than she could bear.

"Yes, yes, oh, God, yes, oh, Paolo, please!"

And then he was inside her. Minutes later, they came together in long, intense spasms. Through her own loud cries she heard him whisper, "Ti amo, Angela. Ti amo."

The sound of voices and gentle laughter filtered through the half-open bathroom door. Santina stood over Angela, who was seated on the edge of the broad, sunken marble tub, piling her long, full, dark hair up on her head.

"Signorina, if you keep moving around, we will never get this done!"

Angela was impatient. She had put on the dress, following Santina's suggestion that she take off all her underwear first, so that no lines would interrupt the smooth flow of silk as it eased from one creamy shoulder, across each firm breast, and over a slightly rounded belly, to drape itself effortlessly around hips and buttocks, before dropping its hem to slender ankles above feet enclosed in the barest of soft, flat, gold sandals. Now, as Santina artfully arranged her hair so that it would look as though nothing more had been done than pulling it up in one sweep and pinning it on top of her head, Angela was anxious to see herself in all her glory.

Finally, Santina placed a heavily scented gardenia in the top of the heavy coil of hair and coaxed a few tendrils down Angela's long, bronzed neck. As Santina stepped back to admire her handiwork, Angela heard Paolo's step on the stairs. He did not enter the bathroom but stood outside against the door, Campari and soda in one hand, a cigarette in the other.

"Angelina," he staged-whispered in a cajoling singsong, "I think it's time now, cara. The guests are waiting to see you."

Angela rose and presented herself to Paolo. His eyes told her what the mirror would late confirm. Breathlessly, he reached out and took her hands. Holding her lightly, as though she were an apparition that would vanish if he made a sudden movement, he kept her at a full arm's length, allowing her to fill his eyes before whispering, "Venere." Venus.

Only then did Angela smile. "Paolo, go ahead. I'll come in a minute."

Angela had to see for herself. She had never worn a gown before. Not even at her wedding. As she stood in the center of the dressing room, she could see herself reflected on the mirrored walls from every angle. Each bronze and white reflection told her over and over again the kind of bare truth that only a mirror can tell. The dress that had looked like "nothing" on the hanger and now fitted itself around Angela's sleek form was magnificent in its simplicity. Angela had never before looked more beautiful.

The guilt she had felt about betraying Frankie that had marred the perfection she had been sharing with Paolo suddenly melted away as she recognized that she *was* extraordinary and that her life should be extraordinary as well. With her regal and gardeniaed head held high, Angela swept up the stairs to meet Paolo's friends.

The room was lit softly by candles and tiny starlike lights scattered in the potted lemon trees that dotted the gallery. Lush blossoms were caught up in their branches as though it had just rained flowers through the open skylight. The strings of hidden violins danced to Vivaldi's tune, as bejeweled guests stood in clusters or lounged on gray suede banquettes that lined the walls.

Angela saw no one; her eyes moved about the room seeking Paolo. Then he was walking toward her, casually elegant in a loosely constructed olive green raw silk suit over a silk shirt of a lighter shade of green that was open at the throat. He flashed his traffic-stopping smile as he reached out to her.

"Let me introduce you to everyone." He circled her waist with his arm and firmly brought her to his side while steering her toward a group of guests.

"This is Carlotta Cortillo. Carlotta, Angela Marino."

A tall, black-haired woman, wearing a hand-painted silk kimono that looked as if it should be framed and hung in an art gallery, confronted Angela. Carlotta drew up a hand from its position on her flat, wide hip and grasped Angela's hand firmly. Angela realized that she was shaking the hand of *the* Carlotta Cortillo—daughter of the Spanish artist, Carlos Cortillo.

Angela's newfound self-confidence burned away as rapidly as Capri's morning mists in the sun. She smiled mechanically, a thin film of perspiration forming on her brow. At the same time, she felt cold. Carlotta's heavily accented voice seemed to come from far away.

"So this is Angela, the reason why Paolo has no time lately for his oldest, dearest friends." She turned to Paolo and thrust out her chin, commanding his attention. "Well, she is very beautiful, Paolo. Anyone can see that. Maybe the old, dear friends look a little *too* old now. And perhaps not so dear, eh, querido? I am glad to have met you," she said brusquely, still looking intently at Paolo. "And take care not to get a chill," she added, glancing at Angela. "The wind changes frequently on this island. Ciao." Pulling her kimono tightly around her, Carlotta turned and walked toward the balcony at the far end of the gallery, where drinks were being served.

Paolo silently pulled Angela closer to his side. With relief he noticed that she was still smiling; she seemed not to have noticed Carlotta's maliciousness. She had not seen Paolo's warm brown eyes freeze for a moment and then just as quickly thaw as he turned to her.

"Come. I want you to meet the others."

"Paolo, wait a minute. That was Carlotta Cortillo. Cortillo's daughter, for God's sake. Paolo, are all these people famous?" Anxiously she looked around her, recognizing faces suddenly as they zoomed at her as in a Fellini film.

"Angela, they're just people. My friends. What's wrong? You're trembling, cara."

"Paolo, what am I going to say to these people? What could I possibly have in common with them? They're all famous and rich . . . artists and socialites and God knows what!"

Paolo turned the full warmth of his smile on her. "Listen to me, Angela," he said, drawing her into a corner of the room. "You must not say these things. I will show you. There. Over there." He motioned most imperceptibly with his chin. "You know who that is?"

Angela looked across the room at a tall, good-looking, lithely built young man wearing a white suit, his hair long and layered like a rock star's.

"That's Vitas Gerulaitis. He came from Queens, too. It won't keep him from playing at Wimbledon. And there," he said, motioning in the opposite direction, "the opera singer, Luciano Pavarotti, a baker's son from my hometown. And there is someone you should know. Also from America, from Texas. Jessica Simon. She was a society lady a year ago, now she is a famous author. A star in your country, yes?"

Angela stared. There she was! Jessica Simon! The author of *At Any Price*, the smash best seller that Angela had read in paperback on the plane to Italy! The wife of Arthur Simon of the world-famous Dallas department store Simon-Lewis.

The fragile, fine-boned woman, perfectly coiffed, meticulously made up, and looking as though she might be called upon to be Johnny Carson's guest at a moment's notice, stood chatting animatedly with a middle-aged man who greedily clasped his drink with both hands. Jessica wore a deep red, smartly tailored Adolfo suit; the red blouse under the short jacket was tied with a jabot. A large diamond brooch sparkled on Jessica's lapel, catching and throwing light to the starburst diamonds at her ears. Although all the publicity circulated about the novelist described her as "in her forties," anyone standing close enough to Jessica Simon in anything better than candlelight could readily see that she was an expertly groomed, well-preserved woman in her late fifties.

Paolo noticed Angela staring.

"So you would like to meet Jessica?"

"Wait, Paolo. I haven't written anything yet. I mean, nothing I could even send out for publication. I can't talk to these people. They don't want to meet a housewife, a nobody with a lot of half-baked dreams."

"I see you must learn something, cara. Let me tell you about half-baked dreams. My father was the son of a shoemaker. A *good* shoemaker, a craftsman, but a shoemaker just the same. His father thought he, too, would make shoes. But Cesare di Fiori had a dream. In Modena, where my family comes from, they make cars. Not just shoes. And every day my father is looking at these beautiful cars and dreaming his dream. One day he takes his design to Ferrari. They love him. He works there seven, maybe eight years—they fight: my father's dreams are too big for another man's factory.

"With the money he has saved and the help of friends he made, he builds one car. One dream car—and from there an empire. This I did not see for myself. By the time I was born, my father was already a very rich and successful man. But my sisters, Donizetta and Marcella—they are much older than I—they remember the hard days when my mama—may she rest in peace—and my papa lived in one room with my sisters and ate only spaghetti so my father's dreams could come true.

"Now, my father is a very proud man. He owns many houses, many cars, has many servants. He carries himself like a king—not a shoemaker. But he never forgets. At night sometimes, after the espresso, he sits with a bottle of Grappa, he smokes a cigar, and the stories come out. About the old days. He wants his son never to forget. You see what I am telling you, cara? Dream. Dream big. Dream and work, and it will be yours. But, like my father says, don't forget who you are. What you were. It will keep you pushing on. Now, come Angela, be brave. Tonight you take a step toward making dreams come true. Let's go talk to Jessica."

Paolo and Angela approached the author, who was standing with Rosita Missoni. Rosita and her husband, Ottavio "Tai" Missoni, were the geniuses behind the Missoni design empire—one that featured creations based on daringly patterned knit fabrics. Rosita had flown to Capri to entertain Jessica while Tai stayed in Milan to discuss the possibility of opening Missoni boutiques in the Simon-Lewis stores with the opulent chain's owner, Jessica's husband, Arthur Simon.

Jessica was admiring Rosita's dress as the slender, silver-haired lady turned to give Jessica the full effect of her boldly-patterned garment. Paolo caught Jessica's eye. Angela heard tones of molasses and honey vibrate deeply as Jessica excused herself graciously, briefly grasping Rosita's shoulder, and turned the full attention of her sharp and animated eyes toward Paolo.

In a second, Jessica had taken Angela in, her darting black eyes going over their subject like a mine sweeper. Jessica's alert senses were already feeding information to her computer-swift brain. Data was being recorded, evaluated, and stored in her nearly infallible memory bank. She was meeting a beautiful, young, but unknown woman who was appearing on the arm of a handsome, wealthy, influential—and, therefore, important—young man. This unassuming, somewhat shy woman might someday be someone to know, reckon with, and perhaps use. The circumstances of this introduction, its setting and participants, made the newcomer fit into the "note and recall" category, as opposed to the "dismissable" category.

"Jessica. Beautiful as always. I would like very much for you to meet Angela Marino," Paolo announced, emphasizing his accent as he succinctly pronounced Angela's name, making it sound like that of an Italian contessa.

He bowed from the waist and kissed Jessica's hand elaborately. Angela suppressed an urge to giggle. She knew this display was for her benefit. The shoemaker's grandson was showing her how easy it was to play the part of the prince. And he was making sure that Jessica would be impressed with Angela.

Jessica extended her procelain-skinned hand to Angela as her perfectly outlined and glossed lips stretched over impeccably capped teeth into a dazzling smile.

"Ah'm so pleased to meet you, Angela," Jessica drawled, her extraordinary voice oozing, then vibrating like the bass notes of cello. Clearly this voice had been cultivated to make the most of its low, cultured-sounding resonance, while maintaining the seductive charm of its Southern accents. In fact, Jessica had never had what would be classified as a Scarlett O'Hara drawl. She had been raised in New Orleans, where the accent lacks that particular charm. Jessica's voice was as contrived as her multi-streaked raven pageboy.

Angela was fascinated. She was seeing a star at close range. A keen observer herself, Angela was puzzled by the tautness of Jessica's complexion—particularly around her dark eyes—as it contrasted with the crepey quality of the tiny space of lined skin that peeked out from above the jabot tied almost at Jessica's chin.

"Angela is a writer, Jessica," Paolo was saying as Angela awkwardly tried to release her hand from Jessica's cool, dry clasp. "She is going to write a very important novel." Angela blushed as Jessica almost imperceptibly raised a perfectly waxed eyebrow.

Angela spoke quickly. "I haven't written anything yet, Mrs. Simon."

"Please. Call me Jessica," the author murmured.

"Oh, thank you. Okay, Jessica. I, uh, read *At Any Price* on the plane coming here and it was great. Really terrific. I couldn't stop turning the pages. I only hope that someday I can do half as well."

Jessica narrowed her eyes, then looked amused. She had evaluated the voice. New York. Not Manhattan. One of the outer boroughs, perhaps, or Long Island. Not Brooklyn or the Bronx. Obviously no finishing school—probably a *public* school education. Maybe a state or city college—if any. No threat. No problem. One could afford to be gracious.

"And I'm sure you *will*, my dear. Just keep writing, writing, *writing*! That's what I tell all the young people."

"Oh, I do!" Angela bubbled. "I do! I write in my journal every day! Well, since I've been with—I mean, since I've been staying on Capri, I've been sort of lax, but I intend to get right back to it, and I think if I can go back over . . ."

Jessica was smiling broadly now. Once again she extended her hand. The girl's enthusiasm was getting tedious, she decided. Time to move along. Paolo would be bored with her soon, too, no doubt. Although she *was* rather beautiful. And passionate, too, from the look of her. The girl was so animated, so excited, that her skin was flushed and her breasts heaved and swelled against the fabric of her dress as she spoke. Her eyes sparkle, Jessica thought. Leave it to Paolo: the girl was doubtlessly well fucked—for the moment. Pointedly, she raised her outstretched hand closer to Angela. The girl *was* going on.

"It certainly has been a *pleasure* meeting you, dear. Thank you for saying all those lovely things about mah book. And I wish you all the best. Paolo, you devil, she's absolutely di*vine*."

Angela flushed deeper and shook Jessica's hand again. She felt foolish, like a silly, simpering schoolgirl. She grasped Paolo's arm. He inclined his head perfunctorily toward Jessica and led Angela toward the terrace.

"Paolo di Fiori is slumming!" Jessica mused, her lips compressed with mirth. "I wonder if dear Cesare knows. . . ."

It was not until the sixth shrill ring that they awoke. After the party, they had declared and made love, then drifted, intertwined, into a deep seamless sleep. Paolo sat up, finally, and answered the phone. Angela stirred, then turned on the light and watched Paolo's face as he listened grimly. It was Aunt Renata. Angela's father had suffered a heart attack. It was not clear yet whether or not he would pull through. Angela was to fly home immediately.

The wind whipped through their hair as they stood in the Naples airport at the foot of the stairs leading to the cockpit of Paolo's jet.

"Cara, why won't you at least let me fly over with you? We'll take you home and then turn around. I won't even get off the plane. I just want those few hours . . . I have so much to say. . . ."

"No, I can't let you. I've got to think. I've got to get used to leaving you. Please, Paolo. I'm worried sick about my father. You understand." She reached up to kiss him and felt his urgent lips. He pressed a square, black velvet box into Angela's hands, which she took without thinking, barely noticing it as she looked into Paolo's tear-filled eyes and thought of all she was leaving behind.

"Please take this gift, Angela. Don't open it now. Wait until you are alone on the plane. Arrivederla, Angelina. Till I see you again."

It was not until she had settled in her seat and was heading toward New York that Angela opened Paolo's gift. Through eyes veiled with tears, she opened the note that read:

Angela—
    This cannot be good-bye for us. We love each other and we will find a way. Please accept this gift as my pledge. It shines less brightly than the moments we spent together, but it will remind you, I hope, of the Grotta Azzurra where you were saved and my heart was lost.
                            Yours in eternity,
                            Paolo

Angela folded the letter and slipped it into the journal she kept close to her in her handbag. She held Paolo's gift in the hollow of her palm. It was an enormous, flawless, tear-shaped sapphire on a simple gold chain. Angela put it on immediately, dropping the shining cool stone inside the bodice of her dress where it rested between her breasts. The weight of it against her heart felt crushing, as anguish and longing overcame her.

CHAPTER
5

ELI lit another Marlboro, vigorously sucking in her round, pink cheeks. She blew a fine stream of smoke toward the ceiling and turned to look at Angela, sitting across from her in the Whitestone Hospital's coffee shop. Jimmy, feeling left out of the conversation, absently stirred his coffee.

"All right, Angela. You've met Mister Right. He loves you. You love him. What are you going to do about it?"

"Nothing. Absolutely nothing. I'm married to Frankie. I realize things have not been too great between us—"

Eli jabbed a finger at Angela and interrupted, "And don't forget those rumors about Frankie's girlfriend."

"They're *just* rumors, as far as I'm concerned, Eli. Besides, what am I supposed to do? Run away? My father's recovering from a heart attack. That would set him back, don't you think?"

"I guess you're right for now, but if I were you, I'd reconsider when your father gets well again."

"I haven't burned all my bridges. I gave Paolo your address, so if he wants to write or anything—as a friend, of course—he knows how he can get in touch."

Eli raised her eyebrows. "Right, Angie, Of course. As a *friend*. Boy, I could use a few friends like him!" She shrugged in exasperation and looked to Jimmy, who simply said, "I just wish Angie would go and live with Paolo. It's what you'd really like to do, isn't it, Angie? You can't love Frankie."

Angela's brow furrowed. She stared intently into her coffee cup, as though the answer to her problems lay in the murky liquid. A comfortable, intimate silence descended upon them.

Eli broke in: "And so what are you up to, Jimmy? Are you

going to have trouble making up your classes after spending so much time here at the hospital?"

"Well, my plans have changed a little. I'll still be taking design courses at Parsons, but I'll carry fewer credits and go at night. I've got to help out with Dad's business. He can't be running around with the truck and laying tiles anymore. He'll work in the office, and I'll help out with the labor end of the business full time for now." Eli frowned. "It's all right," Jimmy continued. "I'll be making good money. By the time Dad's feeling better, maybe I'll have saved enough to get my own place."

Angela looked up. She realized that she hadn't asked Eli anything about herself since they had been reunited at Sal's bedside.

"Oh, Eli, I've been so self-absorbed, I didn't even think to ask how you're doing with your work. In your last letter you said you hated your job. Are you still with the Brad Monroe Literary Agency?"

"Oh, yes! Still with Brad Asshole Monroe! Only now I'm an Associate Agent—whatever that means! Actually, I've gotten a pretty good raise, and Brad's starting to take me a little more seriously. When he isn't busy ripping off poor would-be writers—he charges them a hundred bucks just to read their stuff—he actually pretends to listen to my advice from time to time."

Angela smiled. "I always thought of you as the glamorous career woman working for the top literary agent in town, discovering new talent, making important decisions, clinching big deals—"

"Humph!" snorted Eli. "And keeping Brad Monroe's greasy little paws off my tits! It's not all lunches at the Four Seasons with hotshot editors, you know. At least not at my level. I read manuscripts, write reports, make recommendations, and also do copying, typing, filing, and oh, yes—once a week I take a turn as receptionist. One of Brad's success secrets is low overhead." Complaining about the job she thrived on and was beginning to excel at was one of her chief pleasures. Pushing her aviator glasses up on the bridge of her nose, Eli looked at her watch, jumped up dramatically and gasped, "I'm going to be late! I have to meet some turkey my mother set me up with, and I'm late! Jimmy, do you want to share a cab back to Manhattan so you can make your class?''

Jimmy nodded.

"How about you, Angela?" Eli asked.

"Since Dad's resting, I'm going to head home and make dinner for Frankie. I haven't even seen him since I've been back. I've been staying with Jimmy. Now that Dad's so much better, I've got to go back and face the music.''

Eli and Angela embraced.

"I'll call you later," Eli assured her.

Trailing behind Jimmy and Eli, who were absorbed in their search for a cab, Angela left the hospital slowly. Unconsciously she kept a protective hand over the sapphire she wore under her blouse. The reality of resuming life with Frankie was now truly upon her. It could not be delayed or put off any longer. She had been able to avoid him because of her father's illness. She had called him when she arrived and had told him that she would stay with her brother until the danger was past. But now Sal was better and would be getting out of the hospital in a matter of days, and Sal's sister-in-law was temporarily moving in to nurse him. There were no excuses left for her absence. She couldn't help but notice that Frankie had not seemed overanxious about her homecoming and had not even come to the hospital once. . . . Maybe there was something to the girlfriend rumors after all.

She thought of Paolo. Of the comfort and joy she found in his arms. How desire had been fully ignited inside her, a flame she wanted never to extinguish. Desire was an important part of her life now. It had lain dormantly smoldering, and now it was a live fire. Life with Frankie would doom that flame to ashes.

Angela reached inside her blouse and pulled the sapphire out where it caught the sunlight, giving off its own special radiance.

"Hey, Eli, Jimmy. Wait for me. I'm going with you. I want to go to Eli's to make a very important, very expensive phone call.''

Eli stopped and turned around to face Angela. "You wouldn't be calling Italy by any chance, would you?"

Angela nodded, searching Jimmy's and Eli's faces for their reactions. Two wide and spontaneous grins reassured her, and she dashed to the curb to hail a cab, waving her arm with a triumphant flourish.

"Paolo? This is Angela. My father's fine. Much better. The doctors say he'll be all right if he takes it easy. . . . What? . . . Yes? . . . Oh. I miss you too, Paolo. So much. That's why I called."

Listening to his voice so near yet so far away, Angela lost her sense of place and time. She felt as though she were floating somewhere in space, her only connection to the world the voice at the other end of the receiver.

"Paolo, did you mean what you wrote in the letter? . . . Yes? Oh, yes, Paolo. It's beautiful. The most beautiful thing I've ever seen. I wear it always. I'm wearing it now. Paolo, it's Frankie. I can't go back. I could get a flight to Rome now. Or Milan. Eli will lend me the money. I could come today. . . . I . . . what? Your father? . . . Yes, I do want to marry you. But . . . you can? . . . From the Vatican? . . . Yes, I'll wait. I love you, Paolo. I'll wait."

CHAPTER
6

A CUSTOM-MADE silver di Fiori sedan took them, as though they were riding on a cushion of air, from the airport to the foothills of the Apennine mountains. One of Paolo's body-guards drove while the other, Gino, sat in the passenger seat, an Israeli-made Uzi machine gun between them. In the back seat, Paolo and Angela sat close together holding hands.

How quickly it had all happened, Angela thought. Only three weeks had passed since she had telephoned Paolo from New York. In the interim, he had proposed and had sent flowers to the Vaccaro home in Whitestone every day. Frankie had been offered and had eagerly accepted a hand-delivered check for ten thousand dollars. When a courier delivered a large, thick envelope from the Vatican, containing a di Fiori—bought annulment of her marriage to Francisco Marino, Angela knew it was time to start thinking about a wedding dress.

It had all happened so quickly and painlessly. If Paolo had any problems in obtaining the annulment, he did not let Angela know.

Looking out the window at rows of pines flying by, Paolo hoped Angela did not notice how damp his palm was. With his free hand he wiped his brow with his handkerchief for the hundredth time that day, though cool September air flowed through the open car windows. His father was certainly making things difficult. Paolo always knew that his choice of wife would be of great importance to his father. He had known that his approval would be necessary and that it would not be easy to obtain, but he had not expected so violent a reaction when he called from Capri to tell him of his intentions. The things his father said! Without even meeting Angela, he had condemned her as a fortune-hunting American divorcée. Cesare had insinuated that Paolo was a young fool with a fire in his loins that could not be controlled by his brain.

Finally, after heated argument, the master of the di Fiori empire gave his consent. But there were stipulations. Cesare di Fiori had not worked and sweated, connived and contrived, to build an empire just to see it fall into the wrong hands one day. He had not slept with one eye open for forty years to see his vigilance wasted. Even if Paolo *was* the light of his life—the son born late in Cesare's life when all hope for a male heir was lost.

It was Cesare's stipulations that were making Paolo sweat as the sedan approached the wrought-iron gates that interrupted the high stone wall surrounding the grounds of Villa di Fiori. As the car rolled smoothly over the unpaved road lined with ancient cypresses leading to the house, perspiration trickled from Paolo's armpits down his sides. His father wanted the couple to sign the papers immediately—before the wedding, of course. Luca Bafabio, the family lawyer, his sister's husband, would be there. It was all so convenient: The entire family lived at the spacious villa. The papers would have been drawn up, waiting to be witnessed and signed. Angela would agree to forfeit any and all claims to the family fortune. She would receive no inheritance in the event of Paolo's death, but should she produce di Fiori offspring, *they*—Cesare's grandchildren—would be heirs to their father's wealth. Further, Paolo was to agree that no child would be conceived until at least one year after the marriage. This way, Cesare insisted, Paolo would have time to see whether he had indeed made the right choice or had just been led by infatuation.

Paolo had listened to all this, biting his lips to hold back words of anger and disrespect. In the end, he had reluctantly agreed to sign the papers. He and Angela were young. They would live forever! They would still be just as in love when the obligatory year of waiting was up. Then they would start their family. Surely Angela would produce an heir. Those miscarriages she had were unfortunate, but with the proper medical care and emotional support. . . . The thing to do was to sign quietly, marry Angela, and be happy. When the first di Fiori grandchild came along, Cesare would surely have a change of heart. And Papa would grow to love Angela, too, when he realized how sincere and loving she was. Paolo mopped his brow again as they pulled up in front of the massive Villa di Fiori.

Angela had been nursing misgivings about her acceptance by the family when the villa loomed into view. A nineteenth-century English-style formal garden stretched before it and led the eye to the stately baroque facade of sienna-colored stone. The ornate gray-green stone detailing did nothing to add a note of welcome to the forbidding sight. A flat red-tiled roof topped the three stories, surmounted by a stone balustrade and an elaborately decorated cupola. The house had been built in the late sixteenth century for the Estes, one of Italy's most powerful ruling families. After the downfall of the Estes, the villa had been held by the Manzinis, another aristocratic family. In the seventeenth century, the Manzinis embellished the facade, adding a wide curved stairway from the garden to the entrance. They also added the pediment above the entrance where the di Fiori crest was now displayed, bright and new against the centuries-old stone.

Cesare had bought the villa from the last impoverished Manzini in 1940 and had carefully preserved the integrity and traditions of the estate as though his own family had inhabited it for hundreds of years.

Paolo was leaning against the car lighting a cigarette when, helped by Ettore, Angela emerged squinting in the afternoon sunlight.

"Paolo, nothing you could have told me would have prepared me for this. This house, Paolo, it's a palace!" Angela exclaimed in an excited whisper.

Paolo laughed nervously. He finished his cigarette slowly, buying time to collect himself for the encounter ahead. With his hands on her shoulders, he placed Angela squarely in front of him and appraised her appearance. She looked fine. Better than fine, she looked beautiful. The pearl gray suede Roberta di Camerino suit he bought for her looked properly subdued and elegant. The rose-colored silk blouse complimented the hues of her perfect skin, and the gray kid bag she carried was neither too large nor too small. The gray leather pumps she wore could have been taken from one of his sisters' closets. They all would approve. They would find nothing to criticize, nothing they could point their fingers at later and say, "These tacky, tasteless Americans!"

Angela flashed her glorious smile at him as Paolo hugged her. He felt guilty about assessing her appearance as though she were an object on exhibit, when in his heart he felt she was without flaw, but he wanted to see her through Cesare's eyes—through Donizetta's and Marcella's—and to be sure that they too would find her perfect.

The brief embrace was just the assurance Angela needed. Paolo led her up the stairs and through massive wooden doors into the vaulted marble-floored hall that led to elegant reception rooms that looked to Angela as though they belonged in New York's Metropolitan Museum of Art, not in a home where a family lived. The entrance hall alone was larger than the Vaccaros' house in Whitestone. It was entirely devoid of furniture, and the walls were frescoed. At the far end was a wide marble staircase, and an arched corridor to the right led to a grand ballroom that Angela's ever-alert eyes could just see into to glimpse the seventeenth-century furnishings.

A uniformed servant appeared and greeted them in Italian. Paolo frowned when Angela extended her hand toward the man Paolo introduced to her as Marco. Embarrassed, she withdrew her hand and nodded. Marco behaved as though he had not noticed the faux pas and led them to a closed door that he opened and entered before them.

The room was grandly proportioned. Faded tapestries depicting scenes of fifteenth-century ladies grouped outside a castle hung on the walls, and an enormous Persian rug covered most of the marble floor. At the far end of the room, a low table, surrounded by chairs, was set with china and silver for tea. In the chair to the right of the table sat Donizetta di Fiori. Tall and extremely thin, she wore a silk print shirtwaist dress, and her sparse, graying hair, pulled back from her long, pale, lined face, was tied with a ribbon at the nape of her slender neck. Her moist eyes, large and dark as Paolo's, stared questioningly at Angela. Next to her sat Marcella, a shorter, plump woman wearing a while silk blouse and beige skirt. Her thick salt-and-pepper hair was cut short and was brushed severely away from her somewhat puffy face. She had been facing her husband, the avvocato Luca Bafabio—a tall, thin, dour man who wore a dark brown three-piece suit with a gold watch chain—and turned now, wreathing her face in a smile as she saw her brother enter the room.

When he saw Angela, the avvocato rose, and from behind his chair stepped Cesare di Fiori. Although in his seventies, Cesare still presented an imposing appearance. His gray wool suit fit his long, angular lines perfectly. His movements as he stepped forward to greet his son and their guest were those of a younger, vital man. He held high his large head with its wavy, thick white hair. Animation emanated from his strong, still handsome features, the most prominent of which was his long, straight, Roman nose. His skin was deeply creased around clear blue eyes that were startling against his tanned skin. His smile dazzled but his piercing eyes remained watchful and opaque. He quickly and warmly embraced Paolo, kissing first one, then the other cheek. Paolo returned his father's greeting heartily and grasped his arm.

"Papa! This is Angela Vaccaro. My fiancée. Angela, this is my father, Cesare di Fiori."

Cesare leaned forward and enveloped Angela's hand in his own two strong, brown hands. Then he kissed her, too, as he had Paolo.

"Welcome to our home, Angela. I can see now why my son has spoken of little else since he met you. You are a very beautiful young lady."

Angela blushed. "Thank you, Signor di Fiori."

"No. No *signore*, Angela. You will be my son's bride very soon. You must call me Papa. Now, come and meet your sisters."

As far as Angela was concerned, dinner was a disaster. They did not even seat her next to Paolo. Donizetta had said something about them all getting to know each other better this way, so Angela sat stiffly next to her, while Luca and Marcella sat across the long, wide table. Paolo sat forlornly at the foot of the table, while Cesare reigned from the head. For the "occasion," they gathered in the formal dining salon, furnished in the Directoire style of the early nineteenth century. Silent, white-gloved servants placed dishes before her, and then whisked them away after she had absently picked at a few morsels. Few words were spoken. The only remarks addressed to Angela were those that would have been made to any visitor who had traveled a long way. How was the weather in New York? How was the long plane ride?

Donizetta and Marcella glanced at her repeatedly, sneakily, so as not to be caught staring impolitely, then they exchanged looks across the table, communicating the way siblings can, with no words, in the language of nuances expressed by a slightly raised eyebrow, a curled lip. Angela saw it all. It was a language she and Jimmy shared, too, and knew well.

Paolo, perfectly aware of what his sisters were doing, sat in a miserable silence. He answered the few questions addressed to him with words of one syllable or with sullen silence. His rudeness was not noticed by anyone but Angela. Only when Cesare spoke to him directly did Paolo give a thoughtful reply. The dinner dragged on. The avvocato Bafabio stared shamelessly at Angela throughout, his narrow, oxblood eyes glistening with lust.

After the espresso was served, the family rose in an obviously rehearsed movement, leaving Angela and Paolo alone at the table. Before he left the room with a cordial glass in his hand, Cesare turned to his son and glared at him sternly. Paolo colored and sighed. When they were alone, he sat down in the empty chair next to Angela.

"Cara. It was difficult, no? Really, they are very good people. Very kind. When they get to know you better, they will love you almost as much as I do. Do you believe me?"

Angela looked into her lap at her tensed, clasped hands. She would have given anything in the world for Eli to barge in and make one of her raucous comments, or for Jimmy or Sal to suddenly appear and tell her everythig was all right. She felt so lonely, so deserted. Paolo sensed her distress. Discreetly, he brushed her hair with his lips and pulled a handkerchief from his pocket to wipe his moist brow.

"Angela, with my family, things are so complicated. We are very strong in business, you know that. My father is like a lion when it comes to Di Fiori Automobili. It is a company, I told you, he built himself from nothing. And this house. He bought it just a few years before I was born. Before Mama died. It is his dream that generations of di Fioris should live here. Royalty of a new age. You understand? This is what he lives for. He does not understand what we have, cara. Our love. He thinks maybe you will leave me, although we know it will never happen. He is old now, though still strong. But he wants assurances . . . that the di Fioris will go on forever. In this home. Always the power behind Di Fiori Automobili—"

Angela placed her finger across Paolo's lips. "I understand what you're telling me, Paolo. Your father thinks I'm a scheming divorcée from America. He thinks I'll divorce you and take the house after he's gone. Or the family fortune, right?"

Paolo tried to protest. He did not like hearing it put so bluntly. Angela would not let him speak.

"You want me to sign something. I'll sign, Paolo. Whatever you say. I know—a prenuptial agreement. Like Jackie Onassis signed. I don't care. If you say it's okay. Besides, as far as I'm concerned, you're the only part of the di Fiori fortune I want." She smiled up at him and waited for him to kiss her. He wiped his brow instead.

"There is more, cara. My father wants us to wait one year before any babies—"

"But Paolo, I told you about that. I don't even know if I can have babies!" Angela's eyes filled with tears.

"Cara, you *will* have babies. I know it. But we must wait. Then, when our first little one comes, you will see the lion become a lamb. We will tear up the papers. Everyone will be so happy. A di Fiori grandson—or a little girl—living in this house, growing up here, a new generation! Then my father will be assured. You see?"

Angela felt a gnawing, acid feeling growing in her stomach. She could do anything Paolo asked of her to insure that his family would accept her—but have a baby? It might just be a physical impossibility. Her doctor never said that she couldn't bear a child, but he didn't exactly encourage her to try again, either. Another failure would be more than she could take, Angela knew. Since she had met Paolo, she had managed to put her disappointment behind her, but now the painful issue was cropping up again.

"Paolo," Angela insisted, "let's face this now. What if I can't?"

"Angela, I don't care. Not now. Please, my love, let's get these stupid papers signed and let's get *married*. Let's go to my father now. He is waiting with Luca. Come on or we'll be too tired to make love!"

"Never!" Angela retorted, smiling and relieved.

Cesare di Fiori sat back in his massive carved wood and leather chair. From behind his desk he emanated invincibility. Here in his office he was king. Absolute monarch. When he sat behind that mahogany, leather-topped, gilt-edged piece of furniture, he was in complete control. From the wood-paneled, book-lined room, he ran an empire, making decisions that involved billions of lire, changed lives, and fashioned events. It was from this position of power that he would present the prenuptial papers for signing.

Luca stood beside the desk, a sentinel, arms crossed over his chest. In front of the desk, two simple damask-upholstered chairs faced Cesare. Angela and Paolo entered the room silently. There could be no doubt for whom the chairs were intended. Angela and Paolo sat down at a nod from Cesare. Marco entered, carrying a silver tray. He placed a brandy snifter before Cesare, inclining the tray toward Paolo, who shook his head, indicating that he had no desire for a drink. Cesare inclined his head slightly toward Paolo. Paolo took the snifter. Angela took a cordial glass half-filled with Strega, a more "suitable" drink for a lady than brandy. Luca took a snifter from the tray, placed it on Cesare's desk, and crossed his arms again. His gaze fell upon Angela's face, then traveled down to the cleft between her breasts, slightly visible between the lapels of her tailored blouse. There his reddish eyes stayed for the remainder of the interview, adding to Angela's discomfort.

When the servant had gone, Cesare raised his glass. "To the health and happiness of my son and his beautiful bride. May they live a hundred years. May they have happy, healthy children," he said, not smiling. Automatically, they all raised their glasses. Paolo and Angela murmured their thanks and sipped. The bitter flavor of the Strega startled Angela. She struggled to remain pleasantly expressionless.

"Now," Cesare said, setting his glass down, "my son has explained these formalities to you, has he not?" Angela nodded. "Good. If you have any questions, I want you to ask Signor Bafabio. Luca. He is our family lawyer. Our avvocato. Because your father is not well enough to be here—and since he has not sent your family lawyer—I want you to feel free to talk to Luca. But, of course, you are part of our family now, or you will be soon, so Luca is your family lawyer, too. Is that not right, Luca?"

Bafabio smiled and licked his cadaverous lips. "Of course, Signorina," he replied, making a courtly little bow.

Angela felt fear and revulsion wash over her as she looked into Bafabio's shrewd eyes. "I have no questions. I'm ready to sign."

Paolo sighed with relief and rose, and placing his glass on his father's desk, he took the silver Montblanc fountain pen Cesare coolly offered him. He signed the documents his father had produced from a locked drawer, and then handed the pen to Angela, who signed quickly. When it was done, Luca and Cesare smiled. Luca kissed Angela's cheek, his thumb grazing her breast as he grasped her upper arm. "Think of me as your uncle," he said, placing his lips close to her ear.

Unseen by the others, Cesare pressed a button under his desk, and a uniformed maid appeared at the door. "Maddelena will show you to your room now, Angela," Cesare said. "You must be very tired from the long trip. Good night."

Angela looked at Paolo, who shrugged, then winked at her. She followed Maddelena out of the room into the hall and then up the long, curving staircase.

Her room was in the largest guest suite in the east wing of the villa. It was, as Angela had anticipated, enormous, and like the other rooms she had seen, the floor was marble and the paneled walls were hung with tapestries. The canopied bed that dominated the space was wide and so high that a brocade-covered stepstool was needed to climb into it. The bed's satin comforter and top sheet were turned back invitingly.

Maddelena silently showed Angela the adjoining dressing room and the cold, ornate bathroom; then, curtseying slightly, she left, closing the heavy bedroom door behind her.

Angela was alone. She undressed quickly and folded her clothes carefully before placing them on the chair next to the bed. When she opened several dresser drawers, she realized that her bags had been unpacked and her clothes put neatly away. As she unfolded the white satin Fernando Sanchez nightgown Paolo had sent her, she changed her mind and slipped naked between the sheets. She folded her arms under her head and stared across the room at a painting on the wall while she waited for Paolo. It was an eighteenth-century landscape, a pastoral scene that would normally have appealed to her, but she saw it as curiously flat and textureless. The trees, the hills, the little shepherd and shepherdess looked remote, cold, and unreal. Angela herself began to feel hollow, and a cold sensation of dread and isolation flooded her. She longed for warmth, for familiarity. She realized that she was about to cry. Stop it! she told herself. Soon Paolo would come up the stairs and lie down beside her. She would feel his strong, smooth body, smell his skin. Then she would feel loved. Then she would know she was home. She turned away from the painting, resting on her side to wait for Paolo.

Paolo, who had risen when Angela stood to leave the room, was now seated again. Luca occupied the chair Angela had vacated. Although Cesare remained behind his desk, all three men were more relaxed.

"There's just one more thing, Paolo," Cesare said in sonorous Italian. "Something I want to make very clear. The girl is a beauty. A rare beauty. Of that there is no doubt. I am not so old that I cannot understand how a young man such as yourself would be drawn to such a woman. You are, after all, your father's son, Paolo. But I never lost my head. You understand? I give you now a chance to prove to me that this is more than a young man's passion, that it is the love of a mature man for a woman worthy to be his wife. I want no nonsense under my roof!" Cesare paused for the full import of his message to take effect. Luca turned to Paolo and smiled mockingly.

"You are not married to her yet," Cesare continued. "I do not know what you did in Capri—I do not want to know—but in my house she sleeps alone until she sleeps with her husband. You stay in your bed. She remains in hers. Is that understood?"

Paolo flushed deeply. It infuriated him that his father would speak to him this way—especially in front of Luca who was always jealous of Paolo's position as heir and whom Paolo despised. Calling upon what was left of his dignity, Paolo rose. "I understand, Papa," he said calmly. "And now, if you will excuse me, I am tired. I want to go to bed."

Cesare smiled. He could count on Paolo. He was a good son: obedient and respectful. And about the American girl—he would come to his senses. The wedding would be approved graciously. No less than if his son were marrying a virgin heiress. No need for the outside world to know that Paolo was displeasing his father. But the marriage would not last. The girl seemed sweet enough now, but soon her lack of background would not be concealable. Paolo would soon turn to someone of his own kind—once he tired of having her in bed, that is. These fiery passions never lasted long. If Paolo was anything like his father, he'd be looking for new conquests soon enough.

Cesare kissed his son good night and patted him on the cheek affectionately. Luca rose and walked out with Paolo.

"It will be tough tonight, eh, Paolo?" Luca put his arm around his brother-in-law's shoulders and hissed in his ear. "She's a lovely girl, Paolo. Very nice," he continued in an insinuating tone.

Paolo pulled away from his brother-in-law and stared with hatred into his leering, smug face.

"Don't even look at her, Bafabio. I warn you," Paolo spat from between clenched teeth.

Cursing under his breath, Paolo climbed the stairs, flung his clothing all over his room, and got into bed. It was easier to curse Luca for insulting his bride than it was to blame Papa for frustrating him and keeping him away from Angela. Was she waiting for him? he wondered. Well, he would explain in the morning: Papa had said no.

At the opposite end of the villa, Angela grew impatient. She distracted herself by imagining what would happen when Paolo finally *did* come to bed. Dreamily, she stretched her arms up over her head and imagined his hot kisses, his tongue darting between her lips, his hands stroking her shoulders, then her breasts. . . . The room seemed warm to her, and she threw back the covers. Her nipples were hard and taut. Her fingers slipped between her thighs. Where *was* he? She wanted him. She wanted him to make love to her *now*. She fell asleep.

The tenor cleared his throat and straightened his ascot. It was fastened too tightly around his thick neck. Pulling a white handkerchief out of his pocket, he clasped his pudgy hands under his enormous belly and nodded toward the organist. Purely and sweetly he filled the cool air of the cathedral with the strains of "Ave Maria." The rustling and murmurings of hundreds of elegantly dressed, expectant guests stopped abruptly as they listened to Schubert's melody. Then, as the string quartet in the chapel played the first measured notes of Pachelbel's Canon in D, amid increased rustlings and murmurings, Angela floated up the center aisle, a vision in white satin, lace, and pearls. From behind the gossamer veil, the scene before her seemed a softly focused dream.

Angela's eyes swept the cluster of people standing at the altar. They found Paolo, beaming at her from where he stood, resplendent in a dark gray morning coat, beside the gold-and-white-robed prelate. She suppressed a smile as she continued down the aisle. Paolo's eyes were like beacons of light burning through the white mist, leading her forward. She held her head high, feeling the gaze of a thousand world-weary eyes upon her. She felt truly magnificent for the first time in her life.

Numbed by excitement, Angela barely heard the words the bishop addressed first to Paolo, then to her. And, later, during the remainder of the solemn Nuptial Mass that followed the wedding ceremony, she wondered how she had made the correct responses.

The day before, when she had made her confession, the Cathedral of St. Geminian had been dark and silent; today it was transformed, just as she too was transformed. She felt as pure as the petals of the white roses she held in her hands. She felt fresh and new. The hopeless years of marriage to Frankie seemed as though they had happened a long time ago, to someone else. She, Angela, was perfect, whole, ready to be Paolo's bride.

The mass was over. Paolo was lifting her chin. She looked up at him and although he was smiling, his eyes were wet. He bent his head to kiss her. A startling blast of the first notes of the triumphal march from Verdi's *Aida* swelled from the pipes of the organ and interrupted the soft, almost chaste meeting of Paolo's and Angela's lips. Paolo threw back his head and laughed. Gripping Angela by the elbow, he led her swiftly down the aisle, past the massive bronze doors, and into the October sunshine, where the excited citizens of Modena waited with legions of paparazzi to greet the new Signora di Fiori.

CHAPTER
───────────── 7 ─────────────

ANGELA awoke and reached across the bed, but the space beside her was empty. She got up and drew on a pink Chinese silk wrapper before she walked to the French window where the heavy drapes had been drawn back and sheer white curtains billowed in the early summer breeze. The scent of citrus trees in bloom permeated the air, and soft morning sunlight streamed in the windows. Angela threw them wide open and stepped barefoot onto the stone-floored balcony. Looking out over the formal English gardens, she saw straw-hatted gardeners pruning the lemon trees near the stone fountain at the center of the gardens. Closer to the house, two servants were skimming the sparkling surface of the water in the marble-tiled swimming pool. Stretching her arms up toward the sun, Angela breathed deeply, savoring the fragrant air.

Suddenly, Paolo was behind her, his bare arms around her, his wet hair brushing against her skin as he kissed her neck. She turned around, and he stood smiling before her, wearing a bath towel loosely around his hips.

"Buon giorno, cara. You look beautiful this morning."

"Oh, Paolo, you say that every morning, but look what a beautiful day it is! Let's take a picnic somewhere, Paolo, just the two of us."

Paolo put his hand on her shoulder. "Angela, I am not always a man of leisure. You know that. Why do you think I'm up so early today? I have work to do. The new designs are ready to go into production. You wouldn't want the di Fioris to start looking like Edsels because we were picnicking in the mountains, would you?"

"No, I don't suppose so," Angela answered. "And,

anyway, I'm not a lady of leisure entirely either. I have writing to do. I have yet to wear out one ribbon on the typewriter you gave me for Christmas.''

Paolo laughed and kissed her. ''Writing sounds like a good idea. . . .'' he said, then he suddenly snapped his fingers. ''Cristo! I forgot! You are going to be very angry with me.'' He slid his hands down her shoulders to her arms caressingly. He rolled his big eyes and looked disarmingly contrite. ''My sisters asked if you would like to go with them to Firenze today for shopping, and I thought you would like it, so I said, 'Certo, of course she will go.' Angela, you will love Florence: the Duomo, the Uffizi, the paintings, the sculptures—more even than what we saw in Bologna! And the statue of David is in Florence . . . and of course you must buy yourself some Florentine gold on the Ponte Vecchio. You will—''

''Paolo! I don't want to go to Florence with your sisters today. I'd rather set up my typewriter right here on the balcony. . . .''

''But Angelina! Marcella and Donizetta will be so disappointed. The arrangements have been made. How can you hurt them like this? They want only to make you happy. They want to be your sisters, Angela. You must at least meet them halfway! Please, cara. For me. For us. Please.'' He began to move the pink silk of her robe down off her shoulder.

''Paolo, why don't they ask *me* if they want me to join them? Why do they always ask you? I can speak for myself. Maybe we can make it for another day.''

Paolo sighed deeply. ''As you wish, Angela. They will be having breakfast on the patio this morning with Papa. You can tell them when you meet them there.''

''Why don't you tell them, Paolo? You got me into this!''

''Because by the time they are ready to come downstairs, I will be gone to work, cara. So you will have to tell them that you are very busy today and that they will have to make other plans to treat you to shopping in Florence. Okay?''

''All right, Paolo. You win. I'll go, this time.''

''Angela, they are not asking to take you to the dentist. It is a trip to Florence on a beautiful day. . . .''

''All right! I said I'd go. But please don't do this again. Next time ask me first. I'd like to use my typewriter one of these days, you know. I have an idea for a short story in my head, and I'd like to put it on paper. Donizetta and Marcella always seem to have something planned for me. Someplace I *must* go. Some important family friends I *must* meet. They're always taking me someplace, and I don't think they even like me. They always give me these little pained tolerant smiles. . . ."

"Angela! They are my sisters. I beg you!"

"All right, all right, I'm sorry. I'm sure I'll love Florence." Now contrite herself, Angela put her arms around Paolo. He smelled of soap and fresh air. "Where is the statue of David, anyway?"

"Right here, cara," Paolo crooned, stripping off his bath towel. "Aren't you lucky?" He dropped the towel, then slowly eased Angela's robe off her shoulders until it hung about her hips in silky folds. He began stroking her breasts until the nipples hardened. She threw her tousle-haired head back and exposed her throat to the hot sun. She moaned and groped for his hardness as his mouth reached her breasts. Kneeling on the towel now, he pulled her robe off and buried his head between her legs. She moved her thighs slightly apart and arched her back, reveling in the sunlight that beat down on her uplifted breasts as Paolo's tongue delved the wet sweetness inside her. Before she could come, he lowered her down on the soft pile of fabric formed by his towel and her robe. On top of her and inside her, he rocked her gently, aware of the unyielding stone beneath them. Cupping her buttocks in his hands, he brought her to climax, and only then allowed himself the few powerful thrusts he needed to join her in oblivion.

Below the balcony, on the patio, Marco, in a crisp white jacket, was setting the table for breakfast.

The water was icy but refreshing. After the grueling day of shopping in Florence, Angela was enjoying her swim, gliding with strong, even strokes up and down the pool without effort, the swimmer's movements a part of her body's rhythm. Her mind wandered freely as she swam, uninterrupted by the demands of her "family."

What was Eli doing right now? Angela wondered. Her last letter had been so bright, so crisp, so like herself, it made Angela miss her sorely. She wrote of her trials as an agent and how she was struggling against a growing attraction to that new author of hers. It was all so amusing, so bright, the way Eli described it—in light ironic phrases—but it was happening in another world; it didn't seem real to Angela.

And what of her own letters to Eli? How did her life seem to Eli? Like a dream? Here, in the fading sunlight that turned the water golden and cast a shimmering halo around the trees and hills of Villa di Fiori, Angela could easily believe her life was a dream. Paolo's love was sweet, sure, and comforting, but hazy, heavy lust blurred the sharp edges of her senses when he touched her. It could all be a dream. Maybe she *was* living in a kind of fantasy. Only the di Fioris made it real. Their disdain of her pierced the gauzy fabric of her dream like a finely honed blade. They disapproved often. They distrusted her. Even when she wrote in her journal, they were watching her. They asked Paolo to talk to her about what she was writing, fearing that she was writing about them, making furtive notes about the "family." How could she be trusted when she was always putting things down in a little black book? Things she did not disclose to them.

Paolo told her to be more discreet. So she wrote letters to Eli, pouring out her heart. Letters could be sealed and sent far away. And Eli wrote back asking her about the journal. Was she writing? Had she used the new typewriter Paolo gave her for Christmas? A stab of guilt shot through Angela, then abated. How could she write? She was too busy. It was not that Paolo didn't want her to write, but he did have certain expectations. Being a di Fiori carried obligations. It was not like being married to the boy next door. After they had been married for a year or so, she would resume writing. She would write about Italy. Out from under Donizetta and Marcella's scrutiny, she would see more of the country. Right after they were married Paolo had promised to show her the country. It was not his fault that he had reneged. No, Paolo could not be blamed if he had to obey his father and sisters. Things would change soon. This was just a period of adjustment. Yes, that was it. The whole family had to adjust to the new marriage, and as soon as they did—say, in three or four months—things would be just fine. Wouldn't they? Oh, God, I hope so, thought Angela as she climbed out of the pool to dry off and get ready for dinner.

When Angela returned to her room, she took a long, hot shower. There was a light knock on the bathroom door.

"Signora, they are waiting for you." It was Maddelena, now Angela's personal maid.

"All right. Please tell Signor Paolo I'd like to see him before dinner, Maddelena. I won't keep him long."

"The Signore has not come home yet, Signora."

Angela stepped from the stall shower and dried herself vigorously with a rough towel. Damn, she thought, why does he have to work so late!

Angela did not look up from her plate. Without Paolo beside her, she felt an outsider among the di Fiori family. She was relieved when Marco appeared at the table, calling Cesare away for an important phone call. Now she could excuse herself without asking Cesare's permission and withdraw to her room to wait for Paolo.

Just as Angela rose to leave, Cesare returned. His face was ashen.

"A terrible thing has happened," he said, standing stiffly at the head of the table. He paused and then spoke rapidly in Italian. Although Angela now spoke the language almost fluently, she had to strain to understand Cesare's staccato burst of words. "Paolo . . . taken by kidnappers . . . cooperate completely. We are not to go to the police . . . instruct us about the ransom. We must pay or Paolo . . ." Cesare's hands began to tremble uncontrollably. Luca rose to grab Cesare's arm to support him, but Cesare pushed Luca away, saying, "We will handle this. We will come through it. My son will live."

Angela sank silently to the floor.

By midnight, the di Fioris had received many telephone calls. First, the police had called to tell Cesare that Paolo's car had been found on the side of the road a few kilometers from the villa. Luca had tried to throw them off the track by giving them a false story, but the police were too smart. There had been a rash of Mafia-connected kidnappings of Northern Italian industrialists. The police were familiar with the abductors' modus operandi. When they found the unoccupied car, it was only a matter of minutes before their elite corps was tracking leads. And it was only minutes more before the Italian press found out. Then the shocked and outraged neighbors, friends, and distant relatives began telephoning. They had heard the story on the radio, seen a segment about it on the television news. Was there anything they could do to help?

At one o'clock in the morning, Franco Aldorelli, owner of the Aldorelli wine empire, called. His son, Roberto, had been kidnapped and returned a year ago. A huge ransom had been paid willingly by the desperate family. . . . Franco offered his services as an adviser to Cesare and arrived at the villa with his bodyguards two hours later. Cesare was grateful and listened carefully to Franco's instructions: keep the police in the dark, have your lawyer do the negotiating with the abductors so that it never becomes heated or personal, and first and foremost, make them prove that Paolo is still alive.

Four hours later, the kidnappers telephoned. Luca took the call. "Pronto. I am Avvocato Luca Bafabio. I am your contact for the di Fioris. Is Paolo alive?"

A gruff voice replied. "He is alive. He is fine. We want three billion lire. See that you get it soon or Paolo will start coming home to you piece-by-piece. I will call again with further instructions for the transfer of money."

After the kidnapper hung up, Luca repeated the conversation to Franco and the family members gathered in Cesare's office. They all began to chatter at once. All but Franco—and Angela. Having recovered from her fainting spell, she sat in a chair in the corner of the room where Maddelena had led her, with an afghan tucked around her. Since she had come to, she had been shivering and could not stop.

"First," Franco began, silencing the family, "you must try to get the money before the police seal off your bank accounts: it is now illegal to pay ransom to kidnappers. You must assure the kidnappers that although the police know about all this, you are not cooperating with any officials. Now, next time they call, ask them a question that only Paolo can answer. They must bring us the answer to this question, thereby proving to us that Paolo is really alive."

Donizetta shrugged her shoulders and looked at Marcella. "I can think of nothing. Can you?" Marcella shrugged and turned to Luca.

Bafabio shrugged his shoulders. "I don't share Paolo's secrets. Do you, Cesare?"

Franco shook his head and smiled at the group. "Isn't it

obvious? Ask his wife! There must always be secrets shared by man and wife, no?"

As one, they turned to face Angela. She stared at them vacantly, fingering the sapphire that hung, as always, around her neck. She held it as though it were a holy medal. Her large green eyes were open wide. They waited for her to speak. It was the first time they had realized she was in the room with them, and her pale, shocked presence unnerved them further.

Angela shook her head as if throwing off a dream. They wanted something from her. She knew that they all expected her to say something. What did they want?

Franco Aldorelli approached her. Putting a protective arm around her, he knelt down next to her and spoke slowly to her in English. "Signora, I know you are in shock, but you must try to think. We must know if your husband is alive. There must be some secret. You don't have to tell us what it is. When the kidnappers call, Luca will ask a question. Make it as cryptic as you like, but make it so that Paolo will know the answer and let us know if he is alive. Surely there is a secret you share."

Angela almost smiled. A secret? In this house? Then she remembered something she and Paolo had talked about together in whispers only. They had decided to try to have a child. There was a doctor in Rome that Paolo had heard about, a doctor who had helped many women who had had miscarriages before carrying a baby to full term. And they were going to see him soon, before the fall. His name was . . . it was . . . Dottore Montefiore. That was it: Montefiore.

"Here's your question," Angela whispered, her mouth dry with fear for Paolo. "Ask him the name of the doctor in Rome. He'll know what I mean. He'll know and he'll tell us."

For two days they heard nothing. Luca and Cesare sequestered themselves behind the ornately carved oak door of Cesare's office. They made phone calls: to Swiss banks, to Italian banks, to American banks. They looked at the financial records and reports for Di Fiori Automobili over and over and over again. Three billion lire was a lot of money—more than three million dollars. Money that even Angela knew the di Fioris did not have readily available. No, something at Di Fiori Automobili would have to give. Or be given.

Angela's world for those two days was a world of prayer—

and paparazzi. She went to the cathedral in Modena every day to light candles for Paolo's return, and every day she was mobbed by the curious and by photographers. At night, the family circle convened in Cesare's office to go over their plans with Franco. Over and over again, Cesare asked, "How could this happen? We have armed guards. Paolo never went to work at the same time any two days in a row. We took all precautions. The other attempts were easily foiled. Why this now? What was different?"

When, after two days, Gino and Ettore still could not be found for questioning, Cesare had his answer. Aldorelli told him it was not uncommon for bodyguards to betray their master's whereabouts and habits, if the bribes were high enough or if the perfidious hirelings were offered a portion of the ransom. Perhaps, thought Cesare ruefully, their salaries should have been more generous. Maybe then they would not have been tempted.

On the third agonizing day of Paolo's disappearance, the second phone call came. It was recorded. The voice said:

"Avvocato Bafabio? This is The Caller. The answer is Montefiore. Paolo is well. I will be brief. Get the three billion lire and put it in a plain brown suitcase. I will tell you later where to deliver it. But get this, Bafabio: no police. We want the wife to bring the money. Just the wife. Alone, unarmed, in a Fiat. No fancy di Fiori."

The phone clicked and disconnected. By the following day, full instructions had been given for paying the ransom. The kidnappers threatened to send them Paolo's fingers, one by one, if they did not get the money together in three days. That night, Cesare and Luca met to discuss the ransom.

"Cesare, you have worked all your life to build the company into what it is today. You did it for your whole family. Everyone knows that. The company is what your whole life is about. The money they are asking you for is outrageous. If you borrow that money against our assets, you will jeopardize our growth for the future. Is that what you want for the company? For Paolo?" Luca asked as he sat across from Cesare, leaning over, placing his face close to the older man's.

"No. I don't want to destroy my dream. But I won't lose my son, either. I must do what those criminals ask of me."

"That's where you're wrong, Cesare. They are thugs.

Brutes. They want the money you have slaved and sweated a lifetime for. And they'll take what they can get. What's the difference to them if it's three billion or maybe one billion? It's more money than they've ever seen or are likely to see. They will take what you give them. Trust me, Cesare. I have spoken with lawyers who have handled these things. You must bargain with these people. They may ask for three billion, but they never expect to get it. . . ." Cesare's full attention had been captured. Luca continued. "And Cesare, for law-respecting people like ourselves, we must bring in the police. We must cooperate with them to some extent. We are not bandits! Here is my plan: Angela takes them the money—say, one billion lire—plus some plain paper for the weight. Without Angela's knowing, the police follow at a safe distance. Before they can count the money, the police will have killed the dirty bastards who abducted your son. What do you think?"

Cesare frowned. "I think I cannot answer you hastily. . . ."

"Of course, my father," Luca replied solicitously, "but remember, it is the animals who took your son and now want to rob your company who are rushing you. Not I."

A great shroudlike silence fell over the house. Donizetta and Marcella spent their days in the oldest room in the house—the chapel that had once been used by the Estes for family masses, sitting on carved stone benches with their rosaries, whispering prayers endlessly.

Unable to escape photographers and reporters, Angela had given up visiting the cathedral in Modena. She stayed home. In her room. Sometimes she prayed, sometimes she cried. But always she was waiting. Waiting as though an answer would come to her if she was only quiet enough to hear it. Waiting as though Paolo would send her a message on the soft breezes that drifted in her open windows. She avoided Donizetta and Marcella assiduously. She took only anxious long-distance phone calls from Sal, Jimmy, or Eli. All she could tell them was that she was all right. And that she was waiting. Nothing else.

When dawn broke on the third day, Cesare was still in his office in the dressing gown he had put on the night before. His eighth cup of espresso sat untouched in front of him. It had taken him all night to make a decision. He had conferred with

Luca until midnight. The avvocato's words had been frank and painful. What were the chances that Paolo still lived? They had heard nothing for three days. And why had it taken two days for them to come back with the secret word from Paolo? In those two days anything could have happened to Paolo. Although this was a painful question, it was a realistic one. And Cesare was nothing if not a realist. Luca understood and respected this. That is why he had felt compelled to lay out all the possibilities, no matter how unpleasant, for Cesare's consideration.

Now the day of reckoning had come. If Luca was right, Paolo was probably lost forever. What was left? Only Di Fiori Automobili. That was all that mattered now. And the three billion lire that would have to be removed from it, like a healthy limb wrongly amputated, would leave it a hopeless cripple. No. Cesare himself would die before he would see that happen.

In the ghostly light of false dawn Cesare, seated alone behind his desk, opened a strongbox. Inside it were three billion lire. Cesare counted out one billion in small and large bills, and placed them on his desk. He closed the box and locked it.

Later, while Maddelena helped Angela dress for the rendez-vous, Luca went to Cesare's bedroom where the patriarch was finishing a solitary breakfast. "Trust me, my father. I know what I'm doing. The suitcase has been weighted perfectly. The real money is on top; the blank paper is buried beneath it. The police will be tailing Angela so discreetly that she will never know she is being followed. This way we are covered. If my brother is alive—and I pray God he is—he will be in his wife's arms before the bastards know they've been tricked. If they find out too soon, the police will close in and wipe them out," Luca whispered intensely into Cesare's ear.

"I understand, Luca. But if my son is alive—"

"And I pray God this is so," Luca interrupted.

"I want no one hurt. I want my son back safe if he—"

"I explained it to you. It cannot fail," Luca said.

It was night. Angela trembled from fear and cold. She had insisted upon wearing the white sundress that Paolo had found her in when he rescued her from the Blue Grotto. She drove slowly on the unfamiliar roads, a map and a flashlight lay at her side along with the all-important plain suitcase. How foolish she had been, she thought. Paolo's complex relationship with his father, the coldness of all the di Fioris toward her—these problems seemed so unimportant now in comparison to the events of the last few days. The only thing that mattered was getting Paolo back. She chewed her lip nervously as she carefully steered the Fiat sedan around the curves of the deserted unpaved mountain roads. Fortunately, Paolo had taught her to be a skilled driver. As the car climbed higher and higher into the black Apennines, Angela envisioned the joyous reunion, but her tense, shuddering body betrayed her fear. These have been the six worst days of our lives, she thought, but they'll be over soon, and that's what's important.

Suddenly, the road ended in a cul-de-sac. She had arrived. As she was instructed, she got out of the car, leaving the headlights on. She stood waiting with the suitcase in her hands. If only she could stop shaking! Her legs barely supported her. She heard the sound of gravel crunching under tires. She saw the headlights of a car. They drew closer, blinding her. Footsteps approached. The bag was snatched from her hands and—he was there. Blinking in the harsh light, she saw him. He looked fine. He was rubbing his eyes and stumbling toward her, but he was all right, he was smiling. He was alive! He could see her now. He opened his arms and came toward her. He was safe. He was coming home.

More gravel crunched under rapidly turning rubber. The air was filled with a mechanical whirring. Without thinking, Angela threw herself to the ground, so fast and so hard that she tasted dirt and blood inside her mouth. Paolo dove, too. She saw him drop to the ground only a few feet from her just as the noise stopped. The air was still. The car was gone. Guided by the beams from her headlights, she crawled to Paolo.

"It's all right now, darling. It's over. We can get up. We can go home." But Paolo lay still. Panicked, she reached out and threw her arm around his shoulders, shaking him. "Paolo, get up. It's not safe here. Let's go!" When he did not answer, she pulled on him, tugging his body until he turned over in her lap and showed her his bloody secret. He lay utterly still, his body covered with wounds that, like red mouths, spilled Paolo's life from their betraying lips. Paolo's deep brown eyes seemed to look at her, but for the first time they were empty of feeling; they did not see her.

Angela moaned. She continued to plead with him to get up, to come back with her to the car. Then, his silence denying her irrational hope, she screamed. The sound was inhuman, torn from her throat. She held him and rocked him and wept. When they found her, exhausted, shocked, and bloodstained, she still held Paolo in her arms.

CHAPTER
8

ELI WALSH began riffling through the stack of mail that had piled up on her desk all day, routinely tossing the newly submitted manuscripts onto the haphazard stack at her right—the "slush pile"—and the small envelopes and periodicals to her left. *Saturday Review* and *The New Yorker* were pushed aside to be read carefully at home, and Eli grabbed *People* and began flipping the pages. She stopped abruptly at a photograph of Paolo and Angela di Fiori standing proudly before the Angelina, the Di Fiori–built racing car that had just won the Grand Prix. Was this the third or fourth time she had discovered Paolo and Angela in the pages of *People*? She smiled involuntarily, remembering that day back in October when for the first time Paolo di Fiori and his new American bride laughed up at her from the magazine's cover. Then she remembered the other reason that day was so deeply etched in her memory. That was the day she had met Larry Gould.

"'Italy's Prince of Wheels Marries his Cinderella,'" Eli read aloud from the magazine's cover. "Jesus H. Christ! And only six weeks ago, Angela thought *I* was the one with the glamorous life!"

Eli was hungrily taking in the description of Angela's wedding gown when she became aware of another's presence in the room. She hadn't heard the door open or close nor noticed the man walk over to the desk, although she was supposed to be functioning as relief receptionist.

"So that's the kind of reading employees of the Brad Monroe Literary Agency prefer," he said with a sneer. "No wonder I'm having so much trouble getting an answer on my manuscript."

Eli raised her eyes and met those of a very impatient-looking young man. He was tall and rangy, with a strong-featured face framed by curly black hair. Eli suspected that a pipe lurked somewhere in the bulging pockets of his rumpled herringbone sports jacket. She managed to smother a mocking smile. She was sure he taught English at some college.

"Good afternoon, sir," she said in her most businesslike tone, shoving the magazine under a manuscript. "Might I be of assistance?"

"Yes, you may. My name is Larry Gould. I'm here to see Brad Monroe. It's concerning my manuscript, *Levy's Lament*."

Gould was looking past Eli, not at her, and his tone could not have been more condescending had he discovered her snapping gum and filing her nails.

Eli smiled sweetly. "I'm so sorry, Mr. Gould, but Mr. Monroe is out of the office at present. Did you have an appointment?"

"Yes. Yes, I did, dammit! And I'd like to see him," Gould snapped, recovering from a hurt and bewildered look that briefly turned down the corners of his brown eyes.

"I'm Elizabeth Walsh," Eli replied politely. "May I help?"

"I doubt it!" Larry said. He turned sharply and made for the exit, slamming the door behind him.

"Nice guy!" Eli said under her breath. Why did they always have to take it out on the underlings when Brad screwed up an appointment? Eli wondered. Who was this Larry Gould anyway?

Then she remembered: *Levy's Lament* had come in a month or more ago. Eli had passed it on to Brad without looking at it or giving it another thought. But after encountering its cranky author, she was curious. There was something appealing about Larry Gould despite his attitude: his good looks, and the hurt she saw when she told him that Brad wasn't in. It betrayed a vulnerability beneath the arrogant facade. Maybe she'd just take a quick look at *Levy's Lament*. God knows when it would get out of Brad's slush pile otherwise. It might be awful, but at the very least, the manuscript might reveal something about the rather attractive Mr. Gould.

* * *

"Brad, you've got to read this. I don't care what you think of the title. This manuscript is good. Very good. This guy Gould is a *writer*. He kept me reading until two in the morning. It's funny. It's sensitive. It's—Brad, you've got to read it yourself."

"All *right*, Elizabeth. I'll skim it and let you know what I think. Now, would you please take these proposals and return them with the standard rejection letter?"

"Okay, Brad. Yessir! And thanks." Eli picked up the rejected manuscripts from Brad's desk and left his office. And after I'm done with your typing, she thought, I'll be back to bring you your coffee and shine your shoes. Why had Brad bothered to promote her? Didn't the title Associate Agent mean anything? She knew that when she had been an assistant it had meant only that she was a secretary. But Brad was still treating her like his "girl." What did she have to do to prove her abilities?

Eli sat down at her own desk and resigned herself to her task. That afternoon, as Eli was getting ready to leave for lunch, Brad appeared at her desk.

"Elizabeth, I believe you're right. I've given the Gould manuscript a cursory look. This Larry Gould has a very particular voice. A bit bizarre, perhaps, and somewhat vulgar, but he is rather unique. I think we'll handle this property. I like developing new talent."

"Wait a minute, Brad. I discovered him, and I want to handle him."

Brad Monroe peered down at his young employee with astonishment. It was the first time he had seen her show such strong conviction. "All right, Elizabeth. I always knew you had an eye for good writing. That's why I promoted you. I wondered, however, if you had the gumption to put yourself on the line for a project that you believe in. It takes more than taste to make a good agent. If you can be so sure of yourself concerning this project, perhaps you can handle an editor when you're trying to sell it."

"You won't be sorry, Brad," Eli said with uncharacteristic softness. "I really think I can do something with this."

"Elizabeth, I'll permit you to take on *Levy's Lament*, but under my supervision, of course."

Eli grabbed her phone and dialed Larry Gould's number.

"This is Elizabeth Walsh from Brad Monroe calling," she said. "I was wondering if you could come in tomorrow at ten to discuss your manuscript. We think it shows promise."

"Thank you, Ms. Walsh," Larry said curtly. "I'm looking forward to meeting Mr. Monroe."

"Your appointment is with me. See you at ten, Mr. Gould," Eli said triumphantly and hung up the phone.

The next morning, Eli slipped on the jacket of the navy blue suit she had bought at Saks during her lunch hour the day before. This was going to be her first meeting with a client of her own, and she wanted to be taken seriously. But why did she feel jittery? Larry Gould was probably having his first meeting with an agent. He didn't know how an agent should conduct herself and her business any more than she did. Besides, Brad had prepared her for this morning's meeting and they had gone over Gould's manuscript with meticulous care. And Eli had seen Brad himself handle author conferences with aplomb. All she had to do was follow his example—and stay calm.

Eli gave herself a last glance in the mirror. Something was wrong. In her new three-piece suit she looked more like some stuffy lawyer on her way to plead a case than a literary agent. She grabbed the handle of her closet door and pulled, praying that the closet's contents would not—just this once—spring out and attack her. Rustling through thrift shop cashmere sweaters with "pearl" buttons and a kaleidoscope of ethnic blouses and dresses and skirts, she finally found what she was looking for. After a brief struggle with the door to get it closed again and a few well-chosen expletives, Eli unfastened the top two buttons of her white cotton blouse and tied a jaunty bright pink and purple deco-patterned scarf around her neck. She reappraised herself in the mirror and happily approved the readjustment. She quickly pushed her oversized aviator glasses up from where they habitually slid on her nose, and was on her way.

Larry Gould bounded up the long flight of stairs from the subway to the street, his long legs taking the steps three at a time. He didn't know why he was in such a rush; he was almost forty-five minutes early for his ten o'clock appointment. He had been up before six and had nursed himself through five cups of coffee before leaving his one-bedroom apartment on

West Ninety-third Street. Today was the day. The first step to finally seeing his dream come true.

Larry couldn't remember ever not wanting to be a writer. Writing and reading had been his passions since childhood. While his friends were outside playing ball, Larry was indoors discovering Hemingway and Proust. Invariably, when a book was presented in English class as required reading, Larry had already read it. As the editor of his high school literary magazine in Teaneck, New Jersey, he unabashedly published some of his own short stories and essays. At Rutgers, where he majored in English Literature, he was the book reviewer for the school newspaper. As a graduate student and teaching assistant at New York University, where he now taught full-time, Larry kept writing—first short stories, then a more ambitious project, his first attempt at a novel, *Levy's Lament*. Several of his recent short stories had been published in obscure literary magazines with limited readerships, and not without some critical acclaim. But his file of rejection letters was thicker than most of his story manuscripts. Now, this was it—the real thing. He had taken a chance with his novel, and an agent had shown interest in it. He was on his way to becoming that most honored and admired creature on earth—a published novelist.

As Larry reached the top step and encountered the hustle-bustle of Fifty-third and Fifth, he forced himself to slow down. Stopping and looking into the window of the Doubleday Bookstore, he chuckled to himself. Before long, his book, too, would be on display in the window for all the world to see. He glanced at his watch for the fiftieth time since he left home. Forty-three minutes to go. He decided to go into the bookstore and kill some time. As he rounded the corner and headed toward the revolving door, Larry didn't notice the "receptionist" from Brad Monroe rushing past in a frenzy.

Eli didn't see him either. She had other things on her mind as she hurried into Eleven East Fifty-third and headed toward the elevators. It was almost nine-thirty! She could just hear Brad now, as the elevator sped up to the twenty-third floor: "Elizabeth! I'm so pleased you could join us today. I was afraid I was going to have to deal with Mr. Gould myself." She didn't need any lectures from Brad this morning, thank you. She was nervous enough as it was. Dashing from the elevator to her desk, she quickly glanced through the open door at

Brad's office, then breathed a sigh of relief when she saw his chair unoccupied.

Eli was stubbing out her third Marlboro when the phone rang. "Have him wait a minute, Sally," she told the receptionist. "He's ten minutes early, and I need time to finish getting my act together." Eli put down the receiver and knocked over her half-full coffee container in one swift motion.

"Good move, Walsh!" she yelped, as coffee splashed onto her lap. "Why don't you just dump it over your head?"

By the time Eli removed the traces of spilled coffee from her desk, the floor, and her brand new suit, Larry had been sitting in the reception area for almost fifteen minutes.

"Okay, Ms. Agent," she told herself as she stood and smoothed her skirt yet one more time, "this is it. The moment of truth. Go get 'em!"

Larry was looking apprehensively toward the double glass doors that led into the offices when Eli emerged.

Larry blushed with embarrassment when he saw her.

"The other day—I'm sorry I was rude to you."

"Let's just start off fresh, okay?" Eli said, leading Larry back toward her desk. "Anyway, your tantrum at the reception desk made me curious enough to take a look at your manuscript. I remember when it came in. I just smirked at the title and passed it on to Brad, sight unseen."

"Now wait a minute, Ms. Walsh. I didn't come here to—"

"Now you wait a minute, Mr. Gould. Don't whip yourself into a frenzy before I've finished. Brad didn't pick the manuscript right up either. What I'm trying to tell you is that I read it and liked it. A lot. And I convinced Brad that he should read it. He thinks it's a worthwhile project for the agency. Now you were saying? . . ." She smiled triumphantly, standing behind her desk.

"Okay. I'm sorry," Larry said quietly. "So you're really going to handle my book. What happens next? How soon will you submit it to publishers? How quickly will I have a contract? I've got several specific houses in mind—"

"Hold on a second," Eli said, sitting down and gesturing Larry into a chair that faced her. "You're jumping the gun, aren't you? You skipped a few steps. Don't start planning the autographing parties yet. You're going to have to do some revisions first."

Eli hadn't known quite how she was going to tell Larry this and hadn't looked forward to it, but she had just blurted it out. Lighting a cigarette, she watched him sit back dejectedly, and then saw his expression change from defeat to anger.

"Revisions! I've written this book three times, and I think it's pretty damn good just the way—"

"Jesus Christ! What the hell is wrong with you?" She stood abruptly, pushing her chair back and banging it against the wall. "Can't anybody have a normal conversation with you? Now sit down and let's discuss this like two rational adults, may we please?" Then she blushed when she realized that she was the one who was standing.

"I apologize again. It's just that I strongly believe in my book. And I've worked a long time on it. But don't worry, I'll try to calm down," Larry said.

Eli saw Larry Gould smile for the first time. She hadn't thought he knew how. It was a lopsided smile, and it softened his hard-edged features. His deep-set brown eyes crinkled up at the corners in a way that reassured Eli immediately. She sat down and collected her thoughts before she spoke.

"Larry, there's one thing to remember through all of what I have to say. *Levy's Lament* is already a good book. I think so and Brad thinks so. We probably could submit it just the way it is. All we want to do is make it a better book. The first half of the book reads smoothly, but then you get bogged down in Levy's self-analysis."

Larry started to speak, but Eli was determined to have her say.

"Let me finish. What you don't realize is that you've constructed the character of Julian Levy so well that the reader really knows him and understands what he is thinking. You don't need to stop him dead in his tracks to explain everything we've just been shown. There are a couple of other minor things that will help to tighten it and some loose ends that need to be tied up, but we can take care of those soon enough. First, I want you to correct the major flaw. Why don't you take another look for yourself, and I'll bet you'll see it, too. *Then* we can start talking about submitting the manuscript to publishers. Okay, I'm finished. Talk to me."

Larry hadn't read the manuscript since he had submitted it to the agency over a month ago. He had reworked it so many times he felt it was finally perfect. Now, as he reluctantly reconsidered the section of the manuscript that Eli referred to, he began to suspect that she might be right. She certainly was incisive, he had to admit. Sharp—and pretty, too. Most of the women he met who had Eli's pert and fresh looks weren't worth knowning, in his opinion. But Eli was on the ball. Grudgingly, he realized she had earned his respect.

After Larry left, Eli sat staring into her overflowing ashtray, rehashing the details of their meeting. Had she handled herself well? Had she handled Larry Gould well? He was not the easiest person in the world to get along with. Perhaps he was just trying to mask his insecurities and wasn't doing a very good job of it. Under the surface, maybe he was really a human being after all; the sensitivity and the humor that were in his writing had to come from somewhere. She liked *Levy's Lament* so much that she couldn't imagine not growing to like its author. But it still would be a hell of a lot easier if her first author was a sweet old lady from Des Moines who had written a candy cookbook.

"Congratulations, Elizabeth. I'm quite pleased."

Eli looked up to see Brad Monroe smiling down at her.

"You handled our Mr. Gould in an exemplary manner," he continued. "He is a rather egocentric and difficult creature, isn't he? I do have a few suggestions for you, however. Would you care to hear them over lunch at the Russian Tea Room?"

As he spoke, Eli saw that his smile was more lecherous than congratulatory.

"Gee, Brad, could we do it after lunch? I, uh, promised my mother I'd meet her today," she lied. "But thanks. Hey, wait a minute, Brad. I don't get something. I didn't think you were here this morning. You weren't in your office when I came in. How do you know how it went?"

"I wasn't in my office because I was reading a manuscript at Doug's desk, just on the other side of the partition here. I heard every word, clear as a bell." Without waiting for a response, he turned away and walked toward his office. Before walking through the door, he stopped and turned back to her.

"Oh, and Elizabeth, one more thing. Could you *please* try to get here on time in the morning? I was afraid I was going to have to deal with Mr. Gould myself."

But Brad's reprimand could not wipe the satisfied grin from Eli's face.

When Larry called the agency at nine the next morning, Eli Walsh had not yet arrived at work. He left a message and sat waiting for her return call, absently nibbling on a cold slice of last night's leftover pizza. After a few minutes he decided he couldn't wait any longer. He was already late for his first class, the one he dreaded the most. There was nothing worse than trying to teach poetry to a roomfull of freshmen who were taking the course because it was required, not because of any burning interest in Blake, Burns, or the Bard.

Larry dialed the now memorized phone number of the agency again. Success!

"Eli, it's Larry Gould. You were right. I did some cutting, and now Levy's not jerking himself off anymore. Not mentally, anyway." He laughed at his own joke.

"You had me scared for a minute, Larry. I started to think you cut out the best parts of the book."

"No, I cut right where you suggested and then reworked the transitions. It went a lot more quickly than I'd expected, and it was less painful than I thought it would be. Now I want to hear about those other weak spots you mentioned. It's kind of difficult to discuss it over the phone, and Friday's my heaviest day. I've got classes in endless succession straight through."

"Classes?"

"Yes. I teach English at NYU—"

"No shit! I was an English major there: class of '72. Okay, look, why don't you come by Monday afternoon, and I'll take you to lunch."

"I can't wait until Monday, Eli. I want to work on the manuscript over the weekend. How about tonight? I'll buy *you* dinner!"

"Okay, Larry. You're on. Listen, as long as you're going to be at NYU, why don't we meet at the Lion's Head Pub? I live in the Village, so I have to end up downtown anyway. Meet me at around seven, and we can grab a drink and figure out where we want to eat from there."

Larry smiled to himself as he hung up the phone. He felt amazed at the intensity of his reaction. Some of it was excitement about his book, but some of it was mysteriously akin to the feeling he had after Mary Ellen Dowd accepted his invitation to the junior prom. Could the bright little blonde be getting to him? He had always had a weakness for the fair-haired and blue-eyed.

One class dragged on into another at an agonizingly plodding pace. Finally, mercifully, five-thirty arrived, and Larry was through for the day. He walked through Washington Square Park, past the ballplayers, skaters, guitarists, and derelicts who peopled the open square twenty-four hours a day. Normally he walked the perimeter of the park, avoiding numerous confrontations with drug dealers and panhandlers. This time he noticed no one; he was deep in his own thoughts. Would Eli approve of the changes he made? Was she really right about cutting the manuscript in the first place—or had he been taken in by her crisp air of confidence?

He walked along Waverly Place, crossed Sixth Avenue, and headed toward Christopher Street and the Lion's Head. The pub had long been a writers' hangout, ever since the offices of the *Village Voice* newspaper had been located on the same block. Larry walked in and seated himself on a stool at the bar. He ordered a Dewar's and water. While waiting for his drink, he looked around the dark, smoky room. The dust jackets of books by the pub's regulars that lined the walls reassured him. He was certain that almost every one of those authors had gone through a stage of doubt at some point during the prenatal periods of their books. And somehow they'd gotten through it, each and every one of them. The jackets on the walls were testimony to that. And soon the jacket of *Levy's Lament* by Larry Gould would join the display.

Larry turned on his barstool to see Eli standing next to him. Even seated on the stool, he had to look down at her.

"Eli! You're here sooner than I'd expected. Here, have a seat, and I'll get you a drink. What will you have?"

"Give me a scotch on the rocks," she yelled past him to the bartender as she settled herself upon the stool. Then she turned back to Larry. "Christ, what a day I've had. I worked like a coolie. So tell me—how was your day?"

"To tell you the truth, Eli, I didn't really notice. I have to admit that my mind was not on teaching. I was really anxious to see you tonight." Eli's bright blue eyes peered through her glasses at him questioningly. "To talk about the book and everything," he explained.

"Oh. Yes. The book and everything. Well, it's too noisy in here. Let's go somewhere else to eat so we can talk."

An hour and two drinks later, Larry and Eli were seated across from each other in one of the wood and leather booths at the Blue Mill Tavern on Commerce Street. "I'm buying us a bottle of wine to celebrate the imminent sale of *Levy's Lament*," said Eli.

"Hold on. I want to be optimistic, but aren't *you* jumping the gun now? I've made some cuts, but the book's not ready for submission yet." Larry leaned toward Eli and grasped her hand. "But you really believe in my book, don't you? That's so important to me. I've been living with Julian Levy and his 'lament' for so long now that I can't be objective about it anymore."

"Larry, can I ask you something? If you don't want to answer, you don't have to. How much of Julian Levy is Larry Gould? I know all about Julian, but not very much about Larry."

He did not answer her immediately, and she looked searchingly into his opaque brown eyes.

Larry let go of her hand and looked away from her, but Eli's eyes caught his again in the small mirror on the wall over the booth.

Was she being polite? Larry wondered. Or did she really want to know about him?

"I'll have to prepare an answer to that question if my book takes off, won't I? You won't be the last person to ask me about Julian and myself," Larry said. "There are some characteristics of Larry Gould in Julian Levy, I suppose. I'm introspective. I'm, I guess, insecure a lot of the time, too. Like Julian, I care far too much about what everyone thinks of me, how I appear to them. You know—image. But Julian's not my alter ego. I like to think that even at my worst, I'm a lot more normal—whatever that means—than he is."

Though he spoke the words casually, they had been hard for him to say. Glib chat about his work, his opinions, was easy for him. In fact, it would be hard to find a man who talked about himself more—superficially. But an admission to anyone of a possible chink in his armor was not just difficult for him to make—it was nearly impossible. Yet he had just begun doing it. Maybe it was the liquor that had loosened him up. Or perhaps it was the sincerity radiating from the clear blue eyes intently looking into his.

Eli felt a wave of gratified warmth. He was obviously not a man who spoke easily about his feelings. She realized she had reached him, affected him in some way.

Larry deftly switched the subject to his manuscript. Over dinner, they discussed the additional changes Eli wanted him to make. Larry appraised Eli's animated face as they spoke. He was listening carefully, but he was watching, too. She was so artlessly pretty.

Hours later, Larry paid the check and they went outside. They drifted to Morton Street, and Larry stopped at the front door of Eli's apartment house.

"Listen, Eli, I'm going to get working on this manuscript first thing in the morning. I've got a lot more to do. You've been a terrific help. Thanks." He bent way down and kissed her quickly on the cheek.

Eli wanted nothing more than to respond to that quick kiss with one of her own, to reach up and draw Larry to her. She knew she was strongly attracted to this man who was so different from those with whom she had casual, uninspiring affairs. Here was a man she could *talk* to and laugh with, a man who was sure of himself and respected her intelligence and responded to it without feeling threatened. But she also knew that to become romantically involved with a client would be professional suicide at this stage of her career—now that Brad Monroe had given her the chance to finally prove her abilities. No, she could not jeopardize this opportunity.

"Good night, Larry," she said thrusting out her hand and grasping his. "Thanks for the dinner. When we sell the book, dinner's on me, okay?"

"Qkay, it's a deal. Good night." Larry let go of her hand and then turned away from the door and headed for the subway station on Seventh Avenue.

Eli didn't go inside for a moment. Her eyes followed him wistfully until he disappeared around a corner.

* * *

Now, months later, in the solitude of her office after hours, Eli felt sharp longing when she thought of that first encounter with Larry. That longing had grown with each contact.

The shrill ring of the telephone interrupted Eli's thoughts. She glanced at her watch as her hand went to pick up the receiver. Who the hell was calling here at the office at almost eight o'clock?

"Eli? It's Larry," the disgruntled voice reported. "I tried calling you at home."

"What's the matter?" she asked.

"The jacket. It's terrible! I want you to call my editor and get him to change it."

Eli's eyes rolled up. "Whoa! Hold on! What are you talking about? You saw the jacket design months ago. And I can't call them at this late hour, anyway. Their offices are closed. It'll have to wait—"

"I'm not talking about the design. It's the flap copy. It was apparently written by an imbecile. It makes my book sound like *pornography*, for God's sake. Eli, I won't have it!"

Eli sighed. She was used to Larry's overreacting to every step taken by his publisher through the long publishing process, but Larry's "author's jitters" had worsened as publication date approached. But, despite his arrogance, every time Eli spoke with Larry, her attraction for him grew.

"Larry, you're just going to have to sleep on this. I'll call your editor in the morning."

"Okay. I'll talk to you then."

Eli replaced the receiver and stared down at the telephone. The dejection in Larry's voice tempted her to call him back and comfort him. But no, her emotions could not interfere with her business. She decided to go home.

A half hour later, Eli was trudging up the steps from the subway station. As she passed the newsstand at the top of the stairs, she paused to read the *New York Post* headline. She cried out aloud when the word screamed up at her: KIDNAPPED! was proclaimed above a photograph of Paolo di Fiori's face. Eli summoned all of her faded energy and started running toward her apartment. She had to call Angela.

CHAPTER
9

THE ALITALIA JUMBO-JET swept its way effortlessly westward, far above the vast blue-gray expanse of the Atlantic. In the first-class cabin, Angela di Fiori sat stiffly in her seat. Only a casual observer would have missed the change in Angela's appearance. Her beauty was unmistakable, irrevocable, but the innocent softness that had made Angela more than beautiful, that had made her pretty, was gone. Overnight, subtle curves had hardened into angles. Her face was pale and darkly shadowed, and her lips tightly drawn. The most dramatic transformation had taken place in Angela's eyes. Only weeks ago, those large green eyes that had danced and sparkled like two perfectly cut, matched emeralds were now as dull and opaque as puddles in the rain. Beneath those lightless eyes, red patches appeared where tears had been rubbed away, roughly and often.

Angela sat up in her seat and pulled her sweater more tightly over her black linen summer dress as a chill crept through her body. Then her hand settled unconsciously on the sapphire around her neck. She shuddered, remembering the events of the last six days.

Donizetta di Fiori had taken charge immediately following the murder of her brother. Cesare, shattered by the death of his son, was a broken old man, in no way capable of making even the smallest decisions. So Donizetta had arranged everything: the stately funeral in the Cathedral of St. Geminian where less than a year ago Angela had become Signora Paolo di Fiori; the burial in the gardens of the villa, where Paolo now shared a grave with his mother; and the removal of the American widow from Villa di Fiori.

There had been no discussion of whether Angela would remain at the villa to live. It was not necessary. There was nothing left at the villa for Angela. And the di Fioris gave her no reason to stay. They had arranged for her to fly to Rome in their private jet, where she would meet a connecting flight that would take her to New York. There, she would stay in the di Fioris' Murray Hill townhouse under their "protection." All of Angela's personal possessions, her clothes and her jewels, would remain hers, but the prenuptial agreement she had signed precluded any claim on the di Fiori fortune.

Angela listlessly picked up a copy of *Time* magazine that the flight attendant had offered soon after takeoff. Angela had not seen a newspaper or magazine since the tragedy. Absently flipping the pages, Angela barely glanced at them until she was stopped by Paolo's face staring up at her from next to a headline that read: "The di Fiori Gamble." Gamble? Angela wondered. What gamble? Every force within her wanted to close the magazine. Whatever the story said, she did not want to know. But her eyes wouldn't stop. If there were circumstances involving Paolo's death that had eluded her, she *had* to know. As her eyes avidly read down the page, the shattering story of Cesare di Fiori's attempted deception of the kidnappers was made clear to her. When the police caught the kidnappers and retrieved the ransom bag, reporters learned that it had been filled with more plain paper than money.

The shock of the truth hit Angela like a blast from a just-opened furnace. "OH!" she cried out as the magazine plummeted to the floor. "Oh, my *God*!"

A flight attendant rushed up the aisle to Angela's side. "What's wrong, Mrs. di Fiori?" she asked in an alarmed voice. "Can I help you?"

Angela shook her head. No. No one could help her. She knew now more than ever that she could not go to live in the di Fiori townhouse on East Thirty-eighth Street. She would not be watched by and held accountable to the heinous di Fiori family. And she had already tried to explain to her father, in a hasty transatlantic telephone call, that she could never return to dependency and live in Whitestone. She would have to find another solution.

The plane landed at Kennedy Airport and taxied to the gate. Angela realized she would have to work quickly. She had to evade both the bodyguards, who would be waiting to escort her to the di Fiori townhouse, and the reporters and photographers, who would surely be swarming about, ready to record her arrival.

Swiftly, Angela pulled off the silk scarf that held a loose ponytail at the back of her neck, then she covered her head with it, tucking in every wisp of her hair. She reached into her handbag for tissues and a mirror. She wiped away the light traces of makeup she wore. She put on large, dark glasses and was ready.

The plane pulled into the gate, and Angela lingered so she could lose herself in the horde of tourist-class passengers. She held her jewelry case in one hand and the one suitcase she hadn't checked in the other. She couldn't worry about her other luggage now. There was no time.

Stepping off the plane, Angela peered through the crowd of disembarking passengers, her eyes scanning the walls of the terminal in search of a telephone. Good, there was a row of them just inside the gate. She raced to one of the phones, dropped in some coins, and dialed. Then she heard Eli's voice.

"Thank God you're home. Please wait for me there," she said breathlessly. She hung up without waiting for a response and anxiously headed toward customs.

Not daring to look to either side, she offered her bags to the customs inspector with her declaration of purchases. It took a few minutes to clear the jewelry, most of which was antique. After she presented the appropriate documentation, Angela's bags were stickered and she headed toward the exit sign.

Miraculously, there were no shouts from reporters of "Angela! Angela!" as there had been at the airport in Rome, and no camera strobes flashed in her eyes. No arm reached out to escort her to a waiting limousine. Without looking back, Angela broke out of the crowd and ran through the automatic doors. She spotted the black limousine parked at the curb, and walking past it, hailed a bright yellow cab.

An interminable forty minutes later, the cab pulled up in front of Eli's apartment building on Morton Street. Angela turned around and apprehensively looked out the back window, praying that she had not been followed. When she saw Eli standing in front of the building, Angela quickly let herself out of the cab and fell into the safety of Eli's welcoming arms.

* * *

Angela didn't function for three tortured days and two restless nights. After having pushed herself through the ordeal of Paolo's wake and funeral and the lonely trip home, her stamina collapsed. She couldn't eat, despite Eli's coaxing and cajoling. She couldn't distract herself with reading, and she didn't dare open her journal. That would only force her to focus her thoughts.

At night she would awaken—sometimes from the sound of her own moans—her sleep shattered by gruesome nightmares in which Paolo's murder was reenacted in all its grisly horror. On the third night, utter exhaustion forced her to sleep uninterrupted. When she awoke, she voraciously devoured the breakfast Eli had made before going off to work. She carried her tea into the living room, feeling better than she had since the first night when she had learned of Paolo's kidnapping. Maybe today she would be able to call her father. She longed for Sal to hug her, to give her comfort he had offered so often when she was a girl, but she wanted to wait until she could show him she was strong and truly all right. She couldn't bear the thought of upsetting him and possibly causing him another bout of heart trouble.

Angela walked to the front window, feeling new energy at the prospect of resuming her life. She smiled absently as her eyes fell on two boys playing catch on the sidewalk. Then she noticed a long, dark car pulling up in front of the building. She watched a uniformed driver get out of the front seat and open the back door to allow the car's passenger to emerge. The blood in Angela's veins froze as she recognized Luca Bafabio.

"Whatever you're here for," Angela said as she opened the door, "get it over with quickly."

Luca strode into the room, and she saw that he carried a leather attaché case.

"As you know," he began, "our family is only concerned for your welfare. We have been terribly worried, not being able to reach you at the house in Murray Hill. Your sisters asked me to make sure you are all right."

"I'm all right, and now that you've seen for yourself, you can go back to Villa di Fiori."

"But Angela, you are not where you should be. A di Fiori cannot live here in this hovel in this kind of a neighborhood."

"I'm perfectly content here with my friend, thank you. Away from the—"

"And I also come with a very generous offer from the family," he interrupted, taking a seat on the sofa and opening the attaché case on his lap. "An account has been established in your name at the New York office of Banco di Roma. Every month, the sum of five thousand dollars in American currency will be deposited in the account and will be at your disposal. The only requirement is that you live in the East Thirty-eighth Street townhouse and conduct your life in a manner befitting a di Fiori."

Angela stood listening as Bafabio spoke, her anger rising by degree with each word. "In a manner befitting a di Fiori?" she asked mockingly. "And which of the living di Fioris shall I use as my example? *Which one?* Donizetta or your own Marcella, who holds everyone not in her exalted position in contempt and disgust? Or should I look up to the noble Cesare, who loved his cars and his money so much that he couldn't part with them to save his *own son?*"

"Angela! I beg of you, do not speak like this," Bafabio reprimanded. "I would not wish to have to report—"

"The only thing you'll have to report is that I threw you out! I don't want any di Fiori generosity. I won't touch money that could have saved my husband's life. Now get out, Bafabio. Go back to Modena and tell my dear 'sisters' that I don't care to hear from them again!" She wrenched open the door and stood glowering at the startled man as he hastily snapped shut his briefcase and stood.

"You are making a very big mistake. The family will not take this insult lightly—"

"Good-bye, Avvocato Bafabio," Angela said as evenly as she could, her body shaking with rage. She watched him walk out of the apartment and waited to close the door until he had disappeared behind the elevator doors. She went to the window and numbly watched the dark car pull away from the curb, then turned and sank onto the sofa as tears of outrage flooded her eyes.

Angela stayed huddled on the sofa all day. She was utterly spent and desperately afraid. The reality of her situation crowded in on her. What would she do? What did she have to back up her brave claim that she could take charge of her life, that she could be independent? She had no job, no money, no direction. It wouldn't work, staying here, existing aimlessly, imposing herself on Eli.

Suddenly, Eli burst into the room. "Whew!" she exclaimed, tossing her briefcase onto the small desk that stood next to the door. "What a wild day I had! I sold my sixth novel!" She turned toward Angela, and her eyes fell onto her listless friend. She was startled by the puffy red patches of flesh encircling Angela's glassy eyes.

"Angela! What's the matter? This morning I thought you were starting to feel better." She rushed across the room and sat on the edge of the couch as Angela mumbled incomprehensibly and started to sob again. She stroked Angela's unkempt hair. "Come on, Ange. Tell me. Please let me try to help you."

Angela caught her breath and smeared wetness from under her eyes. "Oh, Eli, what am I going to do with myself?" she sobbed.

Eli looked into the depths of Angela's eyes. "You're going to live, Angela. You've survived, and now you're going to *live*."

"Live? How? I can't—"

"First of all, you're going to start writing that novel."

Angela began to protest, but Eli would not be interrupted.

"Look at your situation positively. You have no commitments or responsibility to anyone but yourself for the first time in your life. Here's the perfect opportunity."

"What can I write about? I can't just sit down and—"

"Write about what you know, Ange. That's what you've done all along. Look in your journal and at the letters you sent me. You've been more places and seen and felt more than a lot of people our age. And no one I know is more observant than you are."

Angela sat up. Eli's enthusiasm was beginning to lift her spirits, yet she still needed convincing. "Eli, I appreciate your encouragement, but I can't write my life story. It would be too painful right now. And besides, who'd want to read it?"

"I'm not talking about your autobiography, I'm talking about your *experience*. You could write a wonderful, lush romance, say, about an American girl who goes to Italy, for whatever reason you want to make up, and falls madly in love. Of course you'll fictionalize, but you can use what you've seen, done, and felt."

"I don't know. I'll have to think about it."

"Okay, that's a start," Eli said, getting up and going over to her desk. She reached into a drawer and pulled out a bundle of envelopes. "Here are your letters, Ange. I've saved every one. Why don't you take a look at them while I change."

Angela stared at the bundle that Eli placed on the coffee table, thinking about the memories and feelings it contained. Maybe she could dig into her soul and write about a wonderful love that bloomed under the Mediterranean sun. Perhaps it would help her sort out her feelings, her joy, her despair. She would be forced to face her emotions, but at a discreet distance, through her heroine. And Eli was right. Up until now, she had always placed the needs of others above her own. She had always deferred. She had let others define her direction, make the choices for her. Writing, the one thing she had always wanted to do, was something she could now throw herself into, something that would give her purpose and direction. And if she was successful, it would give her her independence. Yes, writing could be her salvation.

"Okay, Ange. Now that I've got my playclothes on, how about going out for a walk? You haven't set foot out of this place since you got here."

Angela looked up to see her friend clad in an unmistakably pink print sundress from the fifties, turquoise anklets, and white sneakers. She couldn't help smiling at Eli's outrageous outfit. "Sure, Eli. It'll probably do me some good. Let me wash my face and run a brush through my hair. I must look like a wreck."

Soon Eli and Angela were strolling in the shade of the trees lining the streets of the Village. A warm gust of wind flew into Angela's face and lifted her thick hair. She was suddenly reminded that, yes, *she* was still alive.

"Feel a little better now?"

"Yes, yes, I do. But there is one thing that's bothering me about writing a book. One little problem you left out. What do I live on until I finish my book and maybe get it published?"

"You're rich, remember?"

Angela stopped and turned to her friend. "No, Eli," she said quietly, "I signed an agreement before Paolo and I were married. There's no inheritance. Nothing. And I wouldn't take any money from the di Fioris. My brother-in-law Bafabio was here in New York to see me this morning with an offer of an allowance. I threw him out."

Eli stared blankly at Angela. All along she had assumed that despite everything Angela was at least financially secure. Then Eli made a quick decision. "Stay with me, Ange," she said. "I've got to pay the rent anyway. Consider everything else as a loan, sort of an investment I'm making as an agent in a promising author. You can pay me back when we sell your book. It'll work out. I promise."

"Oh, Eli, thanks," Angela said, hugging her friend. "But I don't know. That's something I'll have to think about."

Wordlessly, they walked to the end of Christopher Street, occasionally stopping before the window of an antique shop or a boutique. Angela felt pleased and proud that Eli wanted to be her agent, but it was out of the question to allow Eli to support her while she wrote her book. She'd have to think of another way, no matter what sacrifices had to be made. She'd find any kind of job that would pay for her shelter and food if she had to. But she was going to write, she was sure of that now.

They turned down West Street, heading for the Morton Street Pier. Reaching the end of the pier, they settled themselves on its weathered edge, each staring silently down into the Hudson River. The red sun was finally sinking behind the odd conglomeration of smokestacks and high-rises across the river in New Jersey, but it didn't disappear before splattering its last rays across the rippling river.

The surface of the dark water shone like beautiful jewels in the sunset, Angela thought. Jewels! She had found her answer. If she sold her jewelry, she could buy a year, maybe two. In her emotional confusion, she had not thought of the jewelry. She closed her eyes tightly to summon Paolo, then she spoke to him silently. "Oh, caro, when you gave me those gifts, you didn't know how much they could one day mean to me. Please know that I'm going to do this only because I have no other choice. Thank you, Paolo. Thank you for giving me another new life." Her tightly shut eyelids held back her tears.

* * *

Angela briskly pushed her way out of Sotheby Parke Bernet, Manhattan's premier auction house, relieved to have completed her distasteful task and anxious to be on time for her lunch date with Eli. Now, a week after returning to New York, her new life could begin. Replaying the morning's events in her mind, she reached up to reassure herself that her cherished sapphire still hung beneath the tawny jacket of her suit.

When she had spread out the contents of her jewelry case on the deep blue velvet pad set on the cherrywood Chippendale desk in the appraisal room, Sotheby's Mr. Jeffreys had looked longingly past the other jewels toward the sapphire hanging between her breasts.

"A perfect pear, Mrs. di Fiori," he had purred.

"I beg your pardon?" Angela was unsure whether the sapphire or her bosom was the object of Mr. Jeffrey's appreciation. She squirmed uncomfortably in the stiff leather wing chair.

"The shape—it's absolutely perfect. An exquisite sapphire."

Angela's hand automatically rose to enclose the precious gem.

"I believe we can fetch quite a handsome sum for it, Mrs. di Fiori. Certainly, that one piece alone is worth far more than everything else here. If you would just take it off so I may examine it more closely . . ."

"No. I'm sorry, Mr. Jeffreys, but I can never sell this sapphire. It was the first present my husband gave me, before we were married." Oh, there had been so many other gifts, she thought. Paolo had given her so much, both before and after the sapphire. But what he had given her could never be bartered or traded; it was all deep within her heart. The sapphire could have been made of paste for all Angela cared. To her, it was the enduring symbol of her love for Paolo, all she had left of him materially, and it would never leave its sacred spot near her heart.

"What about your wedding ring, Mrs. di Fiori? I see that you're not wearing one. Has that already been sold?"

My God, Angela thought, this guy ought to audition for a membership in the di Fiori family. He might make it—he's certainly heartless enough.

"If you must know, Mr. Jeffreys," she replied coolly, "my

ring is with my husband. Now, can we please get on with the business I came here for? The pieces I've brought with me this morning are all that are for sale."

Mr. Jeffreys flicked the switch of the small black high-intensity lamp that stood at one side of the desk and placed a tiny jeweler's loupe against his left eye. He picked up Angela's diamond and platinum bracelet, the one she had discovered on her wrist when she woke one morning at Villa di Fiori after Paolo had gone off to an early business meeting. "This is just to celebrate another day with you," Paolo's note had said.

"Ah. This bracelet," Mr. Jeffreys intoned, "must be twenty carats all combined. The center diamond is flawless, as beautiful as its owner, if I may say. . . . It could fetch up to . . ."

Angela did not hear. Twelve pear-shaped, thirty marquise-shaped, and thirty-six round diamonds were struck by the small sharp beam from the lamp, and her eyes were blinded by light and tears. The few pieces of jewelry scattered on the velvet pad before her symbolized a part of her time with Paolo: the bracelet, the diamond and sapphire earrings he had given her to commemorate the first anniversary of their meeting at Capri, the gold and intaglio choker that had been his present to her on the eve of their wedding.

". . . and this choker . . . quite unusual . . . Etruscan revival . . . a striking specimen . . ."

As Mr. Jeffreys's appreciative murmurs brought Angela back to the business at hand, she nervously dabbed at her eyes, hoping that he had not noticed her tears. She cleared her throat.

"Well, Mr. Jeffreys, can you give me some idea of the total worth of these pieces?"

Mr. Jeffreys's steely eyes settled lewdly on Angela's breasts as he ceremoniously closed the calfskin folder containing the pad on which he had been taking notes and folded his hands on top of it. He sat back in his leather wingback chair before he spoke, his eyes still gazing at the spot where Angela's breasts cleft to cradle the sapphire.

"Well, Mrs. di Fiori, unless you'd like to reconsider my earlier proposition . . ."

"You've heard my answer, Mr. Jeffreys."

"I'm afraid, then, that I would have to estimate the total worth of these pieces to be somewhere between thirty and thirty-five thousand dollars. This is an estimate, of course, less our commission. The final value will be established at auction."

"How soon can you sell them?" Angela asked. Then she realized that she seemed too anxious, and sat back in her chair, trying to compose herself.

"Usually it takes from two to three months. Catalogs have to be produced, the pre-auction exhibition scheduled. . . ."

"Tell me, Mr. Jeffreys"—Angela leaned forward again, placed her arm on the desk, and edged her hand across the highly polished desktop until her delicate forefinger almost touched the simple gold cufflink on his starched white cuff— "is there any way that this matter could be sped along? This is a very trying time for me, and I'd like to get this sale over with. I certainly would appreciate anything you could do to help." She gazed at him longingly, hoping he would not be able to discern what she really felt. She needed cash—the quicker, the better.

Mr. Jeffreys's cool composure was visibly softened. "Well, Mrs. di Fiori," he began slowly, "there is a sale scheduled for a week from today. The exhibition of merchandise opens tomorrow, but I may be able to slip your things in, once my appraisals are confirmed. This is not a regular practice, but I'm sure that in your case, we can make an exception." Smiling slyly, he placed his icy hand over hers.

Angela withdrew her hand from his as gracefully as she could manage, and, crossing her legs, leaned back against the high hard back of her chair.

"Oh, Mr. Jeffreys," she murmured, her eyes downcast, "I don't know how I can ever thank you!"

"There are a few papers here for you to sign, but after that, if you would permit me to take you to lunch?"

Angela responded with a sweet smile, as she took his pen and scrawled her signature in the places he indicated. She replaced the pen and stood before she spoke.

"Thank you again, Mr. Jeffreys, but I'm busy for lunch today. I'm meeting with an old family friend at Burger Heaven!"

Before Mr. Jeffreys could regain his composure, Angela was out of the room, down the elevator, and safely on the street. She suppressed a giggle as she let her hand leave the sapphire in its place beneath her suit jacket and raised it to hail a cab. She couldn't wait to tell Eli the story.

Only minutes later—Eli was on time for once and was waiting outside her office building when Angela arrived—Eli and Angela were sharing a table amid Formica and fluorescence at Burger Heaven on East Fifty-third, with two cheeseburgers deluxe.

"Christ, Ange." Eli laughed as she wiped ketchup from the corner of her mouth. "You outsmarted that stiff at his own game. Good for you."

"Yeah, good for me." Angela laughed cynically. "I've just gotten rid of almost all I have left of Paolo."

"Come on, you know that's not true."

"I suppose you're right. I've got a lot more than some women will ever have," Angela murmured in response.

"Sure you do. Take me for example. I've been so busy trying to become Superagent that I haven't had time for a relationship. Remember that old expression the guys in high school used to use? The four Fs? Well, that's me. Find 'em, feel 'em, fuck 'em, and forget 'em. Not that many of the men I've met are worth much more than that."

"Eli! What are you talking about?" Angela sputtered, returning her cheeseburger to her plate. "What about Larry Gould? You found him. Now what about the rest? I know from your letters that you're crazy about him."

"I'm definitely attracted to him, could probably even fall in love with him if I gave myself the chance, but I can't allow myself to get emotionally involved with a client. Especially one so important to my career."

"But his book, *Levy's Lament*, is coming out soon. Can't you—"

"Nope. Can't. I think this book is going to establish Larry, and his publisher will want him to do another, and then we're right back to square one. Besides, there are still foreign rights to be sold on *Levy's Lament*, and hopefully there will be a movie sale. That's the torture of it. I'm on the phone with him a couple of times a week. Anytime I can find an excuse to call. Believe me, I'd much rather be talking about him and me than his royalties and the agency's ten percent."

"And does he call you?" Angela asked, looking squarely across the table.

"Does he? At first I thought it was just author's jitters, but now I'm convinced the attraction is mutual. Just this morning he called to remind me that we have a 'client-agent' date to go out to celebrate. Bound books of *Levy's Lament* will be in on Friday, so Larry and I are having dinner on Saturday night." She pushed aside her last French fry and paused to light a cigarette. "Christ, Ange," she exclaimed in a puff of smoke, "I'm nervous. Whenever I'm with him I'm afraid he'll see that I want him."

Angela took a long thoughtful sip of her Coke. She wanted to encourage Eli in her quest for love, and she was certain that if anyone could handle the precarious coexistence of a personal relationship with a professional one, it was Eli. As much as Angela didn't want to advise Eli to take a gamble with her career, she wanted so much for Eli to be able to experience the joy and contentment she had found with Paolo.

"This may sound ridiculous," Angela began tentatively, "but I think you should go for it. Take the chance. You've already cemented your business relationship with Larry. You believe in his work, and he trusts you, so your dealings with him shouldn't be jeopardized."

"Maybe you're right. I just don't know. If I lost him as a client, I'd be really upset. He was my first one, and I believe in him more than any of the others. That's what makes my job worth it. Sure, I love making the big deals and making money for the agency, but a big part of the satisfaction is getting good writers published."

"Listen, Eli, you've encouraged me to make the two biggest decisions of my life. The first one, to go back to Paolo, was right. And the second one, to finally start writing, is going to be right—it's got to be. Now, I'm telling you to make a decision. If you don't at least try, you'll always wonder what could have happened."

Eli looked thoughtful for a moment, then stubbed out her cigarette. She glanced at her watch, then she looked back at Angela mischievously. "Come on, Ange, let's get out of here!" she exclaimed, her lips curled up in a conspiratorial grin. "I've got only forty minutes before I have to get back to the office, and we've got to go and buy me the sexiest dress in the world for Saturday night!"

CHAPTER
10

ELI stretched out luxuriously in her bed, thinking about the last three weeks. So this was what if felt like to be in love. Nothing she had previously experienced had prepared her for this. From the first moment she and Larry had held each other right here in this bed, she had been electrified, newly charged with a power she had never felt before. Larry had admitted, as they lay together in the afterglow of lovemaking, that he, too, had hesitated. He had not wanted to ruin his relationship with his agent, but once he had a finished copy of *Levy's Lament* in his hands, he could restrain himself no longer. Since that Saturday night the two new lovers had seldom been apart.

Although they had agreed it was best to keep the relationship a secret from the publishing world, Eli was glad that they could be seen together without raising suspicions. After all, an agent and her client had a perfect right to spend time together.

Their lovemaking was always wonderfully intense. They had quickly discovered each other's secret erotic zones and gloried in their mutual pleasuring. Even this evening's lovemaking, which had only lasted moments, filled them with satisfaction. After Larry's last class that afternoon, he had come to her apartment for a nap before they went out. When Eli came home from work, the sight of his long, lean body, dark against the crisp white sheets, aroused her immediately. She stripped off her clothes and straddled his hips, readying him with her hands. Then she slid forward and down, taking him deep inside her, rocking back and forth in an ever-quickening pace. Still not fully awake, Larry came in shuddering spasms, as Eli cried out in exultation. Then she had curled up next to him and dozed off. Now, she stretched again and, opening her eyes, reached across the bed. Hmmm, she thought lazily after finding that Larry was gone, he must be in the shower.

As Larry rinsed shampoo from his thick, curly hair, his eyes closed tightly to shut out the soapy foam, he felt a pair of hands slithering toward his groin and a warm, wet body sliding up against his wet back.

Larry opened his eyes and turned to see Eli smiling up at him playfully. "What the hell are you up to now, wench?" he exclaimed, as his penis began to stiffen in Eli's hands.

"Ha! I'm not through with you yet!" She laughed. Then she bent down to take him into her mouth.

Larry was incredulous. This woman he had fallen in love with never ceased to amaze him when it came to sex. He had to admit that in the past three weeks Eli had uncompromisingly introduced him to many aspects of the world of Eros that had been only fantasies to him before. And she never seemed to tire. Even after their most elaborate and lengthy bouts of lovemaking, when they both had reached climax several times, she would be ready for more, coaxing him to readiness.

Larry leaned back against the cool wet tile, not knowing whether to heed his body's yearning for more or his knowing that if he did they were going to be late.

"Eli," he said huskily, "you know that if you keep doing that, we're not going to get to Angela's on time."

Eli let him slip out of her mouth just long enough to answer but not before substituting her agile hands. "Hey, don't worry. If I ever showed up on time, Angela would think there was something wrong with me. And besides, I could get you off in two seconds. You're almost too easy. The trick with you is to prolong it. That's what I like best—driving you crazy first. And one more thing, Mr. Gould—"

Larry chuckled to himself. Eli was the only woman he had ever known who could converse and give head simultaneously.

"—I want to have you well satisfied," Eli continued, not missing a stroke, "before you finally meet Angela. After all, I know how your eyes can wander, and she *is* gorgeous."

Larry bent down and lifted her up. As water splashed between and around their slippery bodies, Larry thrust his tongue into her mouth. He kissed her long and hard, then bent down to thrust his tongue between her legs. He licked and stroked, and heard her begin to moan above him. His tongue nipped and darted at her throbbing clitoris, as her hands clenched the curls on his head, guiding him back and forth. Then he felt her pulling him up. He knew what she wanted. Larry entered her smoothly, and after a few short strokes, he heard her gasp in ecstasy.

Out of the shower, as they playfully dried each other, Larry questioned Eli.

"Are you really worried about my meeting Angela? Is that why you've put off introducing us for so long?"

"No, that's not the reason. Although I suppose any woman might be subconsciously a little nervous about introducing her lover to a beautiful woman like Angela. She just hasn't been receptive since she got back last month. I've only seen her once or twice a week myself. She's needed some time to sort herself out, and she's trying to get started on her book. I'm the one who talked her into having this little dinner party tonight, just to get her back into some kind of social routine. And I think meeting you will help her. You can encourage her, since you've gotten your first book published. You're a good example. The new apartment should help, too. Even though it's tiny and it's practically unfurnished, it's the first place she's ever had that's her own. And if she can actually get started writing, well, she'll really be on her way."

Fifteen minutes later, Larry and Eli were across the street, climbing four narrow flights of stairs to the ramshackle studio apartment Eli had helped Angela find.

When Angela heard their knock, she got up from the new convertible sofa that served as her bed and put her wineglass on the table Jimmy had resurrected from the Vaccaros' basement in Whitestone. She was nervous. Nervous about having her first guests in her own apartment. Nervous about doing something "normal" for the first time since she returned to New York. Nervous about meeting Larry Gould, not only because he was a real writer, but because he was Eli's new lover, and she wanted to like him and to make a good impression.

As soon as Angela opened the door, Eli stood on her tiptoes and kissed her friend heartily on the cheek. "Angela di Fiori, meet Larry Gould."

Larry shook Angela's outstretched hand, staring. Eli was right. Angela *was* gorgeous. She was a knockout.

"Hello, Larry," Angela said with all the cheer she could muster. "I'm so glad to finally meet you. Eli's written and told me so much about you that I already feel like we know each other."

"Okay, enough pleasantries, you two," Eli interrupted. "I don't want you to get too well acquainted." And she gave Larry a playful jab in the ribs.

"Oh, stop it, Eli," Angela said with an embarrassed laugh. "Come on in and let me get you both a drink. Wine okay?"

Angela handed glasses of red wine to Eli and Larry, and Eli proposed a toast. "To my two favorite clients: Angela di Fiori and Larry Gould. May they both make me lots of money."

Angela laughed as they all touched glasses. "Eli! For God's sake, aren't you being a little optimistic? I haven't even set up my typewriter yet. I'd like to make my own toast—to the imminent success of Larry Gould's *Levy's Lament.*"

Glasses clinked again as Larry allowed himself another long hard look at Angela and smiled. He was going to like her. "Angela, I see you've got an advance copy on the table. You must have liked it if you're toasting its success."

"To tell you the truth, Larry, I just started reading it. I've been so busy getting myself organized in this new apartment. . . ."

Larry's smile wilted.

"Anyway, from what Eli's told me," Angela continued, "I just know it's going to be a smash."

"Angela, what's this wine? It's absolutely delectable," Eli broke in smoothly.

"Oh, it's Barbera d'Alba. Do you like it?"

"Yeah, it's really great, but you'd better get to like California jug wine for now. At least until you get your book written and published. How are you progressing anyway?"

"Every morning for the last month—since I've been in this apartment—I've been going to set up the typewriter and work on the outline. I've got some ideas, but I can't get started."

"Well, how about this for inspiration? Larry's publisher is already asking what Larry wants in advance for his next book, and *Levy's Lament* hasn't even been seen in the bookstores yet. All we have are terrific prepublication trade reviews, but the word of mouth in the industry has been fantastic, and that's what gets the ball rolling."

"That's wonderful, Eli. Larry, congratulations. That's a great reason for starting a second novel, but how did you get started on the first one? What motivated you to sit down and begin?"

"The burning desire to do it," Larry said crisply. "Without that, you can just forget it."

"Oh, Larry," Eli jumped in, "don't be such a pompous ass. You're not Saul Bellow yet, you know. You've got to remember that Angela's in a completely different situation than you were when you began working on *Levy's Lament*. She *does* have the burning desire, but she's got a lot of other things going through her mind, too. She'll start when she's ready, won't you, Ange?"

"I hope so, Eli," Angela said softly, staring into her empty wineglass, "I hope so. It's just so frightening. I'm not sure if what we've talked about will really work. It's not really writing if I just fictionalize my life with Paolo. I don't want to just take the easy way out."

"Believe me, it's not the easy way out. It's still going to be a lot of hard work. Listen, Ange, it's going to work. You've simply got to start writing."

After Eli and Larry had gone home, Angela lay awake in bed, trying to sort out her feelings. She knew she was frightened. Ever since writing her first compositions in elementary school she had harbored the dream of becoming a writer. But up until now it had only been that, a dream, something to look at from far away. Now she would have to face it squarely; she woud have to prove to herself that her dream was not just an ego-protecting fantasy. But what if she wrote her novel and it wasn't good enough to be published? Or what if it was published and was a flop? These were possibilities she would have to deal with. They had never been part of the dream, but they were certainly part of the reality.

Angela began thinking about Diana, her heroine, and her bittersweet affair with Giancarlo, the married Italian industrialist she meets in Italy on a research trip for her master's thesis in art history. Fragments of a plot began to take shape in Angela's mind as characters began to come to life. Secondary characters drifted into her consciousness as the story of Diana and Giancarlo began to unfold. Angela turned on the light, sprang out of bed, and put on water for coffee. Then she went straight to her closet and reached for her typewriter—the one Paolo had given her last Christmas, the successor to the old portable that Mama had given her those many Christmases ago. She placed it—along with her letters and journals— squarely on the old table from Sal's cellar and plugged it in, then inserted a fresh sheet of paper. As the pot on the stove began to steam and whistle, she began to type: *Blue Grotto*, a Novel by Angela Vaccaro.

CHAPTER
11

SNEAKERS with silk? It was foul-ups like this that made Eli
late. She was on her way out the revolving glass doors of her
office building when she realized she still wore her running
shoes—the shoes she and thousands of smartly, carefully
dressed New York business women wore for their healthful
walks to work each day.

Eli raced back inside the building and headed for the
elevator bank. God! she thought, looking down at her feet,
they clash too. Her bright yellow-and-blue Nikes were not at
all complementary to the peach-colored antique silk dress Eli
wore with a long, knotted strand of pearls and big pearl
earrings. She raced back to her desk, stripped off the sneakers
and the white socks she wore over pale pantyhose, and slipped
into the black patent leather T-strapped, low-heeled shoes she
kept in her canvas briefcase.

Brad Monroe called to her as she hurled herself out the door.

"I can't stop now," Eli cried. "I'm late for lunch at the Four
Seasons!"

Eli briskly walked the short distance to the inconspicuous
entrance to the Four Seasons restaurant on the East Fifty-
second Street side of the Seagram's Building where the
Women's Media Group met for lunch once a month. Several
times a year, a "program" was offered. Eli had suggested
Larry Gould for the program next month when he and several
other speakers were to discuss "Women's Image in the
Media." Eli did not relish the task of telling the program
committee that Larry would not be able to come. On the spur
of the moment Vassar had invited him to teach a special
creative writing course, and, at Eli's insistence, he had

121

accepted. Although she hated the idea of his leaving the city, she knew it was the right thing for him to do.

Levy's Lament had been published a year ago, and in that year Larry had become something of a literary celebrity. Eli feared he would never settle down to writing again as long as he stayed in Manhattan to gloat in the heady cocktail-party-circuit atmosphere. He had become the darling of the critics and the intelligentsia, and he played the role to the hilt. Successful parties all over town and in the Hamptons that summer had required the presence of Larry Gould to ensure that they had cachet. And Eli had willingly accompanied him everywhere.

But when his book hit the best-seller lists, what had been merely bothersome became unbearable. Eli found it increasingly difficult to fix a smile on her face while hearing Larry tell for the billionth time how he wrote *Levy's Lament*. As much as she loved and supported him, the thought of reading one more article entitled "Gould's Lament?" actually sickened her. She urged him to extricate himself from the circle of sycophants that was tightening around him and threatening to squeeze the creative juices from his body. He needed solitude to think and write. As long as there were toadies around to tell him he was a star and a genius, he would never be motivated to begin his second book. Besides, even though Larry's success had made Eli's name important too, she had other clients, Angela among them. Larry, if allowed to, would consume all Eli's time and attention, leaving nothing for her other clients.

It hadn't been all that difficult to convince Larry to take the job. The idea of a school as prestigious as Vassar wanting him to join the faculty was one more note of flattery in a symphony of praise and acceptance that Larry perpetually enjoyed. Although Eli had half-jokingly teased him about running wild after the pretty, wide-eyed co-eds, she had encouraged him to go.

Eli entered the marble foyer and bounded up the stairway to the Grill Room where she cast a quick, discreet, comprehensive look around the room, as she always did. It was here in this lesser of the two dining rooms that the giants of publishing gathered at lunchtime to make their deals, see each other, be seen by each other, and to exchange the gossip that the industry thrived on. Beyond the square, polished wood bar, up another short flight of stairs, she spotted two superagents being courted by two supereditor regulars. Eli hoped they would notice her and register that she too was important enough to be lunching at the Four Seasons. No one would suspect that Eli was here for a meeting, not to clinch a big deal.

Eli then swept through the Pool Room, so-called because its tables bank a twenty-foot marble pool, and up the stairs to the private room where the Women's Media luncheons were held. Just as Eli stopped at a table to pick up her name tag, Linda Fine, the editor who had purchased the paperback reprint rights to *Levy's Lament*, appeared at Eli's side.

"Great to see you, Eli. You look marvelous. I expected to see you gaunt and haggard."

"Why's that?"

"From having to schlep Larry Gould around. Did I tell you I went to school with that pompous jerk?"

Two pink spots appeared on Eli's cheeks. Now was obviously not the time to make her affair with Larry public knowledge. Eli replied evenly, "You think Larry's a pompous jerk? A lot of people would disagree."

"Oh, sure, he's hot now, but I knew him when he ws a horny newspaper editor at Rutgers. He was just like his character, Julian Levy. The biggest jerk-off artist in his fraternity. Pretentious as hell. Always after all the blond, tacky townies. Definitely had a thing for blondes—" Linda stopped herself short as Eli ran her fingers through her own blond curls.

"Well, you know what I mean—the super-WASP-type blondes." Linda continued, "My assistant's sister goes to Vassar, and she says he's up there right now having a hot one with some very horsey, toney, long-legged number from Virginia or Connecticut or something. You know the type. She's one of his students."

Eli barely touched the buffet salads, pâtés, and rare roast beef she had listlessly piled on her plate as Linda continued chattering about rumors of a big-name author changing publishers. Eli's mind and heart were not on gossip or food. She was deeply hurt. Had Larry really betrayed her? Had he gone the literary groupie route? What he had been in college, Eli didn't care. But was he fucking his students and making a horse's ass of himself? Or was what Linda had said just more mindless gossip based on little more than what people expected to hear?

Eli hadn't had as much contact with him as she'd expected to since he left in early September, but he told her it was because he was so busy, so involved in the new manuscript. She believed him and kept her distance. Could he have been holding her at arm's length so he could be free to screw around?

Dozens of conversations buzzed around Eli, who sat looking forlornly at the crème caramel the waiter placed in front of her. She pushed it away, removed her badge, and slipped unobtrusively from the restaurant.

She walked back to her office in a trance. Her assistant had to tap her shoulder to get her attention when she returned. "Hey, Eli! Here's a package that came by messenger while you were at lunch. I think it's the Gould contract."

Eli opened the envelope. It was the Gould contract. She would have to call Larry. But not just yet. First she went to the ladies' room and splashed cold water on her face. She fluffed her hair, straightened her dress, and took several deep breaths. She would call Larry as though she had heard nothing. Love was based on trust. She wouldn't fall prey to the gossip-mongers. Larry was innocent, she told herself fiercely. He loved her and she loved him. But perhaps it was time for a visit to Vassar.

Eli's arrival in Poughkeepsie took Larry by surprise.

"Eli! It's so good to see you!" They embraced warmly, and Eli fairly skipped with joy into the bedroom. She was confident from the warmth of his greeting that he still loved her and was faithful. She began to strip off her clothes. First, she tossed aside the heavy Mexican sweater she wore, then slipped out of her baggy faded jeans, revealing lacy white underpants. She sat down on Larry's bed and yanked off her Frye boots and socks. She had her turtleneck sweater pulled up over her head when Larry asked, "Eli, what are you doing?"

"What does it look like I'm doing, turkey?" Eli laughed. She threw the sweater across the room and shook out her golden curls. She stood up, bare-breasted, and faced Larry.

With her hands on her hips, she challenged him playfully. "Well? See anything you like?"

Larry stared at her for a moment and then turned away. "Eli, for God's sake, you just got here! Where's 'How are you? What's new?' You haven't even given me a chance to look at my contract!"

Eli's bravado evaporated. She picked up her sweater and covered her breasts. "I'm sorry. It's just that it's been weeks since we made love, and I thought you'd be as eager as I am."

"Well, it's been weeks for me too, Eli, but you don't have to jump me, for God's sake. You're so . . . so *aggressive* sometimes!" As soon as Larry said it, he was sorry, but there it was. His statement hung suspended in the silence that followed while Eli picked up her clothes and dressed. Tears flooded her eyes and rolled down her cheeks, but her mouth remained set in a firm line until she tied the belt of her Mexican sweater and swung her bag over her shoulder.

"I don't know what's wrong with you, Gould, but I'm not going to stick around here and find out. You've obviously got some kind of bug up your ass. Sign the goddam contract and send it to my office. And one other thing: you'd better be well into writing that second book. Your publisher doesn't hand out fifty-thousand-dollar advances to one-book wonders."

Back in the city, Eli decided that she was too angry to go home and do nothing. After dropping off the rented car, she headed straight to the Buffalo Roadhouse, a bar near her Morton Street apartment.

"A Bloody Mary," she said to the bartender, "with an extra heavy hit of vodka."

Angrily chomping on the obligatory celery stalk, Eli thought about her "lost" weekend. She had planned on a drive up the Hudson Valley to enjoy the October foliage. It was to have been a cozy, romantic weekend. They would have driven up into the mountains, climbed for a while, and stopped at a farmstand to buy crisp Macoun apples and maybe a pumpkin. Then, with their cheeks glowing, their bodies pleasantly exhausted, they would have gone back to Larry's little apartment and made love, over and over again.

But Larry had ruined it all. He had some pain-in-the-ass

problem that had made him lash out at her, and although she had the satisfaction of having the last word and making a dramatic exit, she was desperate to know what was really wrong between them. Perhaps the rumors about Larry *were* based on truth. What then? She remained calm. Maybe Larry was frustrated because his writing wasn't going well. His behavior didn't necessarily mean that he was having an affair. He needed some time without her, apparently. Fine. She would stay away. No calls. No visits. Not for a few weeks, at least. Eli left some bills on the bar and walked home alone.

Eli called Larry shortly after Thanksgiving.

"Hi, Larry," she greeted him airily. "How have you been doing? Writing a lot?"

"Eli! How are you?"

"Fine, just fine."

There was an awkward pause. "Eli, I am truly sorry for the way I acted when you were here. I should have called to apologize, but I haven't been in touch with anyone lately. I've cut myself off from everything, and I've just been writing."

"Good! That's what you're there for. I'm glad you're writing."

There was another pause while Eli held her breath.

"Look, Eli, I'd really like to see you."

Eli exhaled and casually said, "I'd like to see you, too. Is there any manuscript for me to read?"

"Yes, I have several complete chapters. And I think I may have hit a few problems—"

Eli interrupted, "Look, Larry, I'll come up and work with you, okay? But let's cool it on the personal level. I haven't heard from you in a long time, and I'm not really sure where we stand. Maybe we can talk about it when I come up."

"Yes, that's exactly what I want to do, Eli. Please. Why don't you come up this weekend?"

"Fine. I'll see you Saturday, sometime before noon?"

"Oh. Well, I have a tutorial session on Saturday, and I—"

"Okay. No problem. Leave the key under the mat. I'd rather read the manuscript without you anyway. I'll just let myself in and get to work. If it's okay with you."

"Perfect. See you Saturday."

* * *

Eli was looking in the top drawer of Larry's desk for a pencil with a good eraser when she found the poems. She hadn't known Larry to write poetry, so her curiosity was piqued. She pulled out the typed pages.

Only you can make me a woman
With you I can be free—
Your proud member
reaches to the depth of my soul
making me whole. I am yours to the end of time. . . .

Holy shit! Some lovesick co-ed is writing this crap to Larry, Eli thought. And she's had his "proud member"! Eli was nauseated, but she couldn't be sure what sickened her more— the poor quality of the writing or the fact that Larry had betrayed her with a student who signed herself "Alison Fairchild."

She forced herself to read the rest of the doggerel. It told her everything: Alison's adoration for Larry, the way she worshipped him (on her knees), and how he alone could teach her the ways of pleasure.

Eli was stunned. How could anyone she loved be such a fool? This Alison girl was obviously young, inexperienced, and silly. She worshipped Larry's fame, not Larry. She was no better than a groupie! A literary groupie! Is that what Larry wanted—a slavish admirer who asked nothing but to bask in the warm light of his celebrity?

Eli was angrier than she had ever been in her life, but she finished critiquing what Larry had written and typed up a three-page report before she let loose the tears of pain and rage. Then, on a fresh piece of paper, she wrote him a personal note and left the apartment.

When Larry returned, he found his manuscript in a much-improved state and Eli's editorial memo before he found her handwritten note:

Larry—
    I was looking for a pencil when I found the "poetical" ravings of a Gould-struck co-ed. (I made the mistake of reading them.) You're a vain fool. I'd like nothing better

than not to have to deal with you ever again, but I have an obligation to you professionally. I am your agent. We are bound by contract.

Please confine your future correspondence with me to business.

Eli Walsh

CHAPTER
12

ANGELA opened the window in her tiny apartment and let in the bracing April morning air. The manuscript was finished. Angela had written and rewritten. She had agonized and triumphed, learning more about herself in writing about the creatures of her imagination than she had ever expected to, and had finally experienced the thrill of accomplishment. She had held the bulky manuscript in her hands again and again, riffling through the pages, saying over and over again to herself: I did this. I made this. I *created* this. This big, thick manuscript exists because *I made it happen.* She felt like hugging herself and dancing. Yesterday Eli had taken the manuscript home to read that night. It was taking every bit of Angela's willpower not to call Eli at the office to ask her what she thought. She desperately wanted to hear what Eli had to say.

Writing was a strange, powerful process. And it was terrifying. Angela had poured her heart out onto paper, given the performance of a lifetime—said everything she had wanted to express about her life with Paolo through her characters—and there was no one there to either applaud or to boo her off the stage. No one to tell her that she had been too immoderate or had not given enough. How she *longed* to hear what effect her words would have on another human being.

The time she had spent writing had been a time of nourishment for Angela's soul and intellect. She had faced the typewriter bravely each morning. On those days when thoughts and words would not flow at all, Angela had taken long solitary walks, thinking often of her mother, Paolo, the babies she had lost.

Most afternoons Angela stayed home and read—classics,

popular novels, biographies, anything and everything. If she was going to be a real writer, she had to do her homework.

Because Eli, Jimmy, and Sal worried that Angela was becoming too isolated, too introspective, too solitary, they gave her a year's membership to the New York Health Club on Thirteenth Street. Angela had been delighted and added a daily swim and exercise class to her routine of walking, reading, and writing. Now, a year and a half after she had begun to write, *Blue Grotto* was finished, and Angela felt the stirring of spring and a sense of expectation. What adventures lay ahead? Whatever they were—she felt ready.

The phone rang. Angela jumped and grabbed it on the first ring. "Ange, it's Eli. I loved it! I loved *Blue Grotto*. I have a few suggestions for improving it editorially, but don't worry, there is no major revision necessary. The point is, I think I can sell it!" Angela's heart pounded with excitement. "By the way, why are you using Vaccaro instead of di Fiori?" Eli asked.

"Because I don't want to use Paolo's death to sell my book," Angela replied breathlessly. "This is *my* book, and I have to know if I'm any good. I want some publishing house to buy my book because they think it's good, not because they think that the di Fiori name will sell," Angela said.

"Angela, I'm telling you it's good. And not as your best friend, as your agent." Eli sighed. "Oh, hell. It doesn't matter anyway. It's been almost two years since there's been any publicity about you. And they say that the public has a short memory. If you want to go with Vaccaro, we'll go with Vaccaro."

"You do understand, don't you, Eli? I don't want to be judged by what happened to me in the past. I don't want my book bought because my husband was killed or because he was rich and famous. And I sure as hell don't want to be associated with any of the living di Fioris."

"Don't worry about it, Ange. With *Blue Grotto* we can't lose. Christ, you can call yourself Joe Schmoe and this book will sell. It's got 'commercial property' written all over it. And the paperback rights! Angela, it will go for a fortune to a paperback publisher."

"Great! What happens next?"

"Make the changes I've suggested—"

"I know, I know. But after that?"

"Then I'll send copies to a few editors, people who I think would appreciate this kind of book and whose houses know how to market a commercial book like *Blue Grotto*. Then I'll set a closing date for offers. Then we'll evaluate them and choose the best. The whole process will take at least a month—so you'll have to be patient."

Eli had another call to take, so they said good-bye quickly. Angela would have loved to talk to Eli for hours, asking her all sorts of specific questions about what she thought about the book, but she knew she was one of several authors in Eli's burgeoning stable. She vowed then and there never to take advantage of Eli's friendship. Even though Angela's window faced Eli's across the narrow stretch of Morton Street, Angela would not drop in for hand-holding sessions and advice about her book.

Angela wished she could do more for Eli in return for all Eli had done for her. Now that Angela was no longer openly and actively mourning, now that she had put her own pain in perspective—although she was still tormented by persistent nightmares about Paolo's death—Angela wanted to help Eli through her carefully concealed pain and disappointment. Although Eli rarely spoke of it, Angela sensed that Larry's infidelity had been a great blow—a blow that had left no bruise but had left Eli bleeding inside. Angela resolved to do what she could to draw Eli out, to help her work through her sense of betrayal.

Zabar's was packed. Why is it, Eli wondered, that no one in Manhatten ever has an original idea? Everyone thinks and plans in herds and packs. It was obvious that several hundred of the thousands that would soon crowd Central Park to hear the New York Philharmonic concert planned to bring a picnic dinner purchased at Zabar's. A dense crowd of casually but carefully dressed Manhattanites, shouldering sacks with bottles of wine and blankets, formed stubborn clusters at each counter, as they jostled aggressively to eye the culinary delights, and not incidentally, each other.

Eli waited on line among the hordes in their Calvin Klein and Ralph Lauren sports clothes to pay for her purchases: two slender loaves of crunchy French bread, Triple Crème cheese, duck liver pâté with green peppercorns, tortellini salad with crisp oil-glossed vegetables, and a fragrant strawberry and kiwi tart for dessert. Then she hurried across Broadway to buy the all-important champagne.

The entrance to the park on Central Park West at West Eighty-sixth Street was jammed with clusters of people waiting for their groups to assemble. Eli stood on tiptoe to see over the heads of the crowd pressing against her. She spotted a familiar long arm waving a rolled-up blanket. Thank God!

"Angela! I was beginning to think I'd never find you!"

"That's why I wore red! And why half the others here did too," Angela exclaimed, laughing. "I walked all the way up here to work off some nervous energy." Angela pointed to her bright blue Adidas sneakers. "I've been a wreck since you told me that three editors are considering *Blue Grotto*."

Eli pursed her lips, her eyes danced, but she said nothing. Angela helped Eli with her armload of packages.

"Hey, what's this? You've got two bottles of champagne in here."

"Oh, I sold a book today," Eli said. "I thought we should celebrate."

"You what? . . ." She searched the crowd for Jimmy's face.

"There he is!" Eli cried, waving her arms to catch Jimmy's attention. "Now we're set!"

The three of them were swept with the crowd into the park toward the Great Lawn. Once they'd scrambled for a space to spread their blanket and had settled in with their bags of food and drink around them, Eli made her announcement.

"Angela, now that you're sitting down, I'll tell you the news. I sold *Blue Grotto* today, Ange. I sold it. I sold it."

Angela gasped. Then the two of them yipped and yelped at each other, laughing and congratulating each other. Jimmy's arms encircled them both. Angela quieted down and panted breathlessly. "Who bought it? Tell me everything."

"Angie, I haven't even told you the *best part*!" Eli's voice rose with each word, until she was practically screaming. "You're getting a HUNDRED-THOUSAND-DOLLAR AD-VANCE!"

Angela's mouth dropped. Her widened eyes danced.

"Ange. Hey, Ange. You still with me?"

"Yeah, yes, of course. My God!"

"I know. Could you die! I almost dropped dead when I heard it. I acted cool as a cucumber when Mark Green said, 'You've got a hundred thousand from me. The offer is good until five-thirty.' He's at Heywood and Horne. So I called the other two editors—it was three-fifteen—and told them I had a hundred, and they had until five to make a better offer. They were more than a little pissed off at the pressure because they both loved the book. Well, at one house the publisher was out of the office, and the other editor needed until ten-thirty tomorrow to try to top the hundred. So I figured Mark Green is a great editor, Heywood and Horne is a good publisher, and the offer was fantastic. I didn't want to risk losing it for a possible no-bid or a lower offer. So at five-fifteen I called Green and said, 'It's yours.' Oh, Ange! Christ, I'm so excited."

"You're excited! I don't know whether to laugh or cry or scream or . . ."

"It's a record, Ange. A goddam fucking record! I don't honestly think there's been an author who has gotten that much money for a first novel ever!"

"Jesus, Eli! We did it! When does it happen, I mean, when will they publish? Do I have to sign anything? When do I get my money? And anyway, who is Mark Green?"

"Okay, okay. Take it easy. I know you have a lot of questions, and I'll answer them all as best I can."

"Hey Ange!" Jimmy cried. "Let's get up on the stage and tell 'em you broke a record! That you're going to have a blockbuster best seller!"

"I'm rich, too! I'm going to get a hundred thousand dollars!"

"Mom would've been so proud, Ange."

"Don't I know it." Angela's eyes filled with tears. "I can't wait to tell Daddy."

The two siblings, oblivious to the crowd around them, embraced.

"One hundred thousand dollars!" Jimmy yelled. "That's a lot of Levis."

"Wait a sec, you guys. It's like this," Eli said soberly. "You'll get ninety thousand dollars. You can't forget about the ten percent that the Brad Monroe Agency gets, right? Also, you don't get the full ninety all at once. It's half when you sign the contract, which I won't get until Heywood and Horne draws it up. It's a big company with slow wheels, so let's say four to six weeks. Then you sign. Another four to six weeks go by, then they send me a countersigned contract with a check. Okay. Then you get the rest of the money when the book's published."

"When's that?" Angela asked.

"They're shooting for a March pub."

"March? That's months and months away!"

"Right. Listen, Ange, you don't just add water and stir. It takes a while to produce a book. There's a lot that goes into it. And you'll be learning all about it as you go. In fact, your first lesson starts in two weeks. Mark Green wants to meet you to discuss his editorial suggestions. Mmm. Pass the pâté!"

"Who *is* Mark Green?"

"He's your editor. Really good pâté, eh, Jimmy? And you're lucky, Ange. He's first rate. And he's H and H's editor in chief, so he's got plenty of clout. And, best of all, he is really high on the project. He'd have to be to get Everett Horne to shell out a hundred grand for a first novel. That reminds me. We've got to get something about this record-breaking business into *PW* right away."

"Hold on. Who's Everett Horne? What's *PW?*" Angela asked.

"Horne is the owner of Heywood and Horne. He's a notorious old tightwad. *PW* is a trade magazine—*Publishers Weekly.* All the bookstores get it, and so does just about everyone in publishing."

"When does Mark Green want to see me?"

"He'll probably call you tomorrow to set up an appointment. And Angie, when you go in, you've got to look gorgeous. I mean stunning. I want them to know that they have one of the most promotable authors of all time."

"Is that what you think, Eli?"

"Yes. That's what I *know.* The combination of a great book and a promotable author means we can go all the way. You may need some coaching. . . ."

"Coaching? For what?"

"Oh, you know. Nothing major. A little PR training just to get you used to appearances, interviews, TV talk shows, touring, that stuff."

"I think I'm going to be sick. . . ."

"You'd better not be, Ange. This pâté was eight dollars a pound."

Angela heard a loud "shush!" from somewhere behind her just as Eli uncorked the champagne and the conductor, Zubin Mehta, appeared on the spotlighted stage. A hush fell over the Great Lawn. The music began.

Hours after midnight, Angela lay immobile, spread out on her bed slightly drunk and grinning. It was too much to think about rationally. It was overwhelming. Dreams were supposed to stay dreams, weren't they? But this one was coming true. Her book was good! Someone was willing to pay one hundred thousand dollars for it! Maybe she really was a good writer, a really good writer who might even have written a best seller!

Angela let her fantasies run riot. She dreamed of rave reviews in all the media. She dreamed of being the toast of the town, dressed to kill on the arm of some attractive man who—Attractive man? Angela caught herself. This was the first time she had thought of herself with a man at all, other than Paolo. Yet, here he was, dressed in black tie, tall, charming, correct—and faceless—heading her into a waiting limo. Angela looked down at her long, taut body. She stopped thinking long enough to realize that she felt good. Her nipples had tightened, and between her thighs she felt warm and moist. Angela's breathing quickened. She saw a vague image in her mind of the faceless man. She heard him whispering to her, telling her how desirable she was, how he wanted her. Then she began to explore her body as a new lover might. She moved her hand over her shoulder and down to her breast. She held her nipple between her fingers. The sensation was exquisite. She wondered briefly if all woman adored to be touched this way as much as she did; it always caused an immediate reaction. She grew wetter and felt the pounding between her legs grow more insistent, until it was almost painful.

She began to caress her other nipple, thinking again of the faceless man. Now both nipples were hard. Her other hand slipped between her legs. It had been so long. As she stroked herself slowly and sensually and her pleasure increased, she pushed her finger slowly inside, and a slight spasm ran through her, a portent of the greater pleasure to follow. She was amazed at how wet it was within. Angela moved her trembling finger back and forth inside, brushing it gently against the spot of most intense desire. Gradually, Angela began to lose control.

Angela worked her hand quickly and rhythmically back and forth, in and out. She threw her head back in abandon. Time seemed to stand still, then a primordial sound came from deep within her as her climax spilled and coursed through her body. The orgasm was intense. As her body began to relax and Angela emerged from her trancelike state, she heard the last low notes of her freedom song. The wrenching, primeval quality of the sound frightened her; it reminded her of the deep pain and frustration that had been locked inside. Curling into the fetal position and hugging her knees to her chest, Angela wept with relief. This experience, coupled with the good news of her book, convinced her more than anything ever had that she was alive! She was here *now*. She had needs and desires, aspirations and talent. She was she. She was Angela. She lay on the bed, smiling while tears ran off her cheeks onto the pillow.

When she woke the next morning, she thought instantly of her book. "I did it, Mama, I did it. I'm sorry you didn't see your dream for me come true, Mama, but it's happened. I wish you could know, oh, God, Mama, I wish you could know that I *did* it!"

CHAPTER
───── 13 ─────

ANGELA appraised her distorted reflection in the cloudy full-length mirror that neatly covered the closet door. The yellowed, chipped walls of the shabby studio were in striking contrast to the elegant and chic woman who stood within them. Angela wore a smartly tailored olive linen suit with a trim skirt slit teasingly but tastefully to show glimpses of her long legs when she sat or walked. The jacket fit perfectly over a red silk camisole that enlivened the dark tone of the suit. High-heeled sandals completed the ensemble.

The shopping expedition to Saks had been marvelous. Angela and Eli had raced around the designer floors indulging their favorite fantasies by trying on outrageous outfits, eventually getting down to the task at hand: outfitting Angela in clothing that was serious and businesslike, yet sexy and feminine enough to show the beautiful author at her best. And looking at herself now, Angela believed that they had succeeded.

Angela glanced at her watch, grabbed her new linen envelope clutch bag from the dresser top, and ran down the narrow tenement stairway to the hot street below to find a cab.

"Well, hi!" a bouncy young woman proclaimed to Angela who waited nervously in Heywood & Horne's reception area. "I'm Lyndley. I loved your manuscript. It was super. Really super. We all thought so. Just follow me."

"Are you Mr. Green's secretary?" Angela inquired politely as she rose to her feet.

"Assistant," Lyndley replied pleasantly but definitely. Angela obviously was not aware there were no secretaries in publishing offices. The young men and women fresh out of impressive colleges who answered the phones, typed the correspondence, did the filing, and made the lunch reservations and travel arrangements were editorial assistants or publicity assistants or even sales assistants. But always *assistants*. Never *secretaries*.

Lyndley jauntily led Angela through a maze of glass-partitioned, thickly carpeted corridors, speaking to her young colleagues en route, apparently pleased with the importance of her task. She stopped at the door of a corner office. "Wait here," she told Angela, her smile still wide and bright. Confidently, she strode into her boss's office, interrupting the handsome editor in chief in mid-swing.

"I'll take that, Mark," she said crisply, disengaging a Rossignol tennis racket from Mark's determined grip. "Angela Vaccaro's here."

"Good. Give me a minute to get my jacket on, then show her in." Mark Green strode across polished wood floors and a Persian rug to his mahogany desk. He took his jacket from the back of the leather-upholstered chair behind his desk and pulled it on. He brushed his brown and silver hair back and straightened his tie. He turned to Lyndley, arms extended, eyebrows raised. Lyndley nodded her approval and left the office.

"He's ready for you now, Miss Vaccaro."

I hope I'm ready for him, Angela thought as she threw back her shoulders and entered the office.

Mark greeted her warmly. He shook her hand and then held it in both of his. His smile made it clear that he was delighted by her, as did the sparkle in his alert gray eyes behind the tortoise-shell-rimmed glasses.

"Angela Vaccaro, this is a pleasure. Elizabeth told me you were an attractive and promotable author, but hers was a gross understatement. And our friend Elizabeth is *not* usually given to understatement, is she?"

Angela laughed. "No, not Eli. And thank you. That's a very nice thing to say." Angela realized that Mark was still holding her hand. There was a moment's awkward silence.

"Well, come and sit down," Mark said, gesturing not toward the chair facing his desk but toward a round table surrounded by four chairs that occupied another corner of the office. Judging from the cluttered appearance of the table and the clean top of the desk, Angela surmised that the handsome desk functioned merely as an impressive showpiece.

When they were seated at the table, Mark launched into a steady, smooth flow of praise for *Blue Grotto*. It was a brilliant first novel, a masterpiece of popular fiction, a pleasure—no, a pure joy to read. Angela heard very little of what he said, but her thirsty ego absorbed the message. She blushed and shook her head as he continued without permitting her to get a modest and polite "thank you" or "now really" in when he took a breath. Then Lyndley stuck her head in the doorway.

"Your reservation is for one o'clock, and it's one o'clock now," she announced in the singsong tone of a mother chiding an errant but indulged child.

"Thanks, Lyndley. Have you been to Manhattan Market?" Angela shook her head. "I'm sure you'll like it. It's not the usual stuffy, formal French restaurant that seems to be in favor among my illustrious fraternity of editors in chief."

Once on the street, Angela felt more comfortable. The streets of New York belonged to everyone. She wasn't on unfamiliar ground anymore. She and Mark exchanged Manhattan small talk about the weather, restaurants, apartments. Angela had been worried that he might talk over her head. After all, he was college-educated, a publishing executive. But his conversation was lighter-than-air. Breezy, full of gentle humor. She knew that he liked her *and* her book, and that gave her confidence.

In a few minutes they were sitting at the table reserved for them at the "New American Cuisine" restaurant. Angela loved the decor: sleek, New York high-tech, softened by the fresh flowers on every table. Floor-to-ceiling windows at the back of the room looked out on a small garden nestled among the buildings.

Mark ordered sea bass with sliced ginger and scallions for them both. Angela was halfway through her meal before she remembered that she didn't much care for fish. She had let Mark order for her because it seemed silly not to. He seemed to require nothing more of her than her smiling attention. As they ate and talked, he kept refilling her wineglass until she was giddy. As he chatted about books and authors, she found herself thinking how attractive he was. She guessed he was somewhere in his forties—and decided he was in great shape. By the time the strawberries in cream were placed before her, she had acknowledged that he excited her as no one had for a long time. There was something about the way he looked at her, the frequent compliments that he interjected, the frankly appreciative smiles that conveyed his sense of expectation— expectation that had more to do with her body than her book. And she was glad.

Apropos of nothing, Mark suddenly glanced up. Gesturing slightly, he indicated a blond woman dressed completely in purple who was sitting with her back to Angela.

"That's Erica."

"Erica?"

"Erica Jong."

"Really?" Angela drained the last of the wine in her glass. "I know Larry Gould," she said, glad finally to be able to show Mark she wasn't totally out of the literary scene.

"*Levy's Lament*? Talented chap." Mark looked at his watch. "Waiter! Check, please!"

Angela wasn't sure if she had said the wrong thing or it was simply time to leave according to Mark's schedule.

She felt better when he smiled graciously and said, "I've got to get back to the office. There's just so bloody much to do right now. But I want you to come back with me. I think we should go over a few of the preliminary editorial changes that I think will strengthen the book. It won't take more than an hour."

Back in Mark's office, they sat together on a leather couch, their knees almost touching. Mark stared into her eyes relentlessly as he carefully outlined his editorial comments. The walk from the restaurant in New York's dense, humid summer air, several glasses of wine, and Mark's intensity made Angela feel sleepy. She could hardly concentrate on what Mark was saying. She did realize, however, that although she had worked out many kinks in the novel under Eli's guidance, her editor was calling for still more revision.

"Just some judicious pruning," he said. His long years of experience with delicate and volatile authors' egos had taught him to avoid words such as "cutting" and "reworking" whenever possible. Angela nodded her head and tried to keep her eyes open. But her head cleared when Mark made his next pitch.

"Right now, I've got so much to do that I won't be able to go over things with you personally, which is what I like to do with a new author, unless we work in the evenings. Why don't you give Lyndley a call tomorrow morning when you've had a chance to look over your schedule, and we can work something out."

There was a light rap on the closed door, and when it opened a head poked into the room.

"Oops. Sorry. Didn't know you had a guest," the young man said.

"That's all right. Come in. I want you to meet Angela Vaccaro, the author of *Blue Grotto.*"

The young man who entered the office looked more ready for the country in his casual clothes than for the executive suite. He grasped Angela's hand firmly and smiled through well-trimmed whiskers.

"Angela, this is Paul Jameson, our art director."

"Hi, Paul. Nice to meet you."

"Miss Vaccaro! This *is* a pleasure! I remember seeing your picture a few times in *People,* but they never did you justice! I wish I had known you were coming in today. I have some preliminary sketches for the jacket for your book. I took the manuscript to Fire Island with me last weekend, and I couldn't put it down. My friends were furious."

Angela laughed uncomfortably. It was hard to get used to constant praise. "Thank you. I'm glad you liked it."

Mark interrupted. "Paul, I'd like a good photograph of Angela for the back of the jacket. Will you arrange for it?"

"Sure," Paul said. "I'll set it up with Scavullo. He's the best. What a fabulous necklace!" Paul exclaimed, noticing Angela's sapphire.

"Thank you. It was a gift from my husband."

"Oh, Paolo di Fiori. You must have had a terrible—"

"Paul, I'm going to want to see a tight mock-up of the jacket for tomorrow's marketing meeting," Mark cut in curtly.

"Right. You got it. Nice meeting you, Miss Vaccaro. I'll be in touch with you about the photographer."

"Yes. You can advise Lyndley, who will be in touch with Miss Vaccaro," Mark said pointedly.

"Bye, Miss Vaccaro."

"Bye, Paul. Nice meeting you. And it's Angela, okay?"
Paul winked and left the office.

"Paul is the number one art director in the business, but he does go on," Mark said after Paul had left.

"I like him. My brother's a graphic artist, you know."

"Is he? Now Angela, you call Lyndley tomorrow and tell her when you have a free evening—and make it soon—and we'll get to work. I'll also have Lyndley arrange for you to meet with Madeline Wood, our publicity director. You'll like her. She's very dynamic." Mark paused to let his cool gray eyes admire Angela's face and body.

Lyndley darted into the room, and Mark stood up. "Your car is waiting." She handed him his tennis racket.

Mark looked at his watch. "Damn! I almost forgot!"

Lyndley widened her eyes in disbelief and retreated wordlessly. Mark stuffed a manuscript, a pile of magazines and newspapers, and his tennis racket into an already half-full briefcase.

"Why don't you let me walk you out? I'd offer you a lift, but I'm going over the bridge."

Within seconds they were on the hot sidewalk outside the Heywood & Horne building. A uniformed man rushed up to Mark and took his briefcase.

"The East River Tennis Club provides the car with membership," Mark said, explaining the black Cadillac limousine parked at the curb.

"That *is* impressive."

"Well, really, they *have* to," Mark replied. "They're in Long Island City. That's over the bridge in *Queens*. How else could one get there?"

"Of course," Angela replied, thinking of the billions of times she had crossed that bridge by public bus or gone under the river by subway.

"Well, I've got to dash off. Grand meeting you, Angela. Truly a pleasure. Give Lyndley a call tomorrow."

"Thanks for lunch, Mark. I'll call tomorrow," Angela called to him as the black car eased into the flow of traffic.

Only now, in the solitude of a cab's back seat, did Angela realize how keyed up she had been through the whole experience. Even the wine- and heat-induced drowsiness did not stop her heart from pounding against her ribs. She took deep, comforting breaths and realized that she was physically exhausted.

Back in her apartment, Angela stripped off her clothes and ran cool water for a bath. She poured herself a tall glassful of Perrier, squeezed in some fresh lime juice, and brought the drink into the bathroom where she lowered her body into the tub. So much food for thought. Angela sipped the bubbly water from the icy glass in her hand and then set it down beside the bathtub. She coiled her hair on top of her head and held it there with both hands. She settled into the cool water, closing her eyes. So much that was new and wonderful was happening. Heywood & Horne was obviously taking her very seriously. She knew this not just because of the important-looking contract she had signed a week ago, nor because a check for forty-five thousand dollars had come to her from Eli's office. She knew it because of the way she had been treated. And Mark . . . well, Mark was an extra she hadn't counted on. But there he was. Attractive and, from the look of it, interested. She would have to give Eli a call as soon as she got out of the tub and get the lowdown on him.

Eli liked working in her office after five. The phones stopped ringing, and she could pore over manuscripts in peaceful solitude. But the cheap bastards who owned the building cut the air-conditioners off at six. Then you did a slow roast since the windows were hermetically sealed. She had the choice between nearly suffocating in the office or going home to work where she could make herself reasonably comfortable.

Eli packed the manuscript of Larry Gould's *My Life Unbound* in the large woven straw bag she used as her summer briefcase. She tossed the pack of cigarettes sitting on her desk into her shoulder bag, gave her glasses a push farther up on her slippery nose, and headed home.

After a refreshing shower, Eli gathered her curls into two short pigtails. Ignoring underwear, she pulled on a pair of faded New York University gym shorts and a white tank top and sat cross-legged on her living room floor with the manuscript in her lap, legal pad and pencil next to her. Although it was not her job to edit the manuscript, she always went over manuscripts before she submitted them to editors, making what suggestions for changes she thought were necessary to get the best offer for it. *My Life Unbound* engaged her as a reader—and as a person—as well as an agent. It was a good book, and Eli read with enthusiasm and pride. It was, as was Larry's first book, clearly autobiographical. It concerned the problems and frustrations encountered by a writer when he achieved his first longed-for fame. It told of the good, intelligent, lovely woman who loved him and how he betrayed her. And in the final chapters it told how the writer matured and came to his senses, how he hoped he was not too late for the woman he loved. After she had read to the end, Eli pushed the pages aside. She wanted to have the good cry she felt she deserved, but it wouldn't come. She was too angry and confused. Her pride had been deeply hurt. Her heart had been broken.

One-night stands were not the answer. She knew that after months of them. It would be so easy to give in to Larry's pleas for a reconciliation. Easy because that's exactly what she longed to do. Reading the manuscript pushed her closer to it. It gave credence to his arguments, to his ardent letters of protestation and declaration. And if he *was* Abraham Liebman, the protagonist of *My Life Unbound*, then he *had* grown, had changed, and perhaps deserved her love.

Eli knew that he was a mere phone call away. He was back in New York, and it was rumored that the Vassar affair was over. But she would not give in. She had lost the first round to Larry—Larry and his co-ed. This time she would win.

The sun was setting, and the first cool breeze of the day scattered the pages of *My Life Unbound* as they lay on Eli's floor. Eli gathered them up and put them in order on her coffee table. The phone rang. Eli sprinted into the kitchen to answer it.

"Eli? It's me, Ange. How are you doing?"

"Shitty. How are you?"

"What's the matter?"

"Nothing, nothing. I was just kidding. How was Heywood and Horne?"

"Great. Terrific. I had so much fun. They *love* the book! And I love my editor! He's gorgeous. Why didn't you tell me?"

"Mark Green? Forget it, Ange. That guy fucks everybody."

"What do you mean?"

"I mean that he has fucked half the women in publishing and probably all of his good-looking lady authors and probably ninety percent of the women at his hotsy-totsy tennis club, probably his assistant, and most likely his maid. And once in a while he probably even fucks his wife!"

"He's married?"

"Is he ever! Old man Horne's daughter. The lovely and untalented Barbara Horne Green. The darling of the Hamptons literary set."

"Mmmm. The more I hear, the more I like. . . ."

"Angela, I am obviously not getting through to you. . . ."

"You sound edgy, Eli. What's up?"

"Oh, nothing. Everything."

"Okay. I'm coming over. Have you had dinner?"

"No. I was too hot to eat when I came home."

"Me too. Tell you what. I'll stop at Amalfi's before I come over. A 'large' with everything?"

"No anchovies!" they shouted together, and still laughing, each hung up.

Angela felt lighthearted and mischievous and in control. With her face completely free of makeup and her hair gathered and clipped haphazardly on the top of her head, she felt more like a teen-ager than a twenty-eight-year-old woman. Wearing a tight T-shirt and skimpy cut-off jeans, she caused heads to turn on her way to the Amalfi Pizzeria. Balancing the pizza box carefully in her arms, Angela turned slowly to give the two teen-agers behind the counter who had been ogling her a good view of her partially exposed backside, and walked out the doorway and onto Bleecker Street. Laughing to herself, she turned down Morton Street and headed for Eli's apartment. She had never deliberately flaunted herself that way, and though she was only playing at it, it gave her a feeling of power she had never known before. If it worked on little boys, why couldn't it work on big boys too? . . . The only men she had ever made love to had wanted *her*. They had made the first moves. Frankie had pushed her to have sex with him in the beginning. And Paolo had seduced her when they first met. And after that there was no need to test her allure. Paolo's lively sexual appetite confirmed it for her. Coming on to men, letting them know she was interested, was a new and exciting sensation. It could be fun. It could give her new power and control.

Angela and Eli sat on the floor happily eating the best pizza in New York. Eli had produced cold beer from her refrigerator, and they both were thoroughly enjoying drinking beer straight from frosty bottles and taking slice after slice from the open box between them on the floor.

"Okay, Vaccaro. What's this about you and Mark Green?"

"I just think it's perfect," Angela said between bites of mushrooms, peppers, and cheese.

"But I told you. The guy is married. Basically, he's married to the boss's daughter. He's not going to throw her over. Not even for you. That's the straight line on it, Ange."

Angela wiped foam from her upper lip with the back of her hand. "Is that how he got to be editor in chief?"

"Are you kidding? Old man Horne wouldn't go for that. He is the absolute epitome of the Protestant work ethic." Eli chewed contentedly on her third slice of pizza, took a healthy gulp of beer, and continued.

"The story is, Mark met Barbara in college. He was at Harvard, she was a Cliffie. Mark had major aspirations then, and Barbara's daddy was conveniently placed at the head of a big publishing company, so naturally he fell in love with her. Actually, she's very nice and attractive, too, so maybe he did fall in love with her. Anyway, after Mark graduated, he married Barbara, and Everett Horne gave him a job in the mailroom."

"You're kidding."

"No. It's true. Mark worked his way up like any other poor slob. Harder, in fact, because Daddy Horne had it in for him. You know: 'Don't expect any special treatment or privileges, young man.' That sort of thing. Not that Mark needed money or anything, though. His family's filthy rich."

"So he's actually good at what he does?" Angela wanted to know.

"He's about the best. I wouldn't say that the guy is deep or anything, but he does have a genius for spotting and developing writing talent, and for knowing what will sell. I wouldn't have given him your manuscript if I didn't think he was good."

"Of course. Well, that's amazing. He worked his way up and everything. What about his wife? Does she know he's fucking around?"

"Oh, yeah. She has to know. She's no fool. Maybe she just likes her life. I mean, they have a great house out in the

Hamptons, and all the big writers gather out there in the summer. She's got megabucks, he's got megabucks. . . . He's had some pretty heavy things going with other women, but he's still with Barbara."

"Well, that settles it. It's perfect. Eli, I'm going to be the next one Mark Green fucks around with."

"Angela, you're nuts! Haven't you heard me? There is no way that man is going to leave his wife. She must have something on him, or maybe he really loves her in some way. I'm not saying that he wouldn't be crazy about you, but Angela, this guy is trouble. He's a very sophisticated, suave, educated kind of guy who likes to put notches on his belt. Forget him. There's a city full of men out there. . . ."

"Eli, you don't understand. I don't want anyone to leave his wife for me. Or even be faithful to me. I'm looking for an *affair*, Eli. I've had true love. I won't find it again. I don't want to. I can't afford to. With Paolo . . ." Angela's eyes welled with tears.

Eli felt that Angela was making a mistake, but as she watched her friend wipe away the tears, Eli decided to postpone further discussion.

"Look, Eli, I want sex. Sex and companionship. Not love everlasting. Mark is handsome and intelligent. He's probably fun to be with. I could probably learn a lot from him, too. If he's willing, I'm willing. He wants me to meet him in the evenings to work on my book."

"Good luck, Angie. I hope he's great."

The friends smiled at each other and ate in easy silence for a few minutes.

Casually, lightly, Eli said, "I got Larry Gould's manuscript today."

"My God! You mean you saw him today, and you let me rattle on about Mark Green?"

"No, I didn't see him. I arranged things so he just dropped it off. The receptionist told him I was out. I couldn't take seeing him today. I had such a rotten morning. I wasn't ready to see Larry at all."

"When was the last time you saw him?"

"Last fall. Just before we broke up. I haven't actually seen him since then, but I've been getting mail from him."

"You never answered any of his letters or calls, did you?"

Eli shook her head.

"Oh, Eli," Angela wailed sympathetically, "admit it. You're still hung up on him."

"I know I am. But I'll get over it. Larry acted like an asshole and now he's sorry. Well, that's just too bad. I suffered. Now he'll suffer."

"Yes, but you're suffering too, Eli. You guys were great together. If there's another chance in the cards for you, Eli, you should go for it."

"I don't know. . . ."

"Is he still teaching at Vassar?"

"No. The summer session is over. Now there's a break until the regular fall semester starts, but I don't think he's going back. He doesn't need the money, and from his letters I gather that he's kind of soured on the whole teaching thing."

"He's through with that co-ed, right?"

"Yeah. That ended a while ago, from what I hear. He's planning on staying in Manhattan and dealing with his new-found fame and wealth. Or something like that."

"Well, he can take lessons from us! Look at how well we're dealing with our new wealth!" Angela laughed, holding her beer bottle aloft.

"Right! Fame hasn't gone to your head, has it, Ange?"

"No, but I hope it does!"

"Really, though, with the money you've got from your book and the money you're *going* to get, you ought to start thinking about doing something."

"I know. That's what my dad says. I need a financial manager. One thing for sure, I need a better apartment."

"Me too. Between you, Larry, and a couple of my other clients, I've become Brad's little star agent. He's scared to death I'm going to whisk you all away and start my own agency. He keeps raising my salary. I can start looking for a new place, too. I'd like to stay in the Village, though. I feel really comfy here."

"Say, Eli, why *don't* you start your own agency? You could work out of your glamorous new digs."

"Don't think I haven't thought about it. In fact, that's my game plan. It's just a matter of when and how. Brad breathes down my neck too much. I'm tired of having to get his approval every time I turn around. He knows I'm good. He just can't give up control."

The doorbell rang, surprising Eli and Angela.

"Were you expecting someone?"

"No," Eli replied as she rose to answer the summons.

Larry entered the room nervously, sweating freely. His hair was tightly curled and slightly damp. Eli stood at the open door, unable to mask her shock.

"Hello, Eli, Angela." Larry's sharp brown eyes swept the room. Angela rose swiftly and began to clear away the beer bottles and the pizza box. She felt self-conscious in her scant clothing. Eli and Angela shot quick looks of dismay at each other for having been "caught" in their sloppiest clothing, fingers full of oil, faces shining with dampness, hair a mess.

Larry's gaze rested on Eli, on the girlish pigtails, the shorts that revealed her round thighs, and at the tank top that clearly exhibited the soft swell of her breasts. Eli felt that gaze and her heart sank. She was at a clear disadvantage: barefoot, sweaty, half-dressed. If she had to see Larry again, she would have preferred to do so behind her glasses and her desk in her office: serene, composed, in command. Now she felt totally vulnerable. Ridiculous, even.

After Angela finished clearing away the last vestiges of their dinner, she said, "Well, I was just going. I'll call you tomorrow, Eli. Nice seeing you, Larry. . . ."

When the door closed behind Angela, Larry found his voice. "Eli, you look . . . you look beautiful."

Eli laughed. "Don't bullshit me, Larry. I look like hell, and I know it. As long as you're here, why don't you sit down? Want something cold to drink?"

"A beer's okay."

Eli rejoiced in the excuse to run into the kitchen. She rinsed her hot face with cold water, told herself to stand her ground, and returned to the living room with a bottle of beer.

"Eli, please. Don't stand over me like that. Sit down. I want to talk to you. I came over uninvited because you won't take my phone calls or answer my letters. I'm back in the city because of you, Eli. Because I want to try again."

Eli exhaled and sat down on the opposite end of the couch.

"I have your manuscript here, Larry. It's excellent. But you know that. You're maturing as a writer. . . ."

"And as a person, Eli. I don't know how I can prove that to
you, but I'm willing. . . ."

"Larry, look. I don't want to talk about all that." Eli wished
that Larry did not look so good—so tall, rangy, and charged
with energy. The way he looked when she first met him. And
loved him. Having him so close to her, it was easy to recall the
feel of his arms around her, what his kisses were like.

Larry's frustration was becoming unbearable. He loved how
she looked. He had meant it when he said she looked beautiful.
She did, indeed. So natural, so unaffected. So lovely. So Eli.
He loved her, and he had to make her see that. Even if she
banished him again, she would have to see that he loved her
and that he was sorry.

"I think we have to talk about what happened between us. I
know I want to," Larry insisted quietly.

All right, Eli thought. You want to open that can of worms,
fine with me. She colored with anger as her thougts of Larry's
embraces gave way to thoughts of his betrayal of her. Eli now
leapt at the chance to get some of her own back.

"Okay. So we talk. You tell me all about how the horsey set
has decided that Jewish authors are ever so tiresome this year,"
Eli spat, her teeth clenched and her voice hard and nasal in an
imitation of a WASP lockjaw accent.

Larry bowed his head and said nothing. Perhaps if she could
empty herself of the venom he deserved to have spewed at him,
they could start afresh. His silence spurred her on.

"Did Mumsy and Daddy not like to see their fair child in the
clutches of the declassé boy from New Jersey?" she continued
in "lockjawese." "Or," she said in her own bitter tone, "did
your girlfriend just get sick of hearing about your favorite
subject: Lawrence Gould, author par excellence!"

Larry met her blazing eyes with a pleading look. She was
really making it difficult.

Eli was feeling a surge of power and excitement at being
able to let her fury loose on Larry, yet she secretly hoped he
would stop her. She wanted him to grab her in his arms, to stop
her mouth with kisses. Anger and desire struggled within her;
she wanted to express all the pain and hurt he had caused—she
wanted him to feel it. But she also wanted to be forgiven for
her outburst—and she wanted to forgive him, too. Larry's
stubborn, unflappable silence only pushed her to say worse

things, more insulting things; she needed to stretch the tension to the breaking point so she could cry in his arms. Even if he reached out and shook her, it would be all right. . . .

"Where are all your fine words now, Larry?" she prodded. "Has your co-ed's poetry not inspired you? What was it she liked about you? Something about a 'throbbing member,' wasn't it? What happened, Larry? Did your member just stop throbbing, or—" Eli flinched as Larry moved. She almost expected him to strike her. But he stood up slowly instead. Calmly, he walked to the door. He turned as he reached for the knob and faced her. He sighed deeply, said, "Good-bye, Eli," and left, closing the door quietly behind him.

Eli heaved the manuscript off the coffee table and missed the door by yards. After long, silent moments, she sat down on the floor to gather up the pages of the manuscript. Feeling hopeless and totally overwhelmed by the storm of emotion that had raged through her, she pushed the pages away from her and broke into exhausted sobs.

CHAPTER
—————14—————

CAROL VOLIN didn't like to be late to marketing meetings. She knew just how important it was to choose your seat, not to just take whatever place was left. The canny subsidiary rights director also knew it was wise to place yourself close to the seat of power, which, depending on which way the power seesaw was tipping, was either at the end of the conference table occupied by Mitchell Schaeffer, the marketing director, or at the other end where Mark Green, the editor in chief, took his position.

It was well known throughout the company and in the industry that Everett Horne would name a publisher within the next two years, and that the obvious candidates were Mitchell Schaeffer and Mark Green. Everett Horne kept both ambitious men on a tight rein, favoring one then the other, while maintaining overall control. The various marketing department heads were constantly shifting loyalties as power and favor ricocheted between Mark and Mitch. Nobody wanted to be on the wrong team when the final choice was made. That the intense rivalry and constantly changing power structure caused the recycled air of the offices of Heywood & Horne to reek of tension and discord mattered little to Everett Horne, who knew that having two first-rate executives working under pressure at top capacity was the best thing in the world for the H & H bottom line.

At no time was the tension worse or more apparent than on Wednesday morning at the marketing meeting in the conference room. The tension was heightened by the fact that nearly all the rest of the meeting's attendants were women, and Mark and Mitch grandstanded for approval and points, challenging each other's business know-how and manhood while picking the brains of the female department heads.

As Mitchell Schaeffer tapped his pencil on the polished wood conference table, the hum of conversation and paper rustling stopped as all attention focused on him. The fight was on.

More than any other department head, Carol Volin enjoyed the struggle. She could afford to: she had a vice presidency and the most power among her peers. As subsidiary rights director she generated millions of dollars selling rights to H & H's books to paperback houses, book clubs, magazines, and to television and film producers. The income from Carol's department showed clearly on the computer print-outs under her own "sub rights" code and frequently meant the difference between a red or black bottom line on a book's final profit and loss statement.

And Carol knew how to flatter the Old Man. And just to be certain that when the chips fell they didn't fall on her, Carol Volin often slept with Mark and, if she did say so herself, gave Mitchell Schaeffer very good head.

"I'd like to try to stick with our agenda as much as possible today, folks," Mitch said. "We've all got lunch dates, and we'd all like to get out of here at a reasonable hour. Before we discuss the progress of the Fall list, is there anything we need to talk about on the upcoming Spring books?"

Carol turned to Mark Green. "I'd like to know when I'll have final, edited manuscripts of some of our big fiction. I haven't seen a copy of *Lone Star* at all, but with Jessica Simon it's not a problem. It's this new author I wanted to get started with. When will I have a manuscript of *Blue Grotto* to submit to the book clubs? The book's got full selection potential, and both the Guild and Book-of-the-Month have already bought their April selections. I need a manuscript for their next meetings if we're going to have a crack at a main selection. And several of the paperback houses are interested. As soon as the story about the advance broke in *PW*, I got six calls. What do I tell them?"

"You'll have an edited manuscript to submit to the clubs in a week," Mark responded crisply. "We can discuss paperback strategy after you've had a reaction from the clubs. In the meantime, you can tell everybody that our first printing is seventy-five thousand copies and the initial advertising and promotion budget is seventy-five thousand dollars."

Mitch tapped his pencil on the table. "Mark, I'd like to have a look at the unedited manuscript again, too, before we announce those figures. I only had the manuscript overnight before we bought it, and from what I read—and from your enthusiasm for it—I'm sure we'll go with those numbers, but I want to discuss our overall marketing game plan before we go public with it."

If Mark was upset by Mitch's comments, he didn't show it. Mitch had projected the seventy-five thousand first printing and the ad budget before Mark had bought the book. He knew that the real issue was the illusion of control. The editor in chief did not decide how many copies were printed or what got spent on a book, the marketing director did. And subsidiary rights strategy was as much the marketing director's province as the editor in chief's. Since Carol reported directly to Everett Horne, as did both men, she was a powerful player on the field.

Mark continued as though without interruption, "Angela is coming in today to deliver her final revisions and to meet with Madeline."

Madeline Wood looked up. The publicity director's plain, pale face, framed by lifeless light brown hair, took on a lively aspect as she began to speak. "And let me say that I have met Angela Vaccaro, once briefly, and I think she's going to be terrifically promotable. First of all, she looks like a movie star. She's articulate and determined. She's a little shy right now, but we can have her coached. I think she can handle the media. And with some special angling we've got a chance with the talk shows. We should tour her to promote the book. People will eat it up. Poor little Italian-Irish girl from Queens—"

"How about that di Fiori angle?" Mitch broke in.

"No, that's out," Mark answered definitely. "She stands on her own. She's not in touch with the family anymore, and she doesn't want to use her previous asociation with them for publicity purposes."

Madeline's face fell. "Mark, it's a terrific angle. Widow of murdered playboy writes books. We could do a fabulous press release. It would be picked up everywhere. We could get it out on the wires. It's a great off-the-book page feature story.

Without it, I'm not sure what media pickup I can get for a first novelist."

Mitch raised his hand to stop her. "Look, if she's as dynamite as you say she is, we don't need any more. Just see that she gets coached and keep the di Fiori stuff out of the releases. We'll be trading on glamor . . . rags to riches . . . Queens girl makes good. That's our angle. We don't need an unhappy author on our hands. Or *another* one, at any rate."

Unseen by the cloistered executives, the sun climbed in the late September sky. After a long discussion of troublesome sales figures and Mark's renewed assurances that department heads would be receiving manuscripts of *Blue Grotto* next week, the meeting broke up.

Madeline Wood swept her publicity tour schedules, all in their neat manila folders, from the table along with her empty blue china teacup. She glanced at the simple, functional watch on her slender wrist and hurried back to her office. She wanted to freshen up before her lunch date with Angela Vaccaro.

Madeline checked her appearance in the large mirror on the back of her closed office door. Not a pretty face, but the bone structure was there: the wide forehead, the jutting cheekbones, the firm jaw. But Madeline knew the features were without distinction: her nose was short and a trifle fleshy; her eyes were merely brown; her lips were pale, thin, and pressed into service as a smiling machine against what seemed to be their own nature; her complexion was drab, opaque, and etched with thin lines after more than thirty-six years of stretching and folding it into countless forced expressions of happiness and enthusiasm.

Madeline had spent the lonely childhood of the plain and unloved in boarding schools. But during her four years at Wellesley College she had learned that she could fill the void of her loneliness by joining clubs, by linking herself to the more popular girls and supporting them in their campus political endeavors, and by speaking out in class and clearly asserting herself. By the time Madeline graduated and began her career as an assistant in Random House's publicity department, she could hold her own in almost any situation. But after each workday, she returned to her apartment to eat a simple dinner alone.

Now Madeline faced her reflection squarely and gave herself

the Madeline Wood, lady publicist smile. Ten years dropped away even as the thin skin around her dull brown eyes crinkled. Pink color suffused her pallid cheeks as she psyched herself for her role, a part she always played to the hilt. She had the reputation of being one of the best publicists in the business, and to be a publicist you always had to be "on," always bubbling with enthusiasm. And it always had to appear to be sincere. Sometimes it even was.

Down the hall, Angela chatted with Lyndley while she waited for Mark. Lyndley admired Angela's new outfit. In her russet suede divided skirt with a matching slouchy, low-belted tunic, Angela looked the very essence of autumn.

"Angela! You're here! Sorry I kept you waiting!" Mark kissed her chastely on the cheek.

"Here's your manuscript. Just as I promised." Angela produced the reworked pages from a soft leather Fendi satchel she had purchased the day before.

"Now I think you'd better show me where Madeline Wood's office is. I'm late for our lunch date," Angela purred, smiling at Mark.

Lyndley rose from her seat.

"That won't be necessary, Lyndley," Mark said. "I'll take Angela to Madeline's office."

Striding confidently in her new, high-heeled suede boots, with Mark at her elbow, Angela arrived at Madeline's office. The door was closed. Madeline's assistant stepped out from behind her desk, looking dismayed.

"Hello, Miss Vaccaro. Madeline will be with you in a minute. Please wait here." The young woman disappeared into the office. Madeline emerged from her office, deliberately closing the door after her. Her composure was obviously ruffled.

"I hardly know what to say. Something's come up. I feel just dreadful. It's terrible, I know, but there has been some kind of awful mix-up. Apparently I had a long-standing lunch date with another author, and my assistant must have accidentally mismarked my date book. I know these things happen, but—"

Angela interrupted. "That's all right. It's a mistake. I understand. I had to bring Mark the revisions anyway. We can have lunch another time. I know I'm not Heywood and Horne's only author, for heaven's sake."

Madeline's bright true smile broke through. Relief suffused her face. "Angela, you're the first author in history to ever say that! You're a dear for being so understanding. I'll make it up to you."

They all laughed with shared relief that a scene had been averted, but Mark was angry. He didn't like his authors getting short shrift. Really, this was inexcusable. He made a mental note to bring this gaffe to Mitch Schaeffer's attention.

Just then the door to Madeline's office swung open. Standing before them in a cream-colored suit of the lightest, softest wool was Jessica Simon.

"Madeline, are you ready for our—" she began to inquire in her sweet, resonant drawl. But she stopped and noticed Mark and Angela. "Why, Mark! I didn't expect to see you this trip. This is a bonus!"

"I didn't even know you were in town, Jessica! Why didn't you tell me?"

"Oh, you know how I love to play the mystery lady, Mark. I'm here for the store, actually. With Arthur. We're peeking in all the Fifth Avenue windows. Have to keep an eye on the competition! I don't believe we've met," Jessica said, turning to Angela.

Angela smiled. "Oh, yes, we have. In Capri, at Paolo di Fiori's. I wouldn't expect you to remember, though. I'm Angela Vaccaro. I was introduced to you as Marino."

Jessica's expertly made-up eyes widened. She blinked hard. "Of course! You're the lucky Miss Vaccaro I've read about in *PW*! That must be quite a little book you've written. I'm sure Paolo would have been very, well, surprised by all this." She lowered her voice confidentially and continued as though she and Angela were alone. "I was sickened to hear of what happened to your beautiful husband. *Sickened.* The world can be a dreadful place, can't it? I said to Arthur, 'That poor, lovely boy.' Everyone adored him, of course. I told Arthur that women would be tearing their *hair* out. But of course no one has suffered as you have, poor child."

Angela mumbled her thanks for the condolences under her breath. She was not quite sure how to take Jessica's remarks, but the honeyed sound of Jessica's words assured Angela that they were well intended.

Jessica suddenly brightened and spoke in a more public

voice. "Now Madeline and I have to dash off to our lunch, but one of these days real soon I'm going to sit you down and make you tell me just what you've been up to and how you managed to write yourself that little book!"

Mark forgave Madeline as he walked Angela back to his office. He would have done the same thing in Madeline's position. A tried-and-true author has to take precedence over an unknown. Even when it came to lunch dates, their first duty was always to the bottom line. Still, Jessica had one hell of a nerve breezing in unannounced. Knowing her, she had probably hopped on her broomstick to check out the competition the minute she read that H & H had paid a hundred-thousand-dollar advance to a first novelist.

"Well, Angela, I'm free for lunch. Will you join me?" Mark proposed once they were seated in his office.

"I'd love it. Your place or mine?" she teased.

"Your place? The new co-op on Gramercy Park? I thought you weren't moved in yet."

"I moved in last week, but even though it's not decorated or furnished yet, I'd love to show it to you."

Thirty minutes later, with sandwiches supplied by a local gourmet shop neatly packed in a bag and tucked under Mark's arm, the two emerged from a cab in front of a tall, prewar building that faced the private, locked park reserved for Gramercy Park residents.

Angela threw open the door to her one-and-a-half bedroom apartment on the eighth floor. "How do you like it?"

Mark looked at the stark walls and bare polished wood floors. There was not a stick of furniture to be found. Several cartons were lined up against the wall in the spacious, light-filled living room.

"It's got great potential, but how can you live here without furniture?"

Angela wordlessly led him into the bedroom, where a mattress, pillows, and bedclothes lay on the floor.

"This is all I need right now. My brother Jimmy is helping me decorate and select furniture. I didn't bring anything from Italy, and this is the first place I've ever had that I can do exactly as I want. I've got the freedom *and* the money now to buy everything new. I'd like to get a few paintings, maybe . . ."

Mark laughed. "Take it easy, Angela. You're counting on millions from this book from the sound of it."

Angela turned slowly to face him. The time for talking was over. Mark knew why Angela had invited him. It was for the same reason she had been invited to his apartment almost every night for the last month. She could have done most of the manuscript revisions at home. Alone. But what she and Mark had in fact been doing could not have been done alone. Not even with the best imagination put to task.

Under Mark's appreciative eye, Angela stripped to her panties and boots. Just as he reached for her, she pulled away and stretched out on the mattress. It was amazing to her how much she had learned about Mark's sexuality in just a month. These little touches drove him wild: the teasing, the boots. She loved controlling his reactions to her.

Now she was beckoning him from the heap of bedclothes on the floor. She stretched her arms up over her head, so he could see the shapeliness of her breasts. . . .

He went to her, and soon they were locked together, each searching for satisfaction like travelers seeking the same destination, but taking two completely different highways.

The only part of Jessica Simon that was not quivering with rage was her multi-streaked raven pageboy, thanks to the many coats of lacquer meticulously applied every morning by her hairdresser. But the rest of her delicate body shook with the intensity of a jackhammer under her creamy silk ruffled blouse and soft wool suit as her limousine returned her to the Sherry-Netherland where she and her husband Arthur kept a suite for their frequent visits to New York.

Who was this Angela Vaccaro and what had she written? That simpering girl whom Paolo had actually married couldn't *possibly* have written a book, especially one that could receive such enthusiasm and such an advance from Mark.

During lunch at Le Madrigal, Jessica had asked Madeline about Angela and Angela's manuscript.

"I honestly don't know," Madeline had said. "I haven't read it, but at this morning's marketing meeting Mark and Mitch spoke of the book in superlatives: 'surefire best seller . . . tremendous commercial potential . . . great romantic story.' Things like that. And Carol Volin can't wait to start peddling it to the clubs and the paperback reprinters. Anyway, Mark's going to distribute copies of the manuscript next week, so——"

"Get me one!" Jessica rapped. She had heard enough. She threw her napkin down onto her uneaten truite en papillote, rose, and left.

In her pink-and-red suite at the Sherry, Jessica muttered to herself as she poured a double Jack Daniels. "It's bad enough that I've got to worry about competing with Robbins, Sheldon, and now Krantz, not to mention whoever the hell else comes along. At least they're published by other houses. Now I've got competition right under my nose. And it stinks. I can't wait to read this 'surefire best seller.' The gold-digging little Miss Angela doesn't know what she's up against. The publishing industry doesn't call me the Queen for nothing. Mark Green can get as hot and bothered as he wants to about that fast little di Fiori piece, but Jessica Simon has worked too damned hard to become the star author at H and H."

It had all started with *At Any Price*, the book that made Jessica Simon a legend. In the fall of 1972, all of Dallas was stirring with preparations for the fiftieth anniversary of the Simon-Lewis department store. In addition to all the special events planned for the month of November, Simon-Lewis planned to issue a privately published history of the store. And who better to tell the tale but the doyenne of Dallas, Arthur Simon's wife Jessica? She managed to find the time—between appointments with caterers and florists, calls to suppliers in Paris, Rome, and New York, and meetings with store buyers and department managers—to dash off the story of the little clothing store that had grown up to become a retailing giant and a chic trendsetter in the industry.

Influential columnists and newscasters were intrigued by the gossipy, glamorous treatment of the department store story. In New York, Suzy, the *Daily News* society gossip columnist, went so far as to suggest that Jessica's tale would be the perfect basis for a commercial novel.

Mark Green's savvy eye caught the piece in Suzy's column, and he placed a call to Jessica. Not quite two years later, Jessica Simon's *At Any Price* was Heywood & Horne's lead novel for the fall selling season. On book publication, Jessica embarked on a whirlwind twenty-city publicity and promotion tour, accompanied by the eager and canny publicist Madeline

Wood. On tour, Jessica successfully used every drop of her
Southern charm to enthrall both the public and the media. After
her first appearance with Johnny Carson on the "Tonight
Show," her proclamation, "Ah have the simplest tastes. Ah'm
easily satisfied by the best," was quoted all over the country by
those who had no idea that the quip belonged to Oscar Wilde.

When Jessica visited bookstores, she bought copies of her
own book and autographed them for the clerks; she started a
file of index cards noting bookstore owners' names and those
of their spouses and children, so she could send them "warm
personal regards" at Christmas. When women queued up in
bookstores clamoring to have their copies of *At Any Price*
autographed by the author, she graciously complimented their
hairstyles and clothes and clucked over their children. As
Jessica blitzed the country, *At Any Price* zoomed to the top of
every best-seller list in America.

Jessica reveled in her newfound fame. Every time another
copy of *At Any Price* was sold, she took it as a personal
compliment. She experienced a new kind of elation she had
never known existed, something that neither her incredible
wealth nor her position in society as Mrs. Arthur Simon had
ever offered. And, more than that, she was loved. She was
adored. She was a *star*.

Swiftly following the paperback success of *At Any Price*
came Jessica Simon's *Almost the Queen*, a roman à clef based
on the life of the Duchess of Windsor. Three months before
publication, Carol Volin sold paperback rights for an unprecedented advance of $2.9 million. Instantly, *Almost the Queen*
appeared on top of every best-seller list. Mark Green and
Mitch Schaeffer decided that another publicity tour would be
unnecessary, but Jessica demanded to once again meet her
adoring fans. Wags in the industry, having witnessed several of
Jessica's "performances," and suspecting that the author had
begun to confuse herself with her new fictional heroine,
dubbed her "the Queen," a name that quickly spread through
publishing's gossip-hungry grapevine.

Now, as her third novel, *Lone Star*, was being readied for
publication, the queen of women's fiction had no intention of
abdicating her throne. Not to Angela Vaccaro—not to anyone.

CHAPTER
15

Heywood & Horne, Inc.

Invites You to Celebrate the Publication of

BLUE GROTTO

A Novel by Angela Vaccaro

AT S P Q R
133 Mulberry Street, New York

March 15, 1979   *eight p.m.*

Black tie

"This is it!" Angela thought as she awoke to greet the gray light filtering in through the open shutters of her bedroom window. All the preparation leading up to this day had been exciting; the shopping trips to provide her with a tastefully glamorous wardrobe for her nationwide tour, and the video sessions with Dorothy Sarnoff, the specialist who had been called in to help Angela project her reticent charm to television cameras that would transmit it to millions of potential book buyers. Angela had been trained to follow the camera's red light and to answer the same questions over and over with a thoughtful pause beforehand. Most important of all, she had been coached to get the title of her book mentioned in each and every interview as often and as deftly as possible.

Sarnoff had declared Angela one her easiest and most successful pupils. Madeline Wood had run the video tapes over and over in her office and had declared Angela a triumph. The pain of looking at herself time and time again on tape had paid off for Angela. Hopes and expectations for success were high.

And there was the book itself. When the revisions were finally completed, Angela had been pleased with the results, although she still wondered if she had the right to call herself a writer and to include her name among those of her greatest heroes. But she had done her absolute best. Of that she was sure. It had been a thrilling day when the package containing the galleys of her book arrived. But the thrill of seeing the words *Blue Grotto* in print was not comparable to the greater thrill she experienced when Mark had taken her to lunch at Lutèce and placed a bound and jacketed copy of the book in her trembling hands. She had examined the book as closely as a mother looks at her newborn baby. She had removed the dust jacket that pictured her smiling face on the back and had run her hands over the sturdy blue cloth stamped with gold that bound the book. Her eyes had filled with tears as she read the dedication: *For Mama and for Paolo*. She wished they could have been there to share this moment with her, the proudest moment of her life.

Now "pub date" was here. The auction among paperback reprinters was being held today; the big party was to be held tonight. Next Monday she would be leaving on her promotion tour. Fear and nervousness gripped Angela when she thought about it. She would be traveling alone, to be met at airports by strangers who would whisk her from place to place to meet more strangers. She would be far from Eli, Jimmy, and her father, and at the mercy of the thousands of people who would know her only as the author of her book, as she was described in the press and seen on television.

The book reviewers would have their day. If they chose to, they could say she was silly and talentless. Or they could say she was a wonderful writer. Or worst of all, they could simply choose to say nothing, find her book unworthy of any attention. Madeline warned her not to be hurt by a lack of review attention. She explained that popular fiction rarely got reviewed seriously unless it was by an established author.

Even after the positive review she received in February from *Publishers Weekly*, Angela was scared. Would others who did review her book be as kind?

Angela swung out of bed. She had overslept, and it was

almost time to meet Eli at "The Teabag"—Eli's name for the Russian Tea Room. And there were still errands to do: she had to pick up her dress at Bergdorf's and go to Bendel's to have her hair and makeup done.

At one P.M. Angela was ushered to a table among those that lined the walls of the narrow front room of the glittering Russian restaurant next to Carnegie Hall. The sight of the cheery multi-hued decor and the welcoming gleam of the highly polished samovars that decorate the room made Angela fall in love with "The Teabag" at first sight. She had heard it was a chic place to lunch, a place where big Broadway and Publishers' Row deals were made, and was pleasantly surprised by the warm, lively, and inviting atmosphere.

Eli was waiting for her, seated on a red banquette.

"This is Brad's table. He lets me use it when he's at the Four Seasons or '21' or some place else," Eli hissed in greeting.

"It's very nice," Angela said, taking a seat with her back to the entrance.

"Nice nothing. It's fantastic. Look at this location! I can see everyone coming in. And there's no way they can miss us. Smile, Angela. There's Daisy Maryles of *Publishers Weekly* with Simon and Schuster's publicity director. See? She's looking at you."

"Eli, do I have to smile at everyone who walks through the door? How will I eat?" Angela asked, craning her neck and swiveling in her seat.

"Not everyone, silly. Just publishing people and media people. Don't worry. I've got my eye on the door. I'll tell you when to glow."

Angela and Eli both decided to celebrate the glorious pub day with blini. Angela plopped another dollop of sour cream onto the center of a crêpe while Eli caught her up on the latest goings on at the Brad Monroe agency.

"Brad is such a schmuck, Ange. You know, I've had to give Carol Volin my home number for reports on today's auction just to keep out from under his nose. Carol's letting me know, blow-by-blow, how the whole thing progresses. I have to do it from my *home*, for God's sake! Otherwise, Brad, the asshole, would be leaking all the details to the press, making himself the big hero of the deal. He even sneaked a copy of your manuscript to one of the paperback houses behind my back.

God, was I pissed! I have to watch him like a hawk. Now he's bending over backward to please me. He's even letting me use his table here. But nothing will prevent him from putting himself in the limelight once the offers for the paperback rights start to climb!"

"Eli, I've got goosebumps. We're talking about *Blue Grotto*!"

"I know, I know. It's a big day for both for us. My first big auction. I'm consulting with Carol Volin on your behalf every inch of the way! And for you—well, you're coming out with big bucks and lots of publicity, no matter what. I mean that quarter-of-a-million floor bid Delano Books put in!"

"But maybe no one will bid, and Delano will automatically get my book for two hundred and fifty thousand dollars."

"Take it easy. They're bidding now. They've been hyped into a frenzy, and the readers' reports have been sensational. The *PW* review didn't hurt either. Not to mention all the money and promo H and H is putting behind the book. The paperback people know *Blue Grotto* has to be a best seller."

The two women laughed conspiratorially and clinked their icy glasses of vodka, toasting each other, *Blue Grotto*, and friendship.

Right after lunch, Eli began rooting in her large leather bag for her credit cards. "I've got to go. The next round of the auction is starting in a few minutes."

"Well, what should I do? Should I go with you?" Angela asked.

"No. Just run your errands, then try to get some rest before the party. It'll be a big success, I'm sure. Madeline's parties always are. Leave it to her to come up with the idea of having it in Little Italy. It's reverse chic! I love it! I'll call you later and keep you posted when anything important starts to break."

Across town in a studio apartment on Central Park West that looked out over the park, Carol Volin was having an orgasm. "Oh, God, oh, fuck, oh, good!" she cried as she greedily grasped the head buried between her thighs. It was over. She composed herself quickly, shook out her unruly, springy black hair, and sat up.

"You want a cigarette? Oh, I forgot. You don't smoke. Not even at times like this."

Mark Green sat up next to Carol and grunted in confirmation. He was exhausted. Sex with Carol was always exhausting. She always insisted that he go down on her, no matter how many times she had achieved orgasm before—during foreplay and while they were fucking. It was a solid rule with her. Some form of payment she exacted. It was bizarre and not always pleasant, because she pushed him roughly and often barked commands, but in the end it was worth it. Carol was great in bed. She approached sex the same way she approached everything. It was something to be best at, something to excel at, something to win at. Mark guessed that the cunnilingus that capped the performance was like getting the blue ribbon that hailed her winner and still champion. But, by God, she was good. Technically, no one could hold a candle to her. Not Barbara, who knew him better than anyone. Not Angela, who was far more beautiful, but somehow distant. No. Carol Volin was the best. Probably the best fuck in publishing, Mark mused as he dozed off.

Carol drew hard on her cigarette and sent a stream of smoke toward the ceiling. She clutched the sheet up over her pendulous, full breasts. She felt good. Mark was a borderline lay, but he gave good head. She got the orgasm she was looking for. The big one. The really satisfying one. And she had confirmed a suspicion. Mark didn't realize it, but he had called Angela's name in the throes of his climax.

So Mark really was fucking her. It certainly made sense. No wonder the revisions for *Blue Grotto* had taken so long; it's hard to write when you're lying on your back! Of course Mark would want to draw out the process by which Angela would be dependent on him for advice and guidance.

Carol's thoughts shifted to the auction in progress. It now looked as if the book was really going to go for a lot of money. But in all her ten years of playing the game of poker that is called subsidiary rights, she had never sweated as she had with *Blue Grotto* that day last October.

Carol had just come back from lunch to find her copy of the final, edited *Blue Grotto* manuscript on her desk when her assistant buzzed her. Robin Sussman, the Delano Books editor assigned to Heywood & Horne, was on the phone. It was Robin's job to know what H & H was publishing in hardcover that might be of interest to Delano—the largest paperback house in the country.

"Hi, Robin. How are you? What's up?"

"Well, Carol, that's what I'd like to know. I thought we were friends. What's this I hear about *Blue Grotto*? The word goes out that you people are sitting on a blockbuster, and you don't even call me?"

"Well, I was just about to pick up the phone when you called—"

"Sure, Carol. Look, I'm willing to make a pre-emptive buy-out offer right now, sight unseen."

Carol had to think fast. If Carol took the pre-emptive offer, the book would be sold to Delano without any other paperback house having made an offer and the game would be over. Great—*if* the book wasn't very good. But the book really was good. After reading it, the other paperback houses would all be in fierce competition for it and an auction situation would drive the price sky high. On the other hand, if the pre-empt were sky high . . .

Carol looked at the manuscript sitting on her desk. She hated to turn down sure money, but her gut instinct about this book told her that its best price would only come out of an auction. Carol didn't want to peg a figure for a pre-emptive bid from Delano, she wanted the book free to find its own level, even if it meant some risk. Sweat stood out all over her brow and began to trickle down her face. In a voice as cool as ice, she answered Robin.

"I don't think I can do that, Robin, although I can tell you the book is fabulous. Absolutely fabulous. Sex, glamour, excitement—the works. And have you seen the author? Celebrity material, let me tell you."

"So I hear, so I hear. Of course I haven't read it, but I'll offer you a hundred thousand right now. What do you say? I'm out on a limb here, but you guys wouldn't have paid a hundred thousand dollar advance for schlock. Am I right?"

Carol took a deep breath. She had to think quickly, so quickly. There were many considerations. The hundred thou Robin offered was not a figure to be treated without care. To Everett Horne it meant his initial investment in the book was covered completely. One hundred thousand dollars was hardly the sky, but as a sight unseen offer, it was impressive. Just what could it mean? Carol summoned all that experience had taught her. There had to have been a leak. Someone—perhaps Angela's agent at the Brad Monroe agency—had gotten a copy of the manuscript to someone big at Delano. Maybe even to Harold Jarett, Delano's publisher himself. Wait . . . hadn't she seen Jarett lunching with Brad Monroe at the Four Seasons just two days ago? A common enough occurence, but maybe it was tied in. . . . They must have read *Blue Grotto* at Delano, Carol decided. And they must think it's good. Damn good. That's why Jarett had Robin call: to head Carol off, to keep H & H from opening an auction, so that Delano could get the book wrapped up for a hundred thousand instead of the thousands upon thousands more the book could potentially bring!

"I'm sorry," Carol said evenly. "A pre-emptive offer at that level is out of the question. You'll know why when you read the manuscript. I'll be sending it over with our promotional info very shortly. Look, Robin, since we *are* friends, and because H and H has always enjoyed a good relationship with Delano, I'll accept a floor bid, if you'd like," Carol added, offering Delano the chance to top the last bid by ten percent in the auction she was now sure would take place.

"Well, I'm sorry you won't go for our pre-empt. Will you accept it as a floor bid?"

Carol had to think quickly again. The floor bid had to be high enough to impress other houses, but not so high as to scare them away from the bidding. It also had to be high enough to be acceptable as a buy-out price if nobody else bid. Carol held her breath and then quietly exhaled and inhaled and counted to ten before she spoke. "No, Robin, the minimum floor we'll accept is two hundred fifty thousand."

There was only a brief pause this time on the other end of the line. Carol knew Robin was either authorized to go to a quarter-of-a-million floor for *Blue Grotto* or she wasn't. Since they must have read a copy of the manuscript, the range and kinds of possible bids had probably been thoroughly discussed before the call was made. If Delano were able to make out like bandits with a pre-empt bid of a hundred thousand, great, but successful strategy required a range of fall-back options.

"All right, Carol," Robin said. "you've got your floor. Just three things: First, could you send a copy of the manuscript over tomorrow morning? Second, when will you auction the book? And third, I'd like to know the top bid at the end of each round of bidding.''

"Robin, you'll get your manuscript this afternoon, and I'll get back to you with a date tomorrow morning.''

Carol placed the receiver on its cradle and whooped with joy. She ran to Everett Horne's office to tell him the good news. There, the door was always open to Carol Volin; no meeting was too important for her to interrupt. Horne knew that when she came racing down the hall, it meant money. Usually big money, and a decision that had to be made at the top—and fast.

She crowed her good news and preened before the Old Man. Horne, eternally confounded and bewildered by his intercom system, thundered as always to his assistant, "Nancy! Get Mark and Mitchell in here now!"

In minutes the three vice presidents were standing before the immaculate desk of the owner, president, and publisher of Heywood & Horne. Carol explained how she had gambled, armed with her faith in the book's potential and the house's ability to market a good book and her own instinct. Robin was waiting to hear what date would be set for the auction. Carol needed material to send out, along with copies of the manuscript, right away. All the top paperback houses would want a chance to buy *Blue Grotto*.

"Let's send baskets of blue flowers to all the editors!" exclaimed Carol. "With a fabulous photograph of Angela in something sexy and romantic. We'll bind the manuscript in special blue binders. Advertising can whip up some copy to send out.''

"They'll want all but a written guarantee that this book will be a national best seller,'' Mitch added. "We'll outline our marketing plans and give them our publicity tour schedule. We'll tell them how much we're spending on ads and promotion.''

"Great!" said Carol. "Now, when do I set the auction? When will all the prepublication publicity culminate?''

Mitch was thoughtful for a moment. "Let's see. We've got a big announcement ad in *PW* coming, and we should be shipping bound books by—''

"January thirtieth," Mark broke in.

"Fine. We'll set a March fifteenth publication date. All the stores across the country will have books in stock by then. That's when all our publicity will break, the reviews will start coming out, the ads will run, and I think Madeline is planning a big party for local booksellers and the media that night."

"Then that's it. The auction will be held on March fifteenth," Carol said. "Okay with you, Everett?"

The Old Man smiled his approval and winked at Carol as he would at a favored grandchild. "Good work," he said simply, then turned to a fat file of orders awaiting his happy perusal.

Carol raced back to her office to call Elizabeth Walsh and let her know about the floor, and to chastise her at least a little for letting Delano get hold of the manuscript. This time Carol had triumphed over the curve ball she had been thrown and made a solid hit, but she might just as easily have struck out.

Carol stubbed out the end of her cigarette in the crystal ashtray Mark had thoughtfully placed on his nightstand before he had bedded her, and checked her watch. It was two-fifteen. She lit another cigarette and hungrily drew smoke into her lungs. She was nervous, the way she always was during a big auction, even though she'd gotten two bids before lunch and she was now at $302,500, with at least three more bids to take in the first round. Then there'd be the second round of offers. If she had all five bidders in for at least two rounds, and driving up the previous bid by the minimum ten percent increased required, she'd be out of the sky and into the stratosphere. And if her news was big—really big—she would arrive at tonight's publication party in Little Italy twice the star that Angela Vaccaro was certainly hoping to be. It would be Carol with whom the media would want to speak. She would make publishing news if she got the bidding over the half-million mark.

She'd have to handle the rest of the auction carefully. Very carefully. She would have her assistant pick up a refill of her Valium prescription at the drugstore across the street from the office. Just a little would ease the tension. Keep her cool yet sharp. The orgasm was good, but it hadn't quite done the trick. A little Valium would be just what the doctor ordered.

Angela tried desperately not to think about escalating bids as she raced around town after her lunch with Eli. Flagging a cab, she settled back into the seat to watch Fifth Avenue pass by. As the taxi passed Doubleday's bookstore, Angela saw copies of *Blue Grotto* piled high in the window. Then, in the front window of the new B. Dalton bookstore on the corner of Fifty-third Street, Angela saw a huge color photograph of herself, staring straight at the rushing crowd. Hundreds of copies of *Blue Grotto* stood attractively arranged around the photograph on heaps of blue satin. A giant reproduction of the front of the gold-and-blue dust jacket stood next to Angela's portrait. Angela told the driver to stop. She got out and stood stunned for a moment, clutching her coat around her against the harsh winds, she paid the driver and walked into the bookstore. Inside the store the reaction was instantaneous—the clerks recognized her and ran to greet her.

"We love your book," they told her, wanting to press close, to shake her hand. She responded quickly to their enthusiasm and bought several copies of her book, to sign and present as gifts. The clerks from downstairs, not wanting to be left out, came up and clamored about her, asking her to sign more copies of her book. Soon a throng of people surrounded Angela, and the afternoon shoppers wanted to know what the commotion was all about.

An hour later, the last book in the store was hastily but gratefully signed, and B. Dalton's manager, her eyes shining with delight, put a stunned and triumphant Angela into a cab. So this is fame, thought Angela, leaning back, exhausted. Well, I like it. I like it just fine.

Angela reached for her telephone as soon as she got inside her apartment.

"Eli! It's me. How's it going?"

"Oh, it's *going*, all right. It's going! Whew! Hot and heavy! There are five houses bidding, and we're almost up to half a million, Ange! Brad is going nuts trying to get the details out of me. I won't tell him a thing till it's over."

"Half a million! My God! I never dreamed . . . Eli! You should have seen what happened at B. Dalton!"

"Not now, Ange. I've gotta keep this line free. Look, I may be late for your party tonight—this auction could go on for hours. Talk to you later."

Angela hung up the phone and walked toward her "office." She had set up the spare bedroom of her new apartment as a writing room. With Jimmy's help, she had taken special care in decorating her splendidly cozy office. In fact, she had lavished so much money on decorating and furnishing this room that she had little money left to furnish the rest of the apartment.

Angela took her journal out of a drawer in the antique oak desk. She wanted to capture her impressions of the B. Dalton experience before she became too caught up in the party and the tour. Just as she settled into her overstuffed wing chair, the phone rang.

"Angie, honey? It's Daddy."

"Hi, Daddy. How are you? Did you get the tuxedo? Does it fit okay?"

"Sure, baby. Jimmy picked it up for me yesterday. But there's a little problem."

"I told you to let me buy you one, Daddy. Those rented ones are never as nice—"

"That's not it, sweetheart. I . . . don't feel so good."

"What is it? What's wrong?" Angela's voice rose in alarm.

Sal laughed. "Don't get excited, babe. It's nothing. A little agita, that's all. I ate one of your Aunt Camella's big sausage-and-peppers dinners last night, and I guess I'm too old for all that heavy food."

Angela breathed a sigh of relief. No one could escape agita after one of Aunt Camella's sausage-and-pepper meals.

"Well, you just rest and take it easy, Dad. Did you call Dr. Blumberg?"

"Nah. What for? So he could tell me to take a bicarbonate? I can do that much for myself. But I don't think I can come to your big party, Ange. Not unless I feel a lot better by tonight. I feel bad about it. I was looking forward to seeing all your friends, seeing my little girl looking like a big shot, eh?"

"Oh, Daddy. It's no big deal. There'll be other parties. You just feel better, you hear? Is Jimmy going to stay with you?"

"No, no. You kidding? We gotta have *some* family at this shindig! Aunt Camella and Uncle Tony are here, so don't you worry about a thing. And good luck, sweetheart. Knock 'em dead!"

"Thanks, Daddy. I will. I love you, Daddy. Bye."

Angela pushed worrisome thoughts from her mind as she prepared for the party.

On her way to the bedroom, Angela stopped and picked up

the copy of the *Daily Sun* that had been delivered that afternoon.

Angela was shocked to see her own face, à la Scavullo, staring out at her from page eight. The grainy black and white shot accompanied a story under columnist Mike Brennan's byline.

He had interviewed her only last week! She hadn't expected the story to run so soon. Somebody should have told her it was in today's paper. The second paragraph explained why no one had told her. The article was a scathing put down of the publishing scene. That Mark Brennan must have a problem, Angela thought as she chewed her lip and read. The article barely mentioned Angela, and *Blue Grotto* got no more than a word in passing. Brennan used the event of *Blue Grotto*'s publication to kick off a series about the "hipper hypeier" world of blockbuster publishing; a world where "the rich get richer" and where "spoiled, young, beautiful widows like Angela Vaccaro di Fiori exploit their own lives between glossy, flossy covers."

Tears of anger burned Angela's eyes. She remembered the interview. Her first. She had been so nervous. She had taken special care with her appearance, making efforts to project the sophisticated and glamorous image she had worked so hard on. She remembered nothing about Brennan. Only a pair of relentlessly piercing eyes. She was too nervous to even imagine that he could react to her as a human being. She saw him as a powerful machine who had the power to hurt and expose her; even force her to pull the scabs from old wounds. How quickly she had snapped when he asked about Paolo! In her nervous, uncertain way she had tried to direct his questions toward her book. Afterward, she had no idea how the interview had gone. She had no way to judge. She only knew that she was relieved beyond belief that it was over.

Angela sighed and straightened her spine. I'm going to let this roll right off my back, she thought determinedly. After all, everyone warned me that the press never quotes you right. In this case, this guy missed everything just to make his own point. Fine. I'm not going to take this to heart. I've got a lot more interviews coming up. I can't let myself get discouraged now!

Angela tossed the newspaper on the floor and began to

undress for her bath. I've got a party to go to tonight. In my honor! she reminded herself.

But, she concluded, I hope I never run into Mike Brennan again as long as I live.

The room was filled with glittering groups of people, all sipping drinks and talking. The party was not yet in full swing, and the mood was one of excited anticipation. The guest of honor had not yet arrived, nor had the celebrities rumored to be joining the ranks of authors, agents, publicists, booksellers, and media folk.

Mark Green, handsome in black tie, stood in a corner talking with his wife and Everett Horne. He anxiously stole glances toward the doorway, hoping that Angela would arrive soon.

A waiter approached the three, offering them Blue Grottoes from a tray, a concoction invented by Madeline for this event consisting of blue Curaçao and vodka over shaved ice. Elegant Barbara Horne Green politely refused the curious drink. Mark, feeling that it was his duty to enter into the spirit of the evening, took one, while Everett Horne barked at the waiter and demanded a Scotch with an authority that made it clear that he, Everett, was paying for this damned frivolous party, after all.

Madeline Wood, looking attractive and understated in a mauve chiffon blouse and matching pants, "worked the room." She circulated among the guests, her eagle eye always zeroing in on the faces from the media. She greeted her "contacts" as if they were long-lost loves. Reporters, columnists, representatives from daytime talk shows—none escaped her. She chatted them up, always asking, "Have you met Angela?"

Then Angela arrived. On the arm of her brother Jimmy, she was resplendent in a daring silk dress of the deepest blue. The bodice was fashioned halter style, leaving the luminous flesh between her breasts bare almost to the navel, and the handkerchief-cut skirt revealed flashes of leg to mid-thigh. Her only jewelry was the sapphire.

Her effect on the crowd was electric. Angela radiated beauty, sexuality, confidence, and intelligence.

Madeline greeted Angela briskly. "The producer of the 'Today' show is here. You've got to meet her. She has another

party to go to after this one, but she promised to stay to meet
you. Come on."

Angela nodded and followed Madeline. She exchanged a
handshake and a few words with the woman responsible for
booking authors on that great launching pad for best sellers,
and then was quickly taken in hand by Madeline to join her
"working the room."

Paul Jameson arrived with a tall, dark, attractive man. Paul
and Angela, who had become friends during the course of the
book's production, embraced warmly.

"I'd like to introduce a friend," Paul said.

The dark man broke in, "I love your dress."

"Thank you," Angela replied. "It's a Scott David."

The young man's smile widened.

"This," Paul said with a flourish, "*is* Scott David!"

The young man laughed, as did Angela through blushes. A
feeling of warmth leaped out between the two and Scott
reached out to hug Angela.

"I *love* your clothes!" Angela warbled.

"I love you in them. I've never seen my dress look as well
on anyone!"

Angela was introducing them to Jimmy when Mark Green
appeared at Angela's elbow and led her firmly to the corner
occupied by Everett Horne and his dark-haired daughter.

"Angela, I'd like you to meet my wife, Barbara."

Barbara Horne Green graciously extended her hand and
grasped Angela's heartily. Despite a warm and sincere smile,
her gaze was penetrating.

She knows, thought Angela. She knows or *assumes* I'm
sleeping with her husband, and she doesn't care!

"And you know Daddy, don't you?" Barbara said. Angela
leaned over and kissed Everett Horne affectionately on the
cheek. He always seemed like a kindly grandfather to her,
although Angela had heard from Paul that he could be a terror
to his staff.

"Thank you for this wonderful party, Mr. Horne. I can't tell
you how exciting it is, how much it means to me. . . ."

Everett gave Angela a rare smile. "You're a good girl, and
you wrote a very good book. So just have a good time."

Mark leaned toward Angela, "We're very excited about the

paperback auction. The bidding was still going on when I left the office, and it's not over yet or Carol would be here."

"I know. I can't wait for Eli to get here and let us know what's happening!" Angela looked around the room and was surprised to see an author she had not expected to see tonight. Larry Gould, in an out-of-date dinner suit, holding a beer in his hand, was talking intently to Mike Brennan, the columnist from the *Sun*. Angela excused herself and went to greet Larry.

"Well, I knew you had been invited, Larry," Angela said, pointedly ignoring Brennan, "but I had heard you didn't show up at parties like this anymore. I'm truly glad you came." Angela kissed him on the cheek.

"I've had my fill of publishing parties," Larry responded, "but you know why I'm here. Where's Eli?"

"Well, it's clear you didn't come for an autographed copy of *Blue Grotto*," Angela returned good-naturedly, gesturing toward a stack of books set around the bar. "Eli will be along later. She's waiting for the results of the paperback auction."

Brennan, quick to pick up on useful small talk, asked, "Anything I can run in my column tomorrow? Any record-breaking news yet?"

"Not yet, but I'm sure Madeline will be in touch with you," Angela replied, flashing a chilly but dazzling smile.

Angela felt someone firmly grasping her arm and turned to face Madeline Wood.

"This party's a huge success!" Madeline bubbled excitedly, waving a hand at the packed floor.

"It's quite a crowd," Angela agreed. "Who *are* all these people?"

"Oh, they don't matter," Madeline said. "What counts is that the media is here. Your name and *Blue Grotto* will be showing up in all the columns tomorrow. And you're charming the hell out of all the early morning TV show producers. They love you! I'll be booking you like crazy! Now all we need is some astounding figure for the sale of the paperback rights, and you'll be all over the papers!"

"I'd rather they print something about my book being good," Angela said half to herself.

Madeline raised her eyebrows. "*Publicity*, Angela, that's the name of the game. Publicity—it's free advertising—that's what's going to sell your book," she said firmly.

Angela nodded and allowed herself to be led to the next encounter. As Madeline maneuvered her through the throng, Angela spotted Eli—a bright patch of blazing turquoise in a Betsey Johnson jumpsuit—trying to work her way past a knot of drinkers engaged in lively discussion. Angela had to get to Eli to warn her that Larry was at the party. Then she could decide whether she wanted to see him or not. Angela extricated herself from the conversation and began to make her way toward Eli.

Eli was growing hoarse shouting "excuse me!" and decided to put her small, agile body to use. She squeezed, squirmed, and pushed through the crowd, desperate to reach Angela with her news. Carol Volin's cab had arrived seconds after Eli's and Eli wanted to give her client the news before anyone else did.

Angela had difficulty cutting through the mass of people. She was continually stopped by well-wishers who congratulated, praised, teased, hugged, and kissed her. Smiling wearily, Angela pushed on toward Eli.

"Dammit!" Eli said when she saw Carol Volin slip into the room and blaze a serpentine trail to Mark, Barbara, and Everett Horne. Eli couldn't blame Carol for going after the laurels with which her boss and colleague would rightfully crown her. After all, it was Carol who had spent eight grueling hours on the phone keeping her property hot and desirable in order to pry bid after escalating bid out of her customers. But Angela should be the very first person to know, and her agent should be the one to tell her.

Out of breath, Angela and Eli finally were pushed together in the center of the room.

"Larry's here!" Angela shouted.

"What?"

"I said Larry's here!"

Carol Volin had reached Mark and Everett. She spoke briefly to them. Mark, spotting Eli and Angela together, gave them a wave and a bright smile. He stepped up to the bandstand and spoke to the band leader, who signaled his musicians. A loud flourish silenced the crowd.

"Oh, shit!" Eli said audibly. Mark held a microphone.

"My dear ladies and gentlemen—and people of the publishing industry," Mark began to titters and groans, "I have a great honor this evening. I am happy to announce that the paperback rights to a wonderful book, written by an extraordinary young lady, *Blue Grotto* by Angela Vaccaro—'' Applause interrupted him. ''—have been sold to Delano Books for an advance of *one million dollars*!'' The crowd, tipsy and primed, broke into wild cheering.

Angela gasped as all eyes sought her. She turned to Eli, who nodded and hugged her.

The band began a spirited tarantella as Mark, with the crowd now parting agreeably for him, made his way to Angela. He took her in his arms and began to dance as the onlookers formed a circle around them. The music got faster and brighter as other joined them in the circle. In the blue of faces that sped by, Angela saw Larry's and tried to break from Mark's arms to warn Eli. It was too late. Larry was standing next to a wildly clapping Eli who had not yet noticed him.

The rest of the evening was a confused, disjointed jumble of drinking, dancing, congratulations, and excitement. None of it seemed real to Angela. Hours after midnight, the buoyant but exhausted guests began to leave.

Maybe it's time to call it a night, Angela thought after kissing Mark good-bye and thanking Madeline. She searched the floor for Jimmy and found him at the bar with Paul and Scott David.

"Lovely party, love," Scott David said, "but it seems to be winding down. Let's all go over to Studio. What do you say?"

Paul was enthusiastic. Jimmy begged off. He had an exam in the morning, and he had to get back to Whitestone. Eli and Larry had disappeared. Paul said he had seen them leave together a few minutes before. Angela was pleased.

"Oh, hell!" Angela exclaimed. "Let's go! I'm too keyed up to sleep tonight, and besides, I've never been there!"

Scott's limousine soon deposited them at Studio 54. Getting into 1979's hottest and most exclusive disco was no problem for friends of Scott David. The owner greeted them personally and ushered them to the dance floor, claiming the right, as host, to Angela's first dance.

Scott held court from a banquette in the balcony of the converted theater, and as the lights flashed and the music pounded, Paul and Angela, who was now feeling the effects of several drinks, danced and danced—together and with strangers. They drank champagne and snorted the high-grade cocaine that was discreetly offered them.

Angela hesitated before she took her first "taste" of the drug, but, urged on by Scott and seeing that he seemed to suffer no ill effects from the white powder, she willingly bent to the task of inhaling the stuff through a tube and into her nose.

The effect was subtle. She just felt happier, higher, and more on top of the world.

As the sun rose over the city, Scott's limo whisked her home. Weary but happy, Angela kicked off her shoes and flung them into the bedroom. She followed them and flopped, fully dressed, on the bed, waiting for the burst of energy she would need to get undressed. No nightmare tonight, she thought; she didn't have the strength to dream.

She wriggled out of her coat, then started at the sudden noise. The phone was ringing. It was seven A.M. and the phone *was* ringing. She rolled over and picked up the receiver.

"Angela! Where the hell were you?"

"Jimmy! What's wrong?"

"It's Daddy, Ange. I'm at the hospital. Whitestone Hospital. It's bad, Ange. Very bad. Please come."

"I'll be right there!"

Angela slammed down the phone, grabbed her shoes, and flew out of her apartment.

The city's early workers filled the streets on their way to their jobs. They shook their heads at the sight of a woman standing in the middle of Third Avenue, in a beautiful evening dress screaming frantically, "Taxi! I need a taxi!"

CHAPTER
─────16─────

ANGELA tried to ignore the cramp in her left hand as she scrawled her name in what seemed like the millionth copy of *Blue Grotto*. So this is what being a successful author is all about. It certainly wasn't all glamour and adulation—it was damned hard work. But the hectic pace of the promotion tour was something to be thankful for. There was no time for grief, no unclaimed moments for introspection. Angela had thrown herself into the tour with frenzied dedication, determined not to stop and face the after-effects of her father's sudden death. During the day she functioned like a demonic automaton, meeting and greeting, signing books, turning on her carefully coached charm to answer the same questions over and over for interviewers. At night, exhausted and drained, she had a drink, or maybe two or three, or more, to fall into a heavy, dreamless sleep. She flew from city to city, staying in hotel rooms decorated in glaring shades of orange, aqua, or avocado, dashing from television and radio studios to bookstores, relentlessly running from the pain of her tragedy, from the thoughts that would reopen and deepen all her unhealed wounds.

Angela put down the pen and handed the book to the owner of the smile beaming down at her from the other side of the table. Before another copy of her book could be thrust at her, she turned in her chair to ask the Heywood & Horne sales rep for whatever the hell city she was in today a plaintive question.

"Isn't it time to quit yet, Bill?"

"It's Terry, Angela. Terry Marshall, remember? And no, you're scheduled for another fifteen minutes. Rich's Department Store is my biggest account, and Faith Brunson, the buyer, will have my head if we cut this short. Just look at the line—they love you! Just keep signing!"

"Okay, Terry. Sorry. I didn't even know there were this many *people* in Atlanta, let alone people who could buy my book. I guess I'd better start signing again. My left hand's about to go, but I can always try the right one."

The good-looking young salesman smiled as the author returned to her task. Usually Terry hated the additional chore of babysitting for temperamental H & H authors when their publicity tours brought them into his selling territory. In his opinion, Jessica Simon's recent visit to promote *Lone Star* had been the most devastating invasion of Georgia since General Sherman's. But Jessica's visit had certainly sold books, just as Angela Vaccaro's was doing now. And that was the name of the game. But Angela Vaccaro was an unexpected bonus: beautiful, pleasant, intelligent—and not bad in bed.

Terry wasn't the only man to enjoy Angela's favors during her tour. There had been a talk show host in Cleveland, the owner of a bookstore chain in D.C., a bartender at the Drake Hotel in Chicago. The daily routine of the tour presented a task-packed, day-long, fast-paced pattern, but at night the treadmill stopped with a jolt, leaving Angela lonely, restless, and terrified of her own thoughts.

A few drinks were not enough to distract her from the devastating thoughts that lay perilously close to her well-controlled veneer. Early on in the tour she had begun to encourage the attention she received from men wherever she went, and mindlessly she succumbed to the advances of strangers.

Anglea despised the unfulfilling, unsatisfying sex for sex's sake, but a few hours spent with a warm, attentive body were better than lying awake alone and falling into a whirlpool of despair. Her "lovers" acted as though she were doing them a favor when she spiritlessly bedded them. Their gratitude was short-lived, however, because Anglea insisted they leave as soon as the passionless act was over. She wanted no witnesses to the threatening, inevitable effects of her nightmares, for the nightmares traveled with her. Seeming to feed on Sal's death, they followed her from city to city with new vigor and clarity.

* * *

"Ange, you're a hit! You're on the list! Number seven!"

"Wait a minute, Eli. I didn't hear a word you just screamed. Let me get the phone closer to my ear." Angela rolled over and propped herself up against the pillows, then looked at the travel alarm clock on the table next to the bed. "Eli, do you realize it's five o'clock in the morning?"

"Oh, God, Ange, I'm sorry. I forgot you're three hours earlier out there in San Francisco. I'm still in bed myself, but I couldn't wait to call you with the news. I wanted to be the one to tell you, before anyone at H and H got to you."

"Tell me what, Eli, *what*?"

"*Blue Grotto* is number seven on the *New York Tribune Book Review* best-seller list," Eli said with restrained dignity. "Now for Christ's sake, Angela," she screamed, "*will you please wake up*?"

"All right, I'm awake! I hear you! I'm just in shock! It's fabulous! How about my reviews? Is the *Trib Book Review* going to run one?"

"Now, Ange, I know what it means to you, but don't get your hopes up. If you stay on the list for a while, they may give you a small review, but even if they don't—or if it's lousy— what difference does it make? You're a hit! You're selling! And you'll be going to the ABA next week in triumph!" Eli wished she could see Angela's eyes. She hoped this good news would help melt the iciness she had seen there after Sal died.

At the mention of the ABA, Angela brightened again. The American Booksellers Association convention, traditionally the occasion for publishers to push their big books for the coming Christmas season, was still the event where something currently hot could be hyped into something even hotter.

Because the 1979 convention was being held in Los Angeles, it promised to be bigger and "glitzier" than ever. In addition to the thousands and thousands of bookstore buyers, managers, and owners, and more than a thousand international exhibitors, the movie people would be there too. And Angela would join the ranks of glamorous and famous authors making personal appearances, from novelist Judith Krantz to autobiographer Betty Ford.

"Eli, that's great. Will I see you there?"

"No. Afraid not, Ange. Skinflint Monroe still won't let me

go, even though I'm getting closer and closer to a movie deal on your book—Whoops! Forget I said that."

"A movie deal! Oh, *Eli!* How can I pretend I didn't hear you?"

"You just knock 'em dead at the convention, Ange. Remember now, you're a star! And watch out for Brad Monroe. He'll be trotting himself all over the ABA claiming you as *his* new star. According to him, he discovered you under a rock! Listen, I'll see you in a couple of weeks when you get back to New York. And maybe I'll have some news about the movie deal then. Oh, hold on! Before you hang up, there's someone who'd like to congratulate you."

Eli rolled over and unwrapped herself from the tangle of bedsheets and telephone cord, then she handed the receiver to Larry.

Angela tried desperately to keep up with Madeline Wood, who was fully four steps ahead of her as they made their way through the crowded lobby of the Los Angeles Convention Center.

"Stay put a second," she heard Madeline yell over her shoulder. "I've got to go pick up your badge."

Angela stopped abruptly, and two women bumped into her from behind. She turned to apologize.

"Excuse me, Miss Vaccaro," "So *sorry*, Angela," she heard as she tried to see the two fleeting faces. Neither one belonged to any one she knew or had even met on her publicity tour. Angela had been *recognized*.

"Okay, we're all set. Just pin this on." Madeline was at Angela's side with the badge, which plainly stated: ANGELA VACCARO/BLUE GROTTO/AUTHOR.

Angela smiled as she pinned the badge onto her suit jacket. She didn't need a label to remind her she was an author. The long, exhausting weeks of touring had gradually made it all sink in. Writing her name countless times on the first page of *Blue Grotto* had reinforced it over and over, and now her book was number three on the *Trib's* best-seller list and near the top of every other best-seller list in the country. Angela straightened her badge and smoothed the lapel of her jacket. She shook out her hair and tilted her chin up with pride.

"—and the blue badges are for the booksellers, and the

green ones are worn by the press," Madeline was explaining. "Those last two are the ones you have to be most aware of. Okay, are you ready? It's one-twenty eight, and we're expected in the autographing area in two minutes."

At the smashingly successful half-hour autographing session, Angela signed hundreds of books, yet scores of conventioneers had to be turned away when time ran out.

"Terrific, Angela," Madeline bubbled as they fought their way back through the lobby toward the main exhibit hall. "You were absolutely fan*tastic*! All right, time to enter the lion's den."

When they entered the hall, Angela was overwhelmed by what looked like a three-hundred-ring circus in full performance. A panoply of brightly decorated booths surrounded her, and in the aisles, hordes of people were racing left and right and milling about in clumps. Above the mêlée, the Berkley Books exhibit towered two stories tall, and another announced its featured titles on revolving poster-size book covers raised high up on stanchions like battle-proud shields. Ahead on the right, Angela saw Ballantine's eight-foot-high, traffic-stopping illuminated book jackets, and over there, could it be a human-size Donald Duck prancing down the aisle? Then Angela and Madeline turned a corner, and there it was: flashing parti-colored neon lights proclaiming HEYWOOD (blink) & (blink) HORNE (blink) four times across the top of the sleek silver-gray and chrome exhibit booth, which was punctuated at each end of its sixty-foot length by tall tropical palms.

"Angela, you got here just in time!" Mark Green appeared out of nowhere. He gave her a peck on the cheek and took her arm. "I want you to meet a reporter from the *Los Angeles Times*."

For the next few hours, Angela spoke to booksellers, flashed her ready smile for photographers, and smoothly answered questions from the press.

Angela was animatedly discussing current trends in fiction with the publicity director of a major bookstore chain when she noticed a commotion at the far end of the Heywood & Horne booth. A crowd was pushing its way toward the booth, filling the already jammed aisle. Camera strobes flashed amid shouts of "There she is!" "That's her!" Angela politely excused herself and made her way out into the aisle to acknowledge the acclaim.

"Madeline! Madeline!" Mitch Schaeffer's enraged voice rang through Angela's ears as he pushed his way past her on his way toward Madeline Wood, who stood several paces beyond. *"What's going on?"*

Then Angela literally saw red. For there at the center of the crowd in an Adolfo suit of shimmering cerise silk, on which a huge diamond-and-onyx star-shaped brooch glistened and gleamed in the glare of the lights, stood Jessica Simon, her perfectly coiffed dark head thrown back to unloose a jubilant, throaty laugh. Beneath her brooch, her convention badge was emblazoned with only two words: LONE STAR.

Angela was still seething when the limousine dropped her at her hotel. Madeline's apology for Jessica's sudden appearance failed to placate her. But Angela knew she could not blame the obviously innocent publicity director, who had so carefully plotted the two authors' concurrent tours so their paths never crossed.

It just seemed a little *too* convenient that Jessica "happened" to be in Los Angeles for tonight's party celebrating the opening of the new Scott David boutique in the Beverly Hills branch of Simon-Lewis, and that Jessica had decided it would be a "nice gesture" to drop in at the ABA Convention and say hello to her dear friends, America's booksellers.

Angela walked briskly under the Beverly Wilshire's black-and-gold awning, through the hotel doors, and then practically ran across the elegant lobby to phone Scott David's suite.

"Scott? Angela. I've changed my mind about the party tonight. When I spoke to you this morning, I thought I'd be too exhausted. But I feel great! Can I still take you up on your invitation?"

"Absolutely, Angela. Terrific! Can I call the store and have them send a dress to your room? You're a great advertisement for my clothes. Pick you up about nine-thirty?"

Angela headed for her room and a much-needed nap. Tonight, she decided, she would look absolutely sensational.

The man in the crisp white jacket carefully and efficiently rolled the cart, covered by a soft-pink linen cloth, along the tree-shaded walk, then stopped at the entrance to Bungalow Nine. He inspected each item that had been laid out on the cart. Everything had to be perfect: every plump berry in the china dish flawless, the thick cream icy cold, the strong coffee in the silver pot piping hot, the sparkling silverware precisely arranged. For this was the Beverly Hills Hotel, the legendary "Pink Palace," where impeccable service—the one deciding factor that distinguishes a merely fine hotel from a great one— was a hallmark. Just before signaling his arrival, the waiter straightened the single red rose in its vase and aligned the morning newspapers that lay to one side. There could be no mistakes, especially when serving a guest as demanding as Jessica Simon.

It was almost noon, and Jessica was still lying in bed among piles of pillows. As the room service cart was rolled into her bedroom—the largest of the five in the bungalow she and Arthur had taken for their California stay—she stretched her arms, recalling the magnificent party she had given at the Beverly Hills Simon-Lewis store the night before. It had gone without a hitch. Well, perhaps there had been one little hitch: Angela Vaccaro had shown up. But Jessica couldn't let an inconsequential little thing like that bother her.

As the waiter who delivered her breakfast slipped unobtrusively from the room, Jessica took her first comforting sip of steaming black coffee and picked up the morning paper. She flipped to the fashion/society page, eager to discover just how glowingly the glittering event of the night before had been recorded. Her small dark eyes darted avidly over the page, then a vein in her forehead began to pulsate violently.

"That bitch!" Jessica screamed, flinging the newspaper across the room as her coffee splattered on the satin-covered bed and a Lalique vase of anthuriums crashed to the floor.

A knock on the door intensified Jessica's rage. She would have to get up and answer it herself; Arthur had long since left his bedroom on the other side of the bungalow to take care of business at the store, and Ivy, her maid, had gone into town on one of Jessica's endless errands. She threw on her marabou-trimmed lilac satin negligee and stalked to the door.

"Goddammit, Madeline, you're late," Jessica thundered as she jerked the door open. "And what's more, you're in trouble. I've had all I'm going to take of that upstaging Vaccaro slut."

"Calm down, Jessica," Madeline said. "I left the convention floor just as soon as I could. Now, what's all this about Angela? You were the one who did the upstaging yesterday afternoon. And I had nothing to do with that. So what in God's name are you talking about?"

Jessica slammed the door shut and turned on her heels toward the bedroom to retrieve the newspaper as Madeline apprehensively settled herself on the deep-cushioned sofa.

"I'm talking about *this*," Jessica bellowed, wildly waving the crumpled newspaper at Madeline's anxious face.

Madeline took the paper and saw the photograph. Scott David and Angela Vaccaro were arm in arm, beaming, while Jessica Simon stood to one side, half of her face cropped out of the picture.

Simon-Lewis and Scott David brought out all the stars last night to celebrate the opening of Scott's new boutique in Simon-Lewis's posh Beverly Hills store on Wilshire. . . . Resplendent in a black silk taffeta Scott David gown and oodles of diamonds was Jessica Simon, wife of Simon-Lewis big boss Arthur Simon, and not incidentally the superstar author of that number one smash best seller, *Lone Star,* among others. But the true star of the black-tie bash was the beauteous Angela Vaccaro, the young first novelist whose own *Blue Grotto* has been nipping at the heels of *Lone Star* on all the best-seller lists. Gorgeous Angela arrived on the arm of the handsome Scott David himself, clad in one of Scott's most heavenly creations of red skin-tight sequins from head to toe, slit up the sides to the hips, showing lots of leg, and slit down the front to the waist, displaying lots of cleavage and a huge sapphire pendant. . . .

"Well?" Jessica demanded.

"Jess, I had no idea. I didn't even know she was on the guest list. I certainly had noth—"

"You're the fucking publicity director, and you're letting her get too much goddamned publicity. I want it stopped, you hear me? *Stopped!*" Jessica's voice had by now lost any trace of its cultivated Southern accent. "*I'm* the star at Heywood and Horne!" she shouted. "*Me! Jessica Simon is number one!*"

Madeline gingerly walked over to the fuming Jessica. She placed one arm gently around the fragile woman's shoulders. "I'm sorry this happened, Jessica. Truly I am. Maybe you should just let Angela have her little place in the sun. She'll probably just disappear after all this brouhaha over *Blue Grotto*. She's really no threat to the great Jessica Simon."

"Disappear? Ha." Jessica retorted, pulling herself free of Madeline's arm. "Don't you think I read her damned book? It's good. She can write. She'll be back with another one, and she'll get *more* publicity, thanks to you!"

"Jessica, please. Stop it. I'm telling you I had nothing to do with last night. Don't you think I would have prevented it if I could?"

"Would you?"

"Of course, Jessica. I would have scheduled her to be someplace else where she couldn't interfere with you."

"But you won't stop her, will you?" Jessica muttered.

"No," Madeline said quietly. "I can't do that. Not even for you. And you know how I feel."

"No, I don't. How *do* you feel?" Jessica snapped.

"You know I love you," Madeline replied simply.

"All right," Jessica said coolly. "You love me?" She unbelted her negligee and began slowly to lift the slithery fabric up to the tops of her still-trim thighs. "You love me?" Jessica asked again, pulling the negligee higher, her voice now husky, "then why don't you show me? Go ahead," she cried, seizing Madeline's head and pushing it down. "Go ahead, love me!"

Anglea dropped the newspaper on her bed and smiled to herself mischievously. Last night had been wonderful. She'd give anything to be able to see Jessica Simon's expression just one more time as she and Scott arrived at the celebrity-studded party. She rolled over lazily and gazed at the crumpled pillow beside her. Which one was it? she wondered. Who had she finally left the party with in the wee hours of the morning, when she had been so dizzyingly intoxicated with the evening and the champagne? Who *did* she spend those hours with just before dawn in this bed? She couldn't be sure, but she hoped it was Warren Beatty. After all, she'd had her eye on him all night.

She shook her head and ran her fingers through her hair, then climbed out of bed, padded across the thickly carpeted floor to the window and pulled open the draperies. The sun had reached its zenith in the dusty blue Southern California sky, but Angela was immune to its rays in her air-conditioned room. She stretched her arms languidly and let out a felicitous sigh. A new day was waiting, and it was time to go meet it.

Then Angela remembered with a jolt that she had no place to go, no carefully orchestrated schedule to fill her day. Heywood & Horne had no plans for her today, except tonight's *Blue Grotto* party at the Bistro, and that was long hours away. Angela was faced with the terrifying prospect of spending a day alone for the first time in weeks. She turned away from the window, away from the day. But, no, this was worse; she was trapped by the room's shrinking walls. She *had* to go out. She had to get away from herself.

Twenty minutes later, having hastily showered and dressed, Angela was standing in front of the hotel intently seeking distraction. She picked her way across Wilshire Boulevard's traffic-laden expanse to discover a tree-lined street stretched out before her, glittering with sun and display windows. Rodeo Drive, the street sign said. Rodeo Drive, Beverly Hills's street of dreams, where the wealthy, chic, and curious, the traditionalists and the trendsetters, the stars and the star-struck came to outfit themselves.

With renewed vigor and a gay sense of expectation, Angela fairly skipped down Rodeo Drive, stopping to peer into each invitingly-dressed store window, tempting herself, daring herself to cross the threshold of one of those splendidly elegant shops: Giorgio's, Right Bank, Ted Lapidus, Hermès. Then something caught her eye that she couldn't resist. A sleek wine-colored bag of the richest, most exquisite leather in Gucci's window demanded that she come in and inspect it more closely. It was a bag she had to have.

"That bag . . ." Angela began timidly, having finally captured the attention of the imperious saleswoman, "the burgundy one in the window, there on the left . . . can you tell me the price?"

From behind the bulwark of the counter, the saleswoman's eyes swept over the girl wearing Levis and a plain blue oxford-cloth shirt, her hair pulled back in a wrinkled red bandana.

"That bag is five hundred and twenty-five dollars," she stated icily. "Perhaps you'd like to see something a bit less expensive."

Five twenty-five, thought Angela. Whew! Who would pay that much for a handbag? For a moment she recalled a long-ago visit to the Gucci shop in Milan, when if her eyes lingered on an object for only an instant, Paolo would proclaim it hers. But those days were far behind her—another time, another life. Her sweet, cherished Paolo was gone forever, and so was the seemingly boundless luxury of her life with him. Get out of here, Angela, she told herself. That bag is not for you.

Then it hit her. In one instantaneous flash, she realized for the first time the true magnitude of her own success. The reality of her success had been clouded by Sal's death, obscured by her whirlwind publicity tour, overlooked because of her own firm decision not to look at any aspect of life with a clear vision. Yes, she was rich. Not filthy rich, but rich enough. And if her money couldn't give her everything, she could at least have that bag.

"No, that's the bag I want," Angela announced with a new-found hauteur. "And I'll take it in black, too."

While an exhausted Madeline Wood slept, Jessica sat in one of the silk-covered boudoir chairs on the opposite side of the room, thoughtfully sipping from a champagne flute filled with Jack Daniel's. Something had to be done about Miss Angela Vaccaro, Jessica had decided. The whole affair had gone entirely too far.

Earlier, Madeline had been saying that throughout Angela's tour, Angela had acted with a cool determination, an unstinting professionalism. She was always charming when the situation required; she was never temperamental or rude. She never let anyone down; she always came through. Well, dear little Miss Angela was not going to come through tonight; Jessica had had an inspiration.

"Wake up, Madeline," Jessica hissed, rising from her chair and shaking the sleeping woman. "We've got work to do."

Madeline rose reluctantly, recognizing the determined look on Jessica's face.

"What's this 'work' all about, Jess?" Madeline asked

warily. "This wouldn't have anything to do with Angela Vaccaro, would it?"

"Well, what do you think? Don't ask any more questions. Just get dressed."

"Jess, please. No dirty tricks. Angela isn't harming anyone, and besides, I don't want to lose my job."

"You won't lose your silly job, Madeline. Not while I wield power at Heywood and Horne. And I intend to hold onto my status there as well as on the best-seller list. Angela is going to be stopped. Or at the very least slowed down!"

"Jess, you can't go around fixing every game—"

"Can't I? Where would I be if I had that spineless attitude? I'll tell you! Back in New Orleans waiting for my daddy to recover from the Crash! No, I'm sorry, Miss Righteous. I have always had to grab what I wanted. Ever since my daddy lost his fortune. I've been poor and powerless, my dear, and let me tell you: it isn't noble. It stinks! And it's not going to happen to me again—ever."

"But Jessica, you're not in any danger. You've got a wealthy husband, a fabulous career—"

"A wealthy husband! That's just something to fall back on. Security. And don't think I didn't have to fight to get that! After my father lost his money, I set my sights on Herbert Lewis, the most eligible man in the entire South! And when he married my simp of a cousin, did I let that stop me?"

"No, Jessica, you set your cap for his cousin and partner, Arthur, then fought and scratched to help build the Simon-Lewis department stores into what they are today," Madeline recited wearily.

"That's right!" Jessica snapped. "*I have* said it all before. You can still take a lesson, miss! Now get dressed. We're going out!" Jessica marched toward the bathroom and slammed the door behind her.

Resigned now, Madeline got out of bed, wrapping the top sheet around her bare body, and began to gather up her clothing. She hated Jessica's rampages. When they were over, someone always ended up hurt. But what could Madeline do? She had been in love with Jessica for years and still was.

When she started at Heywood & Horne as an associate publicist, she had already given up any hope of a loving relationship with a man. After a brief lesbian liaison with a high school teacher, her several spiritless affairs with men had ended without any fulfillment, either sexually or emotionally.

Then came Jessica. Madeline was thirty-one when, as senior publicist, she was assigned to accompany the author on her publicity tour. As they traveled together from city to city, Jessica intuited the younger woman's yearnings and established an affectionate relationship with her. After Madeline responded to each of Jessica's carefully plotted advances, Jessica seduced her, beginning an affair that satisfied each woman's special needs. Jessica provided the love and attention Madeline so desperately craved; Madeline was the strong ally Jessica needed at Heywood & Horne, an ally who would make Jessica's interests her own.

As a result of the astounding success of Jessica's tour for *At Any Price*, Madeline Wood was named publicity director at Heywood & Horne, a decision that Jessica clearly supported.

Madeline was grateful to Jessica for both the affection and success that Madeline had reaped from the relationship. There was almost nothing Madeline wouldn't do in return.

Jessica returned from the bathroom, bathed and more determined. She sat down at her dressing table and began to apply makeup with swiftly moving hands.

"Madeline," she snapped, catching the younger woman's reflection in the glass, "not dressed yet? Hand me the phone!"

Angela returned to her hotel room exhausted and elated. An unsmiling bellman was two steps behind her, a haphazard array of packages hanging from each arm.

Just as she plopped herself down on the bed, the telephone rang. She reluctantly picked up the receiver.

"Angela? Is that you, dear? Jessica Simon here. I hope I'm not disturbing you, but I called to extend an invitation."

"Hello, Jessica. No, you didn't disturb me. I just got in from shopping."

"Shopping? How marvelous! I wish I had known you were going, I would have given you a personal tour of Simon-Lewis. But I suppose you did see quite a bit of it last night."

"Yes, Jessica, it was a lovely party."

"Well, that brings me around to the reason I called. I hardly got a chance to chat with you at all at the party, or even at the

convention center yesterday afternoon. I thought perhaps we
could get together for a drink and have that little talk we
promised ourselves way back when in New York."

"I wish we could, Jessica, but I've got the H and H party
tonight, and I'm leaving L.A. in the morning."

"Oh, but I'm right here at the Beverly Hills. Why don't you
come to the Polo Lounge around six. We'll have just one drink,
and then you can go off for your beauty rest. Now, I won't take
no for an answer."

"The Polo Lounge? Well, maybe just one drink. . . ."

An hour later, a cab turned off Sunset Boulevard on to the
lush, verdant grounds of the hotel that had been the Beverly
Hills long before Beverly Hills became Beverly Hills. As the
car slowly curved its way up the drive, Angela—resplendent in
a Zandra Rhodes creation from Giorgio's—peered out the
window to see the famous pink stucco facade through the
numerous royal palms, banana trees, and blue-flowering
jacarandas. When she passed through the lobby she noticed a
fireplace with a fire glowing within. How ridiculous, she
thought, still feeling the effects of the hot, heavy air outside.
But this was Southern California, she reminded herself, a place
where many years ago the word *ridiculous* had taken on new
meaning. She found the Polo Lounge off the lobby and paused
in the doorway at the maitre d's desk.

"Angela!" Jessica's syrupy voice floated over hushed
murmurs, occasional laughter, and the tinkle of glasses and ice.
Angela peered into the darkness of the room in the direction of
the banquettes that faced the entrance. Then she saw Jessica's
bejeweled hand waving at her from a front banquette. Jessica
had claimed one of the coveted tables that were in full view of
all the comings and goings. Angela headed across the room,
and as her eyes adjusted to the dim lighting, she noticed
Madeline Wood at the table. The arbitrator, Angela thought.

"Angela, darling," Jessica crooned, "that dress is an
absolute smash! The perfect thing to wear to the Pink Palace!
How clever. So few can wear that particular shade of pink. I
know I certainly can't. Well, do sit down, dear. Madeline and I
took the liberty of ordering you a Margarita. Margaritas are a
little tradition of mine whenever I come here."

Angela would have preferred a drink less potent, but she

good-naturedly raised her salt-rimmed glass as Jessica proposed a toast.

"To a successful party tonight," Jessica proclaimed.

"Oh, look. Over there," Madeline said brightly. "Isn't that Ali MacGraw leaving?"

"I believe it is," Jessica said with enthusiasm. "And when we came in I saw . . ."

Angela didn't hear a word. A platter of guacamole and tortilla chips had just been brought to the table. She realized that in her shopping frenzy she hadn't eaten all day. She gazed hungrily at the avocado concoction, waiting for one of the others to dip in with the first chip.

". . . you'd be amazed at the famous people who have been in and out of this room," Jessica was saying, oblivious to the tray of food. "The Polo Lounge and the Beverly Hills are just filled with history. Not just Hollywood history, but *literary* history as well. Joyce Haber took a room here so she would have peace and quiet while she was writing *The Users*, even though she lived only a few blocks away! And did you know that Jacqueline Susann used to have one of the kitchen's blackboards brought to her room so she could keep track of her characters?"

Angela took a sip of her drink and smiled. Literary history? The next thing Jessica would tell her, she thought, was that Tolstoy dashed off *War and Peace* next to the pool.

Abruptly, Jessica eased herself around the table and stood. "Would you girls excuse me for a moment? I believe my nose is shiny."

"Well, Angela," Madeline said cheerfully, "are you all ready for the party tonight?"

"Yes, I'm looking forward to it. I haven't been to the Bistro." She finished her drink, and having momentarily escaped Jessica's scrutiny, she grabbed a chipful of guacamole. "Mmmm, this is good," Angela said, taking her first bite. "I haven't had a thing to eat all day."

"The Polo Lounge is famous for its guacamole, in addition to everything else it's famous for. I wish I could try it, but I'm allergic to avocados." Years as a publicist had given Madeline the ability to have something to say about anything.

"Really? That's too b—"

"Well, I'm back!" chimed Jessica, slipping into her seat. "Angela, I see you've discovered the delectable guacamole. I wish I could indulge, but *I* try to take care of my figure. Now, what were we all talking about?"

"Caaaaalll for Miz Angela Vaccarooo! Caaaaalll for Miz Angela Vaccarooo!" A tiny man wearing a brass-buttoned coat was meandering through the room, loudly droning his message.

"Angela! How exciting!" exclaimed Jessica, waving the man toward their table. "You're being paged!" Then she said in a conspiratorial whisper, "If you'd like some privacy, perhaps you'd better take your call in the lobby."

Angela wondered who would be calling. Had Mark sneaked away from his wife and tracked her down, hoping for a quickie before the party? If that were the case, Angela certainly didn't want one of those pink telephones to be brought to the table. She wasn't about to supply Jessica with any gossip.

"Thanks, Jessica. Excuse me." She got up and followed the page out to the lobby.

Jessica smiled. She reached into her bag and rooted about purposefully as a waiter brought the second round of drinks she had ordered. She pulled Angela's fresh Margarita close to her and opened her right hand surreptitiously to allow the powder from two small Seconal capsules to slip into the frothy drink.

"Jessica! What in God's name are you doing. You can't—"

"Shut up, Madeline."

"Jessica—please—she said she hasn't eaten and that—"

"I said shut up!" Jessica hissed, pushing the drink back to its rightful place.

"Wasn't that fun!" Jessica exclaimed when Angela returned to the table. "It's not every day one gets paged in the Polo Lounge!"

"That was strange," Angela said quietly. "There was no call for me."

"Of course not, silly." Jessica laughed. "I was just having a little fun with you."

Madeline grimaced.

"When I went to powder my nose just now," Jessica continued blithely, "I asked to have you paged. Paged in the Polo Lounge! Now you've been initiated!"

"Here's to the Polo Lounge!" announced Angela. She raised her glass and, thirsty from the salty chips she had eaten, gulped half her drink.

Soon Angela felt woozy. The already dark room grew dimmer and began to revolve slowly. Jessica's melodious voice began to sound fuzzy. She had to prop her head in her hand as she finished the last sips of the Margarita. It was time to go back to her hotel and get some rest. She hadn't realized how much she needed it.

"Angela, I believe you're sleepy," Angela heard Jessica say from far away. "I almost forgot I promised to get you back to the Beverly Wilshire for a little rest. Now, don't you worry. You still have plenty of time. I'll have my driver whisk you back and arrange a wake-up call for you at the desk. Come along, Madeline. Let's help this child out to the car. It's time for her nap!"

"No, Ivy, put that away!" Jessica barked at her maid while the hairdresser pulled Jessica's hair into a sleek chignon. "I've changed my mind."

Jessica had selected three dresses to choose from for the party. But when Ivy presented each garment for her employer's approval, Jessica decided against all three. The magenta chiffon Halston would simply not do. Nor would the silver-beaded Galanos. Not even the turquoise taffeta de la Renta was right. For tonight she would be the star of the evening—the only star. Angela would sleep through the entire event. Tonight Angela's humiliation would be Jessica's triumph. How she'd glory in that luscious moment when she would sweep into the Bistro, all eyes on *her!* And she would enter arrayed like an empress.

"Bring me the gold Saint Laurent! The off-the-shoulder one with the matching cape!" she commanded.

At ten-thirty precisely, Jessica alighted from her Bentley and stepped through the cast-iron and glass doors of the restaurant. She hesitated briefly just outside the largest of the Bistro's three private rooms where the party was in full bloom, to savor the delicious feeling of anticipated triumph. She was ready to make her entrance.

Several guests greeted Jessica as she glided into the room,

but her entrance failed to capture everyone's attention. She looked to the center of the crowd to see what drew them like fluttering moths around a bright light. Then the sea of people parted, and Jessica saw her on Scott David's arm. Swathed in white organza ruffles, looking lithe and elegant and thoroughly "right" in the limelight, stood an exultant Angela Vaccaro.

CHAPTER
17

"WHAT IS THIS?" Eli demanded, her blue eyes ablaze, her blond curls trembling with fury. "What the hell is this?"

She slammed a copy of *Publishers Weekly* on Brad Monroe's desk and waited for a reply, her tightly curled fists resting on her hips.

Brad had put down the *Wall Street Journal* when Eli stomped into his office. He raised his chin in her direction and asked, "Hmm?"

"This! This! You . . . you . . ."

"Now, Elizabeth, if you're referring to that harmless tidbit in Paul Nathan's column . . ."

"Harmless tidbit? Who are you kidding? It says in black and white that 'Brad Monroe closed a deal with Aurora Productions for the movie rights to *Blue Grotto*.' Half a million was the figure they quoted. Here," she continued, excitedly jabbing the page, "see for yourself, goddammit. Now who called Paul Nathan? I sure as hell didn't. *I'm* the one *making* that deal, for God's sake, and it's far from closed! It's still in fucking delicate negotiation!"

"Elizabeth, you shock me with this crude display."

"Crude, my ass. Crude is being a limelight-seeking, grandstanding, credit-stealing son-of-a-bitch! What do I say to Len Seligsman? He's the guy at Aurora that I'm supposed to be making this deal with! What do I tell *Angela*? I've been keeping her on tenterhooks ever since she got back from L.A. Jesus, you're too much!" Eli sputtered and breathed hard. The first wave of her rage was spent. Now she would get down to cases.

"Look, Brad. When you went behind my back and showed

199

Blue Grotto to Delano, I thought okay, maybe he doesn't think I know how to handle a big paperback deal. But then you tried to cut me out of the publicity after the paperback auction. I saw you talking to that reporter at Angela's party—it's no wonder he never mentioned my name! I want publicity, too. How else can I build a reputation? But the difference is, Brad, I only want publicity for the work I do! Credit where it's due, man. Fair play, for God's sake! Now you want to take credit for my movie deal. Swell. But now there may be no deal at all, thanks to you."

"Well, I've heard you out, Elizabeth, and I must say you certainly are overreacting. You'll make a good agent someday, Ms. Walsh, if you can just learn to—"

"I *am* a good agent, Brad! That's what burns your ass! Two of my authors are on the *Trib's* best-seller list right now— Larry's number eleven and Angela's number two and holding strong. And those Delano best-seller list bonuses are rolling in. I don't need the Brad Monroe Agency anymore. I'm out of here!"

Brad rose behind his desk. "Don't be hasty, Elizabeth. Of course you're leaving. That's what I'm grooming you to do. That's why I've carefully trained you, so you could leave the nest and go off on your own—when you are ready, young lady, *and you are not ready yet.*"

"You're right, Brad," Eli replied with defiant sarcasm. "I'm not going until you call Len Seligsman and apologize for the—how would you term it?—'ghastly misunderstanding.' Then and only then, I'm packing up my star authors to take to the Elizabeth Walsh Literary Agency!"

"Elizabeth—Eli—you can't expect me to call Aurora. It's ludicrous, it's not—"

"Look, Brad, I'll phone every cranky, disgruntled author on our list and try my damnedest to woo them away from you— which won't be too hard with a few I can think of right offhand—if you don't start dialing that phone right now!"

"Sally, get me Len Seligsman in L.A.," Brad said. "Right now . . . please."

Within an hour, Eli was back in the new apartment on lower Fifth Avenue that she shared with Larry Gould. The contents of her desk were under her arm in a bunchy, unwieldly package, and the Aurora deal was tightly sewn up. Close to a half million dollars' worth of income would be added to Angela's growing fortune.

Larry was surprised to see Eli home so early.

"I left Brad Monroe," she announced flatly.

"Eli, that's fantastic! It's about time!"

"The bastard almost ruined my Aurora deal in yet another of his obnoxious, transparent bids for fame."

"Good. I'm glad he finally provided the straw to break the camel's back. You've always talked about getting out of there, but I was beginning to wonder if you ever would."

"Thanks for being so supportive," Eli said dryly.

"I am being supportive, Eli. I'm sorry he screwed up your deal, but I'm glad you're making the big move."

"Well, he didn't blow it. It came through anyway. Aurora has agreed to pay five hundred thousand."

"Well, that's great! Why are you so sour? Eli, that's terrific news! Let's call *Publishers Weekly*! What a fantastic start for the Elizabeth Walsh Literary Agency!"

"Yeah, yeah. Only don't call *PW* so fast. Brad got to them first before the deal was closed. Seligsman was cool about it, though. He'd just gotten the okay from the money man."

"Angela must be in seventh heaven. I'd love to see *Levy's Lament* as a movie. Couldn't you see Dustin Hoffman playing—"

"Angela! My God! I haven't called Angela!"

"This news will be good for at least an hour on the phone. See you later, Eli."

"No, wait. I have a better idea. Let's tell her tonight at Jimmy's dinner. With everyone there. It'll be more festive. Maybe it will cheer her up. She's been sort of strange and mopey since the tour. I think she's kind of letdown. She doesn't seem to know what to do with herself."

"Fine. So we'll tell her the good news tonight. Now, why do *you* look so miserable? You've dumped Brad, you've made a tremendous deal, and you're about to open your own agency? What's wrong?"

"Larry, I'm *scared*. I've never been my own boss. How do I know I really can run my own agency?"

Larry drew Eli to the living room couch and sat down with her. He put his arm around her shoulders.

"Let's look at the pluses, Eli. You've got Angela. A big star.

Blue Grotto has definitely established her. You'll have no trouble selling her new book at more than double what you got for *Blue Grotto*. There'll be another big paperback deal. Another movie deal . . . this thing can just keep snow-balling. Then there's me. I'm a 'literary light,' according to at least fifty critics. My new book's on the best-seller list, and everyone knows we're an 'item.' Every guy who thinks he's written another *My Life Unbound* or *Levy's Lament* is going to send his manuscript to you. You're got a few more solid authors with blue type—or maybe blue stationery with white type? The spare room's waiting for you, kid. We'll put in another phone. You can hire an assistant once things start moving. . . ."

Eli threw herself into Larry's arms, hugged him, and nestled against his chest contentedly.

Angela presented herself at Mark's door. She took off her dark glasses as Mark ushered her inside and flung her straw bag into a chair.

"Angela, darling!" Mark greeted her.

"Mark, darling!" Angela mocked, bored and peevish.

"Oh, Angela, I can see you're going to be difficult."

"On the contrary," Angela replied airily, slipping off her flat sandals, "I think I'm rather *easy*."

"I wish you wouldn't speak that way, Angela. It doesn't become you, you know."

Angela unfastened her belt buckle and began to pull off her jeans.

"Angela, wait! Can't we talk? Why the hurry?"

"I thought you were on your lunch hour."

"Yes, but Angela, I don't punch a time clock. You've been back from your tour for two weeks. You haven't called me once—we have so much to . . . talk about," he finished lamely.

"Have we? Madeline can fill you in on the details. Your sales figures should tell you anything else you need to know."

"That's not the point, Angela," Mark replied in exasperation. "I know how the bloody tour went. Madeline submitted a full report. But I want to know about you, Angela. About us."

"What is there to say, Mark? Are you getting tired of this? Maybe it's all too cut and dried for you. Maybe you need a change of pace. I know—I'll put on one of those naughty nightgowns you bought me. The ones that are supposed to tempt me to spend the night." Angela removed her jeans, dropped them on the floor, and sauntered to the dresser where she opened a drawer and retrieved a black lace nightgown— and also noticed a feminine-looking, tortoise-shell cigarette case. She undressed and slipped the nightgown on over her head just as Mark, looking forlorn, came in and sat down on the bed to take off his shoes.

"So," he said, pulling at his shoe laces, "you're sleeping with Mitch Schaeffer."

"I had lunch with him last week."

"And went to bed with him afterward."

"So what if I did?" Angela pulled open the drawer and produced the cigarette case. "And who does this belong to? You're not exactly celibate when I'm not around."

"It's Carol Volin's," Mark replied miserably, "and yes, I slept with her, but I don't anymore. And I don't sleep with Barbara anymore either. Angela, when you were on tour, I missed you more than I thought possible. Then when I saw you in L.A. and Barbara was there, and I couldn't—"

"Mark, stop! We've been over this before. We started this thing with an understanding. Let's not ruin it by being foolish, all right? I don't ask who you sleep with. Please return the courtesy. I don't want to be confronted like this. Please don't spoil things."

Angela sinuously lowered herself onto Mark's lap. She had looked forward to this rendezvous too much to let him ruin it. She needed the kind of sex she had with Mark: predictable, uncomplicated, satisfying. She needed it after the nights she had spent unsatisfied on her tour. Most of the men she had gone to bed with seemed to come seconds after she took off her clothes. Few were able to please her.

"Mark," she crooned in his ear, "I want you. I've waited for this." She pressed her mouth against his and slipped her hand under his loosened belt to grasp his erection. Soon they were locked together like adversaries in combat. Mark panted endearments, and Angela urged his hands to stroke and satisfy her. She ground her hips against him, seeking her climax. She pushed and struggled against him as though she were fighting for something he owed her that he would part with only by force. Finally, the battle ended and the two exhausted duelists broke apart.

"Think Carol Volin would mind if I smoked one of her cigarettes?" Angela asked.

Heads turned as Angela made her way through the garden at Tavern on the Green to reach the table where Larry, Eli, and Jimmy waited for her. She wore closely fitted black silk pants under a loose, low-cut emerald green tunic. Angela's hair was brushed dramatically to one side, and a large, perfect gardenia was fastened at her ear.

"Sorry I'm late," Angela trilled. She greeted everyone with kisses and sat down next to Jimmy.

"You picked a hell of a tacky restaurant for Jimmy's celebration," chided Eli as the strains of "Happy Birthday" reached them from the chandeliered, glass-enclosed dining room bordering the garden.

"Well, I think it's fun," Angela retorted. "I don't care if it *is* full of tourists and rowdies. I might just get rowdy myself."

Angela's dinner companions smiled uneasily. Lately it was difficult to tell when Angela was joking.

"Let's order drinks. You guys have finished yours, I see, and I need one. And then Jimmy can tell us what it is we're celebrating tonight."

When the drinks were served, Jimmy raised his glass and said, "To me! The new junior book designer at Heywood and Horne!"

"That's super, Jimmy," Angela cried. "I knew Paul Jameson had looked at your portfolio, but I didn't know he had a job to offer!"

"He really liked my work," Jimmy said proudly, "and I happened along at the right time. One of his designers had just quit."

"Here's to Jimmy's new job!" cried Eli, lifting her glass. "And here's to Angela's next book!"

Angela's face darkened in a scowl. "I don't know about any next book yet. Let's not push things."

"Well, you've got to start sometime," Eli said.

"I said don't push," Angela retorted.

Larry broke in. "Hey! What about telling her your news, Eli?"

"Right. Okay! Ange, we've done it again. Aurora Productions bought the rights to *Blue Grotto* for *five hundred thousand*!"

"A movie! Oh, God, I can't wait," Angela cried. "Who will play the heroine? Who would make a good Diana?"

Jimmy's eyes brightened. "Oh, I think Jane Fonda, don't you?"

"I kind of thought maybe Jackie Bisset. You know, she's dark—"

"Candice Bergen—with a dark wig!" Jimmy shot back.

"Or Raquel Welch in that serious role she's searched a lifetime for. . . ."

"But not Barbra. *Definitely* not Barbra," Jimmy said with mock seriousness.

"Oh, Jimmy, you're right. Can we put that in the contract?"

"What about Giancarlo? The hero?" said Jimmy.

"Hmmm. Oh, that's easy—Giancarlo Giannini. That's a natural. Either him or some other gorgeous Latin. Marcello? He's getting a little old, but . . ."

Larry laughed. "Don't you think these Italian types are a little overrated?"

Silence greeted what Larry had thought was an innocuous remark. Eli shot her lover a warning look. Angela unconsciously place a protective hand over the sapphire around her neck and said, "No, I don't think they are."

Eli bravely forged into the tense silence. "I walked out of the Brad Monroe Literary Agency today—for good," she said.

Angela beamed. "Eli, that's wonderful! Waiter—bring us a bottle of champagne. The best!"

Angela jumped up and ran around the table to hug Eli. Then, after glasses were filled, she solemnly proclaimed, "Here's to the Elizabeth Walsh Literary Agency. Here's to Jimmy's new job. Here's to Hollywood. And here's to the box office smashes of the future—*Levy's Lament* and *Blue Grotto*!"

The happy group proceeded to consume large quantities of champagne, oysters, steak au poivre, red snapper Dijonnaise, and poached striped bass. As the waiter served the Tavern's famous banana fritters with cinnamon sauce and uncorked yet another bottle of champagne, Larry offered his toast: "Here's to the *Trib*'s best-seller list."

"Where it seems I'll always be number two," Angela slurred.

Larry looked hurt. "What's wrong with number two? I wouldn't kick if *My Life Unbound* made number two. I'm damn happy to be at number eleven. A lot of authors would give their left nut to be number fifteen!"

Eli intervened quickly. "I'm sure Angela realizes that, Larry. And by the way, guys, I got my advance copy of the *Trib* in the office yesterday. Larry's moving up to number eight next week!"

"And who's number one?" Angela asked.

"*Lone Star*. Jessica Simon," Eli answered quietly.

"*That*'s my point. That Southern-fried game hen has the spot sewn up. Dynamite won't get her out of there."

"You're still holding at two, and it's a very close second," Eli reminded her friend.

"Oh, I know. I wouldn't mind so much if it wasn't that damn Jessica. She has it in for me. She slipped me a mickey in the Polo Lounge!"

Angela leaned toward Eli and spoke in an intense whisper. "I mean it. If Scott hadn't come up to my room and thrown me into a cold shower and poured black coffee into me, I never would have made it. I was out *cold*, for God's sake! And why do you think Dallas and Houston were canceled from my tour at the last moment? That's Jessica's territory. If I had come near the Texas border, she'd have been waiting there with a posse!"

Jimmy and Eli exchanged glances. Angela was obviously drunk and overwrought.

"Well, never mind, Ange," Eli said brightly. "Your next book will be number one."

"Next book, next book. What next book? Why don't *you* write it, Eli? You think it's easy? You think it's fun? I can't think of a thing to write about. Not a goddamn thing! So you write it, okay? You write the damn book, and I'll be the agent!"

All eyes in the crowded garden found Angela. Her voice had risen to near-shouting level. Jimmy quieted his sister and allowed her to pay the check to avoid another outburst.

"Maybe we'd better get Angela into a cab," Larry suggested. "She looks as though she's had it."

"I'll get her home, Larry. I'm going downtown, too," Jimmy said.

He hailed a cab and helped his sister inside. "Gramercy Park South, then over to West Eighteenth Street." Jimmy started to talk about the apartment he'd just moved into in a Chelsea brownstone, but he noticed that Angela wasn't listening to him.

"I meant to tell you, Ange," Jimmy began, trying another tack with his testy sibling, "you look great tonight. That outfit is really nice."

"You like it? It's a Scott David. I have it in red, I have it in blue. . . ." Angela's voice trailed off wearily.

When they reached Angela's building, Jimmy turned toward his sister and examined her face in the dim light of a streetlamp. He touched her cheek.

"Good night, Ange. And *please* take care of yourself."

"I will, Jimmy," Angela whispered with surprising sobriety. "We're the only ones left now, aren't we?"

Angela fell into a deep sleep easily that night, but a few hours before dawn she dreamed of a glaring light. As the brightness became more intense, her mind's eye clearly saw two headlights boring through mountain mists. She saw herself sitting on a dirt road. Something heavy lay in her lap. A horrible, bloddy burden. And then she saw the eyes. Paolo's stony, dead eyes. There was blood on her hands, blood on her dress. Blood everywhere and cold, dead eyes.

She began to toss and moan. Once again she was awakened by the sound of her own screams, useless cries for help that never, ever came. She sat bolt upright in her own bed, her breath coming in sharp gasps. The hum of the air conditioner was the only sound in the tomblike silence. Angela lay back, hugging her pillows against her trembling frame, and cried herself to sleep.

The house that Eli and Larry rented for the summer on Martha's Vineyard sat on Lighthouse Road, in the tiny, unfashionable "up island" town of Gay Head, far from the more populated, touristy "down island" towns of Edgartown and Oak Bluffs, and the notorious Chappaquiddick. They had deliberately chosen the privacy and quiet of Gay Head so Larry could work on his third book and Eli could read manuscripts and ready herself for launching the agency in the fall.

On a bright Monday afternoon at the end of June, Larry hopped into the rattletrap Volkswagen convertible he kept on the Vineyard and headed toward the Edgartown Airport. He had come a week earlier to open the house while Eli got her business in order so she could take the summer off. And although he had gotten some writing done, he had missed Eli and was eager to get her reaction to his first chapter. He couldn't help thinking as he drove up to where the two women were waiting—Eli jumping up and down with joy at seeing him, Angela shading her eyes and squinting into the sun—that he'd rather be alone with Eli. He'd much rather it was just the two of them.

"Look, Angela! Just look at all this!" Eli exclaimed, turning around in the front seat to face Angela, who sat in the back with the suitcases and her portable typewriter. "This island's got everything! Farms, woods, ponds, streams, the ocean, the Sound. It's paradise!"

"I see, I see. It's beautiful, Eli. You can stop selling me on the place. I'm here!" Angela replied, laughing.

"Well, ladies, how are things back in the Big Apple?" Larry asked, not truly caring.

"Boring, boring, boring," Angela answered.

"Now Angela, you can't expect the routine of a writer's life to match the kind of excitement you had on the publicity tour, right?" Larry said.

"I suppose. . . . " Angela said unconvincingly.

Eli and Larry stole a quick glance at each other, a glance that was not unobserved by the backseat passenger.

"Larry! Let's stop in Menemsha and get some lobsters for dinner!" Eli suggested.

After stopping in the little fishing village, then picking up fresh corn from a roadside stand, the threesome arrived. The little saltbox house was a welcome sight to Eli. While Larry unloaded their bags from the car, Eli excitedly showed Angela the house, leaving her in the neat, little spare room to unpack and get settled.

Angela showered, put on shorts and a halter top, and took a book to the sun deck, where Eli joined her with a manuscript and two glasses of chilled white wine.

Sea gulls soared and cried above them as the sun dipped like a fiery ball into the sea. Eli sat back, put her feet up, and sighed with contentment. "This is what it's all about," she said, sipping some wine.

Just then the stillness was broken by the clattering of typewriter keys. Angela gritted her teeth. The sound was certainly familiar to her, and it had never bothered her before, but by God, it bothered her now. She forced herself to concentrate on her book.

"I think it's time to start dinner," Eli said an hour later.

"Let me help," said Angela. "I can at least make the salad."

"No, that's Larry's job. He thinks he's Craig Claiborne when it comes to salads. I tell you what, you play guest for tonight since it's your first night, and from then on we'll all pitch in, okay?"

"Okay, Eli. But I *will* help with the dishes!"

Eli vanished through the screen door. Angela returned to her book. She was startled a few minutes later by Eli's high-pitched screams and ran downstairs to the kitchen where Larry was playfully threatening Eli with a squirming lobster. Eli was shrieking and laughing. Then with one swift motion Larry plunged the lobster into the steaming pot, and with just as swift a motion he gathered Eli against his chest and kissed her hard. His hand reached for her breast. This isn't going to work, thought Angela as she climbed the stairs to the deck. This is not going to work all. But Angela decided that she owed it to Eli to give the visit a chance.

The next morning, after breakfasting on scones and pastries brought from the Scottish Bake House near Edgartown, Larry went upstairs to hammer at his typewriter. Each staccato tat-tat-tat sounded like a harsh reproach in Angela's ears. "I'm writing, you're not, I'm writing, you're not" the typewriter seemed to say to her.

Eli had suggested that she come to the Vineyard, hoping that solitude would give her time to think about what she would do for her next book. But Angela couldn't think of anything she wanted to write about. She was all played out, she told herself. She had written one book; maybe that was it for her. Maybe she simply wouldn't be able to write again.

At dinner, conversation was light. Though Angela sensed

that Larry longed to talk about his day's work, he avoided any talk of writing in her presence. Angela was miserable, and she felt she was making her friends miserable, too.

One morning three days later, Angela hiked up Lighthouse Road to a clam bar where she emptied six dollar's worth of change into a pay phone.

"Heywood and Horne!" announced a faraway voice.

"Paul Jameson, please." Angela chewed her lips as she waited.

"Paul! It's Angela!"

"Angela! How's the Vineyard?"

"Paul, listen," Angela answered, "is my invitation to your house on Fire Island still open for the Fourth of July?"

"Yes, of course! You can stay as long as you like. You know Scott and I would love to have you."

"It's in the Pines, right?"

"Yup. The infamous Pines."

"Paul—I'll be there! I'll call you tonight when I get back to New York!" Angela hung up the phone and ran to the house. To pack.

The music from Cherry Grove's Ice Palace disco made even the leaves on the trees outside dance to its pounding rhythms. Let the media try to convince the straight world that disco was dying; the gay men—and women—who formed the undulating mass on the dance floor knew better.

As Angela swayed and bounced, bumping against Scott's naked sweating chest, everything inside and outside of her throbbed. Blinding lights and glistening muscled bodies flashed past her eyes as if she were on a carousel gone berserk, and the music rocked with such unrelenting fury that she was sure Grace Jones was standing on *both* sides of her screaming, "I Need a Man."

The night was at its peak, and so was the mescaline Angela had taken, intensified even more by the amyl nitrate Scott had just passed under her nose. She hazily followed the little brown bottle as Scott passed it to Paul, who was wildly dancing beside them. She watched as Paul and his dark-bearded dance partner dreamily inhaled. The powerful amyl rushed through their bodies, luring them into a writhing embrace.

Was this all real? The erotic spectacle wavered in and out of focus as Angela whirled and the lights flashed off and on. Whether it was real or not didn't matter; the atmosphere was charged with sex, and Angela was willing to succumb. For two months, Angela had abandoned herself to the totally sybaritic, hedonistic Fire Island summer scene: drugs, sex, sun—and dancing every night.

"Fucking goddamn whore!" Scott's drug-charged voice rose above the crescendo of the music. Scott violently grabbed at Paul, and then a half-dozen arms were flailing in the air. But moments later, Paul and the dark-bearded stranger had drawn Scott into their embrace.

Angela was left standing alone on the dance floor for only an instant when she felt a warm breath on her ear.

"Hey, come on, dance with me."

She turned toward the soft voice and began again to move with the incessant beat. She looked up into a deeply tanned face, framed by short blond sun-bleached curls. Above an even blonder moustache and a strong straight nose, piercing blue eyes gazed into hers. Angela's eyes followed a drop of sweat as it dripped from the stranger's chin onto his gleaming hairless chest. She watched it with drugged fascination as it slid slowly down his tight washboard belly, skirted his navel, and crept through the few golden hairs that disappeared into the tight jeans with the top button suggestively open. And then she was drawn to the bulge his genitals made in the taut denim. Angela knew she wanted to explore this body with more than her eyes.

Rick had spotted Angela almost an hour before from his perch on the platform next to the deejay's booth, and had been watching her ever since. He had left his after-dinner "trick" back at his house with his housemates, who were preparing for a party. He had promised his handsome young lover of the moment that he would return with a surprise, and what could be more surprising than a woman? Now as Rick watched Angela dance, he knew he'd made the right choice.

Rick pulled a small aerosol can from his pocket and the red bandana from around his neck.

"Ethyl?" he asked Angela as he sprayed some of the contents of the can onto one end of the bandana.

"N-n-no," Angela huskily replied, her throat dry from drugs.

He gave a lazy laugh. "Oh. Hey, now I know who you are. I

saw you on TV. I even read your book. It was hot. Really. Here. Try this. Just inhale." And he laughed again as he thrust the end of the bandana soaked in ethyl chloride into her mouth.

Angela breathed in deeply, and she watched as he sprayed the other end of the cloth and stuck it in his own mouth. They danced languidly for a few moments, connected only by the bandana. Then she felt her entire body going numb, and she fell toward the floor. Strong arms caught her and pulled her up.

"Hey, I'm sorry. You okay? I guess I overdid it. I'm really sorry. Hey. C'mon. Let's go get some air."

With their arms wrapped tightly around one another, Angela and Rick slowly weaved their way down Atlantic Walk. Five seemingly eternal minutes later, they were in Rick's pleasantly cool bedroom. After silently noting that his trick was still asleep under a sheet in the darkened room, Rick gently pulled Angela again into his arms. He pushed his strong hands up under the back of her T-shirt, and Angela thrilled to the hardness of his crotch pressing into hers. The mescaline she had consumed hours ago was only beginning to wear off, and all sensation was blended in lavish delight. As Rick lay her down on the edge of the bed, all feeling seemed to be advancing between her legs with the persistence of flames lapping at tinder.

Angela reached across the bed to waken Rick's sleeping friend.

"Hey . . . what . . . Rick?" The sleepy voice reported in Angela's ear like gunshots. Her senses froze, icy and alert. With a gasp and a cry, she bolted and ran as the young man sat up in bed.

"Hey! What's with her?" Rick asked.

"That was my sister," said Jimmy.

CHAPTER
──18──

ELI stepped back aross the plum-colored carpet and surveyed the room with pride. A large, glass-topped teak desk stood in the corner near the double windows and a smaller one near the door for her newly hired assistant. Three sleek file cabinets stood against the wall in a row, waiting to be filled.

Eli was glad she and Larry had cut the summer a few days short. They had evaded the maddening Labor Day weekend on the Vineyard, and Eli was able to ready her home office while Larry began rewriting his finished first draft. The telephone rang, and Eli picked it up on the second ring.

"Eli, it's Paul. Do you know where Angela is? Her things are gone from the house, but she didn't leave a note or tell us she was going. She is supposed to ride back to the city with us today. I've called her at home, but there's—"

"Paul, slow down! It's not even noon! Angela probably just decided to leave early. You know how unpredictable she's been since she came back from her tour. I'm sure she's fine. Give me a call tonight when you get back, okay?"

When Paul called again that evening, Eli still had not heard from Angela, nor did she answer her phone. Minutes later, Eli and Larry were at Angela's apartment building, where the doorman told them he had not seen Angela all day. Eli shot Larry a frantic glance, and they took a cab across town to Jimmy's apartment. They found Jimmy sitting dejectedly on his stoop when they pulled up.

"Eli!" he blurted. "Thank God you're here. I just tried to call you."

"My God! Something's happened to Angela."

"No, Eli. Nothing's happened to her," Jimmy said quickly.

"No physical harm, anyway. I saw her early this morning on Fire Island and she was okay." Jimmy turned to Larry. "Can we all go for a walk or a cup of coffee or something? I've got to tell you what happened."

Eli and Larry returned home after midnight. Eli was not shocked by Jimmy's revelation. She had guessed that he was gay years before. Her concern was about Angela. Exhausted and worried, Eli went to bed. She was awakened from a fitful and light sleep by the jarring ring of the phone. Hoarsely calling Angela's name before the caller even had a chance to identify herself, Eli held the receiver tightly and listened:

"Eli! I'm in London. I'll be brief. I'm not stopping here; I'm on my way to Dublin. I'm fine, but I had to get away. Please don't worry. I'll write you from Ireland just as soon as I'm settled in."

From the window in her room in the stately, red-brick Shelbourne Hotel, Angela gazed down on St. Stephen's Green. Angela didn't know why she had chosen the Shelbourne. Maybe it was because she had once read that Thackeray stayed there almost 150 years ago and found the hotel to be "magnificently conducted." Or maybe she remembered reading about the Green below her and hoped it would bring her the little bit of peace that Gramercy Park brought her at home.

Angela didn't even know what had made her come to Ireland. Or how she had gotten herself here or why. All she could remember was running, running, running. First she had fled from the house in Cherry Grove, racing along the beach, shoeless, back to Paul and Scott's house in the Pines to collect her things. Then she had boarded the seaplane that returned her to Manhattan. She wanted nothing more than to get away from Fire Island, where her decadence had ripened and then rotted.

Angela knew that thoughts of her mother had forced her weary brain into frantic activity as she had flown back in the seaplane. What would Marie Dugan Vaccaro think of her two precious children now? Her Angela and her Jimmy had realized the dreams she had had for them, but something had gone wrong. Angela couldn't pinpoint the exact moment when the dream had become a nightmare. She didn't know how or why what happened had happened. She only knew that she needed time—and space—to think. She had to find the Angela her mother had known so long ago.

And what about Jimmy? Had she lost him too? She shuddered when she realized her relationship with him might be irrevocably damaged. She wasn't horrified by the revelation that Jimmy was gay. What disturbed her was that he never had discussed his homosexuality with her. Was that her fault? Had she been too self-absorbed to be approachable? She was angry with herself for having let their relationship disintegrate. She and Jimmy had always shared their secrets, even as small children.

The sun had left the sky, and the park below was a quickly darkening spot of green. Angela caught her own reflection in the window and was startled. "All right," she reprimanded the gloomy image before her, "enough! Get up and get out!" She turned toward the luggage rack where her one suitcase lay still unopened. A small smile turned the corners of her mouth up as she opened the case and saw that she had had the presence of mind to pack a few sweaters. She grabbed a denim skirt, a blouse, and a bright Kelly-green Shetland and dug down to pull out her brown leather boots.

After she hastily showered and dressed, Angela went to the mirror to adjust the high ruffled collar of the white cotton blouse under her sweater. The reflection she saw was a far brighter one than the one she had seen in the window only a few minutes before. Realization that she was ravenously hungry—she hadn't eaten in more than twenty-four hours—she grabbed her bag and the guidebook she had bought at the airport and went directly to the lobby. She had no trouble finding the Saddle Room, which the guidebook recommended for its excellent roast beef.

After a dinner of rare prime ribs, steamed new potatoes, coarse brown bread, and a big dish of chocolate ice cream, Angela lingered over her coffee, laced with just a bit of Irish whiskey, reading her guidebook. She noted that the Shelbourne's Horseshoe Bar was also highly recommended as a convivial meeting place. Well, Angela thought as she tossed her American Express card onto the bill, where else do you go after putting on the feedbag at the Saddle Room but to the Horseshoe Bar? She laughed at her own silliness, and then promised herself that she would have only one drink—to toast herself and a new beginning.

Angela hadn't been sitting in the Horseshoe Bar for more than ten minutes when she heard a voice say, "Hello there!" She looked up into a pair of hazel eyes, twinkling from a bearded face.

"Hey, now. You're not mad at me, are you?" the voice spoke again before Angela realized this was actually someone she knew.

The voice and face belonged to Mike Brennan, the columnist for the *New York Daily Sun* who had interviewed Angela in New York when *Blue Grotto* was published. Mike's columns covered a wide range of subjects in a gritty, down-to-earth style. On Monday he would champion the working man, the blue collar worker who lives in one of the "bedroom boroughs" or one of the working-class neighborhoods of Manhattan; and on Wednesday Mike would incisively assess a political crisis or trash the latest "instant celebrity," although Mike himself was something of a celebrity. His name popped up frequently in Liz Smith's column in the *Daily News* and on Page Six of the *Post*, linked with those of some of Manhattan's most celebrated and glamorous women.

A successful novelist as well—his two novels, one about the life of a city cop, the other about corruption in prize-fighting, had hit the best-seller lists—Mike kept a keen eye on the publishing world. Looking into his eyes, Angela remembered Mike Brennan all right. And she also remembered the shock and anger she'd felt when she'd read the result of his interview with her. Now Angela didn't know how to react to this man smiling down at her. She should still be angry, but a familiar face was a familiar face.

"No, I suppose I'm not angry. If you can stoop to conversing with the 'overprivileged widow,' I can at least be cordial. Have a seat."

Mike settled into the banquette. "Now don't hold that against me. I did feel that the quality of your writing showed that you've got some good books to come. I just think you took the easy way out on the first one, that's all. If I insulted you, I apologize. Really. Friends?" He smiled broadly and, Angela thought, irresistibly.

She reached across the table to shake his outstretched hand and smiled back at him. "Okay. Friends."

"Good. So what brings you to Ireland, Angela? Research for a new book?"

"Well, no. Not really. Just a change of scene, I guess. I haven't started another book yet. I just can't seem to find an idea or the inspiration."

"Then why *not* use Ireland? God knows there's enough here to write about to fill more than one library."

"I don't know. Maybe. I just have to do some thinking first." Angela looked down into her glass, half-filled with amber Irish whiskey. Her spirits sank, if only a little, for the first time since she'd left her room.

Mike Brennan silently sipped his beer. Watching her now, he remembered how astonished he had been when he had first met her. He had read her book before the interview and was captivated more by the author's photograph on the back of the dust jacket than by the book itself. No one can really look like this, he had thought.

Then Mike had met her. She had walked into "21" as if it were the winner's circle and she the winner. When she thrust out her hand and confidently introduced herself, Mike couldn't help seeing that, beautiful as Angela looked in black and white, she was unbelievable in full, living color.

"And what about you, Mike?"

Mike suddenly realized that Angela's green eyes had caught his stare.

"What are you doing here?" she continued. "Covering a story?"

"Just finished, actually. I've been up in Belfast working on a series called 'The Children of Violence.' I'm flying back to New York in the morning. How about taking me out for a bon voyage drink? To a real pub. I know this is supposed to be one of the best hotel bars in the world, but it's still like an American cocktail lounge. We might as well be in the Oak Room at the Plaza in New York. Come on, what do you say?"

"Uh, no, thanks. I'm kind of tired. Jet lag and all. Maybe sometime back in New York."

"C'mon, just one round. We'll go to McDaid's. You'll like it. It's Brendan Behan's old hangout. Come on." Mike tossed some bills on the table and got up and took Angela's arm.

Lights twinkled at them through the silvery mist that had
settled on St. Stephen's Green, and Angela inhaled the sweet
moist air.

"It is beautiful here. Really lush," she murmured contentedly, hugging her arms around her against the evening chill.

"Ah, but this isn't Ireland, this is Dublin. If it's the beauty of
Ireland you want to see, you've got to go out into the
countryside. See the greens of the grass and the grays of the
stone, the—" Mike stopped himself and laughed. "Hey, I'm
not trying to sound like a travel brochure, but this country does
inspire me."

"Well, I guess I came to the right place," Angela said
quietly as they turned onto Grafton Street. "I'm desperate for
some inspiration at the moment." Angela's candidness surprised her, and she said no more. Mike did not question her,
and they walked through the crooked streets without another
word.

"Here we are." Mike broke the silence as they turned into
the one-block length of Harry Street. He pointed to the ornate
facade of McDaid's and led Angela to the door. Once inside,
Mike shepherded her past the bar to one of the cozy snugs
toward the back.

The interior of the room was hazy with smoke, and the
regulars stood around the old oak bar or in clumps in the back.
Laughter rose above the warm, thick brogues. Angela expected
at any second to hear a director shout "Cut!" and see the magic
disappear.

"Here's to a new old friend," proclaimed Mike, lifting one
of the foamy dark pints of Guinness that had just been plunked
onto the table, "and maybe her new book!"

Angela raised her mug to return his toast. "You really do
think my book is here somewhere, don't you, Mike? But you
don't know me. How I think, how I feel."

"Ah, but you're wrong there, Angela. I read *Blue Grotto*,
remember? Between the lines I could see a lot."

"I wish you'd said that in your column. But I do want to do
something with more depth this time. I want to force myself
into facing a bigger challenge. Not because you said so or
because of anyone else, I want to do it for *me*. I'm not saying
there's anything wrong with *Blue Grotto*, and I'm not going to
defend it. When I wrote it, it was the book I had to write, for

many reasons. I was just getting my feet wet as a writer and . . . well, there were other reasons, too."

"There you go. Now you understand what I'm trying to say. In *Blue Grotto* there are hints of greater things to come."

"You still haven't answered my question, Mike. Why is my book here? Angela Vaccaro's next blockbuster can hardly be the story of fighting in the streets of Ulster. I can't just do an about-face and write a book that's *completely* different."

Mike laughed. "I'm not saying that, Angela. Not at all. I know you've got an audience who will expect certain things from your new book, and I'm sure that many of your readers would be perfectly content to have *Blue Grotto Two*. What I'm saying is that you can tell a romantic story, but it can be played out against the very real drama being enacted here. Get out of Dublin. Go up to Ulster, to Belfast and Derry. Get into the towns and see it for yourself: Protestant fighting against Catholic, children learning to kill and maim before they can read or write. You have the power to make your readers understand what these people have been struggling against for generations, but first you've got to understand it yourself."

Angela's mind began to race, and the conversation became spirited. Her physical exhaustion seemed to slip away, and she didn't notice the passing of time as one drink became two and two became three. Kindled by Mike, the small flame of an idea flickered in Angela's mind. She felt *good* for the first time in two days, and better than she had felt in months.

It was eleven o'clock, and the barman sounded "Time!" As they walked outside, Angela shuddered with excitement and from the cool night air. Mike threw an arm over her shoulders, and they made their way back to the Shelbourne.

Twenty minutes later, Angela lay in bed. Alone. Mike had walked her back to her room and said good night with a peck on her cheek. Even though she had resolved to swear off casual sex and had made up her mind to turn him down when he made his move, she was somehow disappointed.

Pushing Mike Brennan out of her mind, Angela began thinking about her ideas for her new book. Even though her mind was furiously activated, Angela finally forced herself to get some sleep. She had a lot to do in the morning to prepare for her trip to Belfast.

* * *

Angela arrived at the Connolly Street station just in time to catch the 2:30 train. Supplied with notebooks, pencils, and a small portable tape recorder, along with the morning's editions of the *Irish Times*, the *Irish Independent*, and the *Irish Press* to read on the train, Angela ran to catch the consistently punctual Enterprise. She glanced briefly up through the glass roof of the station to see the yellow ball of the sun beaming down from a pure blue sky. She anticipated the lush greenness she was about to discover, a greenness seemingly created from that vivid yellow and blue.

When Angela got off the train in Belfast after a two-and-a-half-hour ride, all she saw was brown. The buildings, the streets, even the sky was murky and sooty. The only bright glints of color came from the red, white, and blue of the Union Jack flying above the station. Angela quickly scrambled into one of the high Austin taxicabs that stood in a line across the street from the station, and asked to be taken to the International Hotel.

Angela spent three weeks in Belfast visiting the Catholic ghettoes, where vigilantes guarded the street corners and families of six and seven lived in shabby two-room row houses that were little more than shacks. She talked to the people—to the men who couldn't get work because they were Catholic "scum," to the women who weren't able to feed their hungry children, to the people who struggled for a life *before* death.

She went into the saloons, dark windowless huts with dirt floors and bottles of ale stacked in corners, and listened to the fiery discussions. Angela was quick to see that the sectarianism dividing the lower classes was the weapon of the rich and powerful. As long as the working-class Protestants—"Prods" —and Catholics were fighting each other, they could never join together to fight their true oppressors.

Then Angela ventured out of Belfast into the heartland of Ulster, where she heard stories that developed into a dismal pattern. She went northwest through Antrim to Derry, where in a bar she was introduced to a man named Dugan. Maybe he was even her kinsman, but she would never be able to know. The orphaned Marie Dugan Vaccaro had never known enough of her parentage to pass on to her children.

Johnny Dugan took Angela to his home in the Bogside, the Catholic-claimed "free" Derry, to meet his family: his wife

Moira and his sons Sean, Martin, and Liam. The grim wife and the two older boys barely acknowledged the odd-looking tall American woman dressed in blue jeans and a fisherman-knit sweater, her hair piled atop her head under a Donegal-tweed cap. But eight-year-old Liam came running over to Angela.

"So ye're an American? Did ye know President Kennedy?" he asked, his bright green eyes shining.

Angela bent down and ruffled his thick, dirty curls. She looked into his hollow, colorless face, wishing she could do something for him—and all the hundreds like him. "No," she said smiling, "I'm afraid I didn't."

The next day, Angela explored the Bogside from the Free Derry Corner past the Brandywell and up into Creggan. What she saw and heard was the same as what she had experienced throughout her travels: unpaved streets were littered with filth and shattered pieces of glass; children's wails came through the thin walls of the tiny ramshackle houses; gray, glum people plodded along with their heads down.

After a dismal sunset, as Angela was heading back to her hotel, she decided to stop at the pub where she had met Johnny Dugan to have a drink and more talk. Johnny and the barman who had introduced him to Angela welcomed her as she ordered a pint for herself and then one for Johnny. Angela turned on her tape recorder and was questioning Johnny about the riots of '69 that had given the Bogside its name, when Moira Dugan burst into the room.

"Johnny! It's Liam!" she shouted. "The soldiers, they've taken him! And there's fightin' broke out!"

A roar of rough voices erupted as Martin Dugan came running in behind his mother. "We was walkin' from the school," he cried breathlessly above the rumble of noise, "and some Prods on the other side of the street was shoutin' at us. Liam picked up a rock and tossed it at 'em."

Johnny Dugan had not heard his son's explanation. He was out on the street with his wife, followed by the men from the saloon.

Angela jumped up and ran with the angry crowd. Racing along, Angela tried to imagine the sweet-faced boy she had met the night before throwing a rock at anyone.

Three blocks from the pub the crowd swung around the corner where a mob of boys hurled pieces of broken pavement at a solid row of British soldiers that stretched across the street. The soldiers, protected by helmets and shields, were pushing the boys back with their clubs. The men from the bar picked up broken bottles, and they too rushed the soldiers. Angela pushed her way closer and saw Johnny Dugan fling a chunk of cement that landed squarely against a soldier's chest. The soldier fell, his helmet flying. His comrades continued to advance against the mob. There were now almost three hundred men, women, boys, and girls trying to push the soldiers back. A homemade petrol bomb blazed across the dark sky and crashed onto the street in a burst of flames. A soldier's club swung out and hit a young girl. She fell, and her mother shrieked and slashed jagged glass across the soldier's face. A shot rang out, then another.

Angela thought she saw two headlights beaming down a dark deserted road. She screamed.

BELFAST, September 28—Thirty-two terrorists, armed with broken bottles, stones, and homemade bombs, were arrested last night in the Bogside section of Derry, following a riot agitated by one of their group. Among those arrested was American writer Angela Vaccaro.

"Damn!" Mike Brennan flung his copy of the *Daily Sun* across his desk in the city room. "Why in hell didn't someone tell me about this when it came in over the wire?" he demanded to no one in particular.

"What are you talking about, Mike? What story is that?" a fellow reporter asked.

"Oh, nothing. Never mind," Mike muttered as he sat down again. "I'm just the one who sent her there, that's all."

The other reporter gave him a questioning look, but Mike had already retrieved the newspaper. His eyes flicked down the page until he found the news he hoped would be there.

. . . Miss Vaccaro was released this morning after the intervention of the United States Embassy in London. She could not be reached for comment, but according to her New York literary agent, Elizabeth Walsh, Miss Vaccaro is in Ireland for the purpose of researching material for a new book. . . .

Angela finally allowed herself to be convinced by Eli to come home for Christmas, although she would have liked to stay in Ireland longer. She wanted to be absolutely sure that she had all she needed to write a credible, serious novel. *Blue Grotto* had brought her commercial and popular success. This new book had to prove to Angela that she was a truly talented writer. This book had to bring her *critical acclaim*.

By the time Angela booked her trip back to New York, the only flight available was on Christmas Eve itself, and even then she had to do some fast talking to secure the last seat. The plane departed a half hour late, but midway across the Atlantic the Aer Lingus pilot announced they had gained airtime, and he hoped to be able to arrive on schedule at Kennedy Airport.

Angela didn't touch the lunch served by the flight attendant. She frequently balked at airline food—even in first class—but this time it was due more to anxiety than the food's lack of appeal. Angela felt good about going home. She was pleased with her work in Ireland and her renewed dedication, and she was eager to see Eli and Larry. But Angela felt anxious about being reunited with her brother.

Angela's thoughts were interrupted by the captain's announcement: "We are still holding over Kennedy, waiting for clearance to land from the control tower. I apologize for the continued delay." Angela glanced at her Rolex and noted that the plane must have been in a holding pattern for some time. It was already almost an hour behind schedule.

Two hours later, Angela was at Eli and Larry's door. She dropped her luggage and rang the bell. The second the door opened, she began rattling out her explanation for her lateness. "Of course we landed late, and then my luggage was last to come off the plane, then I couldn't get a cab—I had to share one with four other people, for God's sake—and then traffic was so jammed that—"

Over Eli's shoulder, Angela saw Jimmy, smiling his irresistible, dimpled smile at her.

"Hi, Ange," he said. "Merry Christmas." And they plunged into each other's arms.

CHAPTER
19

THE MANUSCRIPT lay on Mark's desk. He leaned back in his chair and stared at it as though expecting it to speak. If it could, Mark would ask it about its future, which seemed most uncertain at the moment. Months ago, Mark had read the outline for a book called *Emerald Isle*. Everett Horn himself had allowed Mark to offer Eli Walsh a five-hundred-thousand-dollar advance for the property without so much as glancing at the painstakingly prepared pages.

"Go ahead," the Old Man said. "That gal Angela has got what they want. We'll make it back in the paperback sale before the first copy is sold."

But now Mark had read the manuscript, and he was worried. Very worried. The truth was that he had only skimmed the outline. When he saw that the plot involved a love affair between an Irish Catholic girl and the British soldier who was later to kill her brother, he thought: Fine. Romance, adventure, danger, passion. The makings of a potboiler. An Angela Vaccaro potboiler. But that was before the manuscript arrived yesterday, and before he had spent the entire night reading it with a mixture of fear and awe such as he had never felt in reading any manuscript before.

It was good. It was better than good, it was great. But would it sell? It had all the ingredients for success: a well-thought out and unique plot, flashes of brilliant description, and swift pacing. But it was literate. More literate, deeper, better written than any potboiler had the right to be. It established Angela, in Mark's view, as a literary novelist. And that made for an "iffy" situation. Potboilers he could push. He knew how to edit them.

Mitch Schaeffer knew how to market them. But *Emerald Isle* was contemporary literature, and that didn't always sell.

Mark leaned forward and rested his elbows on the desk. He massaged his temples as though the pressure at each side of his head would help him compose his thoughts. He needed to be very clear about his intentions.

Okay. This is an undisputably well-written book. It's a major work of fiction, he thought, but it puts my ass on the line. We've paid half a million dollars for it, and we have no guarantees it will sell as well as *Blue Grotto*. The paperback people will take a "wait-and-see" attitude. They won't put up another million just like that. This is 1981. The days of the super auctions are over. We could take a bath unless . . . Mark scribbled some notes on a piece of paper. He needed to get to the potboiler readers and assure them that Angela had delivered the romance and action they crave. That part was easy. Advertising, publicity, and promotion aimed at that audience was a Mitch Schaeffer specialty. But he had to reach contemporary literature readers as well and let them know that Angela Vaccaro had served up a dish that they too could savor. If that market could be made to take notice—then anything could happen. Angela might win the American Book Award, maybe even the Pulitzer. And he, Mark Green, would be known throughout the industry as the man who discovered and nurtured that talent.

There was only one answer: reviews. It was the reviews that got the serious book-buyer motivated. And the prime review to get was the front page of the *New York Tribune Book Review*. With a laudatory review on page one, Mark's new literary reputation would be made, the book would have a chance in both markets, the paperback people would be burning up the telephone wires, and Angela would . . .

At the thought of the flesh-and-blood woman, Mark sighed. When they had dinner at Vanessa's just last week, she told him how lonely she was. She had shut herself away in her writing room for almost a year and a half since her return from Ireland. He had seen her only a few times during that period. She claimed that she saw only him, her brother, and her friends Eli and Larry. The only public event she attended was Eli's wedding to Larry Gould. There was the mini-tour to five cities she went on for Delano's paperback promotion of *Blue Grotto*, but that took only two weeks.

She had certainly changed since she had gotten back from Ireland. She was calmer, more centered, more down-to-earth. But with him, she was more distant than ever. Such a strange affair. It simply did not fit the pattern. By now, Angela should have begun to nag Mark to leave Barbara. The nagging should have then led to the showdown. She should have given him an ultimatum and set some ridiculous time limit. Then she should have tearfully left him—free to make new conquests after she had rightly divined that he had no plans to leave Barbara. But Angela simply refused to fit the mold. She never mentioned Barbara. She never asked him to promise not to sleep with his wife. Angela never asked him anything. As long as Angela was content with the status quo, there would never be the big blow-up or the expected denouement.

And here was the worst of it: Mark *wanted* Angela to beg him to leave his wife. He wanted so achingly for Angela to want him. Angela was never going to fulfill him. He knew that. Perhaps her manuscript would.

He straightened his tie and stood up. Lifting his chin purposefully, he strode down the hall and into Mitch Schaeffer's office.

"Mitch," he announced, "I'd like a few minutes of your time. It's important. And I think Madeline should be in on this, too."

Mitch's assistant, Sharon, discreetly retreated from the office, taking a folder of correspondence with her.

"I'll tell Madeline you need her," Sharon said as she left.

Within moments Madeline and Mark were seated across from Mitch, who lounged comfortably behind his desk. Mitch liked the set-up. Mark was coming to him, facing him across the long, wide expanse of furniture that separated them and displayed Mitch's power. From behind his desk, he had control of the impromptu meeting.

"What's on your mind, Mark?"

"*Emerald Isle*. Eli Walsh's office delivered it yesterday, and I stayed up all last night reading it. It's a winner."

"I never doubted that Angela—" Mitch interrupted.

"Let me finish," said Mark. "It's not a potboiler. It's a very serious book. It has a lot of important things to say about

Ireland, about human nature, about hate, about love. . . . It's written wonderfully. It's a mature book. It should break out of the genre. It's a book for men *and* women. It's for people who want to read a great love story. It's for people who want to—"

"All right, all right, I'll read it. Have Lyndley shoot me over a copy of the manuscript," Mitch said, holding his hand up like a stop sign.

"That's not the bloody point. Of course you'll read it," Mark said crisply. "I want to impress upon you that this isn't another book that you simply apply a marketing formula to. I want this sold differently. I want this to get very special attention. That's why I wanted Madeline in here.

"Madeline," he continued, "I want you to exert all your influence. I want you to push hard for major review attention. I want you to get the intellectual media high on this book. I want you to launch a campaign. Write a special release. This book should get attention from everyone interested in Ireland—everyone interested in peace, for God's sake. Politicians. There must be a million Irish politicians in this country. Get Teddy Kennedy to give us a quote. Get a letter off to Jimmy Breslin. Send a review copy to the Pope. All the big clergy. And most of all, Madeline, *I want the front page of the* Tribune Book Review. That's absolutely the key. I want you to use every ounce of influence you have ever had with the paper and *get that review*!"

Mitch Schaeffer chuckled as Madeline made frantic notes.

"You're crazy, Mark. Ted Kennedy doesn't give a shit about a novel by Angela Vaccaro. You're wasting your time. Jesus! The Pope! Are you out of your mind? And what makes you think the *Trib* is going to give you the front page? I say we take out the *Blue Grotto* file and go the same route. You don't argue with success. Right?"

"Mitch, you haven't heard a bloody word I've said," Mark said.

"What do you think, Madeline?" Mitch asked.

"We've already got quite a bit of prepublication publicity on this book," Madeline began, directing her remarks to neither Mark nor Mitch. She had decided to present the evidence disinterestedly and let the two men fight it out. "We've got all the clippings from the UPI story about Angela's arrest in Derry. The *Trib* carried it, the *Times*, the *Sun*. It was carried all over the country, and Europe picked it up pretty heavily too. Then there was that little press conference we set up when she got back. And don't forget what the press picked up when she was touring for the *Blue Grotto* paperback. They all asked her about her arrest, and she talked a lot about Ireland. So the pumps are primed. And I got a call yesterday from 'Issues and Answers' on Channel Four. They're putting together a panel to discuss the problems in Northern Ireland. They want Angela on the show."

"Marvelous!" said Mark. "Let's book her."

"I don't know," Mitch said. "That's a very controversial thing. I mean, she's a fiction writer, she's got a big audience."

"And it's gotten bigger since the paperback," Mark added.

"Yeah, well, why rock the boat?" Mitch finished.

Mark turned to Madeline, his expression demanding an answer.

"It's publicity, Mitch. I don't think we should turn it down," Madeline said gently.

"Do you think you can get the *Trib Book Review* to go for a page one?" Mark asked, pressing what he saw as his advantage.

Madeline turned to Mitch.

"Go ahead," Mitch said. "Give it a try. I don't think you'll get very far." Madeline and Mark rose to leave.

Mitch called after them, "Hey, Mark! Before you place that call to the Vatican, you think you can let me know when you'll have a manuscript from Jessica? *Lovers and Losers* is a great title, but that's not enough for catalog copy!"

"I'll let you know as soon as I have something," Mark answered.

Damn him, Mark thought. He's always got to have the last word. He's always got to score his points. It was a sore spot with Mark that he had not been able to wrest the new Jessica Simon manuscript out of the author's hands yet. It was late. And getting later.

Before he went back to his desk, Mark poked his head into Madeline's office. The harried publicity director hadn't gotten to her chair yet, but she was already reaching for the phone.

"Please, Madeline, work on the *Trib*. It's the key," Mark said.

Madeline nodded, then closed the door after Mark. She raced back to her desk and placed her call to Dallas.

"Jessica? It's me."

"Well?"

"Angela's manuscript is in."

"Good. Send it out here."

"Well, I don't have it in my hands yet—"

"Then why are you wasting my time?"

"I just thought you should know. Mark thinks it's something, well, special. You know—literary. He wants a big review campaign. Copies out to important people—politicians, clergy, serious writers, statesmen. A totally different thing from *Blue Grotto*."

"Why didn't that slut rot in that Irish jail? Leave it to that scheming bitch to get caught in a filthy brawl and come up smelling like a rose. Now this! I'm fed up!"

"Calm down, Jessica, please," Madeline said. "There's nothing we can do about it. Angela is going to be taken very seriously if Mark is right. Look at it this way: if she gets page one of the *Trib Book Review*, she'll move to a different category, she won't be competing—"

"Page one of the *Trib Book Review*! Over my dead body!" Jessica screeched, her cello voice sounding now like an untuned violin. "I'll put a stop to her literary pretensions. I won't have it! Do you hear me, Madeline? I won't have it!"

"But my job, Jessica," Madeline tried to reason. "I've got to do my job. There's nothing I can do for you."

"Don't worry. As long as I'm Jessica Simon, you'll have a job. So you can stop whining right now. I intend to take care of this myself!"

"But how, Jessica?" Madeline began to ask when she realized that the connection had been severed.

Angela emerged from the dressing room. She would be "on" in ten minutes. She pulled a stray thread off the front of her khaki-colored silk and cotton knit top, and as she dashed to the green room to compose herself, she heard a masculine voice call her name.

Angela looked up, and her heart gave an unexpected little lurch. Michael Brennan! Of course! He was an obvious choice for a panel on the Irish "troubles."

"Mike! Nice to see you," Angela cried. And she meant it. How was it that she never noticed how good looking he was before?

Mike was not tall, but he was well built. He wore his thick, light brown hair carelessly pushed away from his high, clear forehead. His extraordinarily sharp hazel eyes were accentuated by expressive brows. His nose was long, highly arched, and hawklike, his lips full and turned up at the corners. His features were, in all, pleasingly arranged, sharply defined, and set off handsomely by a full, well-trimmed brown beard streaked with light highlights. The last vestige of a summer tan made his light eyes brighter by contrast. He gave Angela a full, unself-conscious smile, which deepened the creases around his eyes.

In a spontaneous motion, he hugged Angela, pulling her close to his chest, where she felt the soft cotton of his shirt and the roughness of his sports jacket.

"My God!" Mike said. "Not since Dublin, Angela! How's the book?"

Blushing and pleased, Angela slipped from his embrace. "It's done, Mike. It's all finished, and I never thanked you."

"Thanked me?"

"For inspiring me. For setting me straight. For being there. For a lot of things."

Mike put his arm around Angela's shoulders and walked with her down the narrow corridor to the green room.

"So tell me about this book of yours," he said, staring at her intently. When Michael Brennan's clear eyes fixed on a subject, they were relentless. His ability to concentrate made people uncomfortable at times but helped him to be the great reporter he was reputed to be. He never missed a detail, he was never less than totally absorbed. When he was after a story, he looked like a bird of prey stalking its quarry with swift, perfectly targeted moves.

Angela bridled under the demand in his question, but encouraged by the friendship implied by his arm around her shoulder, she began to tell Mike about *Emerald Isle*.

He listened to her carefully and questioned her in a direct, informed way that made her feel as though she were being interviewed, but the sensation was not unpleasant. His interest

in her work was so obviously sincere that she felt flattered and
pleased.

All too soon they were on the air and answering the
questions put to them by the host of "Issues and Answers."
Angela found it difficult to concentrate on the panel discussion.
She was still tingling from the touch of Mike's arm on her
shoulders. Her heart was pounding from the way he looked at
her, from the way he encouraged her to talk about her book.

After thirty tedious minutes, it was over. Mike walked
briskly back to the green room, while Angela struggled to push
back her chair, which was stubbornly imbedded in thick carpet.
She wanted desperately to catch Mike before he left. She might
never run into him again. All of a sudden, that seemed almost
tragic. She finally extricated herself and nearly ran into him as
he was leaving the green room, a briefcase tucked under his
arm.

"Mike!" she said breathlessly. "I, uh, wanted to say
. . . to say, uh, to say good-bye."

Mike laughed while Angela blushed and cursed herself for
being so transparent.

"Miss Vaccaro, I had no intention of leaving without saying
good-bye to you. Rest assured. I'd like to get hold of that
manuscript of yours. Could I read it?"

"Oh, I'd love you to! I just gave it to my publishers a few
weeks ago, and I'm working on revisions, but I would love to
hear what you have to say about it."

"Well, I warn you, I'm ruthless when it comes to my
friends' writing. I always say just what I think."

"I'm hoping you will," Angela said. "Look, I could send a
copy over tonight, if you like. . . ."

"Sure, great. I'm at Seven Thirty-four Eleventh Avenue."

"Okay. Well, if you're sure you'll be there, I'll messenger it
over as soon as I get home."

Mike smiled. "That's a deal. So long, Angela."

Angela left the broadcasting studio feeling elated. It's good
for *Emerald Isle*, she told herself. That's why I'm so excited. If
Mike Brennan does a big story on it in his syndicated column,
it'll be terrific for the book. Angela called Eli as soon as she
got home and asked her to send a copy of *Emerald Isle* to Mike
Brennan. At seven the next morning, the phone awakened her.

"Angela! I've just finished *Emerald Isle*. Can we talk?" Mike's voice was wide awake but breathless.

"About my favorite subject?" asked Angela, suddenly wide awake herself. "Of course."

"Good. I'm on my way!"

Angela pulled herself out of bed. On his way? Even if he was coming from his apartment, it wouldn't take him long, maybe fifteen minutes by cab. Angela washed quickly and pulled on jeans and a T-shirt. There was nothing to eat in the apartment. She'd have to run down and get some bagels or something so she could offer Mike breakfast. She gave her hair a quick brushing, slung her bag over her shoulder, and ran to the door. When she opened it, Mike was standing there, leaning against the doorway, panting for breath.

"I ran over, in fact, I ran right past your doorman. I always run in the mornings. I called you from the corner. I hope it's okay."

Angela laughed delightedly. Yes, she decided—looking at his eyes, his hair, his beard, his sinewy arms and legs, the triangle of sweat that stained the front of his thick sweatshirt—it was okay.

Angela led Mike to the bathroom, where he refreshed himself briefly. The weather in New York was still warm, even in late September, and Mike had run a long way.

"I have nothing to offer you," Angela called from the kitchen as Mike emerged from the bathroom with a towel in his hands. "Just coffee."

"Angela, don't ever say that *you* have nothing to offer," Mike said, following her, tossing aside the towel, and grinning.

She turned and stood face to face with him. There was something palpable in the air. In a flash the attraction between them was obvious. They shared an awkward, silent moment, a moment that made Angela almost dizzy with desire, then just as swiftly self-conscious. She was standing before him, very aware now that she was braless under her T-shirt. And he was unabashedly taking all of her in. His smile was pure joy.

"Well, I'll make you that cup of coffee. And you can sit down and tell me all about *Emerald Isle* as experienced by Michael Brennan."

Mike sat down at the small kitchen table while Angela prepared the coffee. "First off, Angela," he began, "it's brilliant. It's a great book. I started reading as soon as I got the manuscript, and I stayed up all night to finish it. That's why I'm here at this ungodly hour. I had to see you—to tell you in person." He paused. "Angela," he continued, "you've got a tremendous talent. You've brought the whole experience to life here. The characters, the plot—"

"Oh, come on," Angela interrupted. "You said you were brutally frank about your friends' writing. You're just being nice now."

"Wait," Mike said. "I *am* being honest. I didn't say the book was flawless. I was coming to the flaws, but I want you to know that I admire and respect what you've done here. A lot of good writers have tackled the Irish thing, but none as well as you have. I mean that."

Angela handed Mike a steaming mug and sat down opposite him at the table. She smiled at him. "Go ahead. I can take it," she said, hoping she could. "What's wrong with the book?"

"It's the fourth chapter," Mike said, leveling his penetrating eyes on Angela's. "I think you rushed the action. Take your time. Develop the relationship between Moira and her son more. . . ."

But Angela was not listening. She was trembling under his gaze. She was unable to concentrate on his words. All she could concentrate on was Mike—sitting there, close to her, sending waves of desire through her. She shifted her position in the hard, high-backed kitchen chair, and her knee brushed his. A shock of electricity jolted her, and she pulled her legs back closer to her chair quickly. Did he feel it too?

Mike had stopped speaking. Apparently a reply was required of her. "Mmm?" she asked. "What? Oh, yes. Moira and her son. The relationship. Right. You're right."

Mike's eyes were searching her face. "Milk," he said.
"What?"

"Milk. I take milk with my coffee."

Entranced, Angela rose.

"I'll get it," Mike said, rising from his chair. Angela noticed a bulge in his gym shorts. He *had* felt the jolt.

"No, I'll do it," Angela protested and walked to the refrigerator.

Mike stopped her. He grabbed her arm. "Angela" was all he said, then his mouth was on hers.

They stood, locked in a tight embrace, while they probed each other's mouths impatiently with tongues and lips. Tighter and tighter they held each other, their bodies straining toward each other. They kissed for a long time, locked together, both consciously holding something back, warning their bodies to go one step at a time.

Mike broke the embrace. He stepped back and touched Angela's hair, then stroked her burning cheek. Roughly he embraced her again, stroking her back with one hand while he held her with the other and whispered her name hoarsely in her ear. Touch me, touch me, please, Angela thought with a fierceness. As though he could hear her, he kissed her again and moved his hands up under her T-shirt until he cupped her breasts. She drew him tighter to her.

He held her while his mouth traveled down her neck. He kissed the light fabric that covered her breasts.

"Wait," she whispered, and broke away from him. Her lips were swollen from his kisses, her face red from the heat of her pounding blood and from the rubbing of his rough beard against her face. She led him to the bedroom, and they lay down.

With sure hands, he slipped off her shirt and jeans. He took a moment to look at her breasts with their hard rosy peaks. Then he lay his head on her bosom and trailed his lips and tongue across the fullness, while Angela stroked his thick hair tenderly.

He stood up and stripped off his clothes, while Angela lay waiting. After what seemed an eternity, he was beside her. He kissed her again, with abandon now, working his tongue in her mouth, imitating motions they would soon repeat, while Angela returned his ardor with joy. He moved his head down and lovingly sucked her nipples. He moved his tongue over her belly, and then buried his fingers between her thighs. He knelt now between her legs. Looking at her searchingly, locking her eyes with his, he entered her. For a moment he did not move. He savored the tight, wet, hot feeling around him and held her to him. Then he began to slowly work his way in.

Angela relished the warm feeling of holding him within her. She let a cry escape from her lips as he began to move. She was ascending that mountain. She felt herself begin the climb to freedom, and it was awesome. Quicker now, harder now, faster now, he thrust. She heard him gasping and sighing with his lips close to her ear. Then she felt it. It seemed to spread like a fire from her womb, through her legs to her toes, her fingers, her neck, her lips, her breasts—she felt shot through with fiery good heat. She cried out and called his name.

They held each other very close for a long time after. Angela felt a fullness and contentment she had forgotten could exist.

Angela awoke first. She showered and splashed herself with her new favorite perfume, Ombre Rose. Humming to herself, she pulled on a freshly laundered Brooks Brothers shirt and began to work at her typewriter. Hours passed quickly as she remained absorbed in the fourth chapter of *Emerald Isle*.

She pushed her chair away from the desk and chewed on a pencil thoughtfully. What was the word she was looking for? Suddenly, two hands held her shoulders. She turned to look into mild, sleepy eyes.

"Mike! I hope the racket from my typewriter didn't disturb you."

"On the contrary, it's music to my ears. Let's see what you've got there."

Mike read the page in the typewriter, over Angela's shoulder, nodding and murmuring encouragingly. Then he kissed her neck tenderly. To Angela's amazement, she felt the renewal of desire. He nuzzled her shoulders and kissed her throat. He stopped when his lips made contact with the cold blue stone Angela wore around her neck.

"Jesus!" he said, lifting the sapphire for a better look. "This is enormous. Did you get this from your royalties?"

"No. It was a gift from my husband."

Mike made no reply. He scooped her up in his arms and carried her to the bedroom. Angela marveled at the strength in his arms.

They were calmer now, their bodies less insistent. With urgency gone, sensuality could thrive. Mike unbuttoned Angela's shirt slowly and deliberately, tantalizing himself by exposing her body in languid stages, arousing her by kissing her body, from the top of her head to the high insteps of her feet.

Mike repeated his exploration of her body, pausing this time to nibble the soft inside of her thigh, while Angela arched her back and sighed. Mike moved his lips closer to the furrow between her legs. She opened to him, and he licked and kissed her, drawing the pearl within the furrow gently between his lips, then releasing it, to flick it quickly and lightly with his tongue.

Angela groaned and grabbed at Mike's thick hair. She tried to stop him; she didn't want to come without giving him pleasure too. But Mike persisted, ever sensitive to her movements, their speed and intensity. Then Angela climaxed with a shudder.

Swiftly, Mike was by her side, whispering, "It is truly beautiful, Angela, so lovely. Pink and mysterious. Deep. Like the inside of a perfect conch shell."

"Well, I'll be damned," Angela said, half to herself.

She had heard that she had beautiful breasts, legs, eyes, hair, lips, ass—but this? Angela did not spend time musing, though. With a burst of energy, she explored Mike's body with her mouth until she brought him satisfaction.

They lay in each other's arms again, relaxed but wide awake. Mike stroked Angela's hair, then he suddenly began to sing. In a hearty voice, Irish-accented, he sang the song that appeared verse-for-verse in the preface to *Emerald Isle*.

"There was a wild colonial boy," he sang out, while Angela laughed and playfully punched his arm. She ended up joining in.

They sang more pub songs, sharing their love for Ireland. Then, still holding Angela in his arms, Mike sat up.

"By God, I'm hungry. Get dressed! We're going to dinner."

Angela showered and dressed, and they went to Mike's apartment in the Clinton section of Manhattan—the area popularly known as Hell's Kitchen. While Mike changed from his running clothes, Angela wandered around the large apartment, the entire top floor of a three-story brownstone tenement. It was furnished with massive dark, old furniture, and the walls of the living room were lined with books. Newspapers, magazines, and manuscripts littered the couch, the faded blue chairs, the hearth rug, and the walnut "partners" desk that was the focal point of the large room.

Mike called to Angela from the bedroom where he was pulling on a pair of jeans. "I don't feel like Elaine's tonight, do you? I mean, that's where I usually end up, but I'd rather go off the beaten track tonight. What do you say?"

"Oh, sure. I don't really care."

Off the beaten track is right, Angela thought as Mike zoomed through the Holland Tunnel in his battered 1968 Porsche.

"New Jersey! You're taking us to New Jersey to eat?" Angela asked incredulously.

"Yeah. There's this great seafood place. Hey! I hope you like seafood."

They were soon standing on line under a red awning in front of the Clam Broth House, Hoboken's famous eatery. Once they were inside, a black-and-white-uniformed waitress led them to a red vinyl booth in the corner of the large, wood-paneled, noisy dining room. They started with a pitcher of draft beer, and over a pot of steamers Angela asked Mike, "Why do you live in Hell's Kitchen?"

"It's the apartment I grew up in. When all of us kids moved away, I decided to keep it. It's big, it's comfortable, and besides, I love the old neighborhood. It's still got that community-within-the-city feel. I know the parish priests and the bartenders. I wouldn't ever think of moving. A lot of my writing is inspired by the place."

"It *is* a big apartment," Angela replied. "Is your family big?"

"Well, like all good Irish Catholics, my parents made lots more good Irish Catholics. There were five of us, and we five have made our contribution too. My sister Deirdre has eight. My mother lives in White Plains with her and helps take care of them all. Kathy has four, Megan never married, and, thank God, my brother Patrick's a priest or there'd be more Brennans than the world could stand."

"Are you the oldest?" Angela asked.

"No, I'm the wee baby mistake my mom and dad made in their passion just before my dad got called overseas. He was killed in the war in 1945, before I was born, so I'm the last. What about you? Where are your folks?"

"Well, my mother and father are dead—"

"I'm sorry—"

"Yes, well it's just me and my bother Jimmy now."

"Is he married?"

"No. He's gay."

"Really?" Mike paused. "Both your parents gone," he said

softly. "That's tough, Angela. And your husband dying that way. I admire your courage."

"Courage?" Angela said with scorn. "Courage? Is that what you think? I remember when my mother died. I was just a kid. I thought I would die too. But I didn't. Then when Paolo died, I thought for sure I'd perish—or go insane. Now my father's dead, too. And you know what? You don't die. You don't go insane. You go right on. You have breakfast. You catch a cold. You write a book. You have a beer. You just keep going. Sometimes I think it's downright obscene." Angela looked down into the foam in her glass mug. Mike reached across the table and took her hand. Angela withdrew it quickly and lifted her glass.

"I'm sorry," she said. "We're here for a good time, and I'm getting so . . . so—"

"I'm having a wonderful time being with you, Angela," Mike said, placing his hand on her once more. She replaced the mug and let him hold her hand tightly in his for a moment.

"Well, anyway, you know how it is to be a kid with one parent, don't you? Losing Paolo, though . . . I can't . . . well, I'd rather not discuss it."

"I think I understand. I never lost a spouse through death, but I went through a divorce. I can tell you that's a pretty rough experience."

"Paolo was my second husband," Angela said, surprising herself again. She hadn't mentioned her marriage to Frankie to anyone in many years.

"I didn't know that," Mike said, raising his brows. "I thought that Paolo was your first husband. What happened?"

"Oh, it was a stupid kid thing. We were too young and ill-suited, besides. We got married right out of high school. It was doomed from the start, I suppose. How about you?"

"I guess my marriage fell victim to the times we live in. After I worked my way through Fordham University, I got a scholarship to the Columbia School of Journalism. I met Susan Mayhew there. She was from this piss-elegant Midwestern family, and I guess she found my poor, rough Irish ways amusing. I'm not putting her down, mind you, we really loved each other, it's just that we were from two different worlds, as they say."

Angela leaned across the table to hear every word of Mike's

story. They barely noticed the waitress when she returned to clear away the empty clam shells and tie lobster bibs around their necks.

"Well, we got married after we graduated, and Susan's career took off like a shot. She was—is—very talented. Anyway, she was offered a job as an anchorperson for a big Chicago station."

Two bright red, steaming lobsters were placed in front of them with drawn butter and lemon wedges. Like automatons, Mike and Angela cracked shells and ate the succulent lobster between long drinks of beer.

"I was still plugging away as a cub reporter five years after we were married! But I wanted to be a writer, not a TV reporter. And I wanted to make it here, on my own turf. I wanted to write about the kind of people I grew up with, the blue-collar city dwellers. You've read my columns. You know."

"So what happened? She left you?" Angela asked.

"Well, it wasn't that cut and dried. She had been doing well all along, and she didn't view what I was doing as really important. She thought I should try to get into TV, too. She couldn't understand that I was in love with the idea of being a *newspaper* man. She didn't see any future in print media. I heard what she was saying, but I wanted to do what I wanted to do. Plus, there was always the big gap between our backgrounds."

"Mmmm," Angela broke in, "like me and Paolo."

"Yeah, well, you know how tough it is."

"Not really. I mean, it was never a problem. Paolo and I understood each other perfectly. Always," she said defensively.

Mike paused and looked at her thoughtfully. "Well, that's very extraordinary and very wonderful. You must have been a great team, the two of you. Susan and I were, I guess, immature. She tired of my 'amusing roughness,' and, quite frankly, I thought her values stank. But I've softened since then.

"In the end, though, it worked out the way it was meant to. She's doing really well in Chicago. She's remarried. She's got a beautiful little daughter, and a year after we were divorced I got my big break." Mike smiled triumphantly as he cracked a lobster claw.

"What was your big break?" Angela asked, spooning sour cream onto her baked potato.

"I got the job at the *Sun*. It was the kind of shitty job that kids out of Columbia J School would cut their arms off for. Less than another year later, I filled in for this old guy, this columnist who was very sick. Then he died, and they gave me the column."

"And the rest is history," Angela said with a flourish.

"Oh, yes! Say, Angela, you look beautiful with sour cream on your nose, do you know that? Why, I'll bet you're the only woman in New York City who really *knows* how to wear sour cream."

Angela covered her face with her napkin. She wiped the cream from the top of her nose and laughed in spite of her embarrassment.

"You know, I was really wrong about you. I've wasted a lot of time." Mike said.

Angela stared at her lobster shell.

"When I did that interview, I thought: Here's Paolo di Fiori's widow. Rich, spoiled—"

Angela spoke without looking up. "I had nothing. They gave me nothing." She said it quietly, simply, and without malice.

"I know. I heard about it later. I thought you wrote *Blue Grotto* for a lark. For attention. I never dreamed you were making your living the same way I make mine. Well, I could see that you were beautiful. But I know lots of beautiful women. I'm not bragging. It's no secret who I go out with, who I see. But Angela, you turned out to be such a wonderful surprise. You're lovely. You're more than beautiful, and your writing—well, you're someone I'd like to get to know very well."

Angela studied her plate.

"Maybe I'm coming on strong, but I feel very strongly," he said, undaunted by her silence. "This morning and this afternoon," he continued, speaking very softly, "were very special. Didn't you feel it too?"

After a few moments, Angela raised her head and smiled at Mike. "Do you think we should order dessert?"

* * *

They returned to Manhattan in silence. Mike parked the car near his apartment building and turned to Angela.

"I want you to come up to my place, Angie. Can I call you Angie? Did they call you that when you were a kid?"

Angela nodded.

"I want to show you what I've been working on. It's that big murder case. I think I have some evidence the police would be very eager to know about. I haven't discussed it with anyone yet. Also, I'd like you to see my etchings," he teased, reaching for her and kissing her.

Angela broke away from the kiss. "No, Mike. Haven't you had enough of me today? Besides, it's really late. I'd like to go home and crawl into bed."

"Crawl into my bed, Angie. Please. Stay with me tonight, Angela." He kissed her again.

"Yes, I'll stay. For a little while," she sighed.

With their arms around each other, they walked the few blocks to Mike's building and then up the three flights to his apartment. He led her into the bedroom where they stood kissing and they began to make love with the same hunger and demand they had felt early that morning.

Angela did not realize that she had fallen asleep until she woke up. Screaming. She'd had the nightmare again. It had come to her even though she was in a stranger's bed, even though she lay sleeping in a stranger's arms for the first time ever since Paolo died. It had found her and gripped her and held her until she cried out, "Paolo, no! Help! Somebody help!"

Mike awoke with a start. Then he realized that Angela was having a nightmare. He held her and rocked her as though she were a child. Still more asleep than awake, she clung to him, throwing her arms around his neck, finding a haven in his arms, her body pressed against his warm, hard chest. He kissed her hair and her wet streaming eyes. "Shhh," he crooned, "it's all right, you're not alone, Angela. I'm here, I'm with you. You're not alone."

Jessica swirled the ice in her tall glass of bourbon. She sat on the brick-paved patio behind "Belle Reine," her Highland Park home outside of Dallas. Her recently "lifted" face was swathed in sunblock, although a huge flowered patio umbrella and a floppy sunhat protected her as she sat near the table that held her telephone and her manuscript.

On nice days Jessica loved to sit on the patio where she could see the pool that she never used and where she could enjoy the sun she took pains to shield herself from. Even if she hated to swim, even if the sun made her dizzy and aged her, she would exercise her privilege.

She had just finished reading several chapters of her new book, *Lovers and Losers*. The chapters were good, in her opinion. Very good. The book was sure to be another number one best seller. Or almost sure. One should never take chances with the really important things. It was okay to gamble, but when the stakes were really high, it was always better to add a little insurance. An ace in the hole was a necessity, in this case. It wouldn't do to have Angela Vaccaro walk off with the pot.

Jessica took a long swallow from her glass. The little sprig of spearmint that Ivy had thoughtfully placed in the tumbler brushed Jessica's nose. She pulled it out between carefully manicured nails and tossed the leaves into the garden that edged the patio.

She folded her hands in her lap contentedly and thought how neat it all was. How very simple and perfect. Monty would be no trouble at all. This would be one phone call it would be a pleasure to make. Anyway, it was always lovely to talk to Monty. They spoke the same language, after all. Monty and Jessica were kindred spirits, Jessica mused, smiling to herself.

She was so glad that Montgomery West, publisher and owner of the *New York Tribune*, had presented her with a golden opportunity, just four short years ago, to show what a good friend can mean to a person in need. And Monty had been so devastatingly in need. It was at the charity ball she hosted at Simon-Lewis's main store in Dallas. It was a benefit for the World's Hungry Children. Or maybe it was for the Blind. Well, no matter. It was a wonderful ball and a rousing success. Even Arthur had a good time that night. Everyone had a bit *too* much fun, and that was the problem. Monty got tipsy. He even wandered out of Simon-Lewis and into the streets of Dallas. One street in particular. What was that little girl's name? Never mind. She was only thirteen, and poor Monty couldn't resist her. He went and got himself arrested! He couldn't ask his wife to bail him out, now could he? She would be very upset. Now, who could Monty turn to in a strange city?

Jessica was so pleased that he had thought of calling her. It was flattering, really. A declaration of special affection. Why, she fairly *ran* to the police station. Good thing—why, *lucky* it was—that Jessica had just a teensy weensy bit of influence with the county sheriff. The whole matter was simply dropped, and the sheriff was kind enough to send her a copy of the statutory rape report before it was destroyed.

Well, it anyone was ever grateful, it was Mr. Montgomery West. Why, he couldn't find words *enough* to thank his dear, good friend Jessica for getting him out of that nasty jam.

Monty was grateful, all right. And Jessica decided to find out just *how* grateful. Front page of the *Trib Book Review* to launch *Emerald Isle* indeed! Jessica would get that stopped right now!

She took another deep swallow of cool bourbon, just to moisten her throat, and lifted the receiver of her white antique French telephone.

"Monty! Monty, darling! Can you ever *guess* who this is?"

CHAPTER
20

"WE SHOULD BE telling ghost stories," Eli said even as she shivered and nestled deeper into Larry's arms.

"I should think Mike's real-life work would be providing all the gore and thrills we could ever dream of," Larry said affably, lighting his new pipe with a long match lit from an ember in the fireplace.

The foursome sat before the hearth on the floor of the house in Martha's Vineyard that Larry and Eli now owned. The autumn night wind rattled at the less than perfectly fitted doors and windows, forcing the two couples to draw closer and closer to the crackling fire, their sole source of warmth and, because they were all feeling romantic, their only source of light.

Mike squeezed Angela's arms as she sat between his legs. "I wish I were dealing with a ghost, but unfortunately our killer is very much a flesh and blood man."

"Emphasis on the blood," Eli said.

"Have you gotten any more letters in addition to the ones you published in the *Sun* last week?" asked Larry.

"Oh, yes. My 'friend' writes me every day without fail. But most of the letters are unpublishable. They are so filled with sick sexuality and bloodthirsty descriptions that if they were printed we'd have a hysterical metropolis on our hands in no time. As it is, everyone is scared silly."

"Well, it's taking the police so damned long to catch the fucker. I mean, he's roaming around killing women, and it seems like there's nothing that can be done about it," Eli said.

"What scares me," said Angela, "is the sheer randomness of it—one day it's a blonde in Manhattan, the next day a brunette's dead in Brooklyn. There's no pattern. Going out on the street now is just a crap shot. There's no reason why he won't get you or me next time," Angela remarked to Eli.

"Well, you two aren't going anywhere at night alone, that's all," said Larry. "You haven't since this thing started, and you're not going to until it's over."

"*If* it's ever over," said Eli.

"Oh, we'll get him," Mike said. "We'll definitely get him. He wants to be caught. That's why he writes to me. He wants to be stopped. These creeps always end up giving themselves away."

"Doesn't it scare you that he's writing you all the time? Why you? Do you think he could turn on you?" Eli asked.

Angela leaned forward and stirred the fire with a poker. She had heard this all before. Wherever the two of them had gone in the last few months, Mike had been questioned endlessly about the "Prince of Darkness" murders. In its fifty-year history the *Sun* had never sold as many daily copies as it had since Mike had begun running the letters he received from the killer who called himself the Prince of Darkness. Mike's name, already a household word in New York, became nationally known as the sensational murders of pretty girls, Jack-the-Ripper style in the nighttime streets of New York, stunned and titillated the country. Every news report cited Mike Brennan as the man to whom the "Prince" wrote and to whom the police turned for help with the solving of this nearly unprecedented case of uncontrolled bloodshed.

"No, I'm not afraid," Mike answered. "He's not out to get me. He considers me a friend. And as long as I'm around and print his letters in the paper, he has what he so desperately wants, what has driven him on this murder spree—the public's attention. Have you noticed that since I've started running something every day, there hasn't been a murder? I don't think he's stopped for good, but the attention he's getting from the news media has apparently sated a part of his hunger. And of course we're selling papers like hotcakes." Mike smiled.

"Why do you think he chose you?" asked Larry.

"My guess is that he's a blue-collar worker here in the city someplace. Maybe a city employee. The kind of guy that reads my column and feels he has an ally in me. The kind of guy who's hidden away in a bureaucratic maze. He feels lost in the combine. A cog in the wheel and all that. He feels anonymous—"

"Well, he's famous now," Angela snorted.

"Well, if he really wanted to be famous," Eli protested, "he should have sat himself down and knocked out a couple of best sellers like you guys!"

"Oh, sure. Piece of cake, right, Larry?" Angela said playfully, lunging toward Eli to shake her.

"Whoops!" said Larry, pulling Eli closer toward him. "Mustn't assault the little mother."

Angela froze in mid-lunge. Mike and Angela both stared at Eli whose face turned bright red in the firelight. Larry smiled down at his wife and kissed the top of her head.

"Sorry. I was supposed to let you tell."

"Oh, shit, Larry," Eli said with a proud smile. "I was going to work it wittily into the conversation. I hate being cornball about this, but, Angela," she said, rushing to her friend's outstretched arms, "I *feel* cornball! I feel so, well, just like all the clichés. I mean, life growing inside me, the glowing feeling, the whole bit! I'm due in April!"

Angela embraced her friend, feeling a bewildering jumble of emotions. She was, of course, joyful for Eli, but there was another feeling swirling inside her, an ache that she didn't understand.

Angela found her voice and congratulated Eli with hugs and exclamations of delight. Mike kissed Eli and shook Larry's hand vigorously. He patted Larry on the back and raised his glass of Irish coffee in a toast. Angela kissed Larry and raised her glass with Mike.

"To a happy, healthy baby, the first, I hope, of many wee ones!" Mike said.

"Spoken like a true Catholic!" Eli cried. "I'd like to try for just one and get it right, if you don't mind!"

"I won't tell the Pope if you won't," Angela said.

"We haven't been on speaking terms since I married out of the church anyway," Eli said, hugging Larry.

"No, really," Mike protested. "I didn't say it as a good Catholic. I meant it. I love big families so much I always assume everyone wants one. I know I'd like to have a big family some day. Lots of kids."

248 *Samantha Joseph*

An embarrassed silence followed. Angela stared at her drink, stirring the hot concoction with a cinnamon stick.

"How 'bout you, Angie?" Mike asked. "Do you like big families?"

Angela felt resentful. Why was Mike asking her this? The subject never crossed her mind. Marriage and children were not for her. She had *been* married. Once dreadfully. Once perfectly. There could be no topping her life with Paolo, so why bother trying? And as for children—her pregnancies had failed, her unborn children had died within her. Life could not grow inside Angela. She was sure of it. Why think about it?

"Well," said Angela sidestepping, "I'm glad Mama and Dad had Jimmy after they had me. Having a brother is one of the best things in my life."

"I'm glad I was an only child," Eli said. "My parents spoiled me, and I loved it."

"I think being an only child did me harm," Larry said. "I think I would've learned more about sharing and consideration if I had had siblings."

"Ah, yes," Eli said with mock resignation. "I've had to teach him everything."

"I'm tired," Angela said. "And we've all got to get up early and head back to New York tomorrow. First thing Monday morning I've got to start correcting my *Emerald Isle* galleys."

"Right," Eli said. "Let's turn in."

Upstairs, Mike undressed silently while Angela packed sweaters and underwear in an overnight bag for the return trip home.

"Angie, honey, you were so quiet tonight. Even when Eli announced her good news. Is something wrong?" Mike asked.

"I don't know what you mean. We've had a great time."

"I guess you were bored by the 'Prince of Darkness' talk. I don't blame you. You've heard it all a hundred times before."

"No. Don't be silly. How many times have you heard me tell everyone about Maze Prison?"

"Strange that you and I are getting so much publicity and glory heaped upon us from others' misfortunes."

"That night I spent in jail has helped me to understand more about the Irish than anything. And in the end, you'll help solve the crime that's frightening all of New York, and my book will perhaps make people more aware. So it's all for the good, isn't it?"

"Yes," Mike answered definitely, "it's all to the good."

Angela stopped packing and turned to Mike. "You should have seen them, Mike, those women I was locked up with in Maze. They were incredible. Their sons, their brothers, their fathers, their husbands dead, arrested, on hunger strikes, but they didn't cry, Mike. None of them cried. They were as dry-eyed as I am now, and full of fight."

"I know," Mike replied, locking into Angela's gaze, "I've seen them. They're incredible, those Irish women. They don't sit and cry. They act. They're realists."

"You mean they're not like me. You're talking about me!" Angela snapped.

"Angela! No, we weren't talking about you at all. What's wrong with you? Why are you so defensive?"

"You were! You were saying that they're stoic about loss, and I'm not. Admit it."

"I was saying nothing of the kind. I'm not a big fan of stoicism when it serves no purpose. I was talking about women who live within a state of war. But, dammit, now that you mention it, Angela, you *do* dwell on the past. You can't tell me that when you get that faraway, teary look in your eyes you're not thinking of Paolo and—"

"That's enough!" Angela hissed. "I'm tired. I want to sleep! What gives you the right—"

"Forgive me," Mike said, putting his arms around her. "I'm sorry. We're both under a lot of stress right now. Maybe we should just go to sleep."

"You're right, Mike," Angela said with remorse in her voice. "I've got a book coming out that's the most important thing I've ever done, and you've got a murderer to worry about. You know, I worry about that nut running around so attached to you."

Mike took Angela's face in his hands and placed his lips close to hers. "Do you worry about me, Angela? Do you really care?"

"Of course," said Angela flippantly. "You're the key to the whole case. Everyone knows it."

Mike sighed. "I just don't understand you, Angela."

"Don't understand me," Angela replied, pushing her breasts

against Mike's bare chest. "Don't figure me out. Just make love to me."

Angela dressed with special care, as she always did before visiting the offices of Heywood & Horne. Jeans and a sweater simply would not do for an appearance by a star author. She was a success, a success that hundreds of people at H & H helped to create, each in his or her own way. They expected her to look successful, and she would not let them down.

Angela pulled hand-tooled Lucchese cowboy boots over her bottle-green tights. She cinched on a heavy silver and turquoise concha belt to accentuate her small waist. Her skirt was a plaid cotton flannel of muted reds, pinks, blues, and greens. It reached to the top of her boots and ended in a demure but playful eyelet-trimmed flounce. Her shirt was a heavy cotton knit. Bright pink and warm, it was collarless and styled in what Scott David called his "Long John" look. Over the pink top, Angela pulled on a natural-colored shoulder bag designed to look like a saddlebag. She shook her long hair and brushed it until it gleamed. Her lightly made-up face shone with health and high expectations.

Mark was on the telephone when Lyndley showed Angela into his office. "I know, Jessica," he was saying as Angela arranged her skirt around her and settled into the couch, alert at the sound of Jessica's name, yet politely pretending to be distracted. "You've never let us down yet," Mark went on. "We're all counting on you. Yes, yes, I have every faith. Especially now that you're in New York to finish up. No, of course I'm not concerned. This is just a 'hello' from your editor, that's all. I know that *Lovers and Losers* will be showing up on my desk any day now. Right. Of course, Jessica. Yes. I promise. No, Jessica, of courst not. Yes. Yes. You take care, too. Right. Thanks. Bye."

So Jessica's book is late, Angela mused. That's odd. She's always the perfectionist.

After Mark put the telephone down, he walked toward Angela with his arms outstretched. "Angela, you're gorgeous! Where have you been keeping yourself? My only contact with you these days is through your agent and the pages you've written. I can't reach you, you don't even return my calls."

"I've just been working hard and fast on the revisions that

you and the copy editors want. I really haven't had a spare moment. Are the galleys in?"

"Of course they're in, Angela, but not so fast. You don't have to dash off, do you? I haven't seen you in weeks." Mark walked to the door of his office, closed it, and locked it.

He sat down beside Angela on the couch. "Angela, you look smashing in that cowgirl outfit. You really look great!" he said, reaching out and cupping her breast.

Angela pulled away.

"What's the matter?" Mark said, unruffled. He stood up and began to loosen his tie. "It won't be the first quickie we've had in the office. Lyndley won't let anyone within a mile of this place when she sees the closed door. Come on. It's been ages, Angela."

"No, Mark it's out of the question. So you can straighten your tie and unlock that door."

"All right, Angela. You're right. Why don't you stick around a while. Say hello to Madeline and Paul, visit with your brother. Then we can have lunch—at my place."

Angela stood up. "Just give me the galleys. No lunch, no fooling around. Just my book, okay?"

Mark flushed with anger. "What is this, Angela? What's wrong with you? I've seen this coming. This wouldn't have anything to do with Michael Brennan, would it?"

"I don't know what you're talking about."

"Yes, you do. We have a news-clipping service here, and every time one of our authors' names appears in print, the article gets circulated. There isn't a gossip columnist in New York who hasn't spotted you at Elaine's or at Regine's, or in some newspaperman's bar with Brennan. I thought you were damned clever linking up with New York's hottest celebrity while this murder thing is on. But I see now that there's more to it." Mark paused. "All right, so you're sleeping with Mike Brennan. Fine. I can adjust to that. That's not a problem. But why should *I* get the cold shoulder?"

"I can't explain it, Mark. It's just not appropriate somehow. I just don't want to go to bed with you any more, that's all."

"I see. No need to fuck the editor anymore, right?" He spat out the four-letter word she'd never heard him use before.

"I don't deserve that, Mark. I know I owe you an

explanation, and if I had one, I'd give it to you. Our sleeping together just seems pointless. I still want you as a friend—"

"Angela, I gave you credit for more originality. I never thought you could really care a lot, but what we had was mutually satisfactory, I thought."

"I know, Mark. I *did* care, in a way. I still do. I don't feel differently about you. I feel differently about me. I just can't see the point any more. I don't know exactly what it is that I want, but—"

"You're in love with Mike Brennan. That's what it is. Why don't you just say so and stop all this nonsense?"

Angela felt a dart of fear at Mark's words. What did she feel for Mike? Why did the idea of sleeping with Mark suddenly feel so wrong? This was silly, she told herself. The affair with Mark was simply stale. Played out. There would be others. There wouldn't only be Mike. That couldn't be. That would be too dangerous.

"No, Mark, I am not in love with Michael Brennan. I've just been seeing a lot of him. It's not love."

"No," said Mark, truly angry now. "I should've known. You couldn't be in love. Not with Mike or me or anyone. You're incapable!"

Tears gathered in Angela's eyes. "Please," she said quietly, "just give me the galleys. I'll have them back to you in two weeks. I'm . . . I'm sorry, Mark."

Mark sighed profoundly. He had expected it anyway. He just didn't expect it today. And he didn't realize how much it was going to hurt.

In minutes, Angela was outside Mark's office with the galley proofs of *Emerald Isle* tucked in her bag. Her eyes were dry and her face composed. Mark had calmed down, kissed Angela's cheek, and told her he looked forward to many happy years as her editor *and* friend. He asured her that steps were being taken to procure the review attention that H & H envisioned at the point of their marketing spear for *Emerald Isle*.

As Angela left him with a kiss on the cheek, he returned to his office, picked up his tennis racket, and "aced" an imaginary opponent. He checked his desk calendar and idly wondered if Carol Volin had dinner plans for that night.

On her way out, after stopping in the art department to visit with Jimmy and Paul, Angela dropped by Madeline's office to reassure the publicity director that she was geared up and ready to promote *Emerald Isle*. Madeline started at the sight of Angela in her doorway and began to shuffle papers on her desk.

"Sorry if I'm disturbing you," Angela began. "I know we don't have an appointment today, but I was talking to Mark and he told me how important it is for *Emerald Isle* to get significant review attention. What are our chances?"

"Reviews? Uh, Angela, let's concentrate on the *Blue Grotto* movie opening in Los Angeles. We can get a lot of mileage from that."

"Yes, I understand, but—"

"*Emerald Isle* will be in the bookstores when the movie opens. Delano will launch the movie tie-in paperback edition of *Blue Grotto* at the same time. I'm working with Delano now to be sure that we all have our timing right. I've even made contact with Aurora. The timing is crucial. Let's not forget it was a number two best seller when it was first released."

"No, I remember. It was behind *Lone Star*, but—"

"Yes, well, maybe it will hit number one as a movie tie-in. Then maybe *Emerald Isle* will hit the list at the same time. Now *that* would be something," Madeline said with her automatic smile.

"Sure, but I'm wondering if we can get the *New York Tribune Book Review* to do something. It would really be the thing—"

"Yes, well, I wish I had more time to spend with you right now. . . ."

"Of course. I understand. I was on my way out anyway."

"We'll be in touch," Madeline called after Angela.

Angela did not feel reassured by Madeline's nervous paper shuffling and avoidance of the review issue, but she decided not to worry. Madeline was a pro, and if anyone had the pull and influence to get the review it was certainly H & H's respected and well-connected publicity director.

It was a fine, clear, crisp fall day, and Angela decided to walk the thirty-odd city blocks home. She wanted time to think before plunging into reading and correcting the galley proofs she carried. Mark's words still echoed harshly in her ears, blotting out all others. "Incapable" he had said. Incapable of being in love. Was that true? Emphatically no. Hadn't she loved Paolo with all the depth and breadth of a poet's passion? No romance had been more perfect, so full to the brim with sweet, unending love. That love had been so flawless, so fulfilling, that it endured even now. She *was* capable of love, Angela thought resolutely. She had loved Paolo and loved him still.

The last guest left at 4:00 A.M., confirming Angela's belief that her New Year's Eve party had been a success. Exhausted, she leaned back on her suede couch and waited as the caterers emptied the ashtrays and collected empty champagne flutes. Angela wiggled out of her flat Charles Jourdan shoes and tossed them aside. She unbuckled the cincher belt that defined the waist of her ankle-length silver silk chiffon lamé dress, a Scott David creation that caught and reflected the soft light from the hundreds of candles placed around Angela's living room.

"It's okay," she told the caterers, "it's fine for tonight. My housekeeper will be in sometime tomorrow, so don't fuss. Mr. Brennan is in the kitchen with the bartender. If you see him there, he'll take care of you."

Several minutes later, the "help" left, satisfied with their generous tips, and Mike emerged from the kitchen, tired but pleased.

"Well, Angela, I think it was a big success," he said, sitting down next to her and nuzzling her neck.

"God, yes. I thought they'd never go home. It's funny who ends up being the last to leave, isn't it? I thought Larry and Eli would stay to the bitter end, but they left pretty early."

"Eli looked cute tonight, didn't she?"

"Yes, but she's only in her fifth month, and she looks like a little house already. I guess she looks so big because she's such a small person."

"And I thought we'd end up putting Mark Green and his wife up for the night, for Christ's sake. Angela," said Mike, suddenly serious, "I'm going to make some coffee. There's something we have to talk about."

"Can't it wait till morning?"

"No. Tired as I am, I won't rest till we've talked. Okay?"

Angela dragged her weary body to the bedroom, stripped off her dress and hose, and, naked, slipped into one of her oversized men's shirts. Comfortably attired and sleepier than ever, she ambled back to the couch and curled up there to wait for Mike and the coffee.

"I've had an offer tonight, Angela," Mike said as they sipped steaming coffee. "One of the newspaper people I invited brought along the city editor from the *Washington Post*. He wants me to come down and base my column in Washington."

Angela felt her heart give a lurch of fear, but she continued to sip her coffee and said nothing.

"It's an excellent opportunity, and the money's very good. I've had several offers recently, but this one is the only one that interests me at all. Of course I can't leave New York and the *Sun* until the Prince of Darkness has been caught. I have to see this case through to the end, and needless to say my feelings about leaving this town are very mixed. And there's another important consideration, the most important one of all." Mike paused dramatically, to be sure he had Angela's full attention.

"It's us, Ange. I don't want to leave New York because I don't want to leave you. But I don't know if we even have a chance. I can't seem to *get* anywhere with you—"

"Don't be silly. You know I'm crazy about you. But this job in Washington—"

"Just tell me you'd rather I didn't go—"

"That's ridiculous. I can't make a decision like that for you."

Mike sighed. "That's what I was afraid you'd say." He paused again. "Angela, are you having an affair with Mark Green?"

Angela's green eyes blazed with anger. "How dare you ask me that? I don't pry into your affairs, do I?"

"There are no 'affairs,' Angela. You know that. There's only you. It's been that way for months now. I'm in love with you, Angela."

Angela felt her heart give another lurch. She began to perspire. She swallowed before she spoke. "I can't help it if you don't see anyone else. I never asked you to make that kind of sacrifice for me," she said sharply.

"Did you hear me, Angela? I said I love you."

"Yes, yes, I heard you," Angela snapped, feling threatened and cornered. "And this is the most ridiculous conversation

I've ever had. I am not sleeping with Mark Green. Okay? Is that what you want? I was, but I'm not."

"Then I'm the only man in your life?" Mike asked wistfully, touching Angela's hair with tentative fingertips.

"Yes!" she said, tossing her head. "You're the only man I'm sleeping with at the moment. What has this got to do with the *Washington Post*?"

"I love you, Angela. These past months have been wonderful for me. The time I've spent with you has been the richest time of my life. You're so good, so strong, so beautiful, Angela, but there's a coldness in you, a wall that I can't break through. If I thought that maybe you just didn't care for me, I'd say 'Okay, forget it,' but I know I mean something to you. We spend so much time together, and the lovemaking—I'd feel it in your body if you didn't care. I know you love it in bed with me as much as I love it with you. I'm not saying that that's everything, but it's a lot. A hell of a lot. I want for us what Eli and Larry have—"

Angela felt her throat close and turn dry. Her heart beat wildly.

"Mike, you're pushing me. Of course I care for you, but *please don't push!*"

"Ange, it's no use. I've told you that I love you. I've told you exactly how I feel. I'm going to find the Prince, and then I'm going to get the hell out of New York. I hope to God I haven't failed you in some way. I don't think I have. I gave it my best shot, but I'll be damned before I spend more time knocking my head against a stone wall." Mike stood up and slipped on his shoes. He retrieved his coat from the bedroom and put it on while Angela remained huddled on the couch.

"I'll have to be around town until this Prince thing breaks, so call me if you need me. But frankly, I'd rather not see you at all for a while. A long while."

Angela stood and followed Mike to the door. The ache in her throat burned away her power to speak, and she did not try because she had no idea what she would say.

Mike turned toward her at the door. He stroked her cheek tenderly. "You are so beautiful," he said hoarsely, "You make it hard to leave. I wish you all the best with *Emerald Isle*. You're a fine writer. I mean it, though you hardly believe it yourself. Take care," he said, kissing her forehead. "Only sweet dreams, Angela."

He closed the door softly behind him, and Angela was alone. A chill gripped her as surely as if a window had blown open and icy winter had leapt into the apartment. She began to tremble violently.

Angela crept into her bed and pulled the thick down comforter up around her shaking shoulders. It did no good. She ran down the hall to her closet and pulled out the Christmas gift she had bought herself with her advance for *Emerald Isle*, a full-length sable coat with a softly peaked hood. She flung it down on top of her comforter and crawled back into bed. But it was no use. Even the sable could not keep her warm. The cold came from within.

She sighed with pain and regret. Why had she spoken to Mike that way? She heard her own words repeated in her head, and she knew she sounded like a bitch. A cold bitch.

Mike was so good, so loving. He was the most important person in her life. She realized that, yet she let him walk away. She did not even try to stop him. And it would have been easy. Three words would have done it, but they were three words Angela could not utter. *Could* not or *would* not? Angela did not know.

Mark Green had said she was incapable of love. He had had that same sad, disappointed, disgusted look on his face when she broke off their affair that Mike had on his tonight.

Oh, why couldn't Mike just let things be? Hadn't they been happy before? Hadn't they enjoyed being together, making love, playing and working together, encouraging each other to be the best that they could be? Why did Mike always have to talk of the future? Of families and children? Of homes and commitment? Why did he have to upset everything this way? Why couldn't anything good just stand still? Why did it always have to move and change and get destroyed?

Angela wept and pounded her fists against the bed. Sobbing loudly, she berated herself for letting Mike walk away. Then she berated Mike for pushing her, for being demanding, for wanting something she couldn't give.

How alone she felt! She needed comfort. But who had held her in the night and made the bad dreams lose their terror? Who had filled her bed and her arms and her body with warmth and sweetness? Mike. It was Mike who comforted her. And now he was gone.

Angela fell into a fitful sleep at nearly 10 A.M. As she sank deeper and deeper, her arms flung out and reaching for some-one not there, Angela began to dream.

She was on the dirt road that led into the foothills of the Apennine mountains. She was there to find Paolo. Suddenly, he appeared from the mist. She ran to hold him, but the mist swallowed him and he was gone. She stood on the road, alone.

CHAPTER
21

"DAMN!" Angela slammed the book shut and threw it down on her desk, as the day's last rays of blue February sunlight steamed in through the window. She was restless. She had been restless for weeks. She had corrected her galleys months ago, then checked page proofs. Now *Emerald Isle* was in the hands of the printers and binders. She would get her first copy any day now, but reviews would not appear until the official publication date, which was still weeks away. Now Angela had nothing to do but wait. Wait for the reception of her book by the book-buying public and, even more important to Angela, its reception by the literary establishment.

Her restlessness was compounded by her warring emotions. She missed Mike terribly—even she could admit that much to herself. A month had passed since their breakup, and she wanted nothing more than to have her anxieties soothed by the security of his strong arms. If only she could call him and tell him how much she needed him, now more than ever. But she couldn't. To begin again with Mike would only reopen the series of questions that had created the schism between them, and she would have to make a commitment that she was unwilling—no, unable—to make.

Angela reached for the telephone on her desk and dialed Eli's number. "How are you, Eli? How are you feeling?"

"Oh, sort of bovine at this point, but okay. What's up, Ange?"

"Well, I know it's kind of short notice, but do you and Larry want to come by for dinner? Or we could go out . . ."

"Oh, sorry, Ange, Larry and I are going to New Jersey to visit his parents. Maybe tomorrow night. Hey, why don't you come with us? Larry's mother won't mind. She'd probably love it—"

"No, I don't think so, Eli, but thanks for asking. Maybe tomorrow night."

"Sure! I'll call you!"

"Oh, Eli, one more thing. Did you have any better luck than I did talking to H and H about the *Trib* reviewing *Emerald Isle*?"

"Well, Madeline assures me that they received the galleys and her personal cover letter. She says she's made all kinds of preliminary and follow-up calls, too. But they won't budge. I don't even want to say this, but it's like they're going out of their way *not* to review you. I don't get it. It's like a barrier we just can't break through."

"Jessica Simon," Angela said.

"Jessica Simon? Oh, Ange, are you still on that kick? You sound like a raving paranoid. What could Jessica Simon possibly have to do with your not getting reviewed by the *Trib*?"

"I don't know, but I'd like to find out."

"Listen, Ange, have you spoken to Mike?"

"See you tomorrow, Eli. I don't want keep you."

Angela hung up, then dialed her brother's number. She knew that Jimmy was involved with a new young man and had promised they would all meet. Why not tonight?

After the tenth ring, Angela again hung up the telephone.

Paul Jameson stuck his head into the "bullpen," the large office where the art department worked. His sharp eyes scanned the room, discovering one lone designer still hunched over his drawing table.

"Hey, Jim, it's after six. Don't you think you should give it a rest? There's plenty of time to finish that."

"I know, Paul, but I want to try a few more sketches."

"Okay, Jim. Your choice. But I've got to run. Scott's showing his new summer sportswear tonight at The Saint. But I'll take a look at your sketches in the morning, okay?"

Jimmy loved his job. Under Paul's tutelage he had learned a lot during the two and a half years he'd been with Heywood & Horne. Paul had once again provided Jimmy with a new challenge to his ability and talent by assigning him his first major book jacket to design. It was past seven-thirty when he decided he needed a break. He got up from his stool and stretched. He decided to take a turn around the floor, hoping to find someone else, perhaps Lyndley or one of the other assistants, working late. At the end of the darkened corridor, light streamed from Madeline Wood's office, and the staccato sounds of her typewriter broke the silence.

When she heard footsteps approaching her office, Madeline started. She spun around abruptly in her chair to face the door, knocking a stack of paper from her desk to the floor.

"Oh! Oh, Jim, it's you."

"Sorry, Madeline. I didn't mean to scare you like that. I saw the light in your office and—"

"It's okay," Madeline said quickly, bending down to the floor.

Jimmy went around the desk to help pick up the scattered papers. "Here, let me help you with—"

"No, it's okay. Really, I can manage. Thanks."

But Jimmy was already picking up papers. He noticed that the words "Lovers and Losers" appeared in the upper right-hand corner of each page. That was the title of Jessica Simon's new book! Only that afternoon Jimmy had heard Mark Green tell Paul that the manuscript still hadn't been delivered. Yet here it was. But why did Madeline have it before Mark? Then Jessica Simon's lilac-colored personal stationery caught his eye. He couldn't help but read the few scrawled sentences when he picked it up:

Maddy, darling—
   L&L is your best writing yet! Now hurry along, my beloved, and finish the last chapter. Mark is getting impatient.

All my love,
J.

   P.S. I had lunch with Monty West, and he sees things our way.

Jimmy looked up from the note into Madeline's stunned face.

"I've got to go now" was all she said.

* * *

Madeline hurried up Third Avenue, perspiring under her Burberry trenchcoat despite the biting chill of the February night air. She looked desperately for a cab, but every yellow car on the traffic-laden avenue was occupied, off duty, or on radio call. Madeline kept walking. She had to get to Jessica's suite at the Sherry-Netherland quickly. She would have to face Jessica and tell her their secret had been unveiled.

How could she have been so careless? She now realized how stupid it had been to work on the manuscript in the office. But it was impossible to work in the confines of her sparsely furnished apartment on East Seventy-fourth Street. Only in her office at Heywood & Horne did Madeline feel truly at home—this was the milieu in which her energy flowed. In her apartment, she was distracted by her own loneliness, a loneliness that would only be compounded if she lost Jessica, which, thanks to tonight's revelation, was now a possibility.

Surely Jimmy Vaccaro would tell his sister every detail of tonight's discovery. It would be only a matter of time before the news was revealed to Jessica. Madeline's anxiety intensified as she anticipated Jessica's wrath. Madeline made a silent prayer that the affair would not be ended and she would not be hurled back into the gulf of loneliness that had swallowed her for so many years. She prayed that Jessica would be able to acknowledge Madeline's years of selfless devotion which began when Jessica, exhausting her field of knowledge with *At Any Price*, experienced difficulty writing her second novel. Madeline was only too willing to help her lover out of her predicament and wrote nearly all of *Almost the Queen*. The overwhelming success of "Jessica's" second book overshadowed even that of her first, and Jessica was more firmly bound to Madeline in order to remain that most wonderful being—Jessica Simon, Author and Star.

For months Madeline had been frantically trying to finish *Lovers and Losers*. This time it had been more difficult. There were too many distractions caused by the increasing pressures of her job.

Madeline hesitated at the hotel door. She couldn't face Jessica yet. She was far too unraveled. She needed some time to collect her thoughts. And she needed a drink.

* * *

Angela was surprised to find Jimmy at her door shortly after eight. He greeted her with a quick kiss and hug and led her into the living room. "Ange, you won't believe what just happened! I came right from the office to tell you." He breathlessly described the evening's events, while Angela listened attentively.

"Jimmy, are you absolutely sure that the letter is from Jessica?" Jimmy nodded. "This is too much. So Madeline's been writing Jessica's books for her! I've always wondered how Jessica could type with those long claws of hers!" Angela paused thoughtfully. "Jimmy, I want you to think hard. Was there anything else in that letter? Anything about me?"

"What do you mean, Ange? It was just kind of a transmittal letter. You know, giving the chapter back to Madeline. You know something, Ange? I get the impression that Madeline and Jessica are lovers."

"That would be the only explanation. Why else would a smart woman like Madeline do anything so excessive for a witch like Jessica?"

"Wait a minute!" Jimmy broke in. "Now I remember the last part of the note. I don't know if it means anything to you, but Jessica said something about lunch with someone named Monty and him doing things their way or something."

Angela started. "Monty West! He's the publisher of the *New York Tribune!* Of course! He's another one of Jessica's society friends! Listen, Jimmy, you stay here. I'll be back soon. Jessica Simon is about to receive an unexpected visitor!"

Jessica sat deep in a chaise lounge amidst the chintz and chinoiserie of her pink-and-red sitting room, voraciously reading Madeline's most recent efforts. Yes, Madeline had outdone herself. Now if Madeline would just hurry up and finish that last chapter, Jessica could get Mark Green off her back just as easily as she had disposed of that other annoyance—Angela Vaccaro.

Jessica was so engrossed in her reading that she didn't hear her maid enter the room.

"Miz Simon," Ivy repeated.

Jessica looked up over her reading glasses and glowered at Ivy. "I told you *no* interruptions!"

"I'm sorry, ma'am, but the lady says it's very important. I told her you don't want to be disturbed, but—"

"Who is it? Miss Wood?"

"No, ma'am. Miss Angela Vaccaro. She says it's important and that you'll want to see her."

Jessica sat up straight. Angela Vaccaro? "Show her into the living room. I'll be out in a minute." She yanked off her glasses and went to the mirror to check her hair, than slashed a fresh coat of color across her thin lips. She tightened the belt of her black-and-gold dressing gown and went to receive her guest.

"Angela!" Jessica called out effusively as she floated toward the living room. "Angela, dear, what a pleasant surprise!" Jessica found Angela standing in the center of the large room, still wearing her sable coat.

"My, my, I don't know what's the matter with Ivy," Jessica gushed. "Why, she didn't even take your wrap or get you a drink!" She started toward the bell to summon the maid.

"It's not necessary, Jessica," Angela stated, her eyes fixed on Jessica's back. "My stay will be brief. I didn't come here for mint juleps and girl talk."

Jessica turned back toward Angela, her eyes narrowed and her eyebrows arched. "I see. Well, then, why don't you just tell me what you *did* come here for."

"Lay off the *Trib*, Jessica. I'm entitled to a review."

Jessica didn't flinch. "The *Trib*? I have no idea what you mean."

"Oh yes you do, Jessica. You're influencing the owner, Montgomery West. I have no doubt that he's one of your friends."

"There is absolutely no basis for your deranged accusation. You're just jittery over your little book. And from what I've heard, you've got good reason."

"Don't be so arrogant, Jessica. I'm not going to let you rob me of my chance. Not any more. I'm warning you, if you so much as—"

Jessica took a step toward Angela. "Don't try to threaten me, Miss Vaccaro," she said with a sneer. "You're way out of your league."

"And don't interrupt *me*, Mrs. Simon," Angela retorted, her eyes blazing. "You're damned right I'm out of my league. My league believes in *working* for success, not fixing the fight. Are you so afraid of letting the best woman win?"

"Get out, you presumptuous fool," Jessica snapped. "I've heard enough. *Get out!*"

Angela didn't move. "I've got more to say," she said evenly. "Your secret has been discovered, Jessica. Madeline was a little too careless."

"You don't know what you're talking about."

"I'm talking about Madeline Wood and the fact that she's the true author of Jessica Simons's books. I know all about it. My brother caught Madeline in her office, writing your book for you."

Before uttering a word, Jessica slowly settled herself into a pink satin slipper chair and decorously spread out the voluminous skirt of her dressing gown. "What do you want?" she asked stiffly.

"Get off my back! Let the *Trib* decide if they want to review my book. I'll take my chances with a good or bad review just like anyone else. I don't really give a damn who writes your book for you, or for what reasons. That's your business. And Madeline's. You can continue your charade, as fas as I'm concerned. But if you ever cross me or anyone dear to me—ever—I promise you I'll make it *my* business to let the whole world know you're a fraud!"

Angela spun around and headed for the door. Before walking out, she turned back to the delicate woman crouched in her chair. "Remember, Jessica, I'm not threatening you, I'm *promising* you. And I keep my promises! Start dialing the phone, Jessica. Call Mr. West right now."

"What's my guarantee you won't expose me?" Jessica wailed.

"You'll just have to trust me," Angela replied.

Madeline didn't see Angela leave the hotel when she looked up from her window-side table in the Sherry's Le Petit Café to order another glass of white wine. Madeline sipped it thoughtfully and slowly, then ordered another. After another hour passed, she knew she couldn't put if off any longer. She would have to go upstairs and face Jessica.

Twenty-two flights above, Jessica Simon stomped savagely back and forth across her living room, downing her third glass of Jack Daniel's since Angela had left. "Damn Vaccaro!" she bellowed. "Damn her brother and damn *Madeline!*" Now Jessica could never use Monty West's dark secret, the trump card she had held for so long. If she did, she'd be the laughing-stock of the publishing industry, an object of scorn to the nation's book-sellers. Even more horrifying, she'd be revealed as a cheat and a fraud to her millions of adoring readers all over the world. Her cherished stardom, the stardom she had spared nothing to claim and to hold onto, would come crashing down around her with tumultuous finality.

And what about that Vaccaro bitch? Yes, Angela had promised that Jessica's secret would remain one, but what reason existed to prevent Angela from disclosing the secret? Why should Jessica take Angela's word as a guarantee? There was no doubt in Jessica's mind that she herself would have taken full advantage of a secret such as this if she were in Angela's position. That's what secrets were for!

As Jessica stalked back across the room to refill her glass, she heard the doorbell ring. "No more visitors!" she shouted to Ivy, who was hurrying to answer the door. Then, having quickly poured another drink, Jessica headed for the door to insure that her command was obeyed.

The door was already open to reveal Madeline standing on the threshold.

"YOU!" Jessica bellowed, her forefinger wildly flailing toward Madeline's face. "You get in here! That will be all, Ivy," she snapped at her maid, all traces of Southern gentility completely removed from her accent. "Go to your room."

Jessica took a gulp of her drink, and her eyes narrowed as they followed Madeline into the room.

Madeline's slender frame began to quiver under Jessica's burning glare. All hope left her as she realized she was too late. Jessica knew. "Jessica, please listen. . . ." she began in a faltering voice.

"Listen? *Listen?* I've already done all the listening I intend to do tonight. That Vaccaro bitch was just up here and told me more than I wanted to hear. How could you be such an imbecile?" she demanded. "After all I've done for you, *how could you do this to me?*"

"I didn't mean—"

"You stupid, ungrateful fool!" Jessica continued, stalking

about Madeline, a tigress circling her prey. "To get yourself caught, and by that slut's brother no less! Why in hell didn't you just write the book in her apartment? Maybe she could have helped with your spelling!" Jessica emptied her glass with a jerk and went back to the bar.

"Please listen to me," Madeline implored, her voice trying to rise above the clanking of bottle and glass. "I didn't want to have our secret discovered. Don't you know that? I would never do anything to betray you."

Jessica whirled around, pushing Madeline away. "Balls!" she snapped, all control having left her. "You want to grab all the glory for yourself, you conniving bitch. I should never have trusted you. Not for one minute."

"Oh, no!" Madeline cried. "No, that's not true! You're upset and you're saying things you don't mean. We love each other!" She reached out to touch Jessica.

"Don't touch me, you disgust me," Jessica snarled. *"Don't you ever touch Jessica Simon again!"*

Madeline felt a slap from Jessica's voice, more powerful than any that could have come from the fragile woman's hand, and she almost fell to the floor. And with that slap came a stunning revelation. Madeline saw her relationship with Jessica with a clarity that she had never permitted herself before. She could see now that Jessica had never loved her; she had used her to hold onto her stardom, the stardom that was Jessica's *only* love.

Madeline felt suddenly free, free of a delusion she had fostered for six years. "Don't worry, Jessica," she stated firmly. "I'll never touch you again. And you'll never see me again. But don't talk to me about Jessica Simon. There *is* no Jessica Simon. She's something we created, and she wasn't worth the effort."

Jessica stood in shocked silence, her shoulders heaving and her face nearly colorless under her heavy makeup. Madeline strode past the enraged woman toward the sitting room.

"Where are you going?" Jessica screamed, fully aware of Madeline's intent. "Don't go in there!"

"I'm only taking what belongs to me," Madeline retorted as she returned with a stack of white paper clutched under her arm.

"But that's mine. It's my new book!"

"No, Jessica," Madeline said, crossing toward the front door. "It's *my* new book. Untitled Manuscript by Madeline Wood. You can read all about it in *Publishers Weekly*. I'll be happy to autograph if for you when it's published!"

"But you can't do this to me," Jessica wailed. "What will I tell Mark Green? What will I tell my *readers?*"

"I'm sure you'll think of something, Jessica," Madeline said as she walked through the open door. "Make something up. Tell them a story. After all, you *are* the great writer!"

Madeline closed the door firmly behind her. As she walked down the hall and waited for the elevator, she heard a glass crash against the door and then Jessica's wild wails.

"That's right. I'm the *Queen*! I don't need you. I don't need anybody. I'll write my book myself. I can do it. I know I can. Why, I'll start right now! IVY!" she shrieked hysterically. "*Ivy, bring me some paper!*"

CHAPTER
22

ANGELA pushed her sable hood back, and all eyes turned toward her as she swept through the revolving doors into the Russian Tea Room. Heads lowered as luncheon companion informed luncheon companion that best-selling author Angela Vaccaro had just walked in. Aware of the stares and whispers but unruffled by them, Angela found her way to Eli's regular table at the front of the restaurant, where she had some trouble getting her shopping bags under the table.

"I should have checked these, but I just have to show you the darling things I got for the baby at Cerutti's," Angela said, greeting Eli.

"Ange, this kid already has twice the wardrobe that I have. Enough is enough already. Hurry up and sit down. I've got something terrific to tell you." Eli was more excited than usual. "The *New York Tribune Book Review* called the publicity department at H and H this morning to request more information about *Emerald Isle*. Of course, they won't say *when* or even *if* a review will run, but the fact that they've inquired means that you're about eighty percent sure of being reviewed."

Angela grinned broadly, not surprised but gratified. "This is such good news, Eli. But believe it or not, I'm twice as nervous as I was when I thought they weren't going to review *Emerald Isle* at all! It means so much to me."

"Don't worry, Ange. Even though we have to expect the worst, off the record I'm betting it'll be a rave review. Hey, I almost forgot! I've got to show you something. Take a look at this hot item!"

Eli pulled a copy of the *New York Tribune* from under the

table where she had been resting it on what was left of her lap. She had a difficult time getting the paper past the round, taut bulge covered in blue-patterned Laura Ashley flannel.

"Read this, read this!" Eli commanded in a choked whisper. Angela read:

PUBLISHING: JESSICA SIMON RETIRES

Jessica Simon, top-grossing author known throughout the publishing industry as "the Queen," has bought back her contract with publishers Heywood & Horne for her upcoming novel, *Lovers and Losers,* announcing that she is giving up writing in order to spend more time with her ailing husband, Arthur Simon, president of Dallas's Simon-Lewis department stores.

"Mrs. Simon feels that her husband has been endangering his health by continuing to run the most successful department store chain in the country. She wants to help him and needs the free time to involve herself more deeply in the day-to-day operation of such a complex and demanding business," says Madeline Wood, Heywood & Horne's publicity director, who herself will be leaving the company in several weeks to pursue a writing career.

Mark Green, editor in chief of Heywood & Horne, expressed his regrets: "We're always sorry to lose a great author, especially when we have had a successful and happy relationship as with Jessica Simon. She is a great talent and a great lady. We wish Jessica and Arthur all the best."

Jessica Simon could not be reached for comment.

Angela tossed the paper across the table toward Eli. "Hmph," she said, "I'll *bet* she couldn't be reached for comment!"

Eli's eyes opened wide. "Is that all you've got to say? Ange, this is unreal! What do you make of it?"

"Well, I can't say that I'm surprised, but I can't say why I'm not surprised either. I don't want to sound mysterious, but I have to be straight and tell you that I thought this was coming. But I can't tell you why because of a promise I made. All I can say is: don't ever say I was paranoid about Jessica Simon."

Eli frowned. "I know you better than to try to pry it out of you, although I get the feeling the review and all this is somehow connected. But you've always kept every secret I've ever told you, from grade school on. All I can say is—Oh, Ange, come on, tell, *please?*"

Angela laughed. "Someday I hope I'll be able to, but for now, let's just forget it."

"Whoa!" said Eli, startled, then smiling. "The baby just kicked me."

"Does it hurt?" Angela asked, reaching over and placing her hand on Eli's belly.

Eli moved Angela's hand higher and to the side, so that Angela could feel the funny, fluttery motion for herself.

"It doesn't hurt," Eli said, "it feels good. I know my baby's in there and fiesty. I wouldn't have it any other way."

Angela smiled. "How wonderful, Eli. Only two months to go!"

Eli turned serious. "You know, Ange, there's no reason why you can't have a baby of your own someday."

Angela's eyes flashed. "There are plenty of reasons why I can't, Eli, so let's not even discuss it."

"That's what you always say, Ange, but you don't know for sure. When you had those misses, you were under Dr. Blumberg's care, and that was years ago. He's a great old guy, but he's an old-fashioned G.P. What if you saw a specialist? A good ob/gyn man—or woman—who knows all the latest developments on difficult pregnancies? There's no medical evidence that says you can't carry a child to term."

"Thanks, Eli, but that isn't what I'm concerned with right now. I've got a fulfilling career, and all I'm interested in is reviews—and maybe another shot at the best-seller list—at the moment."

"I know you have an important career," Eli countered. "So have I."

"Well, you seem to need more than work, Eli. I find my life perfectly fulfilling as it is."

Eli rolled her eyes and drummed her fingers on the table. "Come on, Ange. This is Eli sitting here, not some talk show host."

Angela remained silent until after Eli gave the waiter their orders.

"Okay. I think about marriage sometimes. I think about my

marriage to Paolo, that is. You know we wanted to have a child. We were planning on seeing a specialist in Rome. If Paolo hadn't died, if I had had a baby . . .''

"Don't kid yourself, Ange. You might have become a mother, but then you'd never have become a writer!" Eli said gently.

"Don't be ridiculous! If Paolo had lived, I could have had it all!"

"Nope. Not with Paolo. And that crazy di Fiori family that had him under their thumbs. You would have been miserable and frustrated. You never would have gotten one word published. And how long would you have tolerated your husband's Papa's-boy bullshit?"

Angela looked as stricken as if Eli had just shot her.

"Eli, why are you saying these ridiculous things? Paolo and I were the most perfect, the most happy— Eli, I thought this was going to be a nice lunch—"

"I saw Mike Brennan yesterday," Eli said in reply.

Angela took a deep breath. "So that's what this is all about. Mike Brennan. Eli, for the last six weeks I've been telling you it's over and finished."

Eli began to cut the chicken Kiev in front of her. After five minutes of silence, Angela asked, as neutrally as she could, "So how is Mike anyway?"

Eli looked up at Angela with a smile of triumph. "You don't care, remember?"

"Eli, I'm close to walking out of here and never speaking to you again. Tell me what he said before you end up wearing your lunch!"

Eli laughed, then turned serious. "He misses you terribly, Angela. He came right out and told me. I'll never understand why you let him walk away. I've never seen a couple happier or more right for each other since Larry and me—"

"We've been over all that. So tell me, is he seeing anyone else? I've read in the paper that he's seeing some model, but I want to know if he's serious with anyone."

"You sure are interested, for a girl who's not interested. He misses you, Angela, and I told him that you didn't seem so hot yourself."

"How could you! I'm fine, I'm perfectly fine!" Angela protested angrily.

"Here," said Eli, reaching into her bag and handing Angela a tissue. "You're getting tears and mascara in the blini."

Angela laughed and wiped her tears away.

Eli felt she had hammered at her friend's shell enough for one afternoon. She changed the subject, knowing that her message about Mike's availability had gotten across.

"Listen," Eli said, "I put in a call to H and H as soon as I heard that Madeline was leaving the company. I don't want just anybody handling your tour. I want the best. So they've agreed to hire top publicist on the outside to coordinate the tour. There are two really good ones I want you to meet before they make a choice. I want someone at least as good as Madeline. The tour has to be timed just right so the movie, paperback and hardcover promotion and publicity are all in sync. You'll be in L.A. for the première of *Blue Grotto*, so the kick-off push for *Emerald Isle* will start in L.A. on Saint Patrick's day. Cute, eh?"

"Real cute. Will I meet the stars of the movie?"

"Are you kidding? Right now they're asking Zeffirelli if *they*'ll meet you! Giancarlo Giannini and Nastassia Kinski meet Angela Vaccaro! I can see the cover of *People* right now!"

Angela made a gruesome face and both women laughed.

"Now Ange," Eli said over dessert, "next week sometime you're going to get a call from H and H's new director of publicity. They assured me she's very good, and she'll oversee the outside publicist. You should start thinking about what you'd like to wear to the première at Mann's Chinese Theatre, by the way."

Angela spent the rest of the afternoon buying clothes for the tour. In the back of her mind she fantasized an accidental meeting with Mike, and that fantasy propelled her into Montenapoleone on Madison Avenue, where she purchased slinky silk lingerie imported from Italy. She was weary but elated when she got home that evening at six.

"There's someone to see you, Miss Vaccaro," the new doorman informed her. "He's been waiting for a couple of hours."

Angela's heart began to pound. She ran into the lobby.

"Mike!" she cried, dropping her shopping bags and embracing him and the long-stemmed red roses he carried.

"Early Valentine's Day, Angela," he said, returning her embrace as best he could.

"Oh, I'd forgotten—tomorrow is Valentine's Day!"

They rode up in the elevator, both of them breathless, excited, and nervous. Angela held the flowers, while Mike showed her what else he held in his arms.

"Look, Ange. Look what I found in Doubleday's bookstore today."

It was a copy of *Emerald Isle*.

"I had no idea they were shipping so soon. I just found out today that the publication date is set for Saint Paddy's Day."

Angela brought Mike a beer while he made himself comfortable on the couch. "Did you see my review in *Publishers Weekly*?" she asked him.

"Yep. Just as I suspected: 'A major breakthrough for a major new talent.' What did I tell you?"

"Oh, Mike! You know what it means to me! When I wrote *Blue Grotto*, I felt I had so little control. I was just more or less trying to purge everything in me. But with *Emerald Isle* I really tried to be a writer. If my review in the *Trib* is as good, I'm home free."

"So they're going to run a review after all! That's great. Nothing can stop you now."

"No, nothing," Angela echoed faintly. Suddenly she brightened again. "Mike, what about you? How are you doing? Are you ready to nail the Prince of Darkness?"

"We're keeping it quiet, but we're very, very close. That is, we're pretty sure who it is, we've just got to carefully assemble the evidence and then pick him up."

"That means you'll be leaving for Washington soon, doesn't it?"

"And you'll be heading out on your book tour. . . ." Mike countered.

They both fell silent, aware that they were plunging into troubled waters only minutes after the ecstatic reunion.

"Angela," Mike said suddenly, "let's give it another go. I really have been miserable without you, although if Eli hadn't told me that you missed me too, I never would've had the courage to come back. But here I am. For a while anyway. I don't know exactly when we'll get the Prince. When does your tour start?"

"I fly to California the second week in March," Angela said.

"Okay, that gives us about four weeks together. We're both pretty miserable when we're apart. What do you say?"

"I'd like to try it, Mike, but on one condition."

Mike held up his hand. "I know what you're going to say, and I promise—no talk of the future. We'll just live for these four weeks. So is it a deal?"

Angela smiled broadly. "It's a deal."

The weeks passed swiftly and serenely with the peaceful bliss that comes with a spell of good weather. Mike moved into Angela's apartment, and they shared the time like two misers who together had found a fortune and wanted to keep it all to themselves, not squandering a penny. Yet both Angela and Mike knew that the time was limited, that the bliss *would* end. But neither spoke of it.

Most days, they spent their time quietly working side by side in Angela's writing room. And every night they made love. Sweet, hot, piercing love that made Angela cry out and moved Mike to hold Angela as though he would never let her go.

One Tuesday morning they awoke to watch Angela's interview on the "Today" show that had been taped earlier at the studio. Mike and Angela sat in bed nibbling croissants while they watched the show. At the commercial break at the end of the segment, Mike grabbed Angela, nuzzled her neck, tickled her, and tussled with her until they both fell on the floor laughing. Angela thanked God that Mike was there to keep her from taking herself and her fame too seriously. He reminded her that behind the glossy image she was human and real.

Their last dinner together the night before her departure for Los Angeles was a quiet one. Angela cooked a light meal, and they ate by candlelight at a table decorated with fresh flowers. Neither Mike nor Angela spoke more than a few words. They ate very little as a net of tension tightened around them. Time was almost up, and yet so little had been said.

Realizing that it was futile to try to eat dinner with a choked and closed throat, Angela put her fork down beside her plate, placed her napkin on the table, and looked into Mike's piercing eyes.

Mike lost himself in the green sea of Angela's eyes, and

rising from the table, took her by the hand and led her to the bedroom. Without speaking a word, they lay down together.

Mike kissed her face, her hair, her neck. Softly, softly, he stroked her while she watched him, her eyes wide with expectation and yearning. She pulled his face toward her and kissed him deeply. She burned under his hands.

They took their clothes off quickly and tossed them aside. Angela moved catlike until she was full-length on top of her lover. She kissed his eyes and fed greedily on his lips. She licked his neck, pulling on the skin with her lips as though she would both eat and drink him. Then she lay beside him. Not wanting to wait any longer, he pulled himself on her. She opened her legs, and he pushed himself deep inside her. They were pressed belly to belly, breast to breast, except for flesh kept apart by the hard, blue sapphire that lay between them.

Mike wrapped his arms around Angela so tightly that she could barely breathe. Wave after wave of warm ecstasy flowed through her. She heard a raw sound coming from miles and miles away that was in fact torn from her own throat.

Mike's spasms began as Angela's peaked. He cried out over and over, "Angela, oh, God! Angela!"

Angela loosened her arms around him when he was still trembling with aftershock. A tiny but definite voice inside her said, *It's never been this perfect. Never.*

Silence blanketed them. Angela prayed that Mike would honor his agreement. Even now, nearly at the end, she could not bear to discuss the future. She would not speak of love. She would not give recognition to the power in whose thrall she now lay.

Mike kissed her. He held her enfolded in his arms. She slept.

Through the night, tortured by thoughts of the separation that the daylight would bring, Mike watched Angela while she slept. Her brow was furrowed, but her breathing was gentle and rhythmic. Once during the long night she stirred and cried out. Mike knew she was having the dream. He held her and rocked her as though she were an infant. He smoothed her hair and murmured comforting words in her ear. Now he could tell her how he loved her. She could not object in her half-sleeping state.

The dream *had* come to Angela. She was on the mountain road again. This time she seemed not to know why she was there. She began to search for someone—she was not sure for whom until she called him. "Paolo, Paolo," she called, summoning him from the mist. But her unconscious mind could not assemble his features. He would not be recalled to life. His face would not show itself. His image had begun to fade.

Angela's suitcases stood against the wall. Mike's typewriter and bags stood alongside them. Angela emerged from her bedroom, dressed in an Oscar de la Renta suit and her favorite Valentino boots. She brushed her hair with quick, hard strokes, while wandering through the apartment in search of a misplaced emerald stud earring.

Mike sat at the dining room table reading the morning paper.

"Has that package arrived yet?" Angela called tensely, finding the earring and putting it on.

"No," Mike said, looking up. "Is it important?"

"Important!" Angela snapped. "I'll say it's important! It's an advance copy of the *Trib Book Review. Emerald Isle*'s reviewed on page one."

"All right, Angela," Mike said in placating tones. "I'm sure it will get here before you have to go to the airport."

"I'm glad you're sure," Angela huffed.

Mike shook his head, returning to his reading. He knew why she was being short with him. He understood. She was tense and nervous about the tour. And about them. Angela would go her way; the Prince of Darkness would be caught, Mike would soon leave for Washington; and it would be all over. Nothing would be said, nothing resolved. It would simply end because the four weeks were up and time had run out. What a sad, stupid waste, Mike thought.

The intercom buzzed and a messenger was sent up to Angela's apartment. He passed an envelope to Angela's eager fingers. She tore at it, anxious to read the review sent by Eli.

"Angela," Mike said, "we've so little time, and it's such a long article. Why not read it on the plane? We can talk awhile, now that you're all ready to go."

"Are you crazy?" Angela said. "After all I've been through? This review almost didn't make it, thanks to Jessica Simon. Besides, I've got to know right now if it's a good review or a bad review."

"Angela, for God's sake! Look at me! You can read the review on the plane!"

"It'll only take a few minutes," Angela replied as she sat down and began to read.

Mike exhaled and went back to his newspaper. Angela scanned the page quickly and squealed with delight.

"Mike! This is a rave review! I can't believe it! It says I'm a writer, a real writer. A serious talent. A great newcomer. He caught each and every important thing I was trying to say! Oh, God, Mike, he says I'm a real writer!"

Angela jumped up and flung herself into Mike's arms. He stood and hugged her.

"Of course you're a real writer!" he said, laughing and squeezing her. In her joy, she squeezed him back. Their lips met, and they kissed with the same desperate intensity that had marked their lovemaking the night before.

Angela pulled away. "I've got to make sure the limo is coming to take me to the airport."

Mike held her arm. "Let me drive you, Angela."

"It's not necessary."

"I know it's not necessary, but I'd like to."

"I said I'd take the limo!" Angela rapped, far more sharply than she had intended.

The thin, tense wire drawn between them pulled tighter and snapped.

"Damn you, Angela! Damn you and your fucking limo!"

"How dare you speak to me that way! What's wrong with you?"

"Nothing's wrong with me. It's you that's fucked up. You're the one that's wrong."

"I think you've said enough."

"Not by a long shot. That's the problem. I haven't said nearly enough."

She turned her back on him deliberately and began to walk away. He grabbed her arm and spun her around until she faced him. He held her arm tight enough so that she could not pull free of him.

"I'm sick of this goddam ice maiden pose of yours, and I'm sick of the way we both haven't said a word about us! You've had it tough, no one's going to deny that," he continued through clenched teeth. "You lost your parents and you lost your husband. The perfect husband, to hear you tell it. But Angela, that was six fucking years ago! Let go, for Christ's sake. You're holding onto nothing! A ridiculous idealized memory! It's just a fucking excuse!"

Angela's eyes snapped and blazed. Her nostrils flared, and she yanked her arm free.

"You don't know what you're talking about, you bastard. Paolo was . . . he was . . . he had . . . he . . . we—" Angela's eyes filled with tears, and her voice was strained and raw.

Mike grabbed her arm again, pulling her so close that their lips almost touched.

"You're going to hear me out, Angela. You're hiding behind this Paolo thing. You hold onto that rock around your neck like it was a talisman to ward off evil. And what's the evil, Angela? Are you so scared to love? To get hurt? Tough shit. That's what life is all about. We all get hurt. There are no guarantees. Not for you, not for me, not for anyone. But if you don't risk it, you might as well just go curl up and die. I don't care how many front page reviews you get."

Angela was sobbing now and writhing to get out of Mike's grip.

"Let me alone, let me alone, you don't know what you're talking about! You're just jealous of me, that's it—"

"Bullshit!" Mike thundered.

"Oh, I hate you, I hate you! You just want to hurt me, you just want to hurt me." Angela sobbed.

"No," Mike said softly, finally letting her go. "I just want to love you. But you won't let me. You just won't let me."

Angela dried her tears. She drew herself up proudly. She ran her fingers through her hair, then shook it out.

"I'm taking my bags and waiting for the limo downstairs, Mike. I'm sorry we had to end on such a sour note."

Mike snorted and sneered. "Sour note? Are you for real, Angela? Can you really do this? Can you really pretend we mean nothing to each other? That our parting doesn't tear you up inside? It tears me up. It hurts like hell. But goddammit, I won't compete with a fucking ghost!"

Angela picked up her bags and left.

CHAPTER
—————————23—————————

IT WAS RAINING in Los Angeles when she arrived. There was a limousine waiting at the airport to take her to the Beverly Hills Hotel. As the car swept along Sunset Boulevard, Angela cursed the weather under her breath. It made her angry. She had left a piercingly cold, blustery, gray March New York day and had hoped to find the legendary California sun beaming on her when she arrived in Los Angeles. Instead, she found herself misted by gray rain.

The porter threw open the door of Angela's suite, and she was greeted by large, lush displays of flowers set all over the sitting room. A basket of fruit sat on a cocktail table. Champagne and a silver dish of caviar nesting on cracked ice rested beside the basket.

After the porter left, Angela examined the flowers closely. There were birds of paradise, orchids of rare and varying hue, calla lilies, and anthuriums. Each display held a small white card signed "Len Seligsman, Aurora Productions."

Without testing the fruit, the champagne, or the caviar, Angela went into the bedroom to shed her New York clothes. She then stretched out on the king-size bed in her slip. There was no sound in the room but that of her own breathing and the hammering of her heart in her ears. She thought she would take a nap but found that although she was exhausted, she could not sleep. She got up to get the *Trib* review from her handbag. She wanted to read it again, slowly, to savor and digest every word. Before she returned to bed, she was startled by the beauty of a three-foot orchid cactus in a clay pot sitting on the dresser. She had not noticed it before. She approached it, enchanted by the wide, long, bright blossoms. The card, propped against the earthen pot, proclaimed "Welcome to Hollywood, Len Seligsman."

My God! thought Angela. This guy Seligsman has really gone all out. She remembered that she had a dinner date with him. She automatically pictured him as fat, fifty, slightly greasy, and decked out in too many gold chains, rings, and bracelets.

She replaced the card and touched one of the blossoms, immediately pulling her hand back in alarm. The sharp-edged cactus leaf had pricked her skin. She sucked the wound in her finger, tasting a drop of blood.

"Damn!" she said aloud, suddenly angry and disheartened. Tears filled her eyes, and she threw herself on the bed, sobbing. After several minutes, she tried to pull herself together and read her review, but she felt too much turmoil to concentrate. She irritably tossed the *Book Review* to the floor.

What's wrong with me? she wondered. Why am I so damned miserable? She lay on the wide bed staring at the ceiling. The scent of the flowers hung in the air. Ice melted in the silver champagne bucket and in the caviar dish. The fuit lay uneaten. The pages of the *Trib* were heaped on the floor. Angela's bags filled with carefully packed designer clothes lay unopened on the luggage stand while Angela hugged herself and wept with abandon. She was all alone.

Angela was awakened the next morning by a phone call from Eli.

"How are ya, Ange?" Eli greeted her brightly.

"Oh, pretty rotten, I guess."

"In light of all this great news? You've done it this time. You've really done it! Next Sunday when your rave review appears on the front page of the *Trib Book Review*, there you'll be on the next-to-the-last page!"

"Is H and H running a full-page ad?" Angela asked wearily.

"No, you dope! Although yes, they are, but that's not it! That's the best-seller page. You're number one, Angela! *Emerald Isle* is number one! Didn't you look?"

"No. I saw the review and forgot to look at the best-seller list."

"Angela, what's wrong?" Eli asked sharply.

Angela drew a deep breath. "I don't know. I'm miserable. It's so lonely here. And yesterday it was raining, and—"

"What happened with you and Mike?"

Angela began to cry as her words tumbled out: "Oh, Eli, he's such an ass. He insulted me and said some horrible things, and the worst part is, I'm sure I'll never see him again."

"Whoa, whoa, start over. This isn't making any sense."

"Well, he yelled at me about Paolo. About how he was sick of competing with a ghost. . . ."

Angela repeated for Eli the scene that had taken place before Angela left for California. When she was finished, Eli spoke carefully.

"Ange, maybe he was a little rough. Maybe he should have said things a little differently, but you know he's right. Could be his big mistake was in not shaking you up sooner."

Angela said nothing. She told herself that both Mike and Eli meant well, but neither of them really understood her. They did not realise that her love for Paolo was sacred, that time could not change it. Six years or sixty, it made no difference. Why did they think she was hiding behind it?

"Angela?" Eli said quietly. "Angela, everyone you've ever loved—nearly everyone—is gone. But, for God's sake, you've got to go on loving anyway. Don't you know that? You love Mike, Angie. If I were you, I'd crawl on my hands and knees—all the way to Washington, if need be—just to tell him. Just to get him back."

"Please, Eli, I can't talk anymore. I've got to get ready. I've got a TV taping and an autographing at Hunters Bookstore."

"All right, but take it easy. I'm on your side, don't forget. I want you to be happy. And congratulations on the review and the number one spot."

"Thanks, Eli. Take care. Give my love to Larry," Angela said and hung up.

She decided to wear the blue sequined dress. She needed its brightness to cheer her up. The sparkling bodice was held up by spaghetti straps; the neckline plunged, displaying Angela's breasts and the sapphire flatteringly. The satiny folds of the skirt hugged Angela's hips. She dressed with care and placed drops of Ombre Rose behind her ears, on the backs of her knees, and between her breasts. Len Seligsman had obviously been trying to impress her—he had sent flowers, fruit, and caviar each of the three days she had been in Beverly Hills—and now she was going to "wow" him. As a final touch, Angela draped a white fox stole over her shoulder.

He was not fat and fifty, nor portly and forty. The independent film producer who appeared at the Beverly Hills Hotel with a bouquet of orchids and gardenias to squire Angela to dinner at Ma Maison was closer to thirty and as sleek as a whippet.

He wore a dazzling white dinner jacket and white pleated slacks. His shirt, open to expose only one thin gold chain, was black silk. His skin was dark, smooth, and perfect, as was his carefully styled hair. His dazzling smile was the result of Hollywood's finest caps and bonding man.

Angela's quiet mood had no effect on the young producer. He complimented Angela extravagantly, talked about what "fun" it had been to produce *Blue Grotto*, how many "megabucks" they were all going to earn, while expertly maneuvering his white Mercedes 450SL at seventy miles per hour.

Angela graciously accepted the compliments, smiling through the "shop" talk. She was relieved when they reached the restaurant on Melrose Avenue and wove through what looked like a Rolls-Royce showroom of a parking lot, before screeching to a halt in front of the parking lot attendant.

Over *blanquette de veau*, Seligsman kept up his movie talk, dropping names he assumed Angela would recognize, although she many times did not. He interrupted his constant flow of chatter to nod at friends and celebrities who passed by on their way to and from their tables.

He kept his arm around the back of Angela's chair throughout the meal and spoke in a manner that led Angela to believe that he expected her to sleep with him before the night was over.

Angela grew resentful. He had bought the rights to *Blue Grotto* and had revealed his interest in buying *Emerald Isle*, but he did *not*, however, own the rights to Angela Vaccaro!

Angela withdrew more and more so that by the time dessert arrived, she had barely spoken in the last twenty minutes. Bored, she looked up to see a well-built man of medium height, with light brown hair and a lighter beard, walk by.

"Mike!" she called excitedly, without thinking. "Mike!" She reached out and touched the man's sleeve. When he turned, she knew she had made a mistake. "I'm sorry," Angela said, red-faced, "I thought you were someone else. I thought—"

The man replied affably, "My name isn't Mike, but I'd be glad to change it."

Angela managed a polite smile while wishing she could be swallowed up by the earth.

Len Seligsman barely noticed the incident.

"Let's go back to my place in Holmby Hills," he was saying.

But Angela wasn't listening. The incident of mistaken identity had struck her with the force of a thunderclap. She had known the moment that she realized the man in the restaurant *wasn't* Mike that it was only the sight of Mike, the feel of his arms around her, that would make her happy. She knew that she wanted to be with him, to see him, more than *anything* else.

A strange and frightening idea began to take hold of her. She felt scared and shaky—and exhilarated. The idea burned in Angela's mind like a beacon that could light up the whole world.

As soon as Angela got rid of Seligsman by firmly thwarting his advances, she ran to the phone in her bedroom. She knew it was after three A.M. in Manhattan, but she didn't care. She was in love. She wanted to awaken Mike and say, "I love you. I always have!" She was sure he wouldn't mind being awakened to those words. But wait! What if he had truly meant what he said? What if this time he was really through with her? Well, that was the chance she'd have to take. She had to tell Mike she loved him.

She dialed his number and waited with impatience and excitement as the telephone rang once, then twice, then three times. She finally hung up after the fifteenth ring. He wasn't home. Maybe he was working late. Very late. With the chief of detectives. Or maybe he was having a drink with some of the "boys" from the paper at Runyon's or one of his other hangouts. There was no cause for alarm.

Then Angela had a chilling thought. What if he had already gone to Washington? Had the Prince of Darkness murders been solved? She realized she hadn't looked at a newspaper since the day before she had left for Los Angeles.

Angela paced the length of the bedroom, toying nervously with her sapphire. Realizing that she held the cold stone in her hand, she yanked on it in exasperation. The thin gold chain broke easily, and Angela held the blue gem in her palm.

"Dammit but I've been a fool," she said as if the stone could hear her and sympathize. She tossed the jewel into the small lizard purse she had thrown onto her bed and tried Mike's number again. It was nearly dawn when she gave up and went to sleep.

She did not leave to tape the "Merv Griffin Show" the next day until she had called Mike's number several times. Still there was no answer. She called the *Daily Sun*, but the busy reporters and editors claimed not to know where Mike was. She tried to reach Eli and got her assistant. Ms. Walsh was having lunch with an editor and would probably not be back until much later.

At eleven A.M., Heywood & Horne's Los Angeles sales rep appeared at her door, waiting to take her to the taping. Reluctantly, she let him lead her to the limousine. She tied up the phone in the studio green room trying to reach Mike, while Merv's other guests glowered at her.

Her performance on the show was adequate. She had answered the same questions so many times that she did not need full concentration to get by. After the taping, she called Mike's number again.

As the afternoon shadows lengthened, she grew more desperate and determined to find Mike. She called the *Washington Post*. They had no idea of the whereabouts of Michael Brennan. The city editor of the *Daily Sun* asked her to please stop calling; she was tying up their lines.

Reluctantly, Angela realized it was time to dress for the première. She showered and perfumed herself. A manicurist was sent for, and Angela convinced her to dial the phone for her one more time before she left Angela with wet nails. The hotel salon provided a hairdresser to whom Angela responded listlessly while he dropped celebrity names.

At last, Angela was dress in her black satin Yves Saint Laurent tuxedo. Preoccupied by thoughts of reaching Mike, Angela arrived at Mann's Chinese Theatre. She was the first guest to arrive, as was prearranged by her publicist. She was to stand beside Army Archerd while he interviewed the stars. She was to be on the television screen the whole time, holding a copy of *Emerald Isle* discreetly, but not too discreetly, under her arm. The cameras were to record her first meeting with Giancarlo Giannini and Nastassia Kinski, the stars of the movie made from her book.

Angela strode over the handprints and footprints of Marlene Dietrich, Bette Davis, and John Wayne, and passed workmen setting up platforms and kleig lights. She walked into the lobby where caterers were setting up a bar to serve cocktails and champagne. Newspaper and television reporters clustered with their crews, waiting for the event to begin. Several of the media people recognized her, and camera strobes flashed in Angela's face. She turned on her public smile and began to answer the familiar questions, assuring the readers and viewers of America that this was the most exciting moment of her life. They would never know there was something she thought more exciting than ten movie premières. She was in love. She would have liked to tell them. She would have liked to tell the world. But first she had to tell Mike.

A young movie usher in a tight-fitting double-breasted jacket pushed her way through the press of people that was growing around Angela. The reporters tried to stop her from getting through.

"I've got to get to Miss Vaccaro, please," she said. "It's urgent!"

Angela reached her hand out to the young girl and helped her through the crowd.

"What is it?" Angela asked when they stood side by side.

"There's a long-distance phone call for you. In the manager's office. It's important."

The telephone was placed in Angela's unnaturally cold and shaking hand.

"Angela!"

"Jimmy!" Angela exclaimed, choked. "Are you all right?"

"Yes, I'm fine. I tried to get you everywhere. Ange, there's bad news."

Angela sank into a chair in the manager's office.

"It's Mike. I just heard it on the radio. He's been holed up with the police for two days trying to capture that killer."

Angela felt the iron hands encircle her chest, squeezing breath from her lungs. She was sure Mike was dead.

"Angela! Angela!" Jimmy shouted. "Angie, are you there?"

"Yes," she whispered hoarsely, gripping the telephone. "Tell me."

"There was a shoot-out, and Mike got shot."

Angela could *hear* the shots ring in her head. "No," she moaned, "no."

"But Ange?" Jimmy said. "Ange? Are you listening? He's alive. Do you hear me? He's alive. I don't know—"

Angela was on her feet, crying and laughing incoherently. "Oh, thank God. O Jesus, Mary, thank you. Oh, my Mike is alive—"

"Ange, pull yourself together. Listen, I talked to the police. We won't know anything for twenty-four to forty-eight hours. He's in critical condition."

"Jim! Where is he?" Angela demanded with perfect clarity.

"He's in St. Vincent's in the Village."

"I know where that is. I'm on my way. And thanks, Jimmy."

Angela hung up the telephone and raced through the lobby where celebrities were arriving. After a glittering couple stepped from their limo, Angela slipped in.

"Drive," she said breathlessly, "get me to the airport as fast as you can!"

The driver began to protest. Angela quickly riffled through her purse and pulled out a handful of large bills, waving them at the driver.

"Yes, ma'am!" he said, stepping on the accelerator, pulling the car away from the throng at the curb.

Angela sat back and breathed deeply. Her heart was pounding and she hadn't realized it but she had been holding her breath since she hung up the telephone. As the limo snaked onto the Santa Monica Freeway, Angela thought about what she would find at the end of her journey.

The next hours were crucial, Jimmy had told her. Well, if they were crucial to Mike, she was going to be there beside him, through each and every one of them. She would be there, and if he could hear her, she would tell him all the things she should have told him all along: that she wanted him, that she needed him, and most of all that she loved him. God, how she loved him!

But what if he turned her away? What if he said she was too late, that he couldn't love her anymore? It didn't matter, she decided. She would have to take the risk.

What if Mike was injured so badly that he might be impaired for life? What if he didn't pull through? Those, too, she decided, were risks she would have to take. She had to give him her love.

She thought briefly of Paolo and of the blue sapphire that lay in a purse back at the hotel. Her things could be sent for, and besides, what did they matter? Good-bye, Paolo, she said to herself. I loved you once, and a tiny part of me always will. But that was long ago. Very long ago. Now she thought as she saw Los Angeles Airport loom into view, I'm flying home. To my love. I'm flying home to Mike.

Over 1.5 million copies in print!

Rodeo Drive

BY BARNEY LEASON

☐ 42-054-4   416 pages $3.75

Welcome to the land of silk and money, where the world's most glamorous — and amorous — come to spend their endless nights dancing chic-to-chic under dazzling lights.

Here, against the outrageously decadent background of Beverly Hills — its hopscotch bedrooms and grand estates, posh restaurants and luxurious hotels — is the shocking story of society dame Belle Cooper and her passionate struggle to become a woman of integrity and independent means.

Not since *Scruples* has a novel laid bare the lives — and loves — of people who have everything…and will pay any price for *more*!

A Novel Without Scruples

a novel by
Barney Leason

☐ 41-596-6   448 pages $3.50

With consummate insight and shameless candor, Barney Leason, author of *The New York Times* bestseller, *Rodeo Drive*, weaves yet another shocking, sensuous tale of money, power, greed and lust in a glamorous milieu rife with

From the seductive shores of the Isle of Capri to the hopscotch bedrooms of Beverly Hills, London and New York, Leason lays bare the lives and loves of the rich and depraved, their sins and shame, their secrets and

**Driven by desire, they would do
anything to possess each other—anything.**

a novel by
BARNEY LEASON

Barney Leason, author of *The New York Times*
bestsellers, *Rodeo Drive* and *Scandals*, once again writes about
what he knows best—the shameless sexual odysseys
of the rich, the powerful, the obsessed and the depraved. . .
the ultra-chic, super-elite trendsetters who will stop
at nothing to satisfy their secret

Set against the glamorous milieu of
haute couture designers, foreign correspondents and
political diplomats. . .rife with the pleasure and pain of the
world's most enviable elite—here is the shocking,
sensuous story of those who live and love
only to indulge their insatiable